THIS
BOOK
WON'T
BURN

BY SAMIRA AHMED

Internment

Love, Hate & Other Filters

Mad, Bad & Dangerous to Know

Hollow Fires

Amira & Hamza: The War to Save the Worlds

Amira & Hamza: The Quest for the Ring of Power

THIS BOOK WON'T BURN

SAMIRA AHMED

LITTLE, BROWN AND COMPANY
New York   Boston

Little, Brown and Company
Hachette Book Group
1290 Avenue of the Americas, New York, NY 10104
Visit us at LBYR.com

First Edition: May 2024

Little, Brown and Company is a division of Hachette Book Group, Inc. The Little, Brown name and logo are registered trademarks of Hachette Book Group, Inc.

The publisher is not responsible for websites (or their content) that are not owned by the publisher.

Little, Brown and Company books may be purchased in bulk for business, educational, or promotional use. For information, please contact your local bookseller or the Hachette Book Group Special Markets Department at special.markets@hbgusa.com.

Library of Congress Cataloging-in-Publication Data
Names: Ahmed, Samira (Fiction writer), author.
Title: This book won't burn / Samira Ahmed.
Other titles: This book will not burn
Description: First edition. | New York : Little, Brown and Company, 2024. | Audience: Ages 12 & Up. | Summary: Amidst her parents' divorce and having to start at a new school midway through her senior year, Noor takes a stand against book bans in her small-town Illinois high school.
Identifiers: LCCN 2023028824 | ISBN 9780316547840 (hardcover) | ISBN 9780316548397 (ebook)
Subjects: CYAC: Family life—Fiction. | Books and reading—Fiction. | Censorship—Fiction. | Muslims—Fiction. | East Indian Americans—Fiction. | LCGFT: Novels.
Classification: LCC PZ7.1.A345 Th 2024 | DDC [Fic]— dc23
LC record available at https://lccn.loc.gov/2023028824

ISBNs: 978-0-316-54784-0 (hardcover), 978-0-316-54839-7 (ebook)

Printed in Canada

LSC-C

10 9 8 7 6 5 4 3 2 1

To the lighthouse keepers of democracy,
to the librarians and the teachers, to
the artists and the writers. To the young
people standing up, marching, shouting.
This one's for you.

And, as ever, for T, L, N. I'm only me
when I'm with you.

Resistance and change often begin in art.
Very often in our art, the art of words.
—Ursula K. Le Guin

Between my finger and my thumb
The squat pen rests; snug as a gun.
—Seamus Heaney

CHAPTER 1

Fire isn't the only thing that can burn you.

Fire, at least, tells the truth. It doesn't disguise what it is. What it can do. How it can turn everything in your life into ash in a split second. Sure, it provides heat, warmth. It's a necessity in life. Its tiniest flicker giving the cozy vibes you want on the shortest, coldest nights during Chicago winters—the ones where your mom makes hot cocoa for the family and you snuggle under old kantha quilts watching classic Bollywood movies while snow falls. But for all its cozy comforts, a single lick of flame can scorch the entire earth.

A thin, shiny scar runs along the side of my right thumb. It's small now, barely half an inch long. I was six years old and playing with matches. I didn't even know what a matchbox was. But the red tips of the long wooden matches in the fancy cardboard box with a colorful illustration of a fox and squirrel on the cover attracted my inquisitive hands. I didn't understand what would happen as I struck the match against the side of the box. A satisfying scratching noise and then a tiny whirl of flame caught and stuck to my skin. My dad answered my screams; a split second later, the flame died out.

He examined the skin, rubbing a burn ointment on it as he calmly explained to me what had happened. How close I'd come to real danger. Fat tears ran down my cheeks and plopped onto the counter. "It's okay, beta," my dad whispered as he cradled me close to him. "But you could've been badly burned. You can't play with matches. I might not always be here to put out the fire." I nodded and snuggled in closer, smelling the whiffs of sandalwood soap he bought in bulk from Patel Brothers on Devon Avenue.

That scar became a kind of fidget. A shiny strip of skin I'd rub absentmindedly. At first, it was puckered and rough. As I got older, the scar grew smaller, smoother, but never completely faded. Some scars never ever go away. Some scars remind you that you let yourself get burned. Some scars remind you that pain is a constant companion.

It was a remarkably regular day for one that would change the entire course of my life. A cold morning in December with a weak sun leaking through the low ceiling of gray clouds. Drips of icicles had formed patches of black ice on the pavement overnight, and my dad had gotten up extra early to throw neon blue salt on the steps and sidewalk. My mom ran the beads of a tasbih between her fingers, whispering prayers as she sipped her second cup of chai, a messy pile of books and graded papers next to her laptop, ready for her 9:00 a.m. lecture at the university. Her first cup of chai was usually finished before my sister or I woke up, before my dad sauntered down the stairs, ready for work. My mom liked to take her first cup of tea in the quiet dark of the kitchen by herself. "Chai in the morning should always bring saqoon," she told me once when I'd woken early and found her. *Peace.* "That was your nani's habit, your great-nani's, and now it's mine." When she smiled—in the Indian way, without revealing any teeth—tiny wrinkles showed next to her dark eyes that brightened whenever my sister or I appeared in the kitchen, the sleep still in our voices.

On that deceptively ordinary day, my dad hurried down the stairs, adjusting the collar of his shirt under his gray sweater, which was on inside out. When I told him he was about to commit a fashion faux pas, he shook his head, yanking his sweater off and pulling it back on correctly. It was odd because he was usually meticulous about how he dressed, but maybe it was another sign I'd missed.

My little sister, Amal, was seated at the kitchen island, texting her friends about some ninth-grade drama. I slid a bowl in front of her and poured cereal for both of us.

"Good luck on your presentation today, beta," my dad said to me. "Your thesis is brilliant."

I had to write a poetry comparison for AP English. I picked this famous Bengali poem, *Bidrohi*, by Nazrul, and wrote about how it was inspired by Whitman's *Song of Myself.* The British Raj banned *Bidrohi* because of its anti-colonial and rebellious spirit. And like Whitman's poem, it's about how the individual sees themselves as unique but also as part of the larger world. Nazrul's work inspired revolutionaries. In his time, Whitman was banned, too. Even lost his job because of his poetry. They were both rebels.

I looked at my dad and smiled, noticing the unusual puffy dark circles under his eyes. He'd been working late on a big case the last several weeks. "I am the fury of wild fire," I said, quoting Nazrul's poem.

"I burn this universe to ashes," my dad responded with the next line, then cleared his throat. "One thought..."

Oh no. When my dad got that pensive look on his face, it usually meant I was about to get peppered with questions. "Dad, no, please. I know what you're about to ask. I don't have time to change my presentation!"

"I'm not saying you have to change anything. But did you consider how each poet presented the role of the hero as the ordinary man?"

I scrunched my face up at him. "Dad! I thought you weren't going to ask any more questions."

"That doesn't sound like me. At all. But in case you decide to pursue this topic for, oh, a master's or PhD eventually, don't you think it might be worth interrogating heroism in light of the wars that influenced each writer? Just a suggestion."

I rolled my eyes. "Thanks, but I don't think my five-page paper and slide deck for AP English is exactly PhD thesis–worthy."

"Yet," he added. I braced for the follow-up queries, for a mini lecture. When he started down a path like this, it usually didn't end until he'd gone on about critical inquiry and the opportunities that awaited me at the University of Chicago. I was relieved he was too distracted to grill me any further.

I'd applied early action and received my acceptance the day before. I'd responded immediately. I was officially a Maroon, class of 2027. I was still walking around in a euphoric state while my dad already had my entire life planned. Only he wasn't planning the future I thought he was.

"But no pressure, right?" I smirked. My dad smiled back at me, his tired eyes shiny with held-back tears. He occasionally had these embarrassingly weird, sentimental moments. Not gonna lie, I didn't hate it. I was very much Daddy's little girl, always his coconspirator, whether it was for planning Mom's birthday surprises or for sneaking ice cream before bed. We were a little club of two.

"Dad, you have the nerdiest dreams for us," my sister said, shoveling cereal into her mouth.

Mom chuckled and glanced at my dad, suddenly buried in his phone. "All okay? No issue with the brief?" she asked.

My dad was a professor at DePaul Law School but wasn't teaching—he'd created the immigration and refugee justice clinic, and that was his focus. He was working on an asylum case that had been taking up more and more of his time. "Fighting the good fight." He nodded absentmindedly, still gazing at his phone. "The latest SCOTUS ruling is maddening. The entire line of inquiry was wrong. It's Lawyer 101 to—"

Amal and I looked at each other. We guessed he was about to bust out with his favorite mantra and beat him to it: "Ask all the questions. Be relentless in finding the answers."

He chuckled. "Okay, okay. I see my work here is done."

He began to hunt down his keys, which he always misplaced. "Try the pocket of your blue coat," my mom suggested. She was right, as always. Dad thanked her with a quick kiss on the cheek; then, jangling the keys, he rushed out the door, waving goodbye. He seemed to be in an extra hurry. I wondered if it had to do with the message he was absorbed with earlier.

A few seconds later, he walked back in, a blustery gust of wind following him. My sister and I looked up and then turned back to our breakfasts, only half paying attention to him. "It's colder than I thought it was," he said, reaching for the maroon cashmere scarf that my mom had given him for their twentieth anniversary a couple of months before. He'd gotten her a new teakettle. Thinking about it now, she must've been disappointed. I mean, a teakettle for an anniversary gift? I can't be sure because my mom never said anything, not to me anyway. She's like my little sister that way; she swallows her feelings.

"Very dapper, jaan," my mom said as he pulled the ends through a loop he made with the scarf.

My dad coughed and then cleared his throat before pausing to gaze at us. "My girls," he practically whispered, his voice cracking. "My beautiful girls." I waved away his extreme sappiness as he walked out the door.

We didn't notice until later that the beat-up brown leather satchel he usually took with him every day was sitting by the front door. He never bothered to come back and get it.

He never bothered to come back at all.

When we all got home, Amal said something about Dad forgetting his bag, and when my mom looked at it, her face fell as if she knew something was wrong. That beat-up old satchel was his security blanket, Mom used to joke. She walked over, opened the bag, and reached in with trembling fingers to pull out a note. I looked over her shoulder as she unfolded the paper. A couple of sentences written in my dad's neat, blocky handwriting. Words with enough fuel to turn our lives to ash: *I'm sorry. I can't do this anymore.*

She crumpled the piece of paper in her fist and walked up the stairs. We didn't hear her sobbing until after she slammed her bedroom door shut.

Then we were sobbing, too.

The cruel act of not being loved back by the person you love the most burns like white-hot phosphorus. Maybe it's not that there was no love, just not enough. Maybe they loved themselves more than they loved you. They might've promised they'd walk through fire for you, and you realized too late that they were the one lighting the match.

THREE
MONTHS
LATER

CHAPTER 2

The universe is punking me.

That is the only logical conclusion I can draw from the tragic chain of events that has defined my life the past three months. Destiny sucks. That's just science.

I'm starting at a new school. During the last quarter of senior year. What a joke. Not the funny-ha-ha kind; more like the fate-hates-me kind. After Dad left, his side of the family sorta ghosted us. I guess our existence was too awkward or maybe too painful for them. Sure, my aunties love some melodrama, but we were a living tragedy. There wasn't going to be a big song-and-dance number with a happy family reunion. Dad made that clear. We were never, ever, *ever* getting back together.

Adults get divorced. I understand that. But this? What my dad did, it's a whole other level of betrayal. But what I don't get is how my dad, a lawyer who fights so hard for refugee families to be together, couldn't fight for *our* family. He gave up on us without uttering a word.

He called me once—a week after he left. He'd moved back to London—where he'd lived until he was seventeen. He talked like everything was normal, like maybe I could visit over the summer. I hung up while he was midsentence. I couldn't stand hearing how happy he sounded. How normal. He torched our lives, and for what? He's the one who always pushed us to ask questions, and now he was ignoring the one question only he could answer. He must've known how much it was killing me inside.

After it all fell apart, my mom came up with the brilliant plan to leave everything and everyone we knew behind. Literally. So here we are, in small-town central Illinois, where I know exactly zero people and am enrolled in a school that only has one AP class.

My mom loved our Chicago neighborhood of leafy trees and nerdy liberals. She was always going on about building community. I mean, she was on the board of a bajillion local nonprofits—helping resettle refugees, cleaning up the park, organizing fundraisers for the local children's hospital. Then my dad left, and she uprooted us from everything on the flimsiest hope that we could start fresh.

Nothing makes sense anymore, no matter how hard I try to figure it out.

Here's what I've pieced together: Dad had some kind of toxic midlife crisis that warped his brain. According to a *Psychology Today* article called "Runaway Husbands," my dad is part of an existential dread trend. He could have chosen to buy a fancy sports car, but no, he went for the most dramatic, damaging act possible. The official name for it is Wife Abandonment Syndrome, coined by this therapist named Vikki Stark. There are books and websites with all these women sharing stories like ours—their husband left a note on the fridge, took his golf clubs, and drove away. In the middle of eating pizza, a husband stood up from the table and said he didn't love his wife anymore and left. Some dude called from a work trip and said he wasn't coming home, ever. It's a shock for everyone but the husband, the dad harboring a secret, who created a plan to leave and was ready to step into a new life. I fell down an internet rabbit hole of stories about men giving up. Still, nothing I've read, nothing in the two sentences my dad left us, has given me any *real* answers to the boulder of a question that has been weighing me down for three months: *Why?*

As in, Why didn't my dad give us a single warning that he was going to blow up our lives?

As in, Why didn't he love us enough?

As in, Why did I ever believe a single word that came out of his mouth?

He set a fire and walked away, not caring that it burned down everything he claimed to once love to infinity. Now and forever, I'll be haunted by the words Dad whispered to me when I was little: *I might not always be there to put out the fire.* I didn't realize he meant he'd be the arsonist.

I rub my index finger back and forth over my scar, the ragged edge of my nail catching on my skin. In this absolute crap show of endless uncertainty that is my life, there is only one thing I know for sure: I do not want to go to school today.

I slide a cereal bowl across the squeaky-clean granite counter to my sister, who wraps her shaky fingers around it. I pour the cereal for her. And the milk. I put the spoon in her hand. At first, Amal was the one who seemed to take my dad's leaving in stride. She and my mom were always a twosome, and I thought they were coping together in their own way. Maybe that's why my mom didn't have enough energy for me. I was fine with it because Amal seemed to be okay, pretty good even, but it turned out I couldn't have been more wrong.

"Eat something," I say. "It'll make you feel better." God. I sound like my mother. The one from the Before Times. The Now Mom is at the other end of the counter, prayer beads in hand, apparently oblivious to the nervous panic of her daughters starting at a new school during the last quarter of the year.

"Might vom," Amal says, spooning some milk over the cereal in her bowl.

"It's first-day nerves," I try to assure her. "An empty stomach is probably not the best way to go. Right, Mom?" I turn to my mom, who looks up from her tasbih and gives us a weak smile, nodding at my sister.

"Noor is right," she mutters, touching Amal's elbow. "Eat something, beta." Her voice isn't exactly overflowing with maternal assurance, but it will have to do—it seems like the most energy she can muster these days. The last three months she's practically been a ghost. She looks it, too. Sunken eyes, dark circles. Stray gray hairs betraying her as they slip out from her usually perfect bun. I don't even know if she sleeps well anymore. I don't think any of us do, not really.

———

I start the car as Amal slides in and dumps her backpack by her feet. She seems more awake now, probably an adrenaline burst from anxiety. Apparently anxiety is a natural reaction to the shock and trauma we've been through. *Trauma.* The first time Amal told me about her therapist using that word, I didn't know how to react. Still don't. I guess I wasn't sure what word to use for a dad who leaves his family for no apparent reason.

Asshole. That's a word.

"You ready?" I ask.

Amal nods. "Do I have a choice?"

"I think Dad pretty much took away all our choices," I say.

Amal blows out a puff of air that ruffles her long, sideswept black bangs. "Can we not?"

I clench my teeth. Amal doesn't exactly defend Dad, but she doesn't seem as angry at him as I am. I look over to make sure she's buckled her seat belt, then put this ancient Karmann Ghia into reverse. It's my father's car. He didn't need it in his fancy new life in London.

While he's in London, we're in Bayberry, Illinois, in Champaign County, population 9,438, which is about as far from London as you can get—at least metaphorically. Even our old home in Chicago, which is only a two-hour drive, feels a million miles away. Mom supposedly moved us here to take a great new job at the nearby college that would allow her to spend more time with us, let us start over, together. Yeah, right. More like no one knows us, so they can't whisper behind our backs and give us those pitying looks my mom hates so much.

"You have your schedule, right?" I ask my sister. "Lunch money?"

Amal gives me a double thumbs-up. She's a master at the sarcastic hand gesture.

Everything sucks. We both know it.

"Primal scream?" I ask.

"Primal scream," she responds.

I count down from three, and we both scream at the top of our lungs as I cross the train tracks heading toward Bayberry High, home of the Battling Bulldogs. When our screams subside, I feel better. Like a pressure valve has been released. Amal's shoulders relax from her ears. I think she'll be fine. I hope she will be. She's always been able to make friends easily. Me, I'm mainly interested in making it to graduation on May 13 without combusting. Then I can head back to Chicago for college, and I'll finally be able to breathe again. I can hold my breath for a few months, right? The only upside to Mom randomly picking this tiny town to move to is that the school year starts and ends earlier, so I'll be in a cap and gown a full three weeks before I would've graduated at my old school. Silver lining to parental abandonment: shortest senior year ever.

I pull into the small parking lot of the two-story redbrick-and-glass building. It's modern, built in the last ten years. Bayberry is a rinky-dink town that's also pretty wealthy and white. Which is clear from the kids who are exiting their shiny cars. It's like the Upside Down of Chicago.

Amal and I glance at each other and get out of the Karmann Ghia and head into the building together.

We were told to report to the front office to meet the "school ambassadors" who would show us around and help us with anything we need. I need my family back; can they help with that?

"Is it me or are people staring at us?" Amal asks.

"Definitely staring at the new brown kids in town." I push the blue doors of the front office open as the words slip from my lips a little too loudly. A school secretary—a middle-aged white woman wearing a floral-print blouse—stares at us from over the tops of her reading glasses, a look of surprise on her heart-shaped face. Clearly she heard me.

Oops. *Excellent first impression, Noor.*

"Hi." Amal gives her a cheery wave. "We're the Khans. Uh... obviously."

"Of course, dear," the floral-blouse lady says with a smile. "Amal and Noor, correct?"

We nod.

"We're so excited to have you here. Welcome! I'm Mrs. Wright. Mr. Carter, the principal, is in meetings all day at the district office, but I know he'll want to personally welcome you both."

"Cool," I say, glancing around the small office. Mrs. Wright narrows her eyes at me a little. She can't already dislike me, can she?

She turns toward my sister and hands her a copy of her schedule, which also has her locker number on it, then points to a nerdy cute boy with wavy light brown hair who is standing so quietly at the end of the counter I hadn't noticed him. "This is Blaine. He's the freshman rep on student council and your ambassador. He'll show you the ropes, right, young man?"

He grins, and his blue eyes light up as Amal turns to him, brushing her bangs out of her eyes and giving him a shy smile. Ninth-grade flirting is so adorable. "Absolutely. If you need anything. I'm your man! Well, not your as in *yours* but... uh... well, you know. I... can... help... you."

"It's easier to speak if your jaw is off the floor, dude," a tall, lanky, and possibly desi (what!) boy sitting in one of the yellow chairs against the wall says before standing up. I stifle a laugh and do a double take because, holy unexpected demographics, there are other desis here?

Mrs. Wright tsks and shakes her head as she hands me my paperwork. "Noor, this is Faiz. You'll be in good hands with him." Wait. With that name he might be more than desi, he's also maybe Muslim? I thought Amal and I would be the only ones.

The four of us shuffle out the door as Mrs. Wright picks up a ringing phone. "Freshman hall is this way." Blaine motions toward the left. "That's where all our lockers and most of our classrooms are."

"Senior hall is that way." Faiz gestures to the right.

"You'll come by my locker after school, right?" Amal asks. I nod and smile.

For a second, I see her as a nervous, chubby-cheeked first grader again, and it crushes me a little. I wish I could fix everything for her, for us, but I don't know how. And anyway, when you're a kid, it's your parents who are supposed to make it all okay, and ours can't because they're the ones who broke us.

CHAPTER 3

I'm silent for a second as Faiz veers us toward senior
hall, showing me my locker. I look at the note card with my locker
combination on it, but when I spin the lock it feels too loose,
the numbers aren't clicking, so I lift up the handle and the door
opens—no combo necessary. The lock is busted. Awesome. Not
that I have anything of value besides my phone, which I shove into
my back pocket.

"You can put in a request to get that fixed. There's a form in the
front office," Faiz says. "But, uh...they might not—"

"Get to it this decade?" I guess.

"Something like that."

I shrug, resigned, and grab a notebook, my pencil case, and my
schedule so we can continue the tour. We take a few steps, neither
of us speaking. I take a breath and plunge into the deep end of conversation. "So did you get roped into giving me this tour because
you're...um, desi and—"

"Muslim?" he asks with a laugh. "Pretty much, yeah. At least Mrs. Wright didn't ask if we were related. I agreed so I could save you from getting stuck with an overly peppy member of cheer squad who would've grilled you with a million questions to decide your social worthiness."

I glance up at him with a wry smile. His brown skin is a shade or two lighter than mine, but his eyes are even darker and he's got incredibly thick, long eyelashes. They've got to be hazards when he wears sunglasses. "And *you* can spare me the interrogation because you've already summed up my Thor-like worthiness?"

He grins, and we take another right turn, passing a smallish but cheery-looking school library. "I think I've got you sized up."

"Please, enlighten me."

We pause next to the book return depository, and he gives me a shy up and down. "Well, you're wearing a tee from a band I don't know with an oversize sweater, so you're giving emo, but . . . the look on your face is telling me I should maybe shut up and continue the tour."

I raise an eyebrow. Okay, this guy has a certain adorable charm, but I'm not about to let him in on that. "So what does your flannel shirt and beanie say about you?"

"That I overslept, rolled out of bed, grabbed the first not-too-smelly clothes in reach, and that my hair is absolutely untamed under this hat."

I laugh out loud. I can't help it. This surprises me. *He* surprises me. I'd expected everything to suck about today. But Faiz definitely doesn't suck.

We continue walking down the hall. Faiz has this unbothered, easy gait. It reminds me of when I was little and my dad would take me on city nature walks. Making us slow down and observe what was happening around us. *Slowing down is good*, he said once. *You'll be surprised what you can notice when you slow down.* I suck in my breath. I hate how the good memories of him sneak into my thoughts like little fires I have to put out before they consume me. I clear my throat.

Faiz turns to me, eyebrows raised.

"Are we the only desi Muslims in the school?" I ask. It's impossible to miss how *not* diverse the school is, how heads swivel as we walk by, like I'm an oddity on display.

He sighs. "Yeah, pretty much. There are a couple other Muslim kids in the lower classes, but you and your sister enrolling has seriously upped the diversity at the school. There's maybe eight hundred students in the high school, and over ninety percent are white. And there's only a handful of teachers of color. Like four, maybe five."

"Damn."

"Honestly? I know people are gaping at us as we pass by, but at least some of it is because you're the new girl. I mean, two new students during last quarter? There's probably going to be an article about you in the newspaper."

I groan.

"Welcome to life in a small town." He stops in front of two large doors painted blue and yellow, with glass cases full of trophies and photos of various sports teams on either side. "This is the gym. Avoid it and hardcore jocks if you can."

"Duly noted," I say dryly, then glance at the clock on the wall. Only fifteen minutes until classes start.

"Faiz! Hold up!" a voice calls from down the hall, and Faiz turns to look, a big smile crossing his face as he takes in the girl running up to him. Maybe she's his girlfriend? Of course, I don't know if he's straight or bi or ace or if she...I force myself to stop speculating because I need to learn to mind my own business.

I glance away as a petite girl with a blond pixie haircut and bright blue bangs play-punches Faiz in the arm, then starts chatting with him a mile a minute. She's wearing a glittery black skull T-shirt and sports thick silver rings on both hands. Her heavy eyeliner and silvery gray eyeshadow are perfect. None of this was what I was expecting, but in a good way. Still, I'm wary of the unexpected. It's the unexpected things that can rip your heart out when you're not looking.

"Hi, I'm Juniper," the perky blonde says.

"Nice to meet you. I'm—"

"Noor. I know," she interjects. "Faiz has been talking about giving the new desi Muslim girl the tour nonstop."

Faiz rolls his eyes, then turns to me. "I, like, maybe mentioned it once."

"Yeah, maybe. Once." Juniper winks at him, then turns to me, eyeing my shirt. "Don't tell me you're an American Football fan?" she squeals.

I nod. "They're only the greatest Midwest emo band—"

"Ever!" Juniper and I practically shout at the same time. "Wait. You know that house? The one on the debut album?" she asks.

"Totally iconic," I say.

"It's super close by."

"Oh my God. I hadn't even thought about that. So..."

"Road trip!" we say in unison again, and then laugh.

I think I'm going to like her.

Faiz clears his throat. "Uh, we should probably get going."

Juniper shakes her head. "Never mind him. His musical taste falls between Midwestern Gen X dad and Disney soundtracks."

"Hey!" Faiz says, and pretends to scowl. Juniper gives him a little side hug.

"No shame in loving a musical," I say.

Juniper laughs. "Anyway, what's your schedule?" She glances at the paper in my hand. "Cool. We have AP English together first period. Also gym, ugh, the worst. And you'll eat lunch with us, of course. Ooh, maybe Faiz will even make lunch for you one day like he does for me," Juniper says, elbowing Faiz.

I'm unnerved by how nice they are. Maybe I am as jaded as my sister complains.

"Definitely," he replies. "Lunch. I can also give you the rest of the tour then."

"By 'rest' he means custodial closets and the band room because this is pretty much it," she says, gesturing widely, then looping her arm through Faiz's, directing us toward AP English. "C'mon, let's go find out if they're still letting us read books in English class."

I scrunch my eyebrows and follow behind them as they lead the way. What did that mean? I mean, I know books are being banned all over, but Illinois was actually trying to make sure it didn't happen here. My dad told me about some new law that they were trying to pass in Springfield that was anti–book banning. But it hadn't passed yet. And honestly, living in Chicago, going to a liberal school, book banning wasn't exactly the first thing on my mind, especially since my life became a shit show. But here I am now in a different reality.

As I think about Juniper's offhand remark, I hear my dad's voice: *Ask questions, beta. Find out what's going on. What books won't they let kids read in class?* Dammit. He's going to be in my head forever. Ironic since he obviously never spared me a second thought.

CHAPTER 4

Day two. One day down and way too many to go. I have a pretty light class load. Technically I only need English and PE to graduate. The school counselor pulled me out of lunch yesterday (which drew some looks; this school is seriously drama starved) to review my schedule and apparently only just realized that I'm basically in a physics class I'd already taken and that I have two study halls. She told me they don't usually let kids have more than one study hall, but they made an exception for me. My cup runneth over.

I have study hall right before lunch, so I get a pass to go to the library to see Juniper—she told me she works in there during fourth period and that it's a chill place to hang. I'm still getting glances from people who haven't gotten the *there's a new girl* bulletin, but I bet everybody will know my name by the end of the week.

I walk through the empty halls, lined with blue and yellow lockers, the buzz of fluorescent lights filling the silence. I pause at the library doors. When I was in ninth grade, I served on my school library's Dewey Book Award committee—every year the volunteers read through a selection of young adult novels and choose a short list of finalists for the prize that was named after an old librarian. Then the entire ninth grade voted on the winner, who was invited to speak to us.

Yes. I was a nerd. Am a nerd. But we got free books, got to have lunch in the library, and the other kids on the committee became my closest friends and we'd freely quote from books to each other with zero embarrassment. But I've distanced myself from friends the last few months. I still had lunch with them—before we moved here—but I said no to every study group gathering and ghosted the group chat. It's not that I suddenly disliked everyone; I just didn't know what to say or how to react to the "I'm sorrys" and pitying looks and to the walking on eggshells around me. Maybe I should've tried harder. Sometimes I worry that the only thing I'm truly good at is doing the exact opposite of what's good for me.

A month after Dad left, Amal got super depressed. I blamed myself for being so caught up in my own feelings that I didn't even notice her spiraling. Never saw how bad she was hurting. I mistook her silence for her being okay. I vowed to never let that happen again, and that singular mission became my entire focus. By the time my mom dropped the bomb on us that we were moving, I was barely making any effort with my friends anyway. Figured I was doing them a favor, because who wanted to be around a perpetually snarky buzzkill?

My friend Nayeli still texts me, though, and sends me YouTube links where they're singing gorgeous, acoustic versions of Taylor Swift songs, but I don't know how much longer they'll stick around when all my responses are red heart or flame emojis—the text equivalent of monosyllabic grunts. I feel kinda bad about it. But sometimes it's like I can't even think beyond this moment, right now in front of me. Sometimes it feels like it takes my all to make it to bedtime without exploding into a billion bits of blood and bone and rage.

I can't let myself lose it. My mom barely feels present even when she's in the room with us, and someone needs to be there for Amal. She says she's fine, now, but how can she be? She turned fifteen two weeks after Dad left. What an asshole. Couldn't even stick around for her birthday. Somehow she still isn't that mad at him. I guess sometimes I feel like I have to be angry on her behalf, too.

I take a deep breath before walking into the library. I thought the one good thing about moving away was that everything wouldn't be a reminder of home, of my dad, but I was wrong. Memories follow you like ghosts.

I push through the glass and wood doors of the "Media Center." I'm taken aback by how small it is. Yes, my old school was private and funded by the university and housed the largest collection of folk, myth, and fairy tales in the entire state of Illinois, so I'm spoiled, but this place is only the size of about three classrooms. Like the rest of the school, it's bright and modern looking. There are tables and a small computer lab area and even a few comfy blue and yellow couches.

Juniper is working the circulation desk. She waves me over when she sees me. I pass a bunch of empty shelves and library carts filled with books. "Do you have to reshelve all those?" I ask Juniper.

She harrumphs. "I wish. The butt cheeks on the school board made us pull all those books from circulation."

"Why?" I ask, even though I'm pretty sure I know the answer.

"Subversive content or some bull—"

Juniper stops herself as a petite thirtysomething Black woman emerges from behind a door marked STAFF ONLY. "Ahem," she says. "Juniper, language."

"Bull hockey is what I was going to say, Ms. Clayton."

"Sure." Ms. Clayton smiles and her dark eyes shine. She's wearing a cream-colored skirt with strawberries embroidered all over it and a green short-sleeve blouse that matches the strawberry leaves. Her medium-long locs are pulled into a low ponytail. She's rocking a cherry-red lip.

She walks right up to me with a warm smile. "You must be Noor."

A look of surprise passes over my face.

"Small town. Word travels fast."

I chuckle awkwardly. "Yeah, still getting used to that."

"You're a transfer from Lab High, right?"

I nod. God, it must be hard to keep secrets here.

"I moved down here from the city about three years ago. I used to live in Logan Square."

"No way! I'm a Hyde Parker," I say. I'm oddly excited to meet another Chicagoan here. "Why did you leave the city?"

"To complete my MLS at the university, and then I stayed on when I got this job. And you?"

I'm not ready to give the real answer. I can barely even face the question. "My mom took a teaching job at the college—social sciences department." I glance at Juniper with a pleading look in my eyes. She picks right up on my anxiety. Yesterday when Faiz had asked about my parents, I told the two of them that my dad didn't live with us. I didn't fill in any other details, but I'm sure the sound in my voice and the look on my face conveyed that it was a painful topic.

"I was telling Noor that the school board are a bunch of fascists," she says, letting me have a moment to catch my breath.

Ms. Clayton gives us a neutral nod and then starts taping up butcher paper over the empty shelves. Seems like a weird choice, unless you're trying to draw attention to the books being pulled....

"So they decided that all those books are—" I can't stop myself from asking more questions. This is what my dad would be grilling them about—the who, the what, the why. Figuring out if there was a case here. I cringe thinking of all the times people used to say my dad and I were alike because I have his chin dimple and I loved to argue in that exacting way lawyers do, even as a little kid. I can't lobotomize myself and extract all the Dad influence from my brain.

"Obscene." Juniper uses air quotes as she answers my question.

"That's like what, a hundred books?"

Ms. Clayton sighs and turns back to us. "It'll be closer to five hundred. District policy states that even a single objection to a book results in its removal from the shelves. It's then *reviewed* by a committee before it has a chance of being added back to the collection."

"Like I said, bull hockey." Juniper shakes her head. "A parent finds some tiny thing offensive and they get the book pulled so no one can read it."

My stomach churns. My old school library was the place my friends and I always hung out. If there was ever a book we wanted that wasn't on the shelves, the librarians welcomed requests. "Have they even read the books they're mad about?"

Juniper snorts. "Yeah, right. I think the only things those parents read are Facebook posts from alt-right news and trolls who know how to appeal to the Olds."

"Does the district specify criteria? Is there a rubric?" I take a deep breath. I can feel the low rumblings of anger pulsing through me. I nervously pinch my scar as I hear my dad's questions coming out of my mouth.

Juniper laughs. "Rubric? As if. The form is on the district website. Anyone can fill it out. They don't need to prove that they've read it. They can literally write *indoctrination* as the reason for the objection."

"It's both more and less complicated than that," Ms. Clayton sighs. I'm not sure what she means but what I'm hearing is *I don't want to get into all the details*. "I became a librarian because I believe in the power of story and want to get books into students' hands."

We watch as she walks over to the now hidden shelves and tapes flyers in the middle of the butcher paper. They all have the words BROOKLYN PUBLIC LIBRARY along with a QR code on them. "I shared my thoughts with the board about pulling the books, but they passed the new policy and what they say goes," she continues as she places a stack of the QR codes on a small table in front of the empty shelves. "If I refuse, they'll find someone else to do it. Worst-case scenario, they shut down the library. Recently, a *public* library in Michigan was defunded and forced to close because of objections to a handful of graphic novels by queer and trans authors, and now there is no library within thirty miles of the town."

"Oh my God. Do you think they could do that here?" I ask.

Ms. Clayton shrugs. "That being said, sometimes problems can be addressed creatively, via a side angle." She hands me and Juniper the QR code. I quickly scan it, and when it takes me to the Brooklyn Public Library site, I see that I'm able to check out ebooks even if I don't live in Brooklyn.

I show my phone screen to Ms. Clayton. Her eyes light up. "Welcome to Bayberry, Noor. Feel free to come by anytime during study hall. I'm always looking for volunteers," she says before heading back into her office.

I walk over to the library cart that Ms. Clayton was working by and look through a folder that's resting on top of the books.

"What are you doing?" Juniper whispers.

"Looking for..." My eyes fall on a spreadsheet, and I pull it out from the folder. "This," I say. "The list of books that are being pulled." I impulsively grab my phone from my back pocket and take photos of the hundreds of books that are on the challenged list. Then I realize why; it's like my dad trained me. "Always get receipts," I murmur.

"The list is on the district website, but I don't know how often it's updated."

"Is anyone even talking about this? Trying to fight it? We should go to a school board meeting and..." I trail off when I see Juniper rubbing her eyes.

She sighs. "Yeah. Been there. Done that. People know it's happening, but it's like they don't want to know. Like it's too much effort to care."

"Sorry, I didn't mean to assume you hadn't," I stammer. "My dad works on immigration and refugee law, and he had this one case where a refugee family was being relocated to this Illinois town. A bunch of people tried to fight against it, but my mom worked with him to build community support for the family and get them safely resettled. My mom is big into the 'all politics is local' thing, and my dad..." Talking about my dad makes me feel as if I'm swerving into an emotional crash.

Juniper raises an eyebrow that gets lost in her bright blue bangs. "I get it. But there's, like, maybe fifteen, twenty parents who are super well connected and have the time to complain and show up at every stupid board meeting, so they get their way. They don't care what students have to say. And they object to a lot more than books."

I lean over the circulation desk. *Get all the facts before you jump to conclusions.* How many times did I hear some version of that from my dad when he was working on a case? "What are other issues those parents go after?" I ask Juniper.

Juniper twists the silver snake ring on her index finger and then continues. "Last year, a couple homophobic parents got all ragey because two gay couples went to prom, so now I'm technically not allowed to take my girlfriend to the dance." She pauses.

I bite my lip. So she's not Faiz's girlfriend. *God.* I'm the worst. She's talking about rampant homophobia and my brain goes to cute boy. Shut up, hormones.

Juniper continues, unaware of the synapses misfiring in my head. "By that I mean my hypothetical girlfriend because I don't—"

My anger finally meets my spiraling thoughts. "You should be able to take your imaginary girlfriend anywhere! Banning queer couples is massive discrimination. How is it not illegal? This is public school; they can't do that."

"They get away with it because they're sly haters. And it's not like the school cares about homophobia. I still get called the f-word sometimes. Once someone put a Post-it on my notebook with the d-word on it, and Carter seriously asked me if it maybe had to do with the Earth Science river embankment assignment." Juniper rolls her eyes and grabs a pile of books to scan in as returned.

"What an asshole."

"Yeah. Also, they didn't *technically* ban same-sex couples from going to dances. They banned *all* couples because they know how to hide their discrimination. So now the school only sells single tickets to dances. Obviously, people go around it and have dates. But those parents along with Mr. Carter made their feelings about queer kids very clear between their dog whistles and talk about maintaining a wholesome culture at the school. I'm afraid it scared some kids to not be open about who they are or what they want."

I'm silent for a second because whatever I say can't express how shitty this all is. I give Juniper a sad smile.

"Look," she continues, "I'm not letting anyone shove me into the closet, and my parents have my back. But, like, a ton of those books being pulled are by queer authors. And what if there's some questioning baby queer that needs one of those books? When I read *Leah on the Offbeat* in eighth grade, I was cheering so hard for Leah and Abby to kiss, and it first sort of confused me, but then I was like, wait. Oh my God, my girl crushes make so much more sense now. I'm a lesbian! And then I was like, give me all the queer books. Now they're all getting pulled."

Lab High was the total opposite of this place. We didn't even have homecoming or prom court because, like, a hundred years ago the student body got rid of them for being sexist and non-egalitarian. We had trans and nonbinary teachers. We learned about pronouns in grade school. What the hell kind of place had my mom moved us to?

I shake my head. "I'm glad your parents are there for you." It pinches a little to say that, to remember what I'm missing. "I hate this all so much. Not to be all mushy on main because I know we just met, but I got your back... not that you need me to, or that you don't have other friends, or that—"

Juniper interrupts me with a smile. "I appreciate you. And same."

I wasn't planning on making friends here, but I think that's what I'm doing. Also, if people are being attacked, I can't stand around with my fingers in my ears. It's not just because that's what my dad would want or that I'm used to protests because of the ones my mom took me to; it's because it's the right thing to do. Last year I read Kip Wilson's *White Rose*, a novel about Sophie Scholl, who, along with her brother and a few other German college kids, protested Hitler's horrifying laws by distributing leaflets condemning him. When she was captured, Sophie talked about why she spoke up. Her answer was so simple but totally crushing—*somebody, after all, had to make a start.* The Nazis executed her when she was twenty-one, only three years older than me. That totally guts me every time I think about it. I clear my throat and meet Juniper's gaze. "Have the students ever collectively protested the, um..."

"The wildly fascist shit the parents and school board pull around here? Nah. I mean, Faiz and I went to the school board meeting Ms. Clayton was talking about. We freelance for the school paper and pitched a story about it. The adviser blew a gasket, saying it was controversial clickbait, not news. Weird that the journalism teacher is against reporting facts, huh?" Juniper shakes her head, a sour look of annoyance on her face.

"The less you know, the easier you are to trick and manipulate," I say. I know that from experience.

CHAPTER 5

I step out of the library, my head spinning with thoughts about what my dad might do or say. He'd probably be putting together a task force with my mom to confront the book bans. God. My brain still defaults to imagining my dad here. There are moments when I expect to see him when I walk down the stairs for breakfast. In my brain fog, I forget that he isn't really available to me, even if I have his number. Amal texts him sometimes, but I don't ask her about it. I don't want to fight with my sister over our crappy dad.

Students file into the hallways, hurrying to their next classes, talking loudly, laughing. A few glance at me, but I'm not interesting enough for a second thought. For the most part I'm invisible, which is fine.

I walked out a different library entrance, so now I'm a bit turned around. I've only been here a couple of days but it's embarrassing to be lost. If you live in Chicago long enough, you develop an innate sense of direction because of Lake Michigan. It's east. Chicagoans know where east is even when they can't see the Lake because you just *know* it's there. But in this town, I have no sense of direction. No internal compass telling me where I am or where I need to go.

I turn right with the flow of student traffic but spin around when I realize I'm heading in the wrong direction. I smack straight into a dude. We both drop our books, and because my pencil case wasn't fully zipped, my pens and lip gloss clatter across the floor. Perfect. Excellent. So much winning.

The guy was walking with two friends who don't bother to wait for him or help out—they walk away laughing. When I glance up, I recognize one of them from AP English. I shove the contents of my pencil case back in the pouch and zip it up.

"You good?" the guy asks. He's gathered up my notebook and binder and reaches out a hand to help me up. I stand without taking his hand, brushing the dust off my palms and coming face-to-face— or rather, face-to-chin—with shiny hazel eyes and broad swimmer shoulders. That's why it felt like smashing into a wall. My mouth opens but words don't come out, because the smile on the face attached to those swimmer shoulders is distractingly cute.

"You're half agony, half hope, huh?" he says, brushing his floppy caramel-brown waves out of his eyes.

"What?"

"The quote. Here?" He points at the cover of my notebook and then hands it over.

"Oh! Yeah, thanks. That's mine." *Wow. Profound statement of the obvious, Noor.* "It's a quote...from a book." Oh my God. Apparently when I crashed into this guy, I lost brain cells.

"Jane Austen?"

"Yeah, actually. How'd you know?"

"My mom is a huge Austen fan. That quote is embroidered on one of her pillows. She has Austen towels, T-shirts, and maybe a million tote bags." He shrugs.

I raise my eyebrows as I collect my things from him. "And you? Are you an Austen fan or are you one of those dudes who won't read *girl* books."

He chuckles. "Whoa. Shots fired. The new girl's here to mix it up."

I sigh. "Right. My entire purpose is to wreak havoc on this small, unassuming town."

"We could use more havoc. So wreak away," he says, then pauses. "That didn't come out the way I meant it to. I meant *wreak*, not *reek*." He scrunches his nose to indicate a bad smell.

I laugh. "Wow. That completely clears it up, thanks."

A faint blush appears on his cheeks as he sweeps his eyes to mine. "I meant this place is stale and we could use—"

"Fresh reeking?" I scrunch my nose in imitation of him.

Now he's laughing, too. "Please. Yes. Surprise us with the reeking of your choice."

I glance at the clock: only two minutes to get to class.

"Great running into you," I say. "Literally."

He smirks but, as I head away, calls out, "Hold up! I'm Andrew. And yes, I like Jane Austen."

"Good for you." I smile and continue walking.

"Aren't you going to tell me your name?" he yells after me.

I turn my head back over my shoulder and grin at him. "I thought you said you wanted to be surprised!"

I still don't exactly want to be at this school, but maybe it's not as terrible as I thought it would be.

CHAPTER 6

"They're censoring practically all queer or BIPOC authors!" I say to my mom the next morning at breakfast, desperate to show her how much we don't belong in Bayberry. "It's totalitarian bigotry. Why the hell are we even here? We wouldn't be dealing with this in Chicago."

"Language," my mother says, raising a weary eyebrow at me as she looks up from staring into her chai. That's what she got out of my rant? I swore once. Honestly, does *hell* even count as a swear?

"Mom. I'm talking about books being banned and you're worried about me saying—"

"H-E-double hockey sticks?" My little sister gives me a crooked smile as she puts a Pop-Tart into the toaster.

My mom sighs. "Yes, beta, you're right. It is awful. It's un-American. But there is nothing I can do to change district policy *this morning*. I'm meeting with the dean of the division about my research proposal today and I need to focus on that. There's a lot riding on it." She looks so drawn, gray. I hated the idea of moving. Hate it still. But I thought she'd at least be happy about it since she made the unilateral decision. I thought this was what she wanted. Maybe I shouldn't expect miracles, but she looks more worn out and resigned than ever.

Mom doesn't have time for my indignation. Fine. I pivot to something that I know will get her full attention. "I bet if Dad were here he'd—"

"But he's not here, is he? I am. So you're stuck with me." Her tone is sharp, like she's suddenly wide awake. Then she sighs deeply and rubs her hands over her face, softening her voice. "You have one quarter left before you graduate. Is it too much to ask for some peace around here?" Then she stands and walks away, ending the conversation.

"Sure. Why bother saving democracy," I mutter.

My sister grabs her hot toaster pastry, quickly tossing it onto a pale yellow plate. It's new and plain, like pretty much everything in this house. My mom wanted a fresh start—a *clean slate*, she said—for our new life. At the time, I hadn't realized that meant giving away almost all our worldly goods and replacing them with inexpensive Swedish box-store minimalism. It works, I guess. Everything—dishes, furniture, area rugs—they're all functional and have the added bonus of having zero memories.

Amal narrows her eyes at me as she bites off a chunk of strawberry frosted goodness and chews. "It's only been three days, can't you wait a little longer to take a stand or make a statement or whatever?"

I roll my eyes and stir some sugar into my tea, then zip my

hoodie a little higher. Don't need to show either of them what I'm wearing to school. Once upon a time, she would've supported me, but that was Past Mom. Now Mom would maybe want to kill me a little bit for my clothing choices. I'd say what she doesn't know won't hurt her, but that's a cliché that turned out to be a big fat lie. Because the things my dad hid from us ripped us to shreds.

Amal and I part ways by the front office as she veers toward freshman hall. Because of the way the school is set up and our different schedules, I don't see her during the day.

When I turn into senior hall, I find Juniper and Faiz hanging by my locker. I'm surprised to see them waiting for me. Is this what happens when you go to normie schools? The slightly left-of-center kids naturally gravitate toward each other? Even if they're practically strangers? I scan the hall, observing the various cliques huddled together. Faiz and Juniper pointed them out yesterday— they're mostly high school movie clichés. Band. Theater kids. Jocks (often separated by sport). Cheer squad. Vapers and pot smokers. The D&D crowd. Of course, there's overlap. The handful of other Black and brown students stick out in the sea of white faces. People assume BIPOC kids are always drawn together because they think we're like a monolith, but a lot of times we stick together as an act of self-preservation.

I step toward my new...friends? I still haven't decided if I'm even going to *do* friends here. Real friendship takes energy, and I don't know how many more people I can stand to disappoint. I don't want to imagine what my Chicago friends think of me ghosting them, and I'm too much of a coward to ask. Still, Faiz and Juniper are trying. Maybe I should, too.

"What's up?" I ask, dropping my backpack in front of my locker. "Am I about to get hazed?"

"What?" Faiz's eyes go wide. "No. I mean why would you... we're not..." We lock eyes and I smile, trying to let him know I'm joking. His skin turns a subtle shade of pink.

"A desi who blushes? The novelties of this place will never cease." I spin my combination into the lock, then remember it still doesn't work. Have to put that repair request in.

"Fine, fine. Make fun of the gentle giant," Faiz says, rubbing his forehead.

Juniper, who is dressed head to toe in black except for her sparkly silver Doc Martins, elbows him. "You're calling yourself a gentle giant? Are you a middle-aged dad in the body of a teen boy?"

"Does six one even qualify as giant?" I joke. I almost feel bad for Faiz, with me and Juniper razzing him. But it seems like he's having fun, and when he smiles he gets a dimple in his left cheek, which is alarmingly cute. Even curiouser, I think *I'm* having fun.

"Excuse me. I'm six two, and that makes me a solid foot taller than Juniper, and I've got, like, seven inches on you, I bet."

Juniper shakes her head. "So you're saying size does matter. *To you.*"

I clap my hand over my mouth to stop myself from laughing.

"I thought we were here to talk about that banned books list, not my size... err... I mean height." Faiz rubs an imaginary spot on his forehead as his eyes slide away.

"After chatting in the library yesterday, I thought maybe I'd try pitching another story about censorship to the newspaper," Juniper says.

"Probably hopeless," Faiz says. "Basically everyone knows about it so it's not exactly breaking news." Juniper narrows her eyes at him. "But try, try again, is what I say," he quickly adds, to Juniper's satisfaction. "It's not like Ms. Rove can kick us off the paper for asking for it."

I raise a questioning eyebrow.

"We both took the newspaper class last year," Juniper explains. "You can't take it two years in a row, so we're reporters-at-large. That's what I meant when I said we freelance. Literally for free."

"We don't even get class credit, but it counts as an extracurricular, so..."

"Padding that college résumé one story at a time, though technically you didn't need it." She gently pokes Faiz.

"Oh, are you already in somewhere?"

"I'm going to the CIA."

"The what now?"

"Sorry, the Culinary Institute of America, not the spy organization that violates human rights on the regular."

Juniper rolls her eyes. "He loves making that correction."

Faiz smiles and shrugs.

"I'm going to Pomona for the gender and women's studies program, though my parents are still hoping I'll switch and go to Northwestern so I'll be close by. But not a chance. I may look like I prefer vampire lairs, but give me that year-round vitamin D, baby." Juniper laughs.

"And then the Midwest will lose you forever." Faiz pretends to pout.

"You'll never get rid of me! I would die without your butter chicken!" She nudges him, then turns to me. "So...anyway, we were talking about pitching another idea to Ms. Rove."

I hand my phone to Juniper, and Faiz peers over her shoulder. "Well...look at the challenged books list again—they're mostly by queer or BIPOC authors. Could that be a new angle for a story?"

Faiz rubs his chin. "The last pitch was specifically about whether or not it was censorship. So maybe the angle this time could be about the identities of the authors?"

"Also, like, where does it end?" Juniper says, and hands me back my phone. She turns to Faiz and they start brainstorming pitches.

I dig my nails into my scar. The thing is, stuff like censorship doesn't magically end—an object in motion stays in motion until acted upon by an outside force. That might be physics, but I also heard that from my dad maybe a million times. He used the courts as the outside force, but as he and Mom reminded us, the courts aren't the only tool to make a change. Another tool is protest. I pull a binder and pen out of my backpack, throw my coat in my locker, and turn to Faiz and Juniper and smile as I unzip my hoodie.

I show them my white T-shirt that screams I READ BANNED BOOKS in large red block letters. At my old school, the Dewey Book Award committee sold these shirts as a fundraiser during Banned Books Week. Every year the school librarians put up banned book displays, encouraging us to read some of the most challenged books in the country. The money we raised from the tees went to buy books for less privileged schools.

Juniper nods approvingly. "You're mad as hell and you're not going to take it anymore!" We both look at her funny and she adds, "My mom loves saying that."

I nod, glancing down at my shirt. The thing about being angry all the time is that rage becomes your baseline and you almost start encouraging people to try to piss you off.

CHAPTER 7

Juniper, Faiz, and I stroll through the door of our first-period English class with Ms. Ashe—the only class that feels tolerable—besides my study halls, which I spend in the library. They're also the only two spaces that have this poster plastered on the wall:

IN THIS CLASSROOM, WE BELIEVE:
BLACK LIVES MATTER
LOVE IS LOVE
FEMINISM IS FOR EVERYONE
SCIENCE IS REAL
NO HUMAN BEING IS ILLEGAL

I haven't seen it in my other classes, but it makes me feel more comfortable in here.

Ms. Ashe clocks my T-shirt and winks at me as I take my seat in the front row, closest to the door. There are only fifteen kids in this class, so I could've sat anywhere, but I like to have an exit plan. Learned that from my dad, I guess. As I settle in, I notice a tall guy with shaggy blond hair next to me staring at me with a sour look on his face. He's one of Andrew's friends who was laughing when Andrew and I collided in the hall.

"What's that shirt supposed to mean?" He narrows his dark blue eyes.

"This is an AP class, so I assumed you could read. Should I sound out the letters for you, Ken?" I look at him with mock sincerity in my eyes.

"My name's Richard, loser."

"Well, Dick, keep your eyes on your own paper," I scoff.

Faiz catches my eye behind Richard's head and smirks.

"Is there a problem, Richard?" Ms. Ashe asks, an eyebrow raised. She walks toward us and starts handing out slim novellas to every student.

Richard clears his throat. "The new girl's shirt violates school policy." He looks up at Ms. Ashe as he takes a book from her, his eyes narrowed and jaw taut. He's telling on me? What is this, like, first grade?

I grit my teeth. "My name is Noor, and keep your eyes off my clothes."

He glowers at me. "So you're a special snowflake and the rules don't apply to you?"

"Richard, why don't you leave school policy considerations up to the administration and focus on the book at hand," Ms. Ashe says.

"He wants to stare at her chest!" a student on the other side of the room yells.

"That is enough. All of you," Ms. Ashe says in her stern teacher voice, walking to the front of the classroom, her arms folded over her chest. "I understand it's last quarter. Senioritis is hitting hard, but this behavior is unacceptable. Some of you might have already gotten your college acceptances, but I promise you none of your universities look well upon a poor second-semester transcript or a note from your AP English teacher withdrawing a recommendation."

A few nervous laughs ping around the room. "Understood?" There's a murmur of yeses, and Richard, whose face is now very red, nods silently.

Ms. Ashe turns her back to us, and while she's writing "Candide" on the whiteboard, Richard whispers under his breath but loud enough for me to hear: "Woke bullshit."

I want to respond, but Ms. Ashe starts speaking and I probably won't think of the perfect comeback until it wakes me up in the middle of the night.

"We're about to enter the best of all possible worlds—maybe," Ms. Ashe says. "Over the next week, we'll be studying Voltaire's *Candide*."

I've read it. I've read everything on this class curriculum already. The English department at my old school was way into "academic rigor." *Candide* is a story about the shortcomings of the philosophy of optimism. It's about a super-naïve dude who lives an incredibly privileged life and then becomes disillusioned with pretty much everything he's learned and what he's been told he has to accept.

I tune back in to Ms. Ashe mid-explanation. "...a satire that was actually quite scandalous in its day," she says. "The novel was banned for being blasphemous and challenging the political status quo." She looks right at me as she finishes her sentence. "Book banning has long been used to silence those who want to speak out, those who are unwilling to be gaslit into thinking they're living in the best of all possible worlds."

CHAPTER 8

I'm in the middle of physics when the intercom crackles on and the school secretary's voice chirps over the loudspeaker: "Noor Khan, please report to the principal's office. Noor Khan, please report to the principal's office." I sigh as every head in the classroom swivels toward me and a few oohs float around the room.

Mr. Graham nods at me and gestures at the door without breaking stride as he reviews Newtonian mechanics beginning with his first law: *An object at rest will only move when acted upon by an outside force.* I slowly stand, grab my things, and head out. Of course, I've heard of kids being called to the principal's office over the loudspeaker, but my old school didn't do it that way. A counselor or administrator always showed up in person to get you. You were still having your butt hauled in, but in a less let's-humiliate-students-as-much-as-possible kind of way. But the Bayberry way is apparently name and shame. Noted.

I slink into the front office. There's no noise except for the low-key annoying buzz of the fluorescent lights and the soft clack of Mrs. Wright typing at her computer. She looks up when I walk in and gives me a sympathetic smile as she gestures to Mr. Carter's open door. His back is to me, and he's chatting on the phone. His voice is deep and confident—the kind of tone that makes suggestions seem like commands. He hangs up. I knock softly on the doorframe. He spins around in a large black leather swivel chair that reads more like rich CEO than small-town high school principal.

He's not exactly what I was expecting. First, he seems kind of youngish? Maybe in his late thirties? Early forties? He's tall with broad shoulders and a defined jawline. "Ms. Khan," he says with a wide smile that shows off his blindingly white teeth. "Come in. Come in. Sorry to keep you waiting." He's friendly and welcoming. Maybe I'm wrong about why I was called down here. I've had to check a lot of assumptions about this place the last few days. "Have a seat. Please."

I enter his incredibly neat office. The light streams in through floor-to-ceiling windows that face the side lawn of the school, and there's not a single dust mote floating around the room. A computer sits on his large wood desk, and that's it. There are no folders or stray paper clips on it. I don't trust people who aren't at least a little messy. They're obviously aliens.

"I'm Mr. Carter, the principal. I'm sorry I wasn't here to greet you on your first day at Bayberry. But duty called. I was lucky enough to meet your little sister earlier this morning. A delightful young lady." Okay, this dude may not be ancient, but he talks as if he's living in a 1950s TV show.

I nod and he continues. "I realize you've only recently moved here, but I'm sure you've gleaned that Bayberry is a special place. This community takes a lot of pride in this school. I'm a lucky alumni myself. I can't say I understand how hard it must be to be uprooted and to start at a new school—especially so close to graduation. But you'll find plenty of welcoming folks here and a culture of acceptance. Honoring diversity is one of the key tenets of Bulldog citizenship."

My eyebrows shoot up. I might gag. Pretty sure the phrase "culture of acceptance" is something he picked up from some mandatory professional development seminar. Don't even get me started on "honoring diversity." My old school used that same phrase until we decided to change it to "stewarding diversity" to signify taking meaningful action. Like, you gotta do more than claim you love "chai tea" and "naan bread" and say Happy Diwali to someone who isn't even Hindu but wanting a cookie for the effort.

He clears his throat. "Now, this atmosphere of…um…tolerance and kindness is something that we must all contribute to. Wouldn't want to be the weakest link in the chain, now, would we?" He flashes that toothy smile again.

I nod and force a grin onto my face as I run my index finger over my burn. I'm not totally sure what Carter's getting at because this lecture so far sounds like catchphrase soup, but the panicky feeling blooming in my chest tells me things are about to take a turn for the worse.

He steeples his hands in front of him. "Excellent. I'm glad we agree. Now, while I had hoped this would be purely a social call, I'm afraid we need to discuss the little problem of your sartorial choices."

There it is—the other shoe dropping. I pull my notebook closer to my chest like a shield. I knew this shirt might get some attention—that was the point—but now that I'm sitting here, I can feel myself shrinking in my seat a little, questioning all my life choices. The principal's fake friendly voice echoes around me. Wearing this I READ BANNED BOOKS shirt was a stupid idea. It definitely didn't help my plan to fly under the radar until I graduate. On the other hand, I should be able to wear whatever I want. It's not as if students give up all our rights when we walk into school.

"Look, I understand. You're new." He continues to speak as if this were actually a conversation and not a diatribe. "You might not have had time to read the entire student handbook yet." *God.* Did anyone *ever* read that? He pulls out a narrow blue pamphlet from his drawer—it's titled "Bayberry High School Student Code of Conduct"—and hands it to me. "Provocative clothing is not allowed at Bayberry."

"Provocative? I'm wearing jeans and a T-shirt." My old school had stupid sexist dress codes, too, that seemingly singled out girls—like no midriffs or spaghetti straps or skirts shorter than mid-thigh—but *this* was beyond.

"I think you misunderstand that term, Ms. Khan. By provocative we don't only mean clothing that might be considered lewd."

Lewd?! I'm glad Mr. Carter can't read my mind because it's absolutely cussing up a storm right now.

"We also mean clothing that might distract or interfere with a sound educational environment for all students." He pauses and raises his eyebrows.

"And my T-shirt—"

"Your T-shirt," Mr. Carter interrupts, his jaw tightening for the briefest instant, "is clearly a challenge to school board policy."

"This shirt expresses a statement of fact. I noticed *Huck Finn* on the curriculum here," I say. "Some people might think a novel that uses the n-word so many times might be, uh, provocative, too."

Mr. Carter takes a deep breath, trying to show me how patient he's being. "Your intent is to spread disinformation by willfully misconstruing school policy and to stir up trouble with this fake controversy. It's disruptive to the learning environment. There are no book bans in this district."

My jaw drops. Is he serious? I literally watched while Ms. Clayton pulled five hundred books from our shelves, but he's saying that's fake news? He's gaslighting me, and he's not even subtle about it.

"You'll find I have zero tolerance for political rabble-rousing. I run a tight ship, Ms. Khan. You will report to C-100 for detention today after school." Mr. Carter points to the door, ushering me out.

I stand up, realizing I've rubbed my burn scar so much that my skin is red and angry. This is such crap. I look at Mr. Carter and adopt a compliant tone because I don't want to get in even more trouble. "Is there any way I can serve it tomorrow? I drive my sister home from school and I need to find her a ride."

"You will serve your detention today. Your sister can wait for you in the library, which remains open until five p.m. Abide by the rules, Ms. Khan. That's the easiest way to avoid any friction. Presumably you want what little time you have in our district to be pleasant?" Mr. Carter flashes me a huge smile as I head out the door. "Welcome to our school," he calls out as I leave. "We're so happy to have you."

CHAPTER 9

I skulk into C-100, the designated study hall/detention room. Faiz and Juniper gave me pitying looks when I told them about my conversation with Mr. Carter. Faiz was surprised I hadn't gotten multiple days of detention. Carter's reaction seemed pretty extreme for a T-shirt that didn't have *lewd* images or swear words on it, but Juniper told me he ran the school like his sad little fiefdom. The guy must be real fun at parties.

I hand a detention slip to the deeply disinterested teacher. He looks up from his book and gives me a curt nod, jerking his head toward the desks in the completely empty room.

I head to the back and sink into a chair. I pull out *Candide* from my backpack and stare into the pages. Now I have forty minutes to ponder all the ways my mom is going to be deeply disappointed in me. For setting a bad example for my little sister. For causing trouble during my first week at a new school. I'm lost in thought, catastrophizing about the multitude of ways my mom might nonviolently murder me, so I don't notice another student take a seat next to me. I swivel my head to glare at them because literally every seat is open and they had to choose this one?

It's Andrew. The dude with the floppy hair who I bumped into outside the library. I bite back my smile.

"We meet again, New Girl," he says with a lopsided grin. "I guess you were serious about wreaking havoc. Detention your first week? That's gotta be a record."

I glance at the teacher, who is leaning back in the swivel chair with his feet propped up on the desk and a baseball cap pulled down over his eyes. He's clearly not a stickler for the no-talking-in-detention rule. I turn to face Andrew. "What are you in here for?"

"Busted with cigarettes in the parking lot."

I raise my eyes to his, a look of shock sweeping over my face. "Like, actual cigarettes? Not a vape pen? I didn't think anyone under the age of fifty still smoked."

"Oh, they're not mine. I mean...I don't smoke. Like, not at all. My...um...a family member died of lung cancer, so I would never touch a cigarette."

"Sorry, I—"

"They belonged to my friend James. He doesn't really smoke, either. Kinda has them to piss off his dad. I was holding his pack because he had to run back inside the building. Unfortunately, Carter was outside and caught me with them. No way he was going to let that slide."

"Your friend let you take the fall for him? That's not cool."

"But what, it's cool to narc on your friends?"

"Depends on the reason, I guess."

Andrew pretends to be taken aback. "Cold-blooded. No loyalty, huh?"

"Not unthinking loyalty, no." I turn back to my book.

From the corner of my eye, I see Andrew slouch back into his chair. He sits there for a few moments as I pretend to read. Then he turns back to me and leans across the aisle, narrowing the distance between us. His hazel eyes twinkle under the normally unflattering fluorescent lights. "So are you going to tell me your name, New Girl? Since we've been thrown into this harrowing situation together?"

"It's detention, not a medieval gauntlet."

"Difficult situations bring people closer."

"Hold up. This is as close as you're going to get." I gesture to the space between us.

He looks into my eyes. Pauses. A second. Two seconds. It's starting to get awkward. But I do not want to be the first one to look away, so I whisper, "Are we having a staring contest?"

He breaks into a smile, but still doesn't blink. "I would destroy you."

"Wow. You're giving off real white-man middle-manager false-confidence vibes, Andrew."

He throws his head back and laughs. He doesn't seem worried at all that we're going to get busted for talking in detention. Then again, the teacher up front is snoring, so we're probably okay. "I will have you know that my confidence comes from both practice *and* privilege."

I smirk and shake my head.

"So, *Noor.*" He pauses to make sure I've clocked that he already knows my name. I have, but I don't say anything. As I've learned, it's not that impressive to find out the name of the new girl in such a small school. "Who'd you piss off to cop detention?"

I sigh and start to unzip my hoodie.

"I like where you're headed with this, but detention is a strictly G-rated space."

I roll my eyes. "Calm down," I say, then twist my body to show him my T-shirt. "Carter did not approve. According to him the concept of reading is provocative and basic statements of fact are not protected speech."

"Damn." Andrew's jaw drops. "Not even a week and you're headed to the top of Carter's enemies list. Impressive." He holds my gaze.

My cheeks start to warm and I do my best to ignore the tiny flutters rising in my chest. I chew on my lower lip and shift gears. "It seems like most kids aren't too bothered by the book bans. . . ."

He shrugs. "Maybe because no one thinks it's that big a deal? It's a bunch of uptight parents not wanting their kid to read about sex or whatever. Who needs books for that when you have Netflix?" He chuckles to himself.

I ignore the joke. "Not that big a deal?" I say a little too loudly, and it causes the detention monitor to readjust his arms across his chest, but he doesn't wake up. "Ever heard of freedom of speech? Banning books is some Nazi-level BS."

Andrew raises his eyebrows. "Nazis? That's a little . . . dramatic."

"No," I say flatly. "It's not. In fact, banning books has been a part of the fascist handbook forever. First they ban books, then they burn them. Then they make people enemies of the state." I flinch for a second, realizing I sound like my dad, but I don't let myself get distracted. Standing up to state oppression might be a concept he introduced me to, but he doesn't get to own it.

"I don't think the school board has the power to make you an enemy of the state."

"You're talking to a brown Muslim girl. I don't think you have any idea how little it actually takes to ban a human being."

Andrew sits back and doesn't say anything else. The flirty, bantery moment dissipates, fizzling out like a dying sparkler. "All it takes," I whisper, more for myself than for him, "is for good people to stay silent and do nothing."

CHAPTER 10

My mom is waiting in the kitchen when I walk in, and she does not look happy. Our front door opens directly into our open-concept living area, so there's no place to hide. Amal whispers, "Good luck," as we slip off our shoes before walking farther into the house.

I open my mouth to speak, but I don't get a chance to utter a syllable.

"What were you thinking?" Mom emphasizes every word. Loudly.

Rhetorical question, obviously. But that doesn't stop me. "I was thinking that making a statement against a fascist policy was a good thing. You know, standing up for what's right like you and Dad taught us. Or are we supposed to forget everything from the Before Times?"

My mom winces when I reference my dad. Seeing her react to the word *Dad* like that twists my insides, but if I'm being honest,

I'm not that sorry. This may be the most responsive she's been to me since he went away.

She clenches her jaw. "Don't you dare throw that in my face. I'm not the one who abandoned this family. I'm trying to do what's best for us."

I shrug off my hoodie and leave my shoes on the low shelf by the door. I'm trying to buffer my rage, count to ten, breathe. *Pause between your impulse and action*, some tiny logical voice in my head is saying. But I don't listen. "Doing what's best for us? Are you serious? You dragged me away from school, from my friends, from our home during the last quarter of my senior year. Please, explain how this is best for me. How is this crappy little no-diversity, authoritarian town best for anything?"

"You're not the only one in this family that I have to think about," my mom says, her voice dead calm and soft, but her words are a body blow. Did she really think this was best for Amal? I turn from her to look at my sister and roll my eyes.

Amal's standing with the fridge door open, her face twisted up. She shakes her head at me, urging me to stop. Conflict makes her anxiety spike. I get that. But anger swells in me like a tidal wave.

My mom looks through me with hollow eyes. "We all needed a fresh start. Needed to get away from..." She trails off, then clears her throat and starts again. "You clearly don't always know what's best for you. You've proven that with this little stunt that landed you in detention your first week at school. You have no idea how foolish it is to draw this kind of attention to yourself. How easy it is for them to scapegoat us."

I clench my hands at my sides. "Draw attention to myself? I do that just by existing. This district is, like, ninety percent white and Christian. You think me wearing a dumb T-shirt is going to be the thing that alienates me?" My voice is raspy, and I choke back a sob. When I'm angry, I tend to cry. That's always how I've been. And I hate it.

"I'm trying to keep you safe. I'm the only one left to take care of both of you and—"

"Is that what you've been doing? Because it doesn't feel that way to us."

My sister lets out a small gasp and then whispers, "You don't get to speak for me, Noor." She and my mom exchange glances, sharing some kind of understanding I'm not part of, and it reminds me that when my dad left, it made me the odd one out at home, too.

———

I haven't put anything on the walls in my room. It's a blank slate. White walls. White shelves for my books—a lot of which are still in boxes. Fake wood desk that has my laptop on it. The only thing that feels like me is my bed—I begged my mom to let me keep it. Not that it's special—a platform with drawers underneath it. But it's piled high with a cloudlike maroon duvet. On top of that rests a worn kantha quilt—a beaded patchwork of dark reds and blues that I've had since my nani brought it back from a trip to India when I was in grade school. She isn't with us anymore, but when I snuggle under it, I swear it holds a lingering scent of coconut oil and rose attar that was Nani's favorite, combined with the light smell of the citrus- and yuzu-scented cleaner we used on our old wood floors. I read once that smell is our closest link to memory, and maybe that's why this bed feels like my only safe space. It's the last piece I have of home.

I keep hoping I'll close my eyes and wake up and this will all have been a terrible nightmare. That I'll be small again. That I can wrap my arms around my dad's waist and that he'll pull me up and kiss my forehead and say, "I love you to infinity." Then I'll respond, "I love you to infinity plus two weeks." He'll laugh and won't bother explaining the concept of infinity to me again because he knows what I mean. What he should have taught me is that his infinity had a limit. What he should have taught me is that his love was a promise that he was always going to break.

There's a soft knock at my door.

I jerk the quilt off my head and scooch up so I'm leaning against the wall. "Come in, Amal."

My sister gently pushes the door ajar, shoving a white flag—a paper towel taped to a chopstick—through the door. "I come in peace," she says, then steps through, shutting the door behind her.

"That's what they all say."

She sits at the foot of my bed. "Are you still pissed?"

"What do you think?"

"I think you're always mad. So let me rephrase, are you more ragey than usual?"

I roll my eyes at Amal. "Ha ha. Not *always*."

"Name one time since we moved here that you weren't angry," she says as she turns to me, crisscrossing her legs.

"Last night when I was asleep."

She makes a loud buzzing sound. "False. I can hear you grinding your teeth from outside the door."

I toss one of my throw pillows at her head but she catches it.

Amal looks at me with a little smile. Her wide brown eyes have always been doe-like. It makes everyone around her want to protect her. Me, especially. Especially since Dad left. "Seriously, sis, can't you give Mom a break? I think she's trying her best."

I run my scar over the nubby weave of my kantha quilt as I try to figure out what to say. Mom has felt so absent, but I don't think Amal sees things the same way I do. When I'm not in the room, I can sometimes hear them chatting, even heard my mom laugh with her recently. I chew on my bottom lip. Sometimes it feels like Amal and I have two totally different moms.

Amal continues, "Is part of the reason you're so upset about this book-banning thing because Dad would be?"

I suck in my breath, my eyes start to sting with tears, but I refuse to let any fall. "No! This isn't about him. I'm upset because it's effed up." A shot of outrage pushes me up. Maybe Amal has a point, but I don't...can't let my mind linger on that. I take a deep breath, trying to relax and sound rational. "Imagine if someone took away all the books in your room." Amal's nightstand overflows with a pile of young adult novels—mostly fantasy.

Amal turns to face me. "Duh. I get it. I know you think *someone* has to do something and that the someone has to be you. But—"

"But what?" I ask more curtly than I mean to.

"I don't mean to get all therapy talk on you, but maybe you're angry about a lot more than the book bans but that's just what you're channeling your rage into."

My thoughts wander. Maybe I'm a sucker for lost causes and underdogs. Maybe I'm trying to pick a fight so I can feel something.

Maybe both. I don't know how to respond to Amal because I don't think I can admit that maybe she's right.

"You know," Amal continues when I stay silent, "it's not like Mom's okay with book banning. She can't deal with everything all at once, that's all. She's probably pissed at the world, too."

I feel a stab in my chest. For all the ways I'm like my dad, I sometimes forget that maybe there are ways I'm like Mom, too.

Amal flops backward onto my bed and grabs the one stuffy I have kept. *Fluffy*. A little light brown dog with dark brown ears. Fluffy has been *through it*. The bald spots on his fake fur prove it. She holds him to her chest. "Do you think that's why Dad took the cases he did? Because he felt like he was the someone who had to do something?"

I flop down next to her. "I don't know," I whisper. "I don't understand anything about why he did what he did."

A tear drips down Amal's cheek. She doesn't say anything else. Just gets up and starts to walk out of the room.

"I'll apologize to Mom," I say. I know that's what Amal wants. She wants to avoid any friction. Maybe she believes that it will somehow make our lives normal again. But there is no normal. Not anymore. At least not for me.

CHAPTER 11

Only a few hours until an entire week at this hellhole is in my rearview. The thing is, the last couple of days, Amal's been, well, peppier, than she's been in a long time. I glance at her as she unbuckles her seat belt. I'm happy she's adjusting, but I'm also nervous that it's precarious, an act. Amal seemed fine in the days and weeks after Dad left. Until she wasn't. Until she wouldn't... couldn't get out of bed one morning. I hadn't noticed that she was depressed. But then again, I wasn't paying attention. I was throwing myself into a bunch of different things at school, trying not to think about what was happening to us. Until I opened my eyes and realized the fridge wasn't as full as usual. Sometimes we'd run out of milk. Sometimes there wasn't bread for sandwiches. Sometimes my mom didn't notice at all until I said something to her.

Then I walked into Amal's room one morning to find her lying in bed, fully dressed, eyes open, but refusing to respond to me at all. I called a friend's mom—a doctor at the hospital—and she helped us figure it out. Talked to my mom and helped get Amal into therapy. Amal's been on antidepressants ever since. She's definitely better now. But I can't get her catatonic look out of my mind. I'll do anything to make sure she never feels that way again.

"Why are you staring at me? Do I have cream cheese on my face or something?" Amal asks, and quickly flips down the visor to check herself in the mirror.

"Uh…" I quickly snap back to the moment. "As if I'd tell you and let you miss out on the opportunity to have Blaine point it out," I say.

"Staaaaahp." She stretches out the word and rolls her eyes at me.

"What? Like he hasn't been texting you since the second you met?"

Amal turns to open the car door and throws a wide-eyed innocent look over her shoulder. "He's being nice, okay? Like introducing me to people. Making sure I have everything I need."

"Oh, I'm sure he's happy to meet your needs," I quip, and hurry out of the car before she can throw something at me.

"I meant for my classes!"

We're both laughing as we slam the car doors shut. A whistle comes from behind us. I whip my head around, ready to murder whoever is catcalling us.

It's Andrew, and he's staring at…my car. "A Karmann Ghia, huh? Very retro surfer girl."

"Yeah, I hear the swells in central Illinois are killer," I deadpan. "Beggars can't be choosers." I glance sideways at Amal, who is pressing her lips together, clearly attempting not to make a wiseass remark.

"No. I mean, it's awesome. I love old cars."

"Shocker," I say with a small grin.

"Somebody woke up on the judgmental side of the bed this morning," he says, and steps closer to me.

"That's her preferred side," Amal jokes.

"Hey!" I say as Andrew laughs.

"You must be the smart little sister."

"Yeah, smart-ass." I wink at Amal, who scrunches her nose at me.

"I'm Amal and my sister is jealous of my brilliance and incredible organizing skills." Amal smiles and shrugs her backpack onto both her shoulders. "See you after school? Unless you're planning on getting detention again?" She smirks and heads inside.

Andrew waves as Amal walks away and then turns back to me, his hazel eyes bright and catching the morning light so that they're almost translucent. He gives me a small smile. I tuck a stray strand of hair behind my ear and clear my throat. That's how cool I am. Ready to flirt by clearing phlegm at a moment's notice. He's cute but also kinda blasé about the book challenges, and that bugs me. "Hey. I wanted to ask you about that thing you said in detention. About the book ban?"

"Yeah...I know. I was giving off troll vibes. Sorry, my inner jerk sometimes has a mind of its own." He raises his shoulders and gives me a sheepish grin.

"Oh...I..." I stumble over my words, then laugh a little, caught off guard by his easy earnestness and quick apology.

"Andrew!" a guy from across the parking lot calls out.

We both turn to him. He's tall, lanky, and standing against a red convertible—obviously a vanity buy. I mean, it can only be top down for, like, four months a year. He looks totally unbothered—an attitude I actually envy.

"That your friend James? The contraband cigarette dude?"

Andrew nods.

James waves, then throws me this *look*, which I'm having a hard time interpreting. He lets his eyes rest on mine after giving me the once-over.

"Can I catch up with you later?" Andrew asks.

"Sure. Yeah."

"Cool. See ya," he says, and walks off toward James. I watch as they fist-bump. One of them says something funny because they both laugh. James catches me staring and tilts his chin at me, regarding me with a wolfish grin.

CHAPTER 12

The entire junior and senior classes eat lunch at the same time. With off-campus lunch privileges, though, more than half the kids are gone every day. There are only, like, three places to eat in town close enough to drive to and from during lunch, but Juniper tells me some kids go home or hang in the park across the street.

"Do you guys ever go out for lunch?" I ask Juniper and Faiz as we sit at one of the round tables along the perimeter of the lunchroom.

Juniper shrugs. "Sometimes when the weather is nice. But chili dogs and grilled cheese at the Elms get old real fast. I could go home for lunch, but then I'd miss out on Chef Faiz's lunch du jour," Juniper says.

"I feel so used," Faiz jokes.

Juniper grins and winks at Faiz. "I *also* stay for your witty conversation and because you let me steal your fries." She swipes one of his fries and crams it in her mouth.

"It's a truth universally acknowledged that fries are the best food offering in every school cafeteria in America," I say, and reach over and steal another one of Faiz's fries. He narrows his eyes at me in mock anger.

"You're an Austen fan, too? I love *Pride and Prejudice*, but *Persuasion* is my favorite! I'd take Wentworth over Darcy any day," Juniper says, and plops her Doc Marten'd feet onto the empty chair next to her. I raise an eyebrow. "If I actually liked dudes," she continues. Then raises the back of her hand to her forehead in a mock swoon. "So much longing and unrequited love and doing right by your family and being an old maid at the age of twenty-seven."

I am half agony, half hope.

"Yeah, it's why I think Jane Austen was secretly Indian," I say. Faiz and Juniper laugh, but their laughter fades into the background as my mind wanders to my parents and our family viewing of *Bride and Prejudice* that led to parental inside jokes and a deeply cringeworthy moment of PDA.

My parents have never pressured me about marriage—ever. In fact, if I told them I wanted to get married at twenty-two, they'd have heart attacks. They had a love marriage. That's one of those facts that always gets curious, surprised looks from non-desi, non-Muslim people when they ask if my parents had an arranged marriage or if I'm "promised" to someone or some BS. Nope. But I'm also not allowed to date. That's been the unwritten rule as long as I can remember. Some people are shocked about that, but it's never bothered me. It just is.

My parents met in college. They helped form the Muslim Students Association together. Dad's family moved to the States when he was a junior in high school, so he jokes about how Mom fell for him because of his James Bond accent. My dad says he fell in love with my mom at a protest as she stood shouting "No blood for oil" while hoisting a homemade sign. "She is only five feet, but she stood so tall that day. So smart. So fierce. Always putting her words into action," my dad once recollected with pride in his eyes.

I always thought my dad and I were close; I thought we understood each other. But I read him totally wrong. I've been racking my brain to determine the Why. The real one. One that justifies what he did, like he was in witness protection or had discovered aliens and now was in quarantine. But all my internet dives into Wife Abandonment Syndrome say that there will never be any satisfying answers. And that's enraging. It's also deeply pissing me off that it's called *Wife* Abandonment Syndrome, because my dad abandoned me, too.

I need to understand how we seemed so happy and yet Dad wasn't. "I knew she was the one I'd want to be with forever," he'd say when talking about my mom. I want to know when forever actually stopped meaning *forever* to my dad.

I absentmindedly reach for another of Faiz's fries at the same time he does and our fingers brush. A little flicker of flame travels up my arm, catching me by surprise. I suck in my breath. Faiz briefly locks eyes with me, then quickly pulls his hand away, drawing it into a fist before flexing it and turning to stare intently at the nutrition label on his iced tea.

Juniper sweeps her gaze from Faiz to me and a slow grin crosses her lips. I pretend not to notice.

Faiz suddenly blurts, "Do you realize how many grams of sugar are in this thing? They might as well restock pop in the vending machines."

Juniper tosses a crumpled napkin at him. "Are you a hundred-and-twelve-year-old man? Be a normal teenager. Consume many empty calories that rot your teeth. Live your best life."

Faiz runs a hand through his messy dark waves and nods a little sheepishly.

There's a brief, awkward pause. Where there's an uncomfortable pause, I seek to fill it. "Um, I have a question about the book challenges."

Juniper and Faiz sigh in unison—clearly this is a retread of a conversation they've had a million times. But Juniper kindly gestures at me to proceed.

"That first school board meeting instituting the new policy was like—"

"Three months ago. Right before winter break. They figured they could bury the lede by hiding it in the midst of Christmas." Faiz frowns. "By mid-December this whole town is deep into holiday frenzy."

"And there's only been one meeting since?"

"Yeah," Juniper responds. "That was the January meeting; the February meeting was canceled because of a snowstorm, and—oops!—they conveniently never rescheduled it. My mom told me some parents posted about how wrong and authoritarian the new policy was on the parents association Facebook page, though."

"That's all?"

"The only people who are hyped are the ones who started the

banning—Liberty Moms and Dads," Faiz says, dragging a fry through ketchup.

I nod, familiar with the group—they're a super fashy right-wing group with chapters all over the country.

Juniper continues. "The school board voted three to two to institute the new policy, so it wasn't, like, five to nothing or anything, but Liberty Moms and Dads backed three of the members, so they basically control the board."

"They're the literal worst," I say.

"Faiz and I covered that meeting for the school paper," Juniper said. "The loudest voices were homophobes saying queer authors were 'grooming' kids because their books had, like, two boys kissing or a trans character." Juniper grits her teeth.

Listening to Juniper, thinking of how this must have hurt her, and so many other kids at school... it makes me want to punch someone. Let's face it, though: I pretty much want to punch someone every day. Still, I've had slurs hurled at me from passing cars when I've stepped out of the mosque. I've heard politicians fearmonger about Muslims and sharia law, so I get how scary it is, how unhinged people can be, and I'm frightened for her. "That's shitty."

"My parents went ballistic and wrote letters to the principal, superintendent, and board that they got some other parents to sign. Not that anyone cared."

"They also sent the letter to the local paper, but it wasn't printed," Faiz adds. "Surprise! The owner of the local paper is the school board president. Bonus, he's running for state rep."

"Wait. What? That's a massive conflict of interest. Is it the only paper in town?" I ask.

They both look at me like I have two heads because, of course, it is.

The bell rings and we dutifully trudge out of the cafeteria, loping toward senior hall. I turn my head to the cacophony pouring in with the students returning from off-campus lunch. I feel lucky that Juniper and Faiz have let me slide into their lunch group. Coming here, I was content to fade into the scuffed linoleum tile like used gum. It's how I feel—how I've felt—on most days the last three months. But hearing the happy, boisterous masses of seniors returning from the Elms or DQ...a strange wisp of a thought crosses my mind. That actually looks sorta fun. It wouldn't kill me to have fun, push all the crappy feelings away. Live in a teeny-tiny bit of denial like a treat.

Sigh. Two months left until I can write off this whole chapter of my life and forget about all the reasons my mom moved us to this tiny, bland town—puzzle pieces that I still haven't figured out how to lock together. Faiz and Juniper head to their lockers after leaving me at mine. I smile watching Juniper elbow Faiz while he pretends he's been mortally wounded. They are two pieces in the puzzle that actually fit.

I shake my head, wishing it weren't always so full of thoughts banging around in opposition to each other. I open my locker and a book tumbles out, which I manage to catch with shaky hands.

But the book isn't mine. On the front, there's a sticky note and in neat upright handwriting a message says simply, "Library books under district review cannot be checked out of the library or read on campus. But I heard you read banned books."

I swivel my head around, trying to see if anyone notices me, if I can figure out who put it in my locker. Of course since my crap lock is still busted, it could be anyone. I run my fingers over a moody blue cover of a boy in a hoodie gazing down a city street: *Anger Is a Gift*. My friend Nayeli read it and joked that with that title, it was obviously written for me, so I guess this is a sign from the universe that I should read it, *now*.

Juniper shows up at my locker with her water bottle and a murderous look on her face. We both have gym after lunch. "What's that?" she asks.

I flip over the book and show it to her. "I think it's one of the books from the challenged list. Someone must've put it in my locker."

She reads the sticky note on the cover. "It's gotta be Ms. Clayton, right? I mean, who else would leave books? Stalkers leave, like, scary notes or dead rats, and secret admirers leave flowers and... maybe home-cooked meals?" She grins.

"Ha ha, but she could've handed me the book. I'm in the library all the time." It's true. From the first moment I walked into the library at this school and talked to Ms. Clayton, I knew it would be the one place I could relax, maybe even escape to.

"Maybe she could get fired for that, though? Or at least in trouble." Juniper shrugs. "If a book's been removed, she's probably not allowed to give it to students."

I wind a strand of hair around my finger as we walk to gym class and another period of trying not to get hit by a volleyball. *I heard you read banned books.* The words of the note echo in my mind. Ms. Clayton, or whoever my secret book fairy is, took a risk to leave that book for me. They obviously want me to read it. But reading banned books isn't enough, I don't think. When we moved down here, my plan was to sail through the year unscathed. I've been scathed enough for a lifetime. I didn't ask for this fight, but here I am, *in it*, and I refuse to do anything half-ass. That's how my dad acts, not me. I could consider the book in my locker a gift. Read it, maybe share it with Amal. But every cell in my body is screaming that it's not just a gift. It's a sign that I need to do more.

CHAPTER 13

I join Faiz and Juniper at our usual lunch spot on Monday after my weekend of equal parts sulking and reading *Anger Is a Gift*. I put the book on the table and unwrap my cucumber chutney sandwich.

"Rebel," whispers Juniper as she picks up the book and flips through the pages.

"I'm the kinda girl who likes to live on the edge," I deadpan.

"What are all those tabs for?" Faiz points to the little yellow stickies that peek out of the edge of the book.

"It means she liked those passages, duh. Don't you bookmark the cookbooks you're always reading?" Juniper gently elbows him.

"Usually I dog-ear the pages," he says sheepishly.

Juniper and I gasp in horror.

"Is it good? The novel, I mean, not the sandwich." Faiz scrunches up his face at my lunch.

"Both are badass," I say as I finish chewing a bite. "I'll have you know cucumber, green cilantro chutney, and butter on white bread may seem like an abomination, but it is truly delicious."

"You need help expanding your culinary palate." Faiz shakes his head.

"Ha! My palate is fine," I say.

Juniper sweeps her eyes from me to Faiz. "You two flirt in the weirdest ways."

"We're not flirting!" Faiz and I say at the same time, locking eyes and then immediately looking away. Why do I feel like I've just been busted by an auntie for standing too close to a boy in the mosque parking lot?

"Anyway," I announce, "the book is about a queer Black teen named Moss whose dad was killed by the police. Moss has, like, PTSD. He and his friends fight back against a racist, homophobic school administration that treats them like criminals."

Juniper scoffs. "Of course it's being challenged." Then she places a hand on her heart and adopts a snooty, melodramatic voice. "Can you imagine what would happen to our dear, innocent children if we allowed them to read about police brutality and racism? No, reality is simply too much!"

Faiz grins at her and plays along. "Mon dieu! Students shouldn't have to be burdened with thoughts of scary books while they are hiding from active shooters in their schools!"

"It's so messed up." I shake my head. "Side note: You two are excellent at uptight, concerned-parent voice."

This weekend I fell down an internet rabbit hole researching book challenges. It's not only Bayberry. Book bans have been gaining steam the last few years. When my dad first talked to me about it, it was a handful of school districts; now it's hundreds. They're going after public libraries, too. It started in red states, places like Texas and Florida with far-right governors, but then it spread everywhere, like a virus.

Juniper continues as my thoughts race. "It's like they think if we don't read queer books, kids will no longer 'turn' queer or whatever messed-up idea they have about being gay or trans. They don't realize that seeing yourself in a book can sometimes save you."

"Same with sex ed. They're afraid if health class mentions condoms, suddenly everyone will want to have sex. Like, some kids aren't already, and now they'll be having unprotected sex," Faiz says while he's stirring a yogurt. When he tilts his head up and sees me looking at him, his cheeks immediately flush. "Not that I'm speaking from, like...experience or...anything. Because I'm..."

"A virgin?" Juniper laughs.

That flush in Faiz's light brown skin deepens. My secondhand embarrassment almost has me blushing, too. Obviously, I get it. Juniper clearly doesn't have the desi modesty complex deep in her marrow like Faiz and me.

I give Juniper a look. "What?" She shrugs. "No shame. Seriously. I mean, same boat for me. I'm waiting for the girl of my dreams."

Faiz jumps in to deflect. "But even if mystery girl walked into the cafeteria right now, would you be able to work up the courage to say *hi*?"

Juniper sighs. "In my mind, yes. In reality, probably a lot less likely. It's performance anxiety, okay. Besides, you're one to talk.

You won't even—" Juniper glances at me, but before she can finish her sentence, someone throws a breadstick at her. A voice yells out, "Suck a dick!"

Sprinkles of laughter spread across the cafeteria along with some boos.

A cascade of emotions wash over Juniper's face. Her eyes are glassy with tears but her jaw is set hard and her hands are curled into fists on top of the table. My mind flails around, not sure what to do. I want to reach out and take Juniper's hand or punch the jerk who yelled at her. But I'm frozen. Faiz isn't, though. He pops right out of his chair, his eyes bulging. "Which one of you assholes said that?"

The voices grow silent, and you can feel the uncomfortable shift in the energy around us.

A lunchroom monitor turns toward us, makes a gesture of zipping her lips while pointing at Faiz. Juniper pulls him down into his seat but not before he yells, "Freaking cowards!"

"Faiz, chill. You're the one who's going to end up getting in trouble. It's okay."

"No, it's really not okay," I say. "Should we say something to Carter?" I ask, but immediately realize it's a ridiculous question.

Faiz scoffs. "Like he'd care?"

"Carter's as homophobic as the rest of them. He's just sly about it," Juniper adds. "And he'd find a way to turn this whole thing around on us."

Faiz nods, his face stony. "Yup. And once you land on Carter's shit list, you can never unsubscribe. He starts to find reasons to blame you for stuff—like, if he saw you with that book?"

Juniper dramatically runs a finger across her throat.

I grit my teeth, my body humming with anger. Carter runs this place like a tiny dictator trying to crush any voice of dissent. "You're totally right, Faiz." My brain whirs with an idea that is either genius or deeply not smart. I stand up and push back my chair, listening to the little screech it makes against the linoleum floor.

"I am?"

"He is?" Juniper asks at the same time, incredulous.

I grab the book from the table. "Juniper's right, too."

"A much more believable scenario." She smirks.

"The admin and parents object to this book"—now I'm waving it around, attracting a bit of attention—"because they think the content is *inappropriate*. They want to pretend police brutality doesn't exist. They want to pretend queer kids, especially ones of color, don't exist. They're offended by the mere existence of trans kids." Venom rises inside of me, twisting my stomach in knots. I rub my scarred thumb against my lower lip and swear I can feel it burning.

"Come on," I say, marching out the cafeteria doors, Juniper and Faiz close on my heels.

We flash our IDs at the hall monitor so she knows we're seniors and can leave campus for lunch. I push open the doors, and the pale spring light breaks through an overcast sky. There's a bit of a chill in the air—the last weak wisps of a lingering winter, making goose bumps rise on my skin. Not exactly sure what I'm doing, but my best plans usually come together on the fly, when I can't overthink them.

"We only have, like, fifteen minutes left for lunch—it's not enough time to leave and go anywhere unless you wanna ditch, in which case, I'm game," Juniper says. Faiz nods and shoves his hands into his pockets.

I walk past the flagpole, scanning the front parking lot, which is reserved for teachers and visitors, and then pick up my pace as I scurry across the street toward the small park. There's no playground or anything. It's a square of grass surrounded by a low hedgerow of bright green boxwoods that pop against the grayish day. There are a few large maple trees with picnic tables scattered around them. In the far corner, some students huddle together, vaping. Whiffs of smoke float over to us, mixing with the taste of burnt petroleum in the air from the new asphalt driveway of a nearby church. A handful of students eat lunch.

Faiz and Juniper follow me to one of the picnic tables. I stop, turning over the book in my hands.

"What are you doing?" Faiz asks.

I suck in my breath. "Something Carter is going to absolutely hate," I say. Then I stand up on an empty picnic table near us.

I hold the book up and start talking. A few heads turn my way. "We've all seen Ms. Clayton pull, like, five hundred books from the library shelves because of a new school board policy. This is one of the books that's been banned because a parent thought it was obscene. Now, because of one complaint, none of us are allowed to check it out. One parent's prejudice shouldn't control what all of us can read." Even though only a few students are paying attention to me, my heart thumps in my chest and my voice squeaks a little as I speak.

Juniper gives me an encouraging little nod. Two other students walk over and stand next to her and Faiz. I continue. "I looked at the whole list of challenged books and almost all of them are by authors of color or LGBTQ authors or queer authors of color." I swallow, pausing for a second to take a breath. "They're saying only some stories matter—cishet white stories. The adults who passed this policy say they're doing it to protect us. They want to protect us from books, but no book walked into a school and killed a bunch of kids. This book ban isn't about protection, it's about prejudice and control." I start talking faster, and Juniper raises a fist and lets out a little whoop.

"This is one of the books that's been pulled from the shelves," I say, holding up *Anger Is a Gift*. We're not allowed to read it *on campus—*"

"But we're not on campus now!" a girl in a gray nubby sweater with auburn hair pulled into a tight ponytail yells from one of the picnic tables.

"Exactly." I smile and open the book to one of the tabs.

I clear my throat. I've never had the best reading voice. My dad is usually the one who read to us in the evenings before bed. When Amal and I were in grade school—after we'd eaten dinner and brushed and gotten into our PJs—we'd join my parents in the living room and my dad would read to us from a novel we'd chosen together. Whenever we finished one book, we'd go to the bookstore together and choose another one. My dad had this soothing tone, and he'd do all the voices of the characters. My mom would sit next to us, sometimes putting coconut oil in our hair and braiding it. We stopped family reading when I started sophomore year. I had too much homework and felt it was too babyish to be read to. My eyes start to sting a little and my throat tightens at the image in my mind, of being a whole family. Oh God, what am I doing? I can't do this. My breathing gets shallow and my hands grow clammy. I gaze up and meet Faiz's twinkling eyes and he gives me an encouraging nod.

I take a deep breath and refocus on the page in front of me. *"Anger Is a Gift* is by Mark Oshiro. It's a novel but also, like, a manifesto, and it's pretty badass." I begin reading a short excerpt that struck me this weekend: "'Anger is a gift. Remember that.... You gotta grasp on to it, hold it tight and use it as ammunition. You use that anger to get things done instead of just stewing in it.'" Once in a while it feels like a line in a book was written specifically for you, like the writer knows exactly what you need to hear, to feel, to know. I didn't ask for all these angry feelings swirling around inside of me, but I get to choose what to do with them.

"Yeah!" a boy in a dark blue hoodie yells. I let out a little nervous giggle, and the handful of other students around join me in laughter.

As I continue reading, there's a feeling in my chest like I'm at the top of a roller coaster. A thrilling kind of lightness that always hits me right before I let out a joyous, terrified scream as we race downward and into a loop. I can't remember the last time I felt this way. The last time I felt like I was breathing without an anvil on my chest. It's like a language I thought I'd forgotten has come flooding back to me.

From across the street, the bell rings and I jump down from the bench as the small group of students scatter to grab their lunches and backpacks and head back in. The boy in the blue hoodie passes me and says, "Tomorrow? Same time, same place?"

"Uh...I guess...Maybe. Yeah?"

He smiles and jogs off. Juniper, Faiz, and I speak in a flurry, talking over each other, laughing, as we head into the building. Such a small thing. Reading a few passages from a banned book. But as I look between the two of them, making plans to meet up after school, I realize that some of that lightness I'm feeling, that moment of defying gravity, comes from being a part of something. I'm standing on some vague, blurry-edged border of belonging. I didn't have a plan to fit in here, maybe stubbornly rejected the whole idea. Being too comfortable means you don't always see the gut punch coming. That's what my dad leaving taught me. But maybe that was the wrong thing to learn. Maybe all I needed to learn was that my dad was a selfish prick who punched a hole in my universe and walked away unscathed.

For the rest of the day, I feel fizzy inside, as if the blood in my veins has been replaced with sparkling water. I had no idea reading a little bit of a challenged book out loud could feel so thrilling. I mean, I wasn't, like, standing in front of a tank or putting a flower in the barrel of a soldier's gun or anything. All I did was read, but in Bayberry that's about as rebellious as it gets. Reading is dangerous because it shows us the truth. Words give us power; that's why some adults want to silence us.

I grab what I need from my locker and slam it shut, then jump back in surprise when I see Andrew leaning against the lockers behind mine, waiting for me.

"You scared the crap out of me!"

"Sorry. I didn't mean to startle you, I was—"

"Engaging in a little light stalking?" I chuckle a bit.

He straightens and cocks his head. "That's kinda harsh. It was mild lurking at most." He smiles.

"Ha! That's what all the pervy stalkers say."

"Noor, I would never." Andrew grows suddenly serious, and I'm reminded that he doesn't really know me. I don't really know him, either.

"I was kidding! I like to walk that weird edgy-humor line sometimes."

"I didn't picture you with a dark side. I mean, you have a Jane Austen quote on your notebook."

"Fun fact, she was a secret goth," I deadpan. "Totally emo."

He laughs. "You're sort of . . . different."

"Uh . . . excuse me?"

"In a good way, I mean." He stumbles over his words. "A cool way. Like, intriguing." It's fun watching him try to pull his foot out of his mouth.

"So I intrigue you?"

He takes a deep breath and brushes away a few soft brown curls from his forehead and gives me a shy smile. "I'm sorry. I'm sorta bad at this, huh?"

"Bad at what?"

"At asking if you'd like to hang sometime, maybe?"

I think about how Amal told me before that it feels like I'm angry all the time. It's true. Usually a constant low-key rage hums in my bones. But maybe I'm still riding the high of the renegade reading session at lunch, because I find myself grinning and nodding at Andrew and saying, "You are pretty bad at this." I laugh a little, and he joins me. "But sure. Let's hang." My mind has apparently temporarily left my body because I kinda think it could be fun.

"Great. I can give you a town tour, too."

"Cool, but what do we do after those fifteen minutes?" I smirk.

"Ha! You're such a snob."

"Don't you forget it," I say, and smile wide. We start walking out together. He's charming and, at least in our few encounters, easy to be around. Like, I don't have to think too much about it. Also, he's cute, which is always a bonus. As we turn the corner out of senior hall, I see Faiz at his locker and wave. He waves back at me, then spies Andrew at my side, and for a brief second, a shadow passes over his face.

CHAPTER 14

There are some days in early spring that hang heavy—
low gray skies, threatening rain, a lingering bite in the air. But there
are other days, like today, when the sun shines so bright and the
light is so full of promise that you believe summer is within your
grasp. It's the kind of morning when the air feels good to breathe.

"What's wrong?" my sister asks as I glance in the rearview mirror.

"I didn't say anything."

"Nooo...but you're acting all weird."

"Weird how?" I ask as I put the car in reverse and pull out onto
the street.

"You're smiling." She throws me a snarky look.

"Oh my God. What devilry! What witchcraft! I had no idea a
smile had crept upon my lips. Pass me my smelling salts before I
faint dead away from the strain."

"Don't worry, Goody Noor, as governor I'll see a witch hanged
for inflicting this upon you! There shall be no good humor in Salem.

Or Bayberry." We both laugh. Amal was reading *The Crucible* last night for class, and during dinner I kept calling her Goody Amal and demanding more porridge and potato stew. My mom missed out on the fake Puritan convo—she stayed late at the office, *again*. Since she started work last week, she hasn't been home much for dinner. I want to believe that she's super busy getting situated at her new job, but I'm afraid she's avoiding me because she can't deal with my questions and complaints.

I'd almost forgotten what laughing with my sister was like. Mainly because every time anything funny happens, I'll laugh and then remember why it feels so unusual. It's like being in mourning, but no one's dead. I've seen Amal do it occasionally, too—stop happiness short. But today she doesn't press the brakes. Instead, she turns the radio louder and starts singing along to the Linda Lindas.

I take a sidelong glance at her as I ease to a stop at a red light. Amal looks well rested. The dark circles under her eyes are practically gone. Her face is brighter. Even if last week was better than I thought it would be, I'm still not willing to say I'm glad we moved, but if being here makes Amal happier even in the tiniest way, I'll take it.

At school, I slide into a parking spot, and before I get out, Andrew appears at the driver's side of my car, startling me. Amal waggles her eyebrows at me. "Don't say a word," I mutter as I turn off the ignition. She feigns shock at the assumption.

"Hi, Andrew," she practically singsongs as she shuts the car door, turning on a syrupy sweet smile. "Noor was *just* talking about you. Weren't you, big sis?"

I lock the car and narrow my eyes at her before turning toward Andrew. "She's concussed."

"She seems extremely lucid and intelligent."

"I'm the brains of the family." Amal laughs. "Noor is the brawn."

"So I've heard," Andrew replies. "I also heard from Blaine that you might try out for swim team next year?"

Amal's face brightens. "Yeah, thinking about it."

"So Blaine's talking about Amal, huh?" I tease.

"Pretty much nonstop." Andrew winks. Maybe I should be annoyed by him being so, I dunno, familiar? Forward? But he's fallen right into the rhythm of our teasing sisterly banter. Somehow it doesn't feel intrusive. It feels nice. So why complicate it? Whoa. I just had a mature, thoughtful moment in real time. Good on me.

Amal rolls her eyes but I can tell she's enjoying the attention.

"I have a lap pool in the backyard. We usually open it during the first week of May. Come over anytime for a swim," Andrew says with a warm smile.

"A lap pool at your house? Your backyard must be, like, huge," I remark, imagining a ginormous suburban McMansion.

Andrew shrugs as if it's no big deal. "Amal, if you want, I can invite Blaine, too."

I clear my throat. Loudly. "I'll obviously be joining as chaperone."

Amal stares daggers at me. "Oh my God. Why can't you act like a normal teenager and not a fifty-year-old auntie?"

I scowl at her and raise an eyebrow, but Andrew jumps in before I can say anything. "Noor's right."

"I am?" I ask before quickly course correcting. "No. I mean, I am. Of course I am."

"Absolutely. I will make sure I have a yardstick and that Amal and Blaine are at least three feet apart at all times," he says. I start to crack up while embarrassment sweeps over Amal's face.

Amal looks from me to Andrew, her mouth agape. "Whatever, it's not like that!"

I play along and add, "And make sure Blaine is in a proper bathing costume. No Speedos or thongs around my little sister!"

"Ewwww. Be normal. See ya later," Amal says, and then turns to start walking away from us when she sees a couple of girls wave to her from across the parking lot.

Andrew turns to me, the wide smile on his face brightening his eyes. "Seriously, though, Blaine is cool. I mean, in case you were worried, and of course you're invited. Anytime."

I nod. "Thanks. Good to know. I haven't talked to Blaine much. Amal thinks I'm overprotective, but ever since—" I pause. I'm not comfortable enough around Andrew to tell him about my dad, so I pivot. "It's that we don't know anyone here."

"No. It's cool. I'm slow to trust people, too."

"Oh, I'm not...I mean, I trust people who deserve my trust. Not that you don't..."

I bite my lower lip and look up at Andrew. It's weird how he kinda gets me. He tilts his head toward school and we start walking in. As I weave around an oddly parked car, he puts his hand on the small of my back and I feel the heat of his skin through my thin sweater. Without thinking too long about it, I lean into the support.

We draw closer to the front doors, where his friend James, Richard, and a couple of other guys are hanging out. James wears expensive dark jeans, a fitted Henley sweater, and Lucky Green Jordans that probably cost two hundred dollars. Everything about him feels curated—as if he's a living social media post. Even the way he leans his body against the building, angled with the perfect amount of slouch and disdain for the world. I can't exactly criticize that, though. I have plenty of disdain for the world, too.

"Andrew, who's your lovely friend?"

Andrew fake laughs and I give him a sidelong glance.

"You're in my gym class," I say to James. "You know my name." I can't figure out if he's rude or just clueless.

James turns his face and looks at the other two guys and scoffs. "I was trying to be polite."

"Active word, trying," I say. Tension rises in the air around us. I can tell Andrew senses it, too, because he's near enough to me that his arm brushes against mine and I can feel his muscles tense.

"Dude. Welcoming much?" Andrew says.

"Nooooor." James annoyingly elongates my name like he's about to go with that old bully favorite of *ma-noor*, as in manure, but he only says, "Seems pretty warmly welcomed." He glances from Andrew to me, eyeing how close we are. I instinctively move a step away from Andrew, but I'm not sure why. I'm genuinely perplexed. There are clearly levels of this interaction that I'm not grasping.

Richard and the other guys snicker.

I start walking away. "See ya."

"Hold up. I'll walk in with you," Andrew says, hurrying to join me. His friends seem kinda like jerks, and I wonder if he's like them and hiding it or if he has bad taste in friends. I'm hoping there's a third possibility.

We walk silently through the main hallway, the usual noisy

pre–first period cacophony filling the building. Andrew and I exchange glances. "James really knows how to suck up all the oxygen in a room, huh?" I say, venturing into a potential minefield.

Andrew shifts his shoulders under his backpack straps. "He loves attention. That's all. He's harmless." His voice sounds casual, but there's a strain of defensiveness in it.

I was about to say something about Richard being a dick in English class, but I stop myself because I feel a current just under the surface. "Have you been friends with James for a long time?"

He nods. "He's cool once you get to know him...."

"And get past the surly attitude," I say.

"He had my back when no one else did," Andrew quickly adds. "When I was having a tough time of it in elementary school and middle school, he was the only friend I could count on."

I get the sense that Andrew wants this conversation to end. Which is fine with me. I'm not sure what else to say and wonder if I'm being too sensitive about the way I've seen James giving me the once-over like I'm being evaluated. As Andrew and I head down senior hall, I see Juniper waiting by my locker. "You guys know each other, right?" I ask, dropping my backpack on the ground.

"Yup." Juniper's normally toothy smile is stretched into a thin line as she nods at Andrew. "How's life on the born-with-a-silver-foot-in-your-mouth side of the tracks?"

My eyebrows shoot up, and I bite back a nervous laugh.

"Well, my personal butler, valet, and chauffeur were gone today, so I had to tie my own laces, drive myself to school, and even pick out my own clothes," Andrew says.

"Clearly," Juniper responds, her voice dripping with sarcasm.

"And how's life in the my-parents-are-both-doctors-but-I-try-to-hide-that-behind-my-heavy-black-eyeliner neighborhood?"

Juniper sneers at him.

"Oh, so you *are* total and complete strangers," I quip. The first bell of the morning rings.

"I gotta run. Talk to you later," Andrew says to me, then turns to Juniper. "A pleasure sparring with you this morning."

"Highlight of your day," Juniper says.

I raise my shoulders in a question when Andrew leaves. "So do you guys hate each other or..."

"He's okay. But his besties, Richard and James, are dickbags."

"Oh my God, right?" I'm relieved it's not just me.

"Especially James. We were lab partners in middle school. He asked me to the eighth-grade formal. When I said no, I didn't like him that way, he acted like there was something deeply wrong with me because who could possibly say no to him!"

"Were you—"

"Out? Nah. Not till ninth. But when I did come out, he stopped talking to me."

"Asshole." I shake my head and open my locker. There's a paperback lying on the top shelf. I pull it out.

"Ooh. Another book?" Juniper says.

I turn it over so we can look at the cover—a photographed silhouette of a young Black boy with his hands raised against the bright lights of a cop car. I read it in sophomore-year English: *All American Boys*. There's a sticky note on this one as well. It has a Toni Morrison quote on it: *The very serious function of racism...is distraction.*

Faiz bounds over as Juniper and I huddle together, flipping through the pages. "What's up?"

I turn to him, his smile wide and his eyes bright as he greets me. "Another gift from Ms. Clayton, I guess. This time with a Toni Morrison quote."

Faiz takes a step closer to me and I sniff sandalwood on him. I suck in my breath. It's like the smell of the Indian soap my dad used. I absentmindedly pick at my scar and take a few deep breaths, trying to quell the fight-or-flight response I'm having, except in my case it's more like fight-or-*fight*. And I do not want to get mad at Faiz for smelling good. I mean, I've been in high school for almost four years, and there are so many worse alternatives to how a boy could smell. How does a simple memory of sandalwood get me so riled up?

"Are you okay?" Faiz asks, touching my elbow. I flinch. Then immediately feel terrible when I see the hurt look on his face. It's not his fault I'm haunted by soap.

Juniper, oblivious to the weird moment that just passed between Faiz and me, reads from her screen. "Looks like *All American Boys* is one of the most banned books in America because of its depiction of police brutality."

"Banned for telling the truth. That tracks," Faiz says, avoiding my eyes.

"And now we have our lunchtime reading."

Faiz adds, "It's a sunny day. So there'll be more people hanging in the park."

"Good," I say. "If you read a banned book out loud and no one's there to hear it, does it make a sound?"

Juniper cocks her head to the side. "You're straining that metaphor so much it's painful."

Faiz laughs. The second bell rings, ushering us to class.

"Don't think you've been saved by the bell," Juniper says to me, waggling her eyebrows. "You still have to explain what exactly you and Andrew are doing together."

I open my mouth to speak, but Faiz jumps in. "FYI, Andrew is a conceited, privileged jerk," he says, and walks ahead of us to class.

I raise my eyebrows in a question to Juniper. "You go ahead, Faiz," Juniper says. "I need to borrow a tampon from Noor."

I give her a quizzical look as Faiz dashes out of earshot. "You need a tampon?"

"No. It's just the fastest way to send most boys running. Even the feminist ones."

I laugh.

"What?" she asks, pulling me aside. "I'm not wrong." Then she lowers her voice to a conspiratorial whisper. "Faiz might kill me for telling you but...in fourth grade, when Faiz was still new at the school, he brought Indian food in a thermos to lunch. Andrew, Richard, and a couple other kids made fun of him, saying his *weird* food stank up the whole cafeteria, basically forcing him to go sit by himself."

My entire body tenses hearing that story—not because it's a surprise, but because I've heard so many versions of it. "That's so sad."

"Yeah, well...I went to go sit next to him and asked him to let me try his food because it smelled amazing—it was rice and chicken korma, and it blew my mind. So he started sharing his lunches with me."

Hearing that story, knowing that Faiz still brings Juniper lunch, makes my heart swell a little. "And that was the start of your beautiful food-centered friendship."

"Pretty much."

Juniper and I walk into AP English and I take my seat by Richard, who wears a constant scowl for me. Glancing at Faiz, my heart twists for his nine-year-old self. I can't imagine what it must've been like for him to be the *only* one. I've never had to deal with that—at least not in school. I hate that Andrew and James were so cruel to him. Little kids can be such assholes. And sometimes, they never grow out of it.

CHAPTER 15

When lunch rolls around, I meet Faiz and Juniper in the cafeteria. They're both grabbing drinks—an unsweetened iced tea for Faiz and an energy drink for Juniper. I frown when I see the silver can in her hand. "Dude, the amount of caffeine and sugar in that could kill you," I say, my mom's warnings practically imprinted in my brain.

Faiz smiles wide, no trace of his earlier ire at Andrew. "I've only been telling her that forever. She refuses to listen."

"Kids today." I shake my head and smile back at Faiz.

"Excuse me, object of your derision right here." Juniper waves her hand between me and Faiz. "Maybe if *someone* had made me lunch today, I wouldn't be resorting to this situation." She pulls out Cool Ranch Doritos from a backpack she's adorned with glittery black skull patches.

Faiz tilts his head and reaches into his bag, producing a foil-wrapped sandwich. "Happy?"

"Is it egg salad surprise?" Juniper squeals.

Faiz nods.

"Is the surprise that egg with mayonnaise is gross?" I ask, pulling a face.

"It's Kewpie mayonnaise!" Faiz looks so disappointed in me.

"This sandwich will change your life," Juniper says.

"Wow. Okay." I raise my hands in mock surrender. "I'll check my egg-and-mayo prejudice."

Juniper reverently hands me the sandwich as we turn to walk out. "You need it more than I do. You ready?"

I force a smile on my lips. "Let's do it," I say, with more confidence than I feel. Another lawyer trick I learned from my dad: Fake it till you make it.

We show our IDs to the hall monitor and step out into the bright yellow sun that's such a contrast with yesterday's grayness. I squint as we cross the street, heading toward the little park. There's a smallish group of kids milling around the benches. Some eating lunch, others hanging out. Waiting. For me? I pick at my scarred thumb, my nerves threatening to get the better of me.

"You okay?" Juniper asks.

"Yeah," I mutter. "Sure."

Faiz touches my elbow. "You look a little pale. You don't have to do this, you know. If you're worried about getting in trouble."

I hate mushy feelings so I would never publicly admit this, but I like having someone ask if I'm okay. But I don't have time to luxuriate in it because I'm struggling with how to explain why I *have* to do this. That it's not ending up on Carter's shit list that's worrying me. That there's an invisible hand pushing me forward. I don't exactly understand it, either. But my dad's words fill my head and part of me thinks that if I can take a chance, on my own, it will quiet his voice and let my own take its place. I need to do this for me to prove to myself that even if I am like my dad in some ways, I'm still me, without him.

I clench and unclench my jaw. Take a deep breath. "It's cool," I say, more for myself than to convince her. We stride into the crowd of ten or so other juniors and seniors. "I got this."

I step up onto the bench of a rickety old picnic table. The bright sun filters through the tender green leaves of the maple tree that gives us shelter. "Uh...hi," I say, my voice croaky. I pause. Random thoughts boomerang through my brain. "I'm Noor. And I read banned books."

Juniper gives me a huge smile and says, "Hi, Noor," and a few others spontaneously join in the greeting. I look out at the group— the kids who maybe don't quite fit in. Kids who found their way to belonging with each other. Kids who I didn't expect to find but did. A smattering of students of color in a district that's mostly white. With a school so small, it's easy to recognize the faces after a few days, but I don't really know any of them. It strikes me that no one here really knows me, either. I count twelve people, including Juniper and Faiz. When I start speaking, the three vapers in the far corner of the park head over, too.

"Challenged books aren't a new thing in America. Stomping out ideas. Forcing us all to think in one way, like we're automatons, is sadly pretty American. But so is speaking out. So is protest." My nerves haven't quieted and an adrenaline surge makes my hands shake.

"Fuck the fascists," someone yells out to scattered laughter.

"Yeah, that part," I say. "Anyway, *they* supposedly don't want us to read certain books because they're harmful"—I make air quotes around *harmful*—"but they don't want to keep us safe, they want to keep us ignorant. Because ignorant people are easier to control...." My mind wanders to a poetry reading my parents took Amal and me to at Women & Children First, a feminist bookstore in Chicago. I remember something the author said and echo it. "And free people read freely."

I open the novel to one of the pages I bookmarked. "This is from *All American Boys*, by Jason Reynolds and Brendan Kiely." I clear my throat, trying to smooth the wobble in my voice. " 'Racism was alive and real as shit. It was everywhere and all mixed up in everything, and the only people who said it wasn't, and the only people who said, "Don't talk about it" were white. Well, *stop lying*. That's what I wanted to tell those people. Stop lying. Stop denying.' "

I look up and a few heads nod along. My gaze drifts toward the school, where I spot Andrew leaning against the flagpole. He gives me a small wave. I didn't expect to see him, and my cheeks heat up knowing he's watching. I look back down at the book and continue reading for a couple of minutes, then jump down from the bench. Juniper hugs me. I get a high five from Faiz, and a few of the other students crowd around. I hand off the book to someone who asks if they can borrow it to read.

"I'm Hanna Kim," an East Asian girl with Dutch braids wearing a WE REBUILD WHAT YOU DESTROY shirt says. "We should make this a thing. My parents went to the January school board meeting to speak out against this policy, but they were basically ignored."

"Hi," I say. "Totally agree. And anyone who wants to read out loud should do it."

"We should also share that list of challenged books with everyone," Juniper adds, smiling at Hanna. "It's buried on the district site like they don't want us to find it." There are a few murmurs of agreement.

A lanky boy wearing ripped jeans and a black T-shirt looks at us through long, dirty-blond bangs. "But a dozen kids reading in a park won't get any attention. *If* that's what you want."

I hadn't thought about it that way. Hadn't considered what I was doing, only that it was messed up that a school was preventing us from reading. But you can't fix a big problem like this unless you make it a problem for everyone.

Faiz nods, shoves his hands into his pockets, and says, "Well, if we want the school board to change the policy—"

"Good luck with that," a boy in a red hoodie scoffs, then walks away.

Faiz continues, undeterred. "If we want them to reverse things, then the goal is to get everyone's attention, right?"

"Yeah." I nod, but my thoughts drift. Honestly, I wasn't totally thinking about the end goal. Sharing these books with other students is awesome, but that can't be it. Not if I meant what I said about us being able to read freely.

"Greta Thunberg started #FridaysForFuture by herself. She stood in front of the Swedish Parliament protesting their inaction on climate change, and eventually it became a global movement," Hanna says, a huge smile on her face.

"We have to start somewhere, even if it's only a handful of us. . . ."

My voice fades as Sophie Scholl's words come back to me. We're not in the position she was. We're not fighting the Nazis in the lead-up to World War II, but I think of the trouble we could get in with Carter, the chaos we could cause. But I think chaos is the point.

Juniper gathers the small group of students and sits at one of the picnic tables to scarf down some lunch. Hanna takes a seat next to her. They're both talking, hands waving animatedly. Someone from the table calls my name. Before I head over, I look back toward the flagpole. Andrew is still there, and now James and Richard have joined him. It looks as if they're arguing, but I can't hear what it's about. Andrew waves his hand dismissively and heads inside the school, with Richard following behind him. James turns toward the park and our eyes meet. He holds my gaze for a second past awkward, so I raise my hand in a halfhearted wave. He doesn't wave back.

CHAPTER 16

"It's not a date. We're going to a coffee shop to study," I say to Amal as she lies across my bed, her head hanging over the side, ankles crossed. There are holes in both heels of her rainbow-striped socks. I know better than to tell her to throw them away. My dad got them for her in our family's low-budget secret Eid gift exchange two years ago at the end of Ramadan. He always got everyone socks. The only surprise was what fun design he'd pick.

Noor uncrosses her feet and clicks her ankles together. "If it's not a date, why have you changed your shirt, like, four times, and why are you wearing lipstick?"

"It's not lipstick—it's a tinted lip balm and my lips are dry, okay?" I blow her a kiss in the mirror. "Besides, technically we're not allowed to date."

"We're also *technically* not allowed to break school rules and talk back to our parents, but that hasn't stopped you." I turn my head to glare at her. She ignores me and sits up. "Do you want me to French braid your hair? You know, for your study *date*."

I roll my eyes and shake my head. My long black hair falls below my shoulders, and thanks to an unexpected drizzle I got caught in after school, it's a bit frizzy now. I grab a skinny scrunchie from my pocket and pull my hair into a messy bun to prove to her (and myself) that it's not a date.

The truth is I kinda thought about bailing on tonight. I've felt weird hanging out with Andrew after Juniper shared the story of him and his friends bullying Faiz in fourth grade. But should I hold fourth-grade Andrew's actions against twelfth-grade Andrew? That doesn't seem fair. Maybe he's not that person anymore. There has to be a cutoff age for holding your past against you. People can change. I think. I hope.

I stop spinning out about Andrew's past and turn back to the present with Amal. "Mom should be home by sevenish. Are you going to be okay till then?" I ask as nonchalantly as possible, because Amal hates when I'm overprotective. Amal would only be alone a couple of hours tops, but it's the first time she'll be by herself in this house. What if something happens to her? What if the house burns down? She could get kidnapped. Mom would kill me and I would let her because protecting Amal feels like my most important job. I bite at my scar, feeling my teeth sharp against the shiny skin, then pull my thumb away to look at the marks. "You know, I could stay home. Or ... or you could come with!"

"Oh my God. I'm fifteen! I'd rather suffer through the worst microwave mac and cheese ever than third-wheel your non-date. Seriously, if you don't go I'm going to tell Mom."

I knit my eyebrows together. "If I don't go on a date you're going to tell Mom I *didn't* break the rules?"

"I thought you said it wasn't a date." She puckers her lips and makes kissy noises.

I choke back a laugh. There's a honk in the driveway. My pulse quickens and my brain races: *It's not a date. It's not a date.* Apparently the butterflies in my stomach have not gotten the message. Way back in a cobwebby corner of my mind, there's a tiny flicker of guilt that I have to extinguish.

"Go already!" My sister hops off the bed and pulls my elbow toward the bedroom door. I catch one last quick glance at myself in the mirror. Ripped jeans, cranberry-red cardigan over a plain black tee, green socks with sparkly silver stripes (Dad, again). I should get rid of these, but I wore these when I took my SAT, wore them for my UChicago interview, and was wearing them when I got my acceptance. They're my lucky socks, even if I know there's no such thing as luck. I nod and smile at my reflection, giving myself my own seal of approval.

I hurry down the stairs, zip up my Docs, give final instructions to my sister, who rolls her eyes at me, and then head out the door. Andrew's silver BMW is pulled up into the driveway, and he steps out when he sees me, the late-afternoon sun dappling his wavy brown hair with golden light. He smiles and then walks around the car to open the door.

"They say chivalry is dead," I say.

"That's only in the big city, New Girl." Andrew winks and gestures for me to enter his car. After I've taken a seat, he shuts the door and walks around to the driver's side. The gray leather interiors are buttery soft and new-car smell permeates the air. It's a four-door, but the back seat is small and surprisingly clean, unlike my car, which is littered with Flamin' Hot Cheetos wrappers, Coke cans, and random extra T-shirts. When my dad drove the Karmann Ghia, it was also a mess, but of law books and thick brown accordion folders. Like father, like daughter. *Sigh.* I used to think that was a good thing.

Andrew presses the ignition button, and the car barely makes a sound. Electric. At least he's eco-conscious. Not that he deserves cookies for that. Not that he's asked for any. Still, I'm keeping a running tab in my head of his transgressions, even the ones I've made up. The less you expect of someone, the less surprised you are when they inevitably screw up. Or screw you over.

"Ready to see the hippest coffee shop in all of central Illinois?" he asks, backing out the driveway.

"*Hip* and *central Illinois* do not belong in the same sentence." I turn to look out the window as the neat lawns and suburban homes float by. "But go ahead and try to prove me wrong. I'll keep an open mind."

"I am half agony, half hope." Andrew smiles but doesn't take his eyes off the road. He's changed his outfit from school. Black Adidas Sambas, jeans, and a charcoal-gray V-neck sweater. He smells like mint soap and freshly laundered clothes. Easing to a stop at a red light, Andrew turns and gives me a look, as if he's guessed that I was evaluating his outfit. I bite my lip and point to an empty field in the distance, the low afternoon sun glinting off silver silos.

"What's, um, planted in that field?"

He laughs. "Corn or soybeans. That's pretty much it around here. Didn't take you for an agricultural enthusiast."

I push my shoulders back and turn to look at him, in a challenge. "Why, because girls can't be interested in farming?"

"No. Because I assumed a city girl wouldn't be fascinated by rural agrobusiness. But in case I'm wrong and for the record, I am one hundred percent in support of girl farmers."

I take a deep breath. "Fine. But FYI, 'girl farmers' are just farmers. You don't call men who own farms 'boy farmers,' do you?"

He gulps. "Fair point."

Whoa. I almost do a double take. He accepted that correction without arguing or throwing the word *feminist* at me as an insult. "Then I'll admit I don't know a thing about planting or seeds or keeping plants alive, but it's not because I'm a girl. It's because I have a talent for killing things."

"That's comforting?" He laughs.

"Also, I don't want to be prejudged... or even *judged* judged."

"This space"—he gestures between us—"is a judgment-free zone. So I'm going to assume you weren't just checking me out a minute ago."

Busted. My jaw drops open. He may be right, but I'm definitely not going to admit it. "You wish I was staring at you."

"You're right, I do," he says without missing a beat.

Oh no. This is banter. We're bantering. Dammit. *Not a date, not a date*, I repeat to myself like a mantra. I will absolutely not succumb to some sparkly eyed boy's small-town charm because I am absolutely, one-hundred-percent not a character in the kind of sappy Hallmark rom-coms my mom and sister love watching together.

We drive through the three-block downtown of Bayberry. Not gonna lie, it's cute. Lined with low-slung brick buildings with big-windowed storefronts. The kind of place millennial couples come for autumn weekends of antiquing and taking Instagram pictures in cornfield mazes on pumpkin farms that sell apple cider donuts. A small hotel in a converted blue-and-gold Victorian home, the Haymarket Inn, sits at the corner of the only four-way stop downtown.

Andrew parks on the street and we grab our backpacks. I keep in lockstep with him as he makes his way to the center of the block. "This place gets pretty packed for the autumn Harvest Daze Carnival and the Fourth of July Freedom Fest. They're actually pretty fun."

"Freedom Fest?" I say, incredulous. "That's giving real supremacist vibes."

"Mostly kids running around with hot dogs and cotton candy and sparklers. And everyone—"

"Is white and Republican?" I deadpan.

Andrew scratches his neck. "I was going to say 'wears the Fest T-shirts that are designed by third graders,' but also . . . yeah, pretty much. Is that a problem?"

"TL;DR? It's not the most welcoming situation for Muslims— especially the only ones in town. Or for Indians, you know, who eat *weird*, smelly food." I try to say this in a way that feels pointed and accusatory, but it sails right by Andrew, which means I'm either losing the power of my snark or he's oblivious. Both dismal possibilities.

"There's Faiz's family and also the Patels, but maybe they're not Muslim?"

I laugh dryly. "I think you're making my point for me."

There's an awkward pause and I almost ask him about the Faiz incident from fourth grade, but I lose my courage when I look into his soft eyes. Not sure if this is my fight to pick or if this is the time to pick it.

Andrew stops in front of a glass door adorned with a logo of a cheery yellow cup of coffee with wisps of steam rising from it. Bright blue letters curve above the cup, spelling out the name of the café: COMMON GROUNDS. When he opens the door, a friendly bell jingles and I'm hit with the satisfying, slightly smoky smell of ground coffee beans. I close my eyes and take a whiff, and for a second I'm back at Plein Air, my favorite café in my old neighborhood. A small, contented sigh escapes my lips.

"So, you like?"

I nod reluctantly, because I hate admitting I'm wrong. It's a cozy space with worn bronze-velvet couches and mismatched chairs around crooked wooden coffee tables. I walk over to a wall lined with shelves. It's full of old travel books—the kind people used before the internet.

"So what do you want?" Andrew asks me as I pull out a guidebook on France.

"World peace. Global nuclear disarmament. No child hungry. The usual."

"You totally have my vote for Miss America," he says, playing along.

I laugh and do a royal victory wave to the imaginary audience. "I usually get a mocha, extra whip," I say, reaching for the front pocket of my backpack to get some money.

"I got this. No worries."

Oh no. No. If he pays he'll think it's a date. Maybe I'll think it's a date. I'm definitely paying for myself. I bite my lip. It might be rude to argue. Then again, arguing about who's going to pay the bill is an Indian art form.

He sees me deliberating and adds, "You get the next round, okay?"

An acceptable solution. I nod and appreciate how he *doesn't* argue.

Andrew walks over to the counter to order our drinks while I plop down on a nubby, worn couch and start thumbing through the French travel book, making up an imaginary vacation.

Andrew returns with two steaming mugs. "A mocha for you and a black coffee for me." He places both gently on the table.

"You take your coffee black like an old man, huh?"

"I prefer my caffeine in its purest form."

"By purest do you mean most bitter?" I spoon off a little of the whipped cream from my mocha and pop it into my mouth before taking a tiny sip.

"I like it because it is bitter...and because it is my heart," he says before lifting his coffee cup and tapping it to mine. "Cheers."

I knit my eyebrows together. "Is that from..."

"A poem by Stephen Crane. Junior year, in American Lit, we had to memorize a poem and recite it."

"I'm impressed you remember it."

Andrew looks at me, taking in the surprise on my face. "Excuse me? Who's judging now?" He chuckles, his hazel eyes bright with laughter.

I smile back. We pull out our laptops and start working on our physics problem sets. The afternoon passes quickly and soon our table is littered with coffee cups and empty plates scattered with chocolate and vanilla cake crumbs. And I've paid my it's-not-a-date fair share. There's a lightness to our chatter as we figure out how to apply Ohm's law to calculate voltage and resistance. We don't talk about anything really personal. Still, I feel myself relaxing into our easy convo, enjoying how comfortable I feel around him.

When I gaze out the windows, I see it's already dark. Time for me to head home. Andrew isn't quite what I was expecting. He's more. Better. I also think about all the things we didn't talk about. The things I'd meant to ask but didn't because I chickened out. About all that stuff with Faiz. About what he and his friends were arguing about at the flagpole the other day. About his choice of friends, period.

Still, it feels good *not* to be angry, *not* to be doggedly pursuing the answers to the million questions rolling around in my head right now. It might be unsustainable, but for now an evening of zero doubts and no catastrophizing is a little gift I'm giving myself.

CHAPTER 17

After grilling me about my non-date in the car on the way to school for a few minutes, Amal sat silently staring at the fields, the side of her head pressed to the window. I knew better than to ask her if she was okay. We both got sick of people asking us that after our dad left. Of course we weren't, duh. Plus my own sadness kept catching me off guard, which made me angry. Angrier. A perfectly nice morning could be ripped apart by a memory. I try to pay attention to Amal because I know how the sucky parts of life can come at you fast.

I keep my eyes on the road, but when we come to a stop sign, I put my hand on her thin shoulder for a brief second, so she knows I'm here. The single most important thing I promised myself was that I'd protect my sister from everyone and everything, even memories. In my peripheral vision, I see her lips curve into a small smile. "I'm good," she whispers.

I search for Andrew but don't find him anywhere in the parking lot. A couple of ninth-grade girls grab Amal, talking a mile a minute. I watch as she walks off with them, smiling, laughing, as if she wasn't in a quiet funk a few minutes ago. That's normal, right? My barometer for normal is so broken. I trudge up to the school, the low ceiling of clouds threatening rain but not yet delivering on that promise. Juniper is locking her midnight-blue bicycle at one of the bike stands. There are punk band stickers all over her helmet, which she takes off and tucks under her arm. When she sees me, a huge grin takes over her face.

"You have to see this," she says, plucking her phone from her backpack.

"I like how every conversation with you begins in the middle."

"Life's too short for niceties." Today she's wearing a yellow Japanese Breakfast T-shirt with ripped red jeans and black beat-up All-Stars. She shoves her phone in front of my face; it's pulled up to a social media post. "Read it."

I look at the account handle: BULLDOGBANNEDCAMP.

"See what I did there? Banned Camp? But books, not instruments."

I roll my eyes and groan. "Life's too short for puns."

"Keep reading."

Beneath a photo of a stack of books, it says, "Join us, the beautiful & the banned. Lunchtime. Schiller Park. Free your mind." A group of hashtags follow it, including #bannedbooks, #fREADom, #bookbans, and #BayberryBans.

I swallow hard. We do need to rally more people to join the cause, but with the reality of it staring me in the face, I worry about the consequences that Carter will be all too happy to deliver. "Do you think anyone will show? Besides us?"

Juniper loops her arm through mine as we head into school. "Have some faith. Not every person's a turd."

She doesn't know she's asking the impossible. Juniper breaks away to chat with some kids from the newspaper while I proceed to my locker. Still no sign of Andrew; usually he's here by now. He could be sick or ditching or running late. Why am I obsessing, though? It's none of my business. It's not as if we had plans this morning. We had coffee last night, that's it. I sigh at the constant ping-ponging of thoughts in my brain and open my locker. There's another book inside: *Ash*, by Malinda Lo. A girl in a white gown against a black cover. It's dramatic and fairy-tale gorgeous. I still haven't directly asked Ms. Clayton if she's the one who has been leaving them for me. I'm worried I could get her in trouble. I'm worried I could get in trouble. We both need plausible deniability.

Faiz comes by my locker to get me for English class, and I hand him the book. He greets me with a warm smile and sparkling brown eyes. The hint of sandalwood on his skin reminds me so much of my dad, it hurts inside my chest. It makes it hard to meet Faiz's eyes, even though I know this has nothing to do with him. "You good?" Faiz asks, noticing my slight wince.

"Yeah. I'm cool." What am I supposed to say? You smell a little like my dad, so being around you is painful? "Did you see Juniper's post this morning?"

He nods.

"You think anyone will show up?"

"Hard to tell. There's literally nothing else happening in this town so some might come for the drama." He grimaces. "So I, uh, texted you last night."

Crap. I'd noticed his text last night: *Kewpie convert yet?* 📚 *I can bring some by LMK.* I saw it when I was at Common Grounds with Andrew and meant to respond when I got home. Tiny flames of guilt lick at the edge of my conscience. I'm about to admit the truth, but it may be more honesty than I can handle this early in the morning. "Sorry. My *do not disturb* was on while I was doing homework. I forgot to check my phone before bed." It's a tiny lie that makes me feel crappy, but I think the truth might hurt him.

Juniper sidles up to us. "What are you two up to?"

"Nothing! Walking to class. What would we be up to?" Faiz blurts.

"Easy, dude. It's one of those throwaway questions, not a pop quiz," she says. "Ooh, is that new Banned Camp reading?" she says, pointing to the book that Faiz sheepishly offers up.

"Just found it," I say. "It looks like a moody queer retelling of Cinderella."

Juniper snags it from Faiz. "You had me at *moody* and *queer*."

Outside at lunch a crowd of around thirty kids surround Juniper. She's sitting cross-legged on top of a picnic table. She's the queen, and we're her loyal subjects hanging on her every word. Her voice is low and drips with honey. There's a husky, emotional quality to it. I'm standing all the way in the back, but I can see she's blinking back tears while she's reading from *Ash*. "Then they took the last step together, and when she kissed her, her mouth as warm as summer, the taste of her sweet and clear, she knew, at last, that she was home."

Juniper closes the book to a smattering of hoots and applause, and Hanna—the junior who talked about Greta Thunberg at our last meeting—gazes at Juniper, mesmerized. Juniper locks eyes with her and I swear I see her blush.

A few people gather around her as Juniper hops down from the table, including Hanna. Juniper grabs some papers from her backpack, gives some to Hanna, and they start distributing them to everyone. They're the flyers Ms. Clayton made with the Brooklyn Public Library QR code. When the bans started, the library began a program called Books Unbanned so that teens anywhere can check out ebooks that might be banned in their hometowns. Gotta love rebel librarians.

"And you get a banned book, and you get a banned book, and you get a banned book," Juniper chirps as she hands out the flyers.

"A star is born," Faiz whispers to me. He was standing on the other side of the group with his D&D crew but found me after people started to disperse. He hasn't said a word to me since our awkward exchange this morning—the one where I lied.

I give him a soft smile. "If our little banned book cabal leads to nothing else besides *that* meet-cute, I'll take the W."

He laughs, then turns to me. He's like a solid six or seven inches taller; I tilt my chin up, smirking at him. My cheeks warm unexpectedly. He gazes back at me for a second, then takes a sudden interest in a pair of squawking birds in the maple tree, so I look away, too. I think I'm the only one feeling those little glimmers of possibility between us because he seems oblivious.

"So you really are a rabble-rouser." Andrew steps up next to me, our shoulders brushing.

"This place could use it," I say, and smile.

"Hey, Faiz," Andrew says in that sort of sullen, head-nod way so many boys greet each other.

Faiz nods at him in a silent, sullen response. There's a pause, the air between the three of us stills, filling with awkward, tense unspoken things. Normally that energy is coming off me, but not this time.

"So...how come you didn't tell me you were doing this again at the coffee shop last night?" Andrew asks.

Crap. I knew lying to Faiz was going to come back to bite me in the ass. I'll have to apologize to him later, make an excuse. A small expression of surprise, then disappointment, quickly passes over his face and he looks away. Part of me wonders if Andrew asked me this on purpose in front of Faiz to needle him. Embarrassment snakes up my spine. I almost apologize but then stop myself, feeling a defensiveness worming its way into my brain. I don't need to report on my daily schedule to Faiz any more than I do to Andrew.

I turn to him. "It's not a secret. You saw us out here before. We decided sort of last minute, and Juniper posted about it this time. That's all."

"It doesn't seem like you'd care about books being banned," Faiz scoffs. "Especially since—"

Andrew cuts him off. "Jocks don't read?"

"That's not what I was going to say, but...are you actually calling yourself a jock?" Faiz shakes his head. "Embarrassing."

"Yeah, so embarrassing to...I don't know, be part of a team, rep your school. Nothing compared to the deep importance of moping around the halls, all emo, pretending your life's terrible."

I stand there flat-footed and closemouthed for a second, trying to figure out what the hell to do. "Can you two chill?" I finally blurt. "All this testosterone spewing is bad for the environment."

Andrew lets out a strained laugh. "Yeah...sure. We cool, man?" he asks Faiz.

"Whatever," Faiz says. He's probably a couple of inches taller than Andrew. But Andrew's bulkier, and he squares his shoulders as they face each other.

There's a moment of silence, and then Faiz walks away without another word, without looking at me.

"Weirdo," Andrew says under his breath as Faiz walks up to Juniper.

"Hey, don't be an asshole."

The bell rings and everyone lazily heads toward school. I start back on my own, but Andrew jogs up next to me. He takes a long breath. "Sorry about that. He's always had it out for me for some reason."

"Are you seriously this clueless? You bullied him when you were kids."

Andrew looks genuinely flummoxed. "Is that what he told you?"

"No, Juniper did." I bite my lip, considering whether I should've kept my mouth shut. Too late. "You mocked him and told him his food smelled weird. Sound familiar?"

"What? When?"

"Like fourth grade."

Andrew pauses as if he's casting his mind back, and a vague look of recollection dawns on his face. "That's why he hates me?"

"Racist microaggressions tend to have that effect."

"Racist?" Andrew scoffs, then presses his lips together when he sees my rage face. "Okay, yeah, I was a little shit then. That was when"—he hesitates—"I had stuff going on." His face looks pained while he's talking, so I don't press it further. "I'll make it right," he says as we walk in the school doors.

I nod, but I'm a bit distracted when I look up.

"See you later." Andrew turns and hurries down the hall to catch up with James.

My own pace slows.

Mr. Carter is standing in the center of the lobby, taking up all the oxygen. Feet in a wide stance, arms crossed in front of his body. He's staring right at me, a scowl on his face. "Ms. Khan," he says, much louder than necessary, as he beckons me over to him.

"I have gym," I say—a futile attempt to get out of this conversation.

"I see you're making friends." He pauses and flashes a wide smile. Not sure if it's for my benefit or for the students and faculty causing a gapers' delay as they pass us in the hallway. *It's all fine. Nothing to see here.*

"I thought we'd come to an understanding. That you'd make efforts to adapt to the culture here at Bayberry High. Follow the rules."

I take a deep breath, running the pad of my index finger over my scar. "Have I broken any?" One thing my dad taught us that *has* come in handy is that lawyers never ask questions in court that they don't already know the answer to. Everything I've done has followed the letter of student handbook policy.

He glances down and chuckles a little, but I'm not sure what's funny. He looks back up at me, his hands at his hips, pulling his suit jacket back. "Since you like stories so much, I'm going to share a little one with you. Did you know that my mom's side of the family were ranchers?"

How the hell would I have known that and is this non sequitur supposed to be interesting? This whole conversation is making me miss gym.

"Over a hundred years. Beef. About an hour south of here, near Oakland, Illinois."

I think I've fallen asleep with my eyes open. I have no idea why I'm being forced to walk down old-person amnesia lane with him.

"I'd spend summers with my granddad on the ranch. There was this bull named Duke—my favorite. Gentle. He'd let us pet him. But once, Duke got angry at one of the ranch hands who was goofing around a bit, and Duke would've gored that man if he hadn't leapt over the fence in time. A bull can kill you that way."

"Mr. Carter, I don't—"

He ignores me. "It's like my grandfather always said: You mess with the bull, you get the horns."

Mr. Carter stops talking, a tight smile on his face, and curtly instructs me to get a late slip from the office. Adults are always sharing weird, probably embellished stories from their childhood to impart some kind of magical wisdom. Sometimes those stories are ridiculous. Sometimes charming. But this time, I'm pretty sure that story was a threat.

CHAPTER 18

It was chilly and rainy for a week. Ah, spring in the Midwest! Carter's warning kept repeating in my head and my nightmares were filled with people getting gored, but I'd avoided seeing him in the halls. I'd expected the rain to slow the momentum we'd started to generate with Bulldog Banned Camp, but it had the opposite effect. Faiz has been acting a little weird around me, but he and Juniper and I continued to hang and post quotes from challenged books and authors on the Banned Camp socials. We've been gaining followers and finding other kids around the country fighting bans, too. Plus, three more books showed up in my locker.

And today the sun shone again and I woke up, for the first time in a long time, feeling like I wanted to be at school, like I wanted to fight these bans even harder. I'm still questioning everything, second-guessing my feelings, but I am going to try to hold on to this momentary belief that I know what I'm doing. It will probably pass soon enough.

Juniper and I walk outside at lunch. Sunlight hits me right in the eye and I blink back a few black blobs before my vision comes into sharp focus again. There must be, like, thirty or forty kids in the park across the street.

I beam at Juniper. She loops her arm through mine, and we practically sprint toward the picnic benches where kids have gathered. Faiz is already there, sitting on one of the benches with some of his D&D crew. He's wearing a flannel over a Star Wars T-shirt and dark jeans, waves of his dark brown hair peeking out from under a black knit cap. I catch his eye and nod; he manages a soft smile. Hanna, the junior who'd had heart eyes when Juniper read last week, skips toward us. She grabs Juniper, and they peel away into the crowd. I watch as they lean toward each other, whispering, laughing, Juniper's eyes dancing every time she looks at Hanna. Juniper is always exactly who she says she is, and I love and envy that about her.

Andrew's in the crowd, too, and he mouths *wow*, with a huge, sparkly eyed grin that gives me butterflies. He and I have been texting and hanging out a little. Nothing serious. But not nothing, either. Then I see James scanning the QR code from one of the flyers that Hanna and Juniper are passing around. Richard has his phone up, filming. I catch Juniper's eye and grimace. She shrugs— it's not as if we can stop him. I mean, we're in a public park; anyone can film anything. But why? And who is he planning on sharing that video with? I think back to something I said to Juniper. *Always get receipts*. It goes both ways, I guess. Those butterflies in my stomach are replaced by knots.

I can't think about that now. I'm always nervous anytime I speak in public and I need to focus. I tuck the book I'm going to read under my armpit so I can wipe my clammy palms against my jeans. I step up onto one of the picnic tables, and the mixed chorus of conversations slowly fades until all eyes are on me.

I take a breath. "Hi," I whisper.

"Louder!" someone yells.

I clear my throat, a nervous smile escaping my lips. "Hi. I'm Noor and I read banned books," I say, feeling the need to reintroduce myself since this is the biggest crowd we've had. I look down at my scuffed Docs and bite my lip, attempting to calm the queasiness in my gut. I do not want to puke in front of everyone.

A few woots and a shout from the middle of the crowd. My eyes sweep to Andrew, who gives me a brilliant smile, a sharp contrast to the scowls on his friends' faces that he seems to be ignoring.

I swallow. "We all know that hundreds of books are being pulled from library shelves. Queer books. Books by authors of color. Stories of sexual assault. All because a handful of parents think we don't have the right to read what we want. That we'll be harmed by reading stories about gay kids or Black kids or trans kids, about survivors, about history. Ironically, the book banners are the same ones who say America is all about freedom. They hate cancel culture, but they have no problem canceling all these books."

"Fascist bullshit!" a voice yells out to a chorus of agreement.

I continue. "The school board passed a policy saying that if even one person objects to a book it gets pulled for 'further review.' But it doesn't say who is reviewing the book or what criteria is being used. They're not calling it a ban because they know bans are wrong, but that's exactly what it is."

"Cowards!" a student shouts.

"You mean assholes," another student yells, and the crowd laughs.

I nod. "Pretty much. Anyway, the policy says the books can't be in school, so that's why we're here, in the park, reading from books they're trying to hide from us." I notice James has started filming me, too. I hesitate, but I can't stop now.

My voice falters, and when I make eye contact with Juniper, she moves closer and stands up next to me. "If they *wanted* to protect us, they'd ban guns, not books!" she yells. There are a few murmured assents, but probably half these kids have guns at their homes. Then she nudges me with her hip, and I hold up the book like a trophy.

"This book, *Monday's Not Coming*, by Tiffany D. Jackson, is a mystery about a young Black girl who goes missing, and no one but her best friend seems to care about it. It's a story about loss and friendship, and it speaks to how violence against Black girls is ignored." I begin reading a passage I'd marked this weekend: " 'I know what you're thinking. How can a whole person, a kid, disappear and no one say a word? Like, if the sun just up and left one day, you'd think someone would sound an alarm, right? But Ma used to say, not everyone circles the same sun. I never knew what she meant by that until Monday went missing.' "

Ugh. Gut punch. I burn up thinking about the racist parents hating on this book because it's so real. The crowd is quiet, like everyone is in their own bubble. That's what a good book does, though—it pulls you into a new world and sometimes even shows you who you are, who you can be. I begin reading a sentence from another page. " 'Well, sometimes the people we love the most can hurt us the most.' " My voice shakes. I'm afraid I might cry, and that feeling hits me like a wrecking ball. I hand the book to Juniper, who touches my arm for a second and continues reading where I stopped.

I sit down on the tabletop, reaching for my water to take a swig. Maybe the promises adults make us become lies because they can't predict the future. Maybe the lies adults tell start as lies they tell themselves. Maybe my dad has no real idea how much his lies have hurt us. Maybe he doesn't care.

The sound of the bell ending lunch echoes beyond the school and into the park, snapping me out of my moody silence. There's a buzz around us as if the crowd is hopped up on too much Red Bull. This is what defiance feels like, I think. A bunch of kids talk to me, and I hear Juniper promise to post all the challenged books on the Bulldog Banned Camp socials. Some students ask if they can read at lunch, too. "The more the merrier," Juniper says. I nod in agreement. This isn't about me. It's about all of us.

I look around for Andrew but he's lost in the crowd; maybe he took off with James and Richard. A big group of us walk across the street together. Faiz slides up next to me and says, "That was pretty awesome. Real chaotic good energy." The earlier tension between us has faded and it's a relief.

"You should read sometime," I suggest.

"Maybe." He shrugs. "I'm more guy-in-the-chair than super-hero. I'll leave that up to you."

"I wish! If I were a hero, at least I'd have superpowers."

Faiz touches my elbow, stopping us as we reenter the school. "You don't need powers to be powerful." There's a warm smile on his face. He's so genuine he almost makes me believe that about myself.

I never feel powerful. Honestly, I'd settle for feeling in control of any part of my life. That's a power I wish I had. We continue walking, but I stop short, right before the turn into senior hall. Mr. Carter is standing outside the doors of the front office, shaking hands with a bald, ruddy-faced man in a navy blue suit and red tie. They're talking but I can't hear what they're saying. I'm interested in what's happening, though, because blue-suit guy is standing next to Andrew with one hand on his shoulder.

"Who's that?" I ask Faiz.

He responds through a clenched jaw. "That's the school board president, Steve Hawley."

"What's Andrew doing with him?"

Faiz looks at me, total surprise on his face. "You seriously don't know? Mr. Hawley is Andrew's dad."

My jaw drops. Andrew's dad is the one behind the bans? He never said a word to me. Maybe this is my karma for all the half-truths and lies of omission I've scattered in my wake. But Andrew's lie sticks in my throat like a bone.

CHAPTER 19

Andrew texted me twice last night, but I didn't respond.
Not sure why he was hiding the truth about his dad from me.
Maybe it's a stupid game to him. Like a dare from one of those
cringey, Cinderella-y nineties teen movies where the popular guy
makes a bet to date the nerdy girl only to discover that when she
takes off her glasses she's gorgeous.

Andrew's car is only three spots over from where Amal and I
park this morning. He's leaning against the passenger-side door.

"Looks like he's waiting for you," Amal says.

"He can wait till hell freezes over."

"Hell hath no fury like my pissed-off sister." Amal places a hand
to her chest, pantomiming shock.

I roll my eyes.

"Why don't you let him explain? Ask him. I mean, you're not
exactly Little Miss Share Everything." I don't think she means it,

but Amal's words cut a little. If I'm not always open about stuff it's because I don't want to get burned. Again.

"Ha ha. Little Miss Spitting Truths. You're the voice of reason now?"

"My wisdom is a gift. You're welcome."

Andrew walks over to Amal's side of the car and says a few things to her as I lock the doors manually, because this car is thirty-five years older than me and there's nothing easy or automatic about it. Amal laughs at something he says and then waves at us as she jogs to catch up with some friends.

"Are you mad at me?" Apparently Andrew was locked and loaded. "Look, if this is about me being an ass to Faiz when—" He talks to me over the hard top of my car.

"It isn't," I snap.

"When you didn't respond to my texts, I figured..."

"Oh, you're used to girls being at your beck and call? Pick that charming habit up from James?" I swear James seems to cozy up with a different girl every week.

"What? No." Andrew seems genuinely offended, but I don't care.

I sigh and adjust my backpack on my shoulders. Tired of having to explain everything. "When were you going to tell me your dad was the school board president?"

Andrew's face falls. "He's my stepdad. My real dad died when I was nine."

"Oh..." That new information smacks me in the chest. I was so ready to rip Andrew to shreds, and now a realization dawns on me. "Wait. Is that what you meant when you said you were a jerk in fourth grade because you were going through some stuff? It was your dad...dying?"

He nods and directs his gaze to the ground. "I was a mess for so long. I hated everyone. I would act out one minute and then sink into this chamber of silence. James was the only one who'd even talk to me or play with me during recess. He didn't leave my side during the wake or the funeral. The other kids treated me like I had a disease. They kept away from me like they thought a parent dying was contagious."

"I'm so sorry." I hate pity sorrys but I'm not sure what else to say. His dad dying isn't an excuse for bullying Faiz, but it's maybe an explanation. A wave of sadness engulfs me. I'm sad for fourth-grade Andrew and twelfth-grade Andrew. My dad may not be dead, but being mad at the world is something I feel in my bones.

After a brief pause, he looks up at me and says in a low monotone, "I guess I should've told you about Steve, but I didn't realize you chose your friends based on their parents."

I feel terrible for Andrew, but it doesn't stop me from getting defensive. "I don't. But you knew I was speaking out against his policies. Seems kinda sus that you didn't say anything. When I saw you chatting with him and Carter yesterday and your friends were filming...well, I was worried you guys were—"

"Narcing on Banned Camp?" He cuts me off with a laugh. "No way. I saw Steve in the hall and said hi because my mom would've killed me if I didn't. Wouldn't you do the same if your dad, or stepdad, showed up at school?"

I would probably feel like punching my dad in the face if he showed up. Not that Andrew would know this because, like Amal said, I'm not a fan of sharing about my dad—it makes me feel like a giant walking wound. But since we're being honest with each other, I suck in my breath and whisper, "My dad left us right before winter break. Couldn't deal with having a family anymore, apparently."

Andrew walks around the front of the car to stand next to me. He reaches out his hand but then draws it away, simply saying, "That fucking sucks."

I let out a surprised laugh because most people who find out about my dad say they're sorry and then get all awkward because they don't know how else to react. Andrew's response feels like a genuine relief.

"He literally didn't bother to come home one day. He left us a note with two sentences saying he couldn't do it anymore." My words start catching, so I clear my throat. "There's even, like, a name for what he did: Wife Abandonment Syndrome."

"Yikes," Andrew says.

"Yeah. I couldn't stop myself from going down that rabbit hole searching for the Why. Apparently, some men abandon their families without ever showing a single sign that they were unhappy. They plan it in secret. They know they're going to leave and how they're going to restart their lives but hide it all from their families. He just—" I quickly brush away a tear that's falling down my cheek. I haven't even told Faiz and Juniper all of this. Only gave them a two-sentence explanation about my parents being separated, and even that felt like I'd cracked my ribs open and exposed my insides.

"Noor," Andrew says softly. "I can't imagine. I'm here, if you ever want to talk about it—like ever—call me. Seriously."

I clear my throat. Talking about my dad might make me feel like the walking wounded, but I'm not about to act that way. It gives my dad too much power. I straighten my shoulders. "Yeah, it's the worst. Still doesn't change the fact that you lied to me."

"I didn't lie. Look, we've known each other, like, two minutes and, well, having your weird stepdad be the school board president kinda sucks. Everyone knows, teachers point it out. It's so not normal. It's even worse now since he's running for office. I know his political stances are kinda BS, but that's him, not me. We don't even really talk about politics at home."

I sigh. "You get that it's a privilege not to have to talk about politics, right? I mean, my entire existence is politicized. Like tons of other people. We don't get the same choice you do to avoid uncomfortable conversations."

He looks chastened. "Maybe not, but do you think it's fair to blame me for stuff my stepdad does? We're not our parents."

I tense, thinking how much I'm *not* my parents, about how Amal said I seem angry all the time. I allow the strained muscles in my back to slacken. It's not even first period and both my sister and Andrew have pointed out ways I've been a jerk. Great start to the morning. The hard edge of my clenched jaw softens. "No, we're not our parents," I say, thinking about my dad, my mom, and all the things they've done that have upset me, things I couldn't change, things they didn't ask my permission to do. I think maybe there's a part of Andrew that understands that.

Andrew smiles. He's so easygoing it relaxes the tense space between us. Maybe I have been too quick to judge. If he's willing to try to make things right, isn't that a good thing? Not like I'm exactly perfect, either. The part of me that's been burned by putting too much trust in people is screaming at me, lighting up warning signs, but maybe Andrew deserves the benefit of the doubt. He's right. We're not our parents. We're not destined to make the same crappy choices they did.

CHAPTER 20

Weird how a little notoriety works. After yesterday's lunchtime reading, more kids are saying hi to me in the halls. I don't feel so invisible anymore. Not sure if that's a good thing. but it is what it is. Like a million other things in my life, I can't change it.

I walk into the library before school starts, working up the courage to ask Ms. Clayton if she really is my book fairy—there was another book in my locker today. But she's sitting at one of the tables next to a student—a ninth grader, I think. I walk up behind them to say hi but then freeze when I see the student sniffle and swipe her nose with the cuff of her hoodie. I turn to the nearest bookshelf, not wanting to intrude, but I'm still listening or, as my mom would note with disappointment, eavesdropping.

"I'm so sorry, Summer. I can't imagine how hard it must be," Ms. Clayton says in a soft voice. "You're brave. Never forget that."

The girl sniffles again. "Thanks. And thanks for, you know, letting me hang out here."

"Of course. Anytime, dear. I want you to feel at home in the library, and my office door is always open."

I hear the girl rummage through her backpack. "Here," she says. "Thanks for this."

I quickly glance at them and see the girl hand a book to Ms. Clayton. "It was awesome."

"Love to hear that," Ms. Clayton says. "And the offer still stands. If you don't want to read at home, you can read in my office during any of your free periods. I have a stack of books on my desk with your name on it."

The girl smiles and stands up. "See you tomorrow."

"Hang in there, kiddo," Ms. Clayton says.

When she gets up, she turns to sees me. "Oh, Noor. Good morning." Then she spies the book in my hand: *I Am Malala*, by *the* Malala, duh. It's her own story about her activism and resilience, about standing up to the Taliban and fighting for the right for girls to go to school. It's bananas that anyone anywhere would want to ban this book. But then again, this school also banned *The Diary of Anne Frank*.

"Read any good books lately?" she asks.

"Yes," I say. "Inspiring ones."

Ms. Clayton smiles. "Excellent. Let me know if you need any more recommendations."

"Thank you," I say. "For everything." I gesture at the book, and Ms. Clayton nods and heads toward her office with a few books in hand.

But a second later, the library doors open and Carter walks in. Instinctively, I turn my back to him and hide the Malala book between my binders like it's drugs. For once, though, he isn't looking for me. I don't think he even notices I'm there.

"Ms. Clayton." His voice booms in the quiet library as he walks toward her. "Can you join me? I'd like to have a word." He motions to her office, and she smiles and walks in. Mr. Carter closes the door behind them.

My blood runs cold. I hope she's not getting in trouble. I edge closer to her office door. At first the voices are muffled, low, and I strain to hear. Then Carter's voice seeps through the door. "As you know, identity politics have no place in our school."

"With respect, all politics are identity politics. And I'd like to have my union rep present for any further discussion regarding—" Ms. Clayton's resolute response is interrupted by the bell ringing. I startle and quickly move away from the door. I have to get to class. I'm trying to avoid any tardies. But as I leave, dread pools in the pit of my stomach.

———

During afternoon study hall, I flip through *Candide* for English class. I'm marking pages with orange sticky notes when the intercom crackles on and Mr. Carter's authority-laced voice booms through study hall.

"Effective immediately, off-campus lunch privileges for all juniors and seniors have been suspended. Students will not be allowed to leave school for lunch and must eat their lunches in either the school cafeteria or the inner courtyard. All exits will be monitored, and anyone found violating this policy will be immediately suspended."

His announcement is met with groans and shouts of *This is bullshit* and *That's not fair*. The teacher tries to quiet us down, but Carter keeps talking because he can't hear us anyway.

"While it gives me no great pleasure to take this extreme action, I'm afraid it is due to the behavior of a few individuals who have plainly flouted the intent of school district policy regarding appropriate reading materials. The school board and I feel this is our only recourse. While most of you did *not* participate in these unsanctioned lunchtime gatherings, I am afraid you must suffer the consequences of the poor choices made by some of your peers, as there has been no formal account of who attended these off-campus assemblies. It is unfortunate that we have been forced into this position." All twenty sets of eyeballs in study hall turn to look at me, most scowling, including some kids who'd actually been at the park yesterday.

There's a gnawing in the pit of my stomach. I honestly think I might vom, so I rush out of study hall before the bell rings. The words of some students chase me out the door: "You screwed us, Noor!" "Go back to where you came from!" Those are the last words I hear before the bell rings and students begin pouring out of class, loud, angry voices filling the hall. I hurry into the girls' bathroom, pushing open the door of a stall before I get sick, knowing that Carter accomplished exactly what he set out to do: paint a target on my back.

CHAPTER 21

A few weeks at a new school and I'm public enemy num-
ber one. For reading! I can't even manage to get in trouble for something truly scandalous. I came to this place with a plan to lie low,
graduate, return to Chicago, and put Bayberry behind me. It was an
easy action plan, but I blew it all up within, like, forty-eight hours
of starting here. One thing about me is I will act on my impulses
without thinking hard about the consequences. *Yell at your mom
and make her feel bad? I'm your girl! Pick a fight with the principal?
Sure, why not! Want to get the whole school to hate you? Challenge
accepted!* The last four months have been an ongoing avalanche of
Things That Suck and me trying to rebuild a mountain in the middle of that landslide, one tiny pebble at a time.

I'm sprawled sideways across my bed, my long hair hanging over
the edge, trying to understand how life can take such breathless,
swift, hairpin turns with zero warning signs. I rub the burn scar on

my thumb, reminding myself that wounds are *supposed* to heal, but if you keep picking at them, they get infected and stay inflamed.

My phone pings. That's, like, the tenth text I've gotten since I raced out of school with Amal after the last bell. I didn't even stop to say bye to Juniper. Or respond to Andrew when I heard him calling my name as I turned out of senior hall. Everyone, and I mean everyone, was staring at me. A few with their eyes full of pity, but most with sour, rageful faces. Off-campus lunch is *the* privilege every kid looks forward to when they start at Bayberry, and now it's gone because of me, just as the weather is warming up and senioritis is about to hit overdrive. Everyone probably hates me. I don't blame them; right now I pretty much hate me, too.

I've probably also screwed over my friends and Amal. Thinking of her diligently doing her homework in her room across the hall makes my heart feel like it's being squeezed in a vise. She's doing okay here. More than okay, actually. She has friends. She's smiling and laughing again, and if my stupid stick-it-to-the-man pseudo rebellion ruins it for her, I'll launch myself into the sun. I can't let things get bad again for Amal. I didn't technically force Carter to cancel off-campus, but it was *my* choice to read those books out loud. I thought maybe I'd pull detention, not ruin the rest of the year for all the upperclassmen. I took a molehill of a mess and turned it into a mountain-size trash heap.

My phone pings again. I groan and sit up, placing my cold palms flat against my tired eyes. I take a deep breath, reach for my phone, and start scrolling. There's a bunch of texts from Juniper reflecting moods ranging from incredulity to straight-up rage to one that reads, *You okay? Call me!* There's a message from Faiz checking in with an orange angry-face swearing emoji. The most recent one is from Andrew: *Want to drown your anger in DQ?*

I *would* like to eat my feelings right now, thank you very much. I text back a simple *yes*.

> **Andrew:** soft serve + rage = two great tastes that
> go great together
> **Andrew:** pick you up in 15
> **Me:** 👍

I feel a twinge of guilt. I haven't responded to Juniper or Faiz. I should. I will. I don't want them to worry, but I also kinda don't want to talk about it. I want to forget, even if only for an hour or two, that I've totally stepped in it. Andrew makes forgetting easy.

When I head downstairs, I see my mom in the kitchen, sitting at the counter, her tasbih between her fingers. She's not doing anything else. Not looking at her phone. Not returning emails or grading papers. Just sitting there, spacing out. It scares me a little.

"Mom," I whisper.

She looks up, a weak smile on her face. I can't remember the last time a smile reached her eyes. "Yes, beta?"

Part of me wants to ask if she's okay. Ask if she needs anything. But I think I'm afraid of the answer, so I don't ask the question.

"I'm going to Dairy Queen with a friend. Cool?"

The Before version of my mom, the Chicago version, the happily married version, would've grilled me: *Are you done with your homework? Who are you going with? When will you be back? Don't forget to brush and floss when you get home!* But the Now version of my mom simply nods an okay. She doesn't remind me of curfew.... Do I even have a curfew anymore? Like so many things between us, it's gone unspoken.

I grab a black wool poncho, embroidered all over with red flowers, that I bought when we were in Rajasthan three years ago. It was the last time we went to India as a family. I bought it from this incredibly good-looking guy at an open-air market in Jodhpur—he was maybe sixteen years old and selling things to support his family. His eyes were piercing, and he responded in this mellifluous Urdu when I spoke to him with my terrible broken accent. His smile was wide and sincere, and I begged my dad to not haggle with him over the shawl. Everyone haggles in India. One of my aunts told me that people are always ready with a sad story to tell you why they have to upcharge you, but I didn't care. No one selling wares at that market was rich or even middle class. They were all barely scraping by. We had so much more, we didn't *need* to haggle. My dad kissed the top of my head, then paid the boy full price. "Enough to feed a family of four for a week, at least," my father told me as we walked away.

Now, as I slip the soft wool poncho over my head, a lump wells in my throat. Not sure who I'm sadder for—the boy or my dad or me. Sometimes a memory reminds you of who you wish you still were. Sometimes a memory can destroy you.

I step outside to a chorus of crickets chirping and some birds singing their evening song. There's a spring crispness in the air. Twilight blooms everywhere around me. I sigh deeply. The air feels good on my skin. But the unfairness of this moment overwhelms me. How gorgeous the night is despite the ugly mess of my life.

How dare you, Nature? Walking around, my entire person a giant bruise, any beauty feels like an affront. It should be gray clouds and storms all day. The stars hidden away, not bursting through the blue-velvet night sky as it fades to black.

Andrew's silver BMW pulls up in my driveway. It's surprising, still—the barely audible purr of the engine, the silvery shine of the paint when Andrew drives under a streetlamp. The showiness. Maybe most jarring of all is Andrew himself. Popular. Athletic. White. He's the opposite of everything and everyone I've ever been attracted to in my life so far. He's the kind of bougie rich kid that my Chicago friends and I used to make fun of. Not that any of us were poor—we were all some variation of limousine liberal. Some of us more limousine, some more liberal. But Andrew... I mean, his stepdad must be a real right-wing, "take America back," angry at the global majority, homophobic, storm-the-Capitol-type conservative. Andrew said he never talks with his stepdad about politics, and a tiny voice in the back of my head is telling me to question that. Maybe they don't need to talk about politics because Andrew agrees with him a little. My breath hitches. No. That can't be true. I don't want it to be true. He wouldn't hang out with me if he believed that xenophobic crap.

On the other hand, I understand not wanting to talk to a parent. I barely talk to my mom. And if my dad ever really tried to get back into my life, I'd ice him out, no question.

Maybe that's why it feels comfortable being around Andrew. We don't have to explain to each other how much our dad situations suck. We both understand the pain of making strangers and even friends feel better when they fall all over themselves, awkwardly apologizing for saying something unintentionally hurtful. Say sorry and move on, okay? That's what I want to say to people, but I can't because it's rude. Instead I tell them it's fine, I'm fine, everything is fine, then get to my room as fast as possible so no one can see me cry. Andrew knows that. He's been there. Understands how raw a wound like that feels.

I walk around the front of Andrew's car and let my fingers rest for a second on the door handle. I shudder, goose bumps popping up all over my arms. The light on the inside of the car flashes on and I see Andrew smiling at me. I'm not sure what I'm doing out here. With him. For the briefest second, I think about making an excuse, faking a headache, going back inside…but I pull up the handle and slip into the car before I have a chance to second-guess myself. I don't want to think about regrets or bad choices or the entire senior class hating me.

An image of my dad's face pops into my mind—he's wearing his disappointed look. The one that says *Are you weighing your choices before you make them?* I squeeze my eyes shut. I won't let a fatherly figment of my imagination judge me. Who is he to chastise my choices, anyway? His choices sucked. *Shut up, phantom dad.*

"Hey," Andrew says, his eyes warm and kind. He begins to lean over, oh so slightly. My pulse quickens, but he draws back, placing both of his hands on the wheel. "All good?" he asks.

Why is it so hard, almost painful for me to answer such a basic question? "Can we please just drive?" I whisper.

CHAPTER 22

We don't say anything. The roads are empty, and as we speed over the smooth pavement, the suburbanish streets of my neighborhood fall away to fields of corn and soy and canola, waiting to burst through the dirt, all that potential energy ready to spring into a summer sea of green and yellow. Andrew opens the car's moonroof. I tilt my head back and my eyes fill with stars. The road is dark and endless, and it feels like we could drive forever.

"Probably don't get starry nights like this in Chicago, do you, New Girl?" Andrew sneaks a quick grin at me before turning his eyes back to the road.

"No," I say, "but we have everything else, like a Great Lake, and public transportation, diversity, and culture. Not to mention restaurants that use spices in their food."

Andrew scoffs. "I'll have you know that at last year's Freedom Fest, the Elms set up their usual food stand but this time their potato salad had paprika on it and it caused a small riot."

I laugh. "Do I even want to know if that's a true story?" I shake my head and turn to look out the window. It gets so dark here. There's a deep inky quality to the night that still catches me off guard.

"I could tell you," Andrew says with a sly grin, "but I like to keep the mystery alive."

"Ha! You're right, paprika is the most enigmatic spice."

We both laugh, and it eases some of the tension that was stuck between my shoulders.

"Still want to go to DQ?" he asks.

"Didn't we already pass it?" I ask.

"Oh yeah, but I guessed you maybe wanted to take the scenic route? Anyway, it's pretty much at the center of town, so a few left turns and we're there."

"All roads lead to DQ?" I smirk. "Ancient Roman but make it soft serve."

Andrew smiles before taking a sharp left turn. "Little known fact, rocky road is a reference to the uneven pavement of the Appian Way."

"It's weird because you seem all normal and charming, but really you're an Austen-loving, poetry-quoting nerd."

"So you think I'm charming?"

My face heats. Is it normal for your pulse to pound in your ears? I let out a nervous laugh. "Figures that's the only part you heard!"

After another left turn, the lights of the DQ come into view. We pull into the last empty spot in the parking lot. DQ is absolutely packed. It's almost depressing how few places there are to go, but at least there's ice cream. Kids are milling around picnic tables outside sipping ginormous drinks or licking up dipped cones before they melt. I see one guy holding a Blizzard upside down over another guy's head like they do in the commercials, and a group of kids are circled around them, cheering for the Blizzard to drop. Smells like teen boredom.

Andrew and I are halfway across the parking lot when I am slammed with the feeling that this is a terrible idea. If I'd thought about it for even, like, half a second, I never would've said yes. I stop walking and Andrew doesn't realize it until he's a few paces ahead of me. He glances over his shoulder, then takes a few long strides back to me.

"You okay?"

"Yeah...no...I don't think I should be here." My brain feels thick, fuzzy.

"Like here in the DQ parking lot, or here in Bayberry, or..." His voice trails off, the question hovering in the air between us.

"*Here*. It doesn't seem like it's a good idea after, y'know, Carter canceling off-campus lunch. Everyone here hates me."

Andrew tilts his head. "That's what you're worried about?"

I shrug. Seems obvious to me.

"It's cool. C'mon, I promise. I know everyone here. It'll be okay." He cups my elbow with his right hand. "I thought you said you wanted to eat your feelings?"

I sigh, giving him a halfhearted smile. I nod and take a reluctant step forward. Andrew gives me a huge grin. "We're going to go wild on the toppings. As far as sprinkles go, the limit does not exist."

The bright lights of the DQ spill out onto the front patio over the tables, where half the senior class seems to be chatting and laughing. Kids are sitting on the backs of chairs and on the tables, and as we get closer, I see the moment like a slow-motion scene in a teen movie. Heads thrown back in laughter, a few couples holding hands, one kissing in a corner where the beams of light don't reach. Virtually everyone is white, which I don't think anyone notices but me. Because when you're the odd one out, you always make a mental note of it, catastrophizing about the things that *could* happen, scanning for exits, forming an escape plan. Sometimes it's the only way to calm my anxiety.

As if he can read my mind, Andrew lightly puts a reassuring palm on my lower back and gives me a little nod as we step into the spotlight.

"Andreeeeeew!" Richard yells out, and then does a double take when he sees me, makes a sour face, and turns to say something to the group he's with before they burst into laughter.

I suck in my breath. This wasn't a good idea. "Do I even want to know what that's about?"

"What what's about?" Andrew asks, clueless.

"Richard's stink eye."

"That's his resting-idiot face. They're just dicking around." Andrew rolls his eyes as if we're sharing an inside joke.

I chew on my lip, trying to convince myself that not everyone is turning to stare at us, that the cupped-ear whispers are not about me. I'm probably being paranoid, but then why is there a burst of adrenaline in my body telling me to run?

As we move through the hushing crowd, making our way to the entrance, the door swings open and James steps out slurping a drink. He's dressed in a conspicuously fitted long-sleeved dark green Henley that brings out his eyes, even under the harsh fluorescence. I hate to say it but he looks hot. If only he had brains, a personality, and wasn't a complete asshole, he'd be almost tolerable.

"Andrew! My dad got us ice time at the rink this weekend," James says, chewing on the end of his plastic straw as he gives me the once-over. "Then we'll bonfire at my place."

"I'm there," Andrew says, and they fist-bump. "Totally going to kick your ass."

"You wish," James says. "Great to see you and"—he pauses, pretending to search for my name—"the new girl hanging out." He sneers a little. He doesn't try to hide it, either.

I roll my eyes. "Were you born this hostile, or do you practice in the mirror?"

James forces a chuckle as he scans the crowd, not making eye contact with me. Andrew laughs uncomfortably. "Relax, I'm just joking around," James says. "Or do senses of humor not exist where *you're* from?"

"What's that supposed to mean?" I straighten my shoulders and look into his eyes, even as he towers above me.

Andrew cocks his head and flicks James's shoulder. "Easy, killer. Your humor is an acquired taste."

"That's one way of putting it," I scoff. James is grating on my nerves, and I know I should leave. I've met guys like him before, but my anger is like an animal ready to pounce, and I don't feel like reining it in.

"Kinda ballsy you showing up here considering you've screwed over the entire senior class, *Noor*." James stresses my name like it's an insult.

"Like there's anywhere else to go in this hick town." The wrong words were out of my mouth before I could stop them.

"You and your loser friends got off-campus privileges taken away. For everyone. Couldn't go have your reading circle jerk in private. No, you had to force your little QR codes and liberal agenda down our throats." James juts his jaw out as he inches closer to me, almost daring me to take a swing at it. And oh, I want to take that dare so much.

Andrew puts his hand on James's chest and pushes him back the tiniest bit. "Dude, what the hell? Carter's decisions aren't Noor's fault."

I'm glad that Andrew said something, but I can feel a wave of rage pulsing through me. I grind my teeth to keep my mouth shut because otherwise I'm one-hundred-percent going to say something I'll regret, even if it's deserved. I ball my right hand into a fist. I've never ever hit anyone and don't know how to throw a proper punch, but right now, I wish I did. My dad would say I need to deescalate. My mom would tell me to get the hell out of here. I take a few slow breaths. The other kids stare at us. Some move closer to grab front-row seats. I do not need this in my life right now.

"I get that you wouldn't understand standing up to fascist rules. You've got Proud Boy written all over you." Oops. Still have to work on that deescalating thing. But when my pulse is pounding in every part of my body, my rage overrides my brain every time.

James nods with his tongue in his cheek. "Nice. Nice girl you got there, Andrew. Maybe you don't realize this, Noor, but you're not in Chicago anymore. And your whole"—he looks me up and down, gesturing at my poncho and ripped jeans—"*urban* vibe doesn't fly here."

I snort. "Urban?" I say, using air quotes as I look down at my poncho. I laugh, step back, and eye James up and down. "As opposed to this"—I gesture at his clothes—"whole try-hard loser look you cultivate?"

I hear a few oohs and stifled giggles from the crowd. James glares at me.

Andrew looks at me, his lips in a straight line. "Let's go, Noor."

I nod. We turn to head back to the parking lot, and someone yells, "Go home, terrorist! No one wants you here." A few people laugh behind my back. My eyes sting, and for a moment my breath is stuck in my body. I've heard those phrases too many times in my life. I want to turn to say something, but Andrew grasps my upper arm. In my anger, I'm trying to form words, trying to find the right thing to say. Even though I know it's useless.

Andrew scans the crowd, anger in his eyes. "Are you okay? I... I'm so sorry. C'mon, let's get outta here."

I glance again at the students on the patio, but they've already moved on to other, more interesting topics, apparently. Why the hell did I engage with James? Feeding a troll is amateur hour.

I lock eyes with Andrew. Give him a small nod. I won't cry. Not here. Not now. That would be like handing all of them a victory. I walk back to the car, seething in silence.

CHAPTER 23

"My friends are dicks sometimes," Andrew says.

"Sometimes?" I say through a clenched jaw, not looking at him even though I feel his gaze on me. Every muscle in my body tenses like I'm still on the starting block in a race where I can't see the finish line and all the other runners have an insurmountable lead.

"Look, I'm really, really sorry. James was totally rude, and I'll find out who yelled at you and force them to apologize."

"What's the point? They'd only hate me more." I sigh.

"Do you want to go home?"

I shake my head. "Not yet." I'm vibrating with anger and I need someplace to calm down, and home isn't it, not that bland house and the blasé gaze in my mom's eyes. I want to go somewhere I can stop time. I don't want to think about my dad or how I'm going to deal with going back to school or how there are still too many days to X out on my calendar before college starts. I don't want to ponder lies or half-truths or lost friends or racist politicians. I'm tired of asking questions and scrambling for answers that are always out of reach.

So I don't press Andrew about why he didn't push back harder against his friends at DQ. Maybe he doesn't know how. Maybe for him that *is* pushing back. Even if he had, it still might've pissed me off because I am *not* a damsel in distress. But friends are supposed to stick up for each other. Maybe he's too scared to say anything. My dad once told me that not everyone could muster moral courage— that's partly why the silent majority exists. I sigh. For now, Andrew is easygoing and doesn't make anything feel pressure-y. If I stifle my questioning, it's easy to hang with Andrew and pretend the rest of the sucky world doesn't exist.

We come to a stop at an intersection, and I finally turn to Andrew, our eyes meet, and I hold his gaze. His mouth is turned up in a slight, sympathetic smile. "I have an idea. Let me try to salvage the night," he says, turning right and pulling into a gas station with a small convenience mart attached.

I sit in silence, counting my breaths. Inhale for four, hold for two, exhale for four, and repeat until I feel calmer. I watch Andrew through the large plateglass windows; he disappears between shelves of snacks. When he comes back out, he holds a paper bag above his head as if it's Simba held aloft by that baboon. I allow myself a small laugh.

He gets in the car and hands me the bag. "What do you think of my choices?"

There are six different ice-cream bars, and I pull out one that's vanilla dipped in dark chocolate. "Good work," I say. For now, I'm pretending ice-cream choices are the only things I have to deal with.

"Don't eat it yet! We're almost there." Andrew takes a few rights until we're on a small dark road, driving through empty fields with no streetlamps.

"This setting has true-crime podcast written all over it."

"There's, like, zero crime in Bayberry." Andrew slows down a bit and takes a left turn.

"It's always the places you least suspect."

The car wheels crunch as we pull over onto the gravel shoulder. "This is it."

"By *it* do you mean the perfect murder spot?"

"Trust me."

"That's what all the serial killers say."

It's dark outside except for the fuzzy glow of a crescent moon. The only sounds are crickets chirping and noises from other insects I can't name and don't particularly want to get acquainted with. The road dead-ends into a small patch of woods. I raise an eyebrow at Andrew, who has walked around the front of the car and is now standing next to me. "Danger, Noor Khan. Danger," I say, a hint of sarcasm in my voice.

"You're afraid of the woods? Don't tell me city girls are freaked out by trees."

"It's not the trees, dude. It's creepy murderers. I'm keenly aware of horror movie tropes, okay? When it's silent, that's when you need to be scared."

"Let's make some noise, then." Andrew gently takes my hand, holding on to the brown paper bag with the other. I swallow. My heart beats like a hummingbird against my rib cage. My first instinct is to pull my hand away. But I pause. Take a breath and thread my fingers through his. A smile lights up his face and we take off running, him tugging me into the damp woods. He howls as a cloud passes in front of the sliver of silvery moon that was lighting our path forward.

I laugh. Decide I might as well lean into the creepy weirdness. Because...it's fun, actually. I'm having fun! Andrew howls again and this time I join. Our voices loud—cymbals smashing into the symphony of hushed night sounds.

Andrew pulls me into a clearing where there's a small pond, a few benches around its edges, and an enclosed gazebo on the other bank strung with fairy lights that twinkle against the still water. Even the most cynical part of me understands how magical this all feels.

"I used to ice-skate on this pond every winter when I was little," Andrew says as he guides us to a bench. There's a chill in the air now, and we sit close to each other.

"You don't skate here anymore?"

"Indoors for most of the year, and in winter, I'm usually at the rink they put up in town. It's big enough for hockey, and the town keeps the ice smooth. At the winter carnival, there are kiddie races on the ice."

"There's a festival for everything here, huh?" I snuggle into my poncho that I'd slipped over my head before exiting the car.

"As you've noticed, there's literally nothing else to do. We have to make our own fun."

"Yeah, I gathered from the DQ."

Andrew presses his lips together as if he's stopping himself from saying something he knows he shouldn't. He takes a beat and then says, "Yeah, that sucked. But I—"

"That sucked. Period. End of sentence," I say, a chilly wariness slithering up my spine. "There's no excuse for it. Calling a Muslim a terrorist and telling us to 'go home' are classics from the racist handbook."

He nods. I can't tell if he's grasping what I'm saying. I also realize I'm running hot and cold between bantery and ragey, but my feelings are a perfect storm of mixed emotions. I practically have whiplash from it. Can't imagine what it looks like from the outside. It's not my job to give him a Racism 101 course, and I also don't want to rehash the evening with a play-by-play, so I shift the conversation to easier things for my own sake, because exhaustion from bigotry talk is real.

"When did you start playing hockey?"

Andrew's face brightens. "My dad got me my first skates when I was four. Been playing ever since."

"Cool. I'm not really a winter sports person. Or, really, any sports."

He turns to me with his eyes wide. "You've never ice-skated?"

I shake my head. "And I would never ever try on a frozen pond because I don't have a death wish. If the ice cracks and you fall through, you'd die from hypothermia, your face pressed up against the cold, hard surface."

He laughs. "That is a weirdly detailed death fantasy. If we're ever ice-skating and you fall under, I will rescue you."

I jokingly roll my eyes.

"But seriously," he says, "you have to try skating. It feels...I don't know...sort of like flying. Especially when you're the only one out there and all you hear is the swoosh of your blades cutting through the ice. My dad would bring me out here all the time. Just me and him."

He looks far into the distance for a moment. His eyes get a little glassy.

"It's a nice memory," I whisper.

"Yeah. Sometimes James and Richard join me now. But I come by myself a lot, too. It's weird, but I think being alone out here is when I feel closest to my dad. Or when it feels like he's closest to me."

I nod.

He takes a beat and then laughs softly. "Does that sound all woo-woo?"

"Woo-woo?"

"That's what my mom calls it when she hears anything about spirits or tarot cards or putting your wishes into the universe."

"No. It doesn't sound woo-woo at all. It sounds nice." I pause. Take a breath. Reach for a feeling I buried. "In a way, I think, I'm kinda...envious."

Andrew turns to me. "Of my dead dad?"

"Oh my God! No. I'm so sorry. That's not what I meant."

"It's okay." He looks at me with a softness in his eyes. "I get it."

"It's like I have all these memories of things my dad and I did together, and I don't know what to do with them. My mom used to call us coconspirators because we'd always do little things we weren't supposed to. You know, like sneak scoops of ice cream before dinner or stay up late to watch random TikToks."

"Mom-designated crimes."

I laugh. "Yeah. Once it was snowing late in the evening. I was in third grade, and when my mom was giving my sister a bath, Dad and I snuck out to go sledding at this little hill behind the train tracks by our house."

"Sounds amazing."

I smile at the memory, despite myself. "It really was. The snow was falling and the drifts sparkled under the streetlamps. The city was so quiet. Only me and my dad and the swoosh of the sled and our howls of laughter..." My voice fades. Sharing this memory, saying it out loud, it's too much. I'm suddenly drowning in sadness. "But those memories—"

"They're all screwed up because your dad left." Andrew finishes my thought.

I nod. "I keep thinking that maybe I can't trust my memories anymore. Like our lives were built on his humongous lies."

Andrew bites his lower lip and turns to look at me, inching closer. "Don't freak out, but when you mentioned the whole Wife Abandonment Syndrome thing, I googled it because I'd never heard of it before."

I raise an eyebrow. My stomach twisting into knots because I'm not sure where he's going with this.

"It seems like dudes who do that—abandon their families out of the blue, cutting them off—are sort of broken."

I sigh. "Yeah. But it's not an excuse," I say, feeling a bit defensive.

"No! No way. I'm only saying that I don't think you should blame yourself for not seeing it, and you definitely shouldn't feel bad for cherishing a memory. He doesn't own them. They're yours, too."

My breath catches in my chest when Andrew says those words. I squeeze my eyes shut and blow out a huge puff of air. "Families can mess you up, huh?"

"Tell me about it."

Andrew reaches into the paper bag and pulls out two ice-cream bars for us. We unwrap them and I lean over and tap my ice-cream bar with his. "To murdery woods that end up kinda cool and not that creepy."

"The night is still young," he jokes, and leans into me a bit. I feel a tingle against my skin, like goose bumps but warm instead of shivery. Then he raises his ice-cream bar and adds, "To the parents and stepparents who make sure we'll need therapy forever."

"Is it that bad...with your stepdad, I mean?" There's a brief pause and I wonder if I've overstepped. "I'm sorry. That was probably insensitive. You don't have—"

"Nah. It's okay. Steve and I...we're not close. He was my mom's choice. Not mine. It was hard at first. Especially since she remarried only a little over a year after my dad died."

"Ouch."

"Yeah. That's why pretty much everyone calls Steve my dad, even though he isn't. He's been in the picture a long time, and it's like they all forgot my real dad existed. My mom doesn't even talk about him anymore. Steve probably wouldn't like it."

"That's the worst." All my edges soften. He wasn't abandoned, but I get how he must feel so alone.

Andrew hunkers down a bit, leaning forward onto his knees. "I was beyond pissed when my mom got remarried. Now Steve and I are sort of like grudging roommates. If your roommate also owned your house, bought your car, and is going to pay your college tuition, and your mom sides with him one hundred percent of the time. I don't get why she's like that. Sometimes it feels like he *allows* me to be in his family, when he's the one that married into mine."

A pained look passes over his face, and it makes me wonder, again, whether that's why he doesn't push back against his stepdad's shitty politics or whether it's a struggle because a tiny part of him agrees.

"I think adults are clueless about how much their terrible choices screw us over." I take another bite of my ice-cream bar. Somehow Andrew's managed to scarf down the whole thing already. When I speak again, my voice is a throaty whisper. "When my dad walked out the door of our old house, he didn't just destroy the future for our family, he wrecked the past. He devastated every memory I have with him. Everyone says I have to get on with my life, but how am I supposed to do that when it feels like it will never stop hurting?"

I sigh deeply. Finally talking about my dad feels like a pressure valve has been released, but it's still so painful. Andrew gently rubs my back, and when I turn to gaze up at him, he looks distraught, like he doesn't know what to say. Maybe I've said too much. When did I suddenly become someone who shares feelings? This is why I don't, because once you do, you want to bury yourself alive. I could've said nothing, pushed everything down, because now my dad ruined this moment, too.

"It's fucked up. I wish I had an answer for you," he says, pulling his hand off my back and wiping away a tear that I didn't realize had fallen on my cheek.

I shake my head a little. Blink. Sniffle. "Ugh. I really dumped a lot on you. Sorry. I hate crying over my dad. He doesn't deserve my tears."

"Maybe... maybe your tears are for you, though, and not him?" Andrew's voice is soft but his words squeeze my heart.

I look into his warm, hazel eyes and let myself melt a little into this moment. With a smiling boy at a magical pond in the woods, under a fuzzy sliver of a moon, the stars popping out against the sky.

CHAPTER 24

My gut told me to ditch school today. I should've listened because it is way smarter than my head.

I stop short as I turn down senior hall. There's a group of people at my locker. One of them is Juniper, but the rest are a mix of athletes and cheerleaders and a few kids from English class. This can't be good. Juniper sees me and gives me a tiny, sad wave. The other kids turn to look and then quickly disperse, some of them laughing. A couple of guys high-five. I screw my eyes shut for a second. God, how much worse can things get?

Asinine question.

Things can always get worse. People can hate you more than you ever thought possible.

Scrawled in fat black marker on the front of my locker are the words *Go home, terrorist*. I reel back, sucking in my breath. No matter how many times people hurl slurs at you, you don't get used to it. The wounds feel sharp and fresh every time.

My jaw drops and I look at Juniper, who moves to hug me, but I put my hand up and she stops. She looks at me with her sad eyes and bites her lip, then directs my gaze toward her locker. I drop my backpack to the floor. I'm not the only one these assholes targeted. *Groomer* and *perv* are scribbled across her locker in the same thick black letters.

Faiz walks up to join us, glancing from my locker to Juniper's, fire behind his dark eyes.

"What the hell?" Faiz's voice is loud. Loud enough for everyone in senior hall to hear. "What is wrong with you assholes?"

I shush him and he snaps his mouth shut. My hands shake so I curl them at my side, tucking my burned thumb into my fist. There's a witch's brew of toxic feelings coursing through my body. My breathing is shallow, and I try taking a few deep breaths but they come out as low grunts. My brain can't form words. Not yet.

"Both our lockers were like this when I came in early this morning to make up a quiz." Juniper's eyes grow shiny as she talks.

I grab her hand and squeeze. I'm still not forming coherent sentences in my brain.

"They're the same words the Liberty Moms and Dads use." Her voice breaks a little.

I'm about to explode into a million burning embers of rage.

"This school fucking sucks," Faiz says.

The bell rings. But we don't move. Other students brush past us, and I hear the not-so-subtle whispers as they do.

"Friggin' deserves worse," one boy says, his words eliciting snickers and laughter from the kids around him, but when I spin around to see who it is, I realize it could be anyone. They're all in on it. They all agree. They all blame me and my friends for destroying their most prized upperclassman privilege: off-campus lunch. I almost laugh out loud at how pathetic it is. At how this measly little bit of freedom defines high school—something to attain for freshmen and sophomores, something to revel in for juniors and seniors. Like it's an achievement to be given the chance to go out for lunch in a town that had no real place to go to in the thirty minutes we get to eat. It was a carrot the administration dangled in front of the students that Carter artfully turned into a stick. But I have no intention of standing still, taking the blows, especially not after this.

I take a few photos of my locker and Juniper's. "I'm going to Carter's office to report this," I say, then ask Juniper, "Can I tell him about your locker, too? Do you want to come with?"

She chews on her lip. "Feel free to show him the photos. But I can't deal with seeing his face. It's ... I don't know. I'm gonna take a minute, call my parents and let them handle it. They're going to be livid this happened again."

I nod. This isn't the first time Juniper's dealt with this. Even thinking about Carter is probably triggering. I watch as she and Faiz head to class. Maybe Juniper's right. It might be smarter to pause and figure out a plan. But I don't have parents who will advocate for me. And I don't want to wait. I take off for the front office, a fireball whirling in my chest.

———

Mr. Carter sits at his desk, a pen poised between two fingers, staring into the middle distance. He turns when he hears me knock on the open door of his office.

"Ms. Khan, take a seat," he says with a quick smile, his voice crisp and professional, pointing to the chairs in front of his desk. His posture is military perfect, his collar starched to a sharp point. "To what do I owe this...pleasure?" He pauses pointedly. In case I somehow haven't understood that I'm absolutely the last person he wants to see in his office besides maybe the angel of death.

"I want to report racist and homophobic graffiti on my locker and Juniper's," I say, and then add, "Uh...it's also vandalism of school property."

Carter leans back in his chair, an astonished look on his face. He cracks the knuckles in his right hand, then his left. This dude is really into the dramatic pause. "Those are some pretty serious allegations."

"I'm not alleging it. I have proof." I show him the photos.

He takes my phone and zooms in on the screen. He shakes his head, a look of disgust on his face. "I see why that is so disturbing. This kind of defacing of school property is cause for suspension."

Carter's reaction surprises me. He's taking this seriously. Of course he's more concerned about the vandalism than the hate, but it's something.

He hands my phone back to me. "Do you have any idea who might've done this?"

I shake my head no.

"Or why?" he adds.

"*Why?* Maybe because they're bigots?" I can't believe he's asking *me* why. The why doesn't matter. It's the who that does.

"I understand you being upset, Ms. Khan. But I'm trying to get the facts here."

"The facts? The facts are some jerks defaced our lockers. Those are the facts." My voice is rising and I feel my neck getting red and blotchy. "The fact is it's a hate crime. Don't you get that?"

"Ms. Khan, I'm going to ask you to watch your language and your tone."

I blow out a puff of air.

Carter continues. "The truth of it is that unless someone steps forward to claim responsibility or some other evidence of who did this turns up, I'm afraid there's not much the school can do."

I scoff. "What about questioning students?"

Carter raises an eyebrow and steeples his fingers. "Would you have us question the entire student body? Some might even say that we'd have to begin by questioning you."

"Me?"

"I'm simply playing devil's advocate here, but it might be suggested that you did this to both lockers and—"

"Why would I do that?" I interrupt.

"A tactic to gain attention—maybe even sympathy—for your cause."

"My cause? You mean to read books?" I say through clenched teeth. I curl my fingers into my palms, digging my nails into my skin to try to control my rage because I'm afraid of what I will say otherwise.

"Ms. Khan, I think we both know you're trying to do more than that. Since you're new here, you are clearly unaware of the history and intricacies of the district's book choice policies. Those books that you chose to read out loud were found to be, among other things, obscene due to pornographic content that parents feel are grooming their kids for homosexual lifestyles."

"Pornographic? Lifestyles? Being gay isn't a lifestyle choice, it's a life." All hope of me keeping my cool is lost because his attitude is so unhinged. "Because two girls kiss it's pornography? Are all the books where a girl and boy kiss getting pulled? Is *Romeo and Juliet* banned now, too? Or...or... *The Great Gatsby*? And *The Scarlet Letter*—I mean, the lady got pregnant by a dude she wasn't married to. Total scandal."

Carter's face turns red and the muscles in his neck grow taut. He forces a smile on his face and stands up. "Thank you for reporting the vandalism, Ms. Khan. I'll have the dean look into it."

Slowly, I stand from my chair, my mind thick with anger and confusion at the turn this meeting took. I start walking toward the door.

"Oh, and, Ms. Khan." I stop and turn to Carter. "I'll be making this announcement shortly, but I'll give you the scoop. Beginning today, the school library will be closed during lunch and after school."

"What? You're closing the library? But kids go there to study during lunch and Ms. Clayton says we're always—"

He cuts me off. "Unfortunately, Ms. Clayton is currently on administrative leave."

I suck in my breath, realizing I've somehow wandered into a minefield. "What...what does that mean?" I whisper.

"You'll find out soon enough anyway," he says brusquely, "so I'll go ahead and tell you. The school board found Ms. Clayton's distribution of QR codes for an unsanctioned third-party library violated district policy."

His words explode like a bomb. Administrative leave basically means Ms. Clayton could get fired. For giving kids access to books, which is, supposedly, her entire job description. My stomach churns and I feel dizzy. I rush out of the office and run to the nearest bathroom to splash cold water on my face. I gaze up into the mirror as the water drips off my chin. I stare at myself. I want to punch my reflection. All I ever do is hurt people.

CHAPTER 25

Today is the longest school day in the history of recorded time—a day filled with dirty looks and nasty whispers and me trying and failing to ignore everything. When the last bell rings, my adrenaline crashes. My head feels thunderous, my body weighs a million pounds. I want to be home. I let out a miserable little laugh. Things are so bad at school that our home here, where I refuse to feel comfortable, now feels like the only safe place for me to go.

I sigh as I lean my shoulder against my locker and aimlessly spin around the numbers of the combination of my still-broken lock. I bet Carter told the maintenance crew not to fix it just to be a jerk. By third period a custodian had painted over the graffiti on my and Juniper's lockers—I'm thankful for that, at least. When I open the door, a small avalanche of folded notes falls at my feet. The laughter around me from the other kids muffles in my ears. I feel that sick, woozy feeling again as I bend down to collect the scraps of notebook paper that seemed to have been slipped through the narrow slats at the top of my locker. I can guess what they say without reading them.

"Are those from a secret admirer? Should I be jealous?" Andrew comes up and squats next to me, handing me some of the notes.

I give him a weary look, like how can anyone be so clueless? "Read the room," I say in a tired voice.

He looks stricken, and honestly, I don't care. He picks up a couple of notes and reads them, shock passing over his face as he takes them in and then looks at the pile gathered at my feet. "Holy crap. I'm so sorry. I didn't realize.... Have you been getting these notes all day?"

I snort. "No, some of the braver students are saying this stuff to my face. *You ruined senior year. Why'd you get Ms. Clayton fired? What the hell is your problem, freak?* Those were some of the nicer things people said." I put all the notes into my backpack and stand up. I should toss them, but I'm going to read them since I'm a glutton for punishment.

Andrew stands next to me. "What can I do? Do you want me to talk to someone? Did you tell Carter about it?"

"Carter?" I guffaw. "He probably left a note himself. He barely cared when I showed him a photo of my locker."

"What about Steve, then? He's always going on and on about civility and how it's been lost in our school and stuff."

I stare at Andrew as I grab the rest of my things and shove them into my backpack. I thought he was kind of getting it, but I was wrong. "Your stepdad. Are you serious? He and Carter are literally the problem. Your stepdad's not going to be the solution. How lucky that you never have to think about that because it doesn't affect you." I slam my locker shut and walk away. I hear Andrew calling my name, but I don't look back.

I head straight for freshman hall to find Amal and get the hell out of school. My brain is on fire and wild thoughts run through my mind at lightning speed. Maybe I should ask my mom to let me join an online school for the last weeks before graduation. We could ask if my old school will let me reenroll virtually. Or I can try to find someone who will let me stay with them in Chicago. Of course, there's no way my mom will let me do any of those things.

When I get to freshman hall, Amal is at her locker talking to a couple of friends. When they see me, they say goodbye to her and hurry away. She turns to look at me, jaw clenched, fury in her eyes. It's so out of character, it catches me by surprise.

"What's up?" I ask. "Why do you look like you're about to throttle someone?"

She shakes her head and hands me a few folded slips of paper. My stomach drops. My breath catches in my lungs. They're exactly like the ones I shoved into my backpack moments ago. I open some with trembling fingers:

Tell your sister she fucked around and now she's going to find out.

Go back where you all came from.

No one wants you here.

YOUR SISTER RUINED THE YEAR FOR US. WE'RE going to RUIN it for you.

Throat punch. My heart sinks. I promised myself that my number one priority was making sure Amal was going to be okay, that life here would work for her. She's laughing again, has friends she hangs out with. She actually likes it here. And because I'm the worst, I dragged Amal into my stupid drama. I did this. I want to scream. Punch a wall. Punch a person. No. Make that *people*.

I sigh. "Amal, I'm so sorry. I never meant for you to get wrapped up in this. I'll—"

She draws her eyebrows together, a genuinely puzzled look on her face. "Why are you apologizing? It's not like you put those notes in my locker."

I rub my forehead. "But aren't you pissed?" Amal might be way more even-keeled than me, but it doesn't mean she's never angry. She's just got an extra-long fuse.

She picks up her bag and shrugs it over her shoulders. "Duh. Obviously. But not at you. If people are this angry that you're reading books, then you're probably doing something right."

I let out a surprised laugh as we start walking toward the exit. "I didn't want you to get blowback from this. I'll stop. I'm going to talk to Juniper and Faiz and the others and we'll stop. I'm going to be graduating soon and it's not worth all of this. I mean, Ms. Clayton got put on administrative leave and could get fired," I say. "Now this"—I wave some of the notes around—"it's not worth risking your safety. Or anyone's."

Amal rolls her eyes. "Seriously? You may be graduating, but *I'm* still going to be here. I don't want to be stuck in some school that fires librarians for letting kids read books because of a bunch of MAGA moms and dads."

I stop and stare at my sister. "Since when did you get to be such a badass?"

Amal gazes at me with her big brown eyes, a hint of sadness in them. "I'm tougher than you think, you know? You don't always have to protect me."

"Yeah, I kinda do," I say, my voice a raspy whisper.

Amal takes a deep breath. "I know things super sucked after Dad left, and I know you were scared with...how I was. I was scared, too. But give me some credit. I'm not going to break."

I squeeze my sister's shoulder and nod, my heart in my throat. Maybe she's right. She does feel healthier, stronger. But I'll never stop looking out for her. Not after everything that's happened.

I push open the school doors and walk into the bright spring day with a hint of summer on its warm breeze, the green smell of freshly mowed lawn wafting over from the soccer pitch. I hurry Amal to the car. I don't want any more incidents. Anyone yelling at me or her. Swearing at us. Hateful words and slurs hurt, but I know how quickly mean words can turn into so much worse.

CHAPTER 26

A bright slant of morning light breaks through my curtains and falls over a stack of books on my desk. It's a collection of the various titles that found their way into my locker over the last few weeks, but the appearances of challenged books stopped the same day Carter told me Ms. Clayton was no longer our librarian. I think of all the kids who won't have Ms. Clayton as their ally at school anymore because she wanted us to be able to read freely, maybe also because she was helping me.

I lie in bed for a second, pressing the tip of my index finger into my burn scar. This tiny mark on my body is a place where I store so many memories. It's a reminder of how easy it is to get burned. I rub the sleep from my eyes and force myself from my bed and step to my desk and my toppling pile of books. I run my thumb up and down the spines. I always thought it was kind of funny to call the bound edge of a book a spine. *A spine.* As if a book is sentient and needs strength to stand.

Illinois is a blue state, but I'm living in a bloodred pocket. Obviously not everyone in Bayberry believes the same thing, but after living in the bubble of my liberal South Side neighborhood in a very liberal city, everything in Bayberry feels like a slap in the face. No Midwestern courtesies for newcomers who supposedly step out of line, not according to what those notes said or the graffiti on my locker. They think outsiders are going to mess up this town. Sounds good. *Mess with the bull, you get the horns*, Carter warned me. Challenge accepted.

I place my palms face down on top of the book pile. *Censorship and book bans are the dying gasps of democracy, but we still have to fight them with everything.* That's something my father told me when waves of anti-CRT laws in public schools started gaining momentum in states with far-right-wing governors in the country a few years ago. Critical race theory, my dad explained, was a legal framework to talk about systemic racism, originally taught in law schools. There were absolutely zero CRT textbooks being taught in middle or high schools. "It's a bogeyman," my mom had added. "All the people saying that white kids will feel bad if they read about, say, chattel slavery or the genocide of Native Americans want to erase history because the truth makes them uncomfortable."

I remember my parents' eyes connecting right then, in one of those ways that adults speak around their kids without saying any words, in their secret language. They smiled at each other and there was such warmth and understanding in their gazes. My first reaction to those gooey parental moments was *Ick, gross, please wait until your kids are far, far away before kissing or even gazing at each other in that way.* But now, looking back on that memory, all I can think is *Damn, my dad should've been an actor.*

My parents met in college at a protest against US incursions in the Middle East. Politics was their love language. They were both always so ready to debate, protest, call legislators. But my mom doesn't yell at the news on TV anymore, doesn't leave circled articles for us to read. She closed the door on that entire part of herself, as if keeping it open would hurt too much because it was her and Dad's thing. I wonder if she misses her old self. I know I do.

My phone buzzes and then buzzes again, pulling me out of the fuzzy tangle of memory. It's a stream of texts from Juniper.

I'm so sorry

I didn't know they were going to run this

There's a link to the school newspaper's website: *The Bayberry High Spectator.* I scan the headline, bile rising to my throat. It reads, BLAMING THE MANY FOR THE ACTIONS OF THE FEW: OFF-CAMPUS PRIVILEGES REVOKED, STUDENTS OUTRAGED.

I skim the article but stop myself when I scroll down to a picture of me at the park across the street from school with a book in hand. My stomach drops. There's also a video clip. James and Richard were both filming that day. Others might have been, too. The caption states, *New student Noor Khan reads a challenged book at Schiller Park during off-campus lunch.*

I guess it's a full-on witch hunt now, and I'm the witch. I plop down on the edge of my bed and bury my face in my hands. I don't know what to do. I want to skip school. But I can't let Amal go in there alone. Also, I want to be there in case Juniper gets more hate or Faiz gets any blowback. Even if he does, I wonder if he'd tell me. He'd probably stiff-upper-lip it so I wouldn't worry. I can't believe my idea—my stupid, stupid idea—has caused such a mess. Ms. Clayton tried to do something, and look what happened to her. Did I think I was going to swoop into this small town and fix it, be the brown savior they'd been waiting for? Ha. Brown girls who try to change the world usually get spat on. We get told to *go home*, like we don't belong here. Like we weren't born here. Like we don't have a right to have opinions. And that can really piss a girl off.

I lie back on my bed. My phone buzzes again. This time it's Faiz: *Don't read the comments.* It's yet another truth universally acknowledged that reading the comments on any article with a clickbait title, especially one about you, is, at best, an absolutely nihilistic idea.

I do it anyway. Because I treat the concept of self-care like it's an urban legend.

Total BS —*Bulldog23*
Groomer —*DAWGMA25*
Hasn't even been here a month and totally screwed us over. —*Joshy2023*
Can't believe she wasn't even suspended. —*CheerSquad*
My parents say she should be expelled. They don't want their tax dollars being wasted on her. —*HHfan4life*
She's Moooooo-zlim. Watch out for the cow tipper terrorists. —*TrippdUp*

LOLOLOLOL —*Joshy2023*

They're infiltrating everywhere. They want sharia law!

—*DAWGMA25*

I stop reading at "sharia law" because I may have little to no impulse control, but there's only so much hate my eyeballs can take in before my brain melts. I turn over onto my pillow and scream into it. I feel icy tentacles of fear creep up my spine, and they collide with the white-hot anger that makes my head want to explode. Yes, I decided to go all rebel *with* a cause when we got here, but we would never have even been here if my dad wasn't a selfish jerk who left us and if my mom hadn't dealt with it by running away to this crap town. I could still be at my old school—it might not have been perfect and maybe I didn't have a million friends, but I had the library kids and the kids at the mosque that I'd known since I was little. I fit there. Walking into my old school didn't feel like running through a field of land mines.

My phone rings. *Rings.* My breath catches because I immediately think it's my dad. He and my mom are the only ones who ever call us on our phones. But it's not him. *Duh.* I answer to my friends' jumpy voices.

Me: You guys are conference calling me?

Juniper: Desperate times.

Faiz: Dude, this sucks.

Me: Yeah.

Juniper: I'm quitting the newspaper in protest.

Faiz: Well, technically we freelance so we can't exactly quit.

Juniper: Fine, Mr. Technicality. But we're not going to
write for them anymore. Period.

Me: What? No! Don't do that, you guys. I don't want that.

Juniper: But we do!

Me: This whole thing is so wild. I can't get my head
around it.

Juniper: Welcome to Bayberry.

Faiz: Also, we're biking over to your house.

Me: What? Now?

Juniper: No. I'm not even dressed. We'll be there in thirty.

Faiz: We're driving to school with you.

Juniper: Because safety in numbers.

Faiz: Also, Juniper hung out with Hanna last night and
she won't spill any details and I figured you could help
me force them out of her.

I think about protesting. Telling them there's no need for them
to worry about me. That I'll be fine on my own. But I don't. I smile
to myself. I'm going to accept this kindness. Also, they'd force it on
me if I didn't.

Me: Shut up! You're always burying the lede! We need
the details. Also, warning, my back seat is a mess of,
like, half-empty Flamin' Hot Cheetos bags and M&M
wrappers.

Juniper: I call dibs on the Cheetos.

Faiz: Of course you do.

Juniper: Breakfast of champions.

We laugh before hanging up. I hurry to get ready. My friends are coming over.

Mom is already in the kitchen and so is Amal. My sister meets my eyes as I trudge down the stairs. There's a soft, sad look in them, and I know she's read the op-ed on the school newspaper's website already. I trust that she hasn't said a word about it to our mom because she's quietly sipping her chai with a faraway look in her eyes, her tasbih resting on the counter. Some people might describe her look as dreamy, even, but I know better, because there's a hollowness to it, like the person she is can no longer find the person she was.

"Salaam, Mom," I say.

She looks up at me, trying to force her smile to meet her eyes. "Salaam, beta. Did you sleep okay?"

"Great. As always," I say, but immediately regret the hint of sarcasm in my voice. "Oh, uh, Juniper and Faiz are coming over in a bit."

My mother knits her eyebrows together in a question, and Amal looks up from eating her cereal, the spoon halfway between the bowl and her open mouth.

"I'm giving them a ride to school. They're new friends."

"Glad to hear that, beta," my mom says, her face brightening. "Hope you cleaned your car." Ah, the tough love of Indian moms.

Amal's laughter turns into coughs and choking sounds. My mom turns to her and gently whacks her on the back.

"Remember when you were little and we told you to look for the mouse on the ceiling after you'd swallowed something a bit too fast like that?" My mom strokes Amal's hair as my sister clears her throat and nods. I catch it then, my mom smiles a real smile, and for a second it feels as if the sun is shining. "You were so worried about that imaginary mouse you made me and your father leave out a little cheese for it at night."

"Surprised we didn't get actual mice because of that," I snort.

My mom turns to me, incredulous. "We took it away after she went to bed, and then one of us would wake up early and put it out again in the morning because Amal would always check." There's a flash of sadness in my mom's eyes.

"I remember that." Amal grins. "You told me the mouse went to live with the other mice in the countryside because I kept asking about him." Amal hugs my mom and my mother leans into it. Amal's closeness to my mom never bothered me, but now it pinches. I haven't hugged my mom in I don't know how many months.

The doorbell rings and I answer it, ushering in Juniper and Faiz, who both take their shoes off without being asked. I make introductions as we step toward the small kitchen.

"As-salaam-alaikum, auntie," Faiz says.

"Walaikum-salaam, beta," my mom responds with a grin. She gives me a little look. I know it's because Faiz's accent is so much better than mine, and for his perfect tameez. *Decorum.*

"Hi," Juniper pips. "Nice to meet you."

"Pleasure to meet both of you. Can I get you some tea or something to eat?"

Juniper and Faiz both politely decline. Faiz adds, "Though I will happily come back for your chai anytime. Noor raves about it."

"Absolutely, beta. I'll have to invite your parents as well. I'd love to meet them. Please give Noor your mom's number."

"Will do, auntie," Faiz says as I mouth "kiss ass" at him behind my mom's back while we gather our things to head out.

The four of us walk into school and every single pair of eyes swivels to us. No exaggeration. When Amal heads to her locker, my first impulse is to follow her, to be her shadow, to protect her. But (1) there's no way she would go for that, and (2) my presence would make it worse. When a few ninth graders catch up with her, one of them looping an arm through hers, I let out the breath I'd been holding. It's a relief to see that Amal has friends by her side.

As I'm watching Amal walk away, out of the corner of my eye I spy Juniper waving to someone as a shy smile crosses her face. I turn and see Hanna down the hall, heading toward us.

Faiz nudges Juniper.

"You said nothing happened between you and Hanna last night," I say, and narrow my eyes at Juniper.

"It didn't! We studied the whole time," she protests with a sly smirk.

"Liar." Faiz laughs.

I bite back my smile because Hanna is drawing closer, her eyes bright and totally focused on Juniper.

I whisper into Juniper's ear, "We need details!"

"A girl never kisses and tells," she whispers back, a pink blush blooming across her cheeks.

Hanna sidles up next to Juniper, a giant toothy grin on her face. Faiz and I share a knowing sidelong glance.

"Hey," Hanna says.

"Hey," Juniper responds.

They keep smiling at each other until Juniper walks into a water fountain. Hanna wraps her arm around Juniper's waist and pulls her away.

"Whoa! Are you okay?" I ask.

"Weird, who put that fountain there?" Juniper jokes, a flush of embarrassment appearing on her cheeks.

"Total hazard." Hanna beams at Juniper.

As we walk on, Hanna turns to me with a sympathetic smile. "Sorry about the crappy *Spectator* op-ed. Little collaborationists."

"Don't read the comments," I grumble.

Juniper, Faiz, and Hanna shoot each other looks.

"What?" I ask. "What did you do?"

"Fought fire with fire." Faiz nudges me a little. Surprising myself and possibly inspired by the cuteness overload of Hanna and Juniper, I lean into Faiz, ever so slightly, a tingle zipping up my arm. But when a whiff of his sandalwood soap floats into the space between us, my breathing hitches.

Juniper shoves her phone in front of my face. The op-ed is pulled up to the comments section. Seventy-two comments. No, a seventy-third just popped up. I scowl. "Read them," Juniper urges.

I scroll past the nasty ones I saw this morning. They're followed by more expressing the same *I-hate-Noor-she's-the-devil-incarnate* feelings. But then...I look up at my friends. There are a slew of counter-messages. Ones calling out the haters for exactly what they are.

You're a bunch of homophobic racists. **—Dawgesome**

The school is banning books. WTF **—HiveMind10**

Ms. Clayton getting fired is BS. **—Swiftie89**

You're fascists. What's wrong with you? **—AughtsBaby**

Censorship is unAmerican. **—OMZee**

There are arguments running throughout the thread basically descending into vitriolic name-calling like all comment sections on the internet. The school newspaper website is public, and, shockingly, it allows anonymous comments. But I guess there have never been issues in the past since the big stories were about new basketball uniforms and the homecoming corn boil.

"You guys did this?" There's a lump in my throat I have to clear away so I don't get all weird and emotional.

They all nod. "Not just us," Juniper says.

"Yeah," Hanna adds. "We texted a bunch of the kids who were at the last park reading."

"We can't let them control the message," Faiz says, our hands casually brushing against each other as we turn down senior hall.

Andrew is waiting for me at my locker, an inscrutable expression on his face that quickly turns frosty when he sees me with Faiz. Juniper and Hanna exchange looks. Andrew and Faiz stare at each other and suddenly the warm vibe around us chills. I thought Andrew promised to do better and figure things out with Faiz. I don't have the bandwidth to call him out. But I also wonder if it's about something more than their past.

After a few awkward seconds of hellos and weird looks, my friends drift off to their lockers and I promise to continue our conversation later, then turn to Andrew. He looks like crap. There are puffy bags under his eyes, the color of newly formed bruises. He takes off the Cubs hat he's wearing and runs his hand through his hair, which is more messy than its normally artfully tousled state.

"I'm an idiot," he says.

He pauses, waiting for me to say something, but I let the silence linger. Another lawyer trick my dad taught me. If you can puncture a space with quiet, the person you're talking to will usually want to fill the hole.

Andrew continues. "I've been super insensitive, and I'm sorry. I'm sorry for all the hate you're getting, and I just read that shitty op-ed on the *Spectator* site and the comments. I didn't realize how many assholes went to this school."

I sigh and start to open my locker. "You never realized it because you're immune to it."

"What does that mean?"

"Most of your friends are cis, het, and white, so you don't *have* to notice it. You're the ones dishing it out, not taking it."

Andrew scratches his chin and the uneven bits of stubble he didn't shave away. "But I don't think my friends—"

I turn to look at him, my mouth agape. "No. No. Stop. Don't even. I thought you were trying to apologize, not deny that some of your friends are racist. Literally, open your eyes." I shake my head. "Look, I don't have time for this. I'm exhausted. My sister and I are both getting hate mail shoved into our lockers. Juniper's gotten homophobic notes. Ms. Clayton is suspended and might get fired. Carter has it out for me, and the school newspaper seems to be doing his bidding. Figure it out on your own."

Andrew steps closer to me, reaches out to touch my forearm, his voice a whisper. "You're right. I've totally screwed up. I'm sorry. I want to make it up to you. I want to do better. I will."

Why are my emotions so mixed up around Andrew? I'm annoyed that I get these warm, gooey feelings about him, and part of me wants to fight them. But they're also so cozy to lean into, and it helps me forget that I'm in the middle of a shitstorm. Sometimes I want to be a normal senior and not one whose life is ever-increasing chaos. But there's also a part of me that wants to lean into the rage and expose all my sharp edges. How am I supposed to function in any normal way when my feelings and thoughts want to fight each other? I lose no matter what.

Andrew smiles at me, and it's kind and warms the space between us. He inches closer. "I'm here for you if you need anything. That includes endless ice-cream bars and bags of Flamin' Hot Cheetos."

I surprise myself with a laugh. "How did you know about the Cheetos?"

"I've stood by your car. That salty, spicy, somewhat chemical smell when you open the door is unmistakable. Also, the empty bags in the back seat. Plus"—he takes my hand and holds it up, sending pulses of electricity down my arm—"the bright-orange-tipped fingers give it away every time. I'm the Sherlock Holmes of junk food detection."

"Your mother must be so proud." I smirk and let my eyes flit up to his.

Our gazes connect for a lingering moment before the bell rings and he slowly lets go of my hand.

CHAPTER 27

"They closed down the comments section!" I practically growl to Juniper and Faiz as I take a seat at our lunch table, which somehow feels more isolated than ever even though it hasn't moved an inch; could be the icy stares in our direction sliding us away. "The opinion piece is still up, though."

Juniper shakes her head. "No surprise. When Faiz and I stopped in the newspaper classroom and brought up the bazillion issues with the op-ed singling you out and naming you, Ms. Rove totally shut us down. Said it was an opinion piece so it didn't have to adhere to the same journalistic standards as a reported story, which—"

"Is a BS excuse." Faiz finishes her sentence. "The *Spectator* has gone full Faux News propaganda for the admin. Facts optional."

"They're not going to stop, are they?" I bite into my sandwich absentmindedly. After trying Faiz's stupidly good egg salad surprise, my sandwich tastes blander than ever. Somehow Faiz converted me to the "elevated perfection" of Kewpie mayonnaise. I bite into my sad turkey, cheese, lettuce on whole wheat. I chew as my mind wanders back to a time I watched my dad question a witness on the stand about a real estate company denying a refugee family an apartment even though they could pay for it. I smile thinking of how he basically maneuvered the dude into admitting his prejudice. The family got an even better apartment because the community started a GoFundMe and they got damages from the company, too. Justice served.

Juniper juts her neck out and stares at me as if she's taking stock of the situation. "You have an evil glint in your eye and I am here for it."

I laugh. "It's not evil, maybe just a moderately sneaky idea. The board and admin claim they're trying to protect us, but it's a lie. People hide behind lies when they know what they're doing is wrong. So we need to figure out how to back them into a corner and force them to say the quiet parts out loud. People always tell on themselves if you give them the space to do it."

Faiz nods. "So do you have a plan?"

"Uh, no, not exactly. Honestly, I went to bed last night thinking we needed to stop pushing back against the book bans, but that's what they want. I don't want to give them that win," I say, taking another bite of my boring lunch.

Faiz smiles and unscrews the lid of his thermos. The spicy, oniony, garlicky smell of keema and daal waft over me, making me forget about everything I'd been talking about. My stomach grumbles. I love my mom's lentils over basmati rice, but it's been so long since she cooked—something she used to love doing. Then he hands a thermos to Juniper. I've been deeply envious of all the lunches he makes them, but when he's offered to make me a lunch, I always say no. It feels a lot to ask even if he's offering.

"You look like you want to make out," he says, then quickly adds, "with my lunch. I mean, you're gazing at me with hungry eyes. Uh...my thermos. You're gazing at my thermos!"

"Is *thermos* supposed to be a euphemism in this conversation?" Juniper bursts out laughing. Faiz and I glance at each other and then quickly look away, embarrassed.

"It's that...I love desi food and it's been a minute since my mom cooked."

"Have you ever tried?" Faiz asks.

"Cooking?" I laugh. "Uh...no. Probably an eighty-two percent chance I'd set the house on fire."

"So there's an eighteen percent chance you won't!" Juniper chirps. "Faiz can teach you! That way you don't always have to look so sad when you watch us eat."

"Yeah...totally," Faiz says, excitement in his voice. "Keema and daal are super easy. I've been making them since fifth grade—it's what made me realize I love cooking."

"You should do it tomorrow, after school," Juniper suggests with an impish smile.

I open my mouth. My first impulse is to say no. I've been trying to push down the occasional fluttery feeling I get when Faiz and I accidentally brush hands or bump into each other because we're just friends and maybe because of Andrew. Because I didn't want to give Faiz the wrong idea. But lately a tiny voice in my head has been whispering that maybe it's the right idea. That's left me so confused because it feels wrong to have feelings for two guys, like

I'm hiding things from both of them. But Faiz's lunch smells so delicious it overwhelms my senses and squashes my doubts. It's a meal. Not a date. Besides, my mom and Amal will be so surprised if I cook dinner. Maybe it's a little thing I can do to make up for being ornery 24/7. I bite my lip. "Okay, but I don't think we have the ingredients."

"I'll bring over everything. No problem."

"It's a date!" Juniper claps gleefully. I furrow my brow at her. She gives me an innocent shrug. "What? I have a vested interest in my friends learning how to cook because I love to eat."

Faiz rubs his face with his palms, then stares intently at his lunch.

"So...," I begin, hoping my face doesn't look as heated as my body feels. I desperately want to shift conversation away from my cooking lesson, which is absolutely not at all a date. A date with a cute desi Muslim boy feels so much more fraught than hanging out at DQ with Andrew. Plus, Faiz isn't *any* desi Muslim boy. He's my friend who is sweet and kind. And who smells like the sandalwood soap that reminds me of my dad so much I have to stop myself from wincing when I'm around him.

It's not logical at all, but I have an innate fear of the desi auntie network, even if we're far from Chicago. There are barely any desis around here, but all it would take is one auntie spying me hanging with Faiz and within three calls everyone in Chicago would know. Then my mom would kill me because she hates being gossip fodder. It was really bad after Dad left. Maybe even a bigger part of the reason she moved us here than I thought.

"Um...what are you two going to do with your free period now that you're not freelancing on the newspaper anymore?" I finally ask.

Juniper chomps on her last fry. "We're going to kick up posting on our Bulldog Banned Camp socials and maybe use our badass investigative skills to track down the jerks leaving those threatening notes."

I get a queasy feeling in my stomach. Sometimes I talk, even act, before thinking. Everyone is taking risks. Too many risks. I know they'll say they can handle the name-calling and the nastiness, but what if it goes beyond that? What if those subtle threats become real? At one of the first protests my mom took me to about refugee policy, I remember seeing counterprotesters, and they seemed so hateful, acting as if refugees were stealing from them. When you challenge the status quo, the people in power who are so used to getting their way tend to push back hard, my mom had warned. I miss that version of my mom—the one that wouldn't yell at me for standing up and taking a risk but would join me. The one who would understand that it was the only right choice.

CHAPTER 28

"What's that from?" Amal asks, reaching toward me over the kitchen counter.

"A bookmark from that tiny bookstore in town," I say, handing it to her. It's bright blue and says *I'm good at judging characters* on it. Hard to miss. "It was shoved in my locker with more hate notes."

Amal frowns. "Sorry, sis."

"You didn't get any today, did you?" I ask. She shakes her head. "You'd tell me if you did, right?" I asked Juniper and Faiz the same question. Juniper's gotten some more nasty notes. And she told me Faiz had a few shoved into his locker as well but tossed them without reading them. I probably should've done the same.

"Yessss, Mom," Amal says, her voice dripping with sarcasm. I'm happy to hear that tone—it feels ... normal. "But seriously, if there's something you should know, I'll tell you."

"You better, or else."

Amal rolls her eyes then and asks, "So why did you clean the counters and shove the pile of mail into a drawer?"

I run my fingers across the now lemony-scented kitchen island. "No reason, really. It's that—"

Amal smiles wide and wiggles her shoulders a little. "Are you expecting company? Company named Andrew?"

"Uh...no." Why do I feel all awkward telling her? "Actually, Faiz is coming over to, um, show me how to cook keema and daal."

"Faiz? Ooh, the plot thickens."

I roll my eyes. "There's no plot, okay? I'm not plotting...with him. I figured we should eat something besides pizza, burgers, and mediocre tacos."

My sister closes her eyes like she's gathering her strength. "Blasphemy! Indians and Taco Bell are like death-till-we-part food besties. I'm burning your desi card."

I raise up my hands. "Forgive me, Mexican Pizza. I never meant to wrong you."

Amal looks satisfied. "So, Faiz. You. Cooking. Or is it *cooking*?" She gives me a big, campy wink.

"Sometimes I forget that your sense of humor is like a cross between toddler and fifty-year-old uncle." I make a face at my sister just as the doorbell rings.

She races me to the door and nudges me out of the way so she can open it. "Hi, Faiz," Amal says, oh so sweetly.

"Hey," he responds, and gives us both a shy grin as he steps inside. I take the grocery bag he's carrying and he slips off his shoes and leaves them by the door. We walk the few steps over to the kitchen. This house is much smaller than our old one, but we do have a large kitchen island, which is great since it's where we spend most of our time when we aren't in our bedrooms.

I put the bag on the counter and Amal immediately starts pulling things out of it: dry red lentils, ginger, garlic, a big fat yellow onion, ground beef, tomatoes, frozen peas, cayenne pepper, garam masala, cumin, turmeric. There's also a large plastic container of plain yogurt. "Let me guess," I say, pointing to it. "There's no actual yogurt in that container."

"Are you even desi if you don't use old yogurt tubs as Tupperware?" Faiz laughs. My sister and I join in. I'd almost forgotten what it was like to share little inside cultural jokes with friends. "Do you also have a cookie tin dedicated to spools of thread?" He looks at me, his dark brown eyes shining.

"Ha! We totally do. It used to belong to my dadi," I say, my smile faltering a little bit. My mom got rid of so many things before we came here, including all my dad's stuff. But she held on to this beat-up blue tin that belonged to Dad's mom. I'd never given it much thought, but now I realize she must've saved it as a memento. Mom and Dad had a whole life together before us, and that's when my dad's family became my mom's family, too. And when Nani died, well...my mom must've felt like Dadi was the last link she had to anything like a parent. The realization crushes me a little.

Amal uncaps the yogurt container. "Rice." She inhales deeply. "Wait. *Basmati* rice."

"Figured I'd precook and save us a step. I wasn't sure if you have a rice cooker," Faiz explains.

"Of course we do," I say, somewhat indignantly.

My sister adds, "But we have no idea where it is, so what Noor means to say is thank you."

I narrow my eyes at her. "Don't you have homework?" I ask.

"Why, do you want to be alone?" Amal responds, a look of angelic innocence on her face, but she knows exactly what she's doing.

"No! I don't want you to get burned is all," I say, using my big-sister tone of voice.

Amal snickers. "Yeah, right. If anyone is going to set the house on fire, it's you." Turning to Faiz, she says, "The fire extinguisher is below the sink." Then she hurries up the stairs. Without looking back at us, she adds, "I'll be doing homework in my room with the music turned up loud so I won't be able to hear anything." I don't need to see her face to know she's probably giggling to herself.

I shake my head. "Never mind her. It's an annoying little-sister thing."

A grin splits Faiz's face. "She doesn't seem annoying at all. I think your banter with her is cute."

My cheeks warm. "So, what do we do first?" I closely examine the various spice jars he brought. I think we have all of them in one of our cupboards, but they haven't been used in a while.

"Wash hands," Faiz says, and walks around the kitchen island to the sink. I'm standing right next to it, so I scoot over a little. He seems at home. Almost more comfortable here than I am. He washes his hands with surgeon-like precision—makes sense since proper handwashing technique is something we've all had ingrained in our brains. I pass him a dish towel to dry his hands before I wash mine.

"Cutting board," Faiz says, and I point to a low cupboard. He grabs it and stands back up and looks to the knife container on the island. He grabs the largest knife and places it on the wooden cutting board. "Now, do you know how to cut up an onion?"

I scoff. "Duh. Of course." I bite my lower lip as my shoulders rise to my ears. "Well...I mean, you peel it and chop it, right? Do the pieces need to be a certain size or something?" I toss the onion up and down in my hand.

He chuckles. "Well, chef, just dice it. Here." As he draws the onion from my hand, our fingers graze and a tiny spark jumps between us. I suck in my breath and try to focus, ignoring the heat spreading through my body. He proceeds to expertly peel and slice the onion. Then he gently places his hand over mine, demonstrating how to curl my fingers under so they don't get in the way of the blade. He continues cutting, tip of the knife blade pointed down into the cutting board until the space is filled with a small pile of tiny, glistening bits of onion. I'm trying to pay attention, but my mind keeps lingering on that spark.

"It's easy." He shrugs and puts the knife down. "Now you do the other half." He turns to me. I pick up the knife and start cutting. My eyes sting and I blink back a few tears. I know it's because of the onion, but it feels like more.

Faiz pulls his phone out of his pocket and plays some music. The sultry, dreamy vocals of Arooj Aftab fill the space. I continue to dice the rest of the onion, a few stray tears slipping down my cheeks. Faiz measures, washes, and soaks the lentils. The rest of the evening moves pleasantly, in a kind of easy rhythm, and soon onions are sizzling in oil, the smell of garlic and ginger wafting around us, and there's an ache in my chest for a feeling I didn't realize I'd even missed. The smell of these simple Indian dishes, my parents, together in the kitchen, as Faiz and I are now, laughing, talking, Urdu music playing. The savory, mouthwatering smells swirl around me, making me miss the home I once knew so badly it almost physically aches.

"You okay?" Faiz asks, a quizzical expression on his face.

I snap myself out of the cascade of memories I've been lost in all evening and brush away my tears with the back of my hand. I clear my throat. "Memories, I guess."

Faiz scrunches his eyebrows. He and Juniper know my dad doesn't live with us—I told them that much, but not much else. I didn't want to go into all the details at the time, and then I never bothered to fill them in. It's still so hard to say the words out loud.

I sigh. "You know how my parents aren't, um, together?"

He nods.

"Well, they used to love cooking together. Now my mom doesn't cook at all. . . ." I look down at my hands. I'm afraid if I look at Faiz, I'll completely fall apart.

Faiz takes a step closer to me but seems to understand that I still need a little space. "Because it reminds her of him? Because she didn't want to be separated?" he asks softly.

I look up into Faiz's warm brown eyes, so full of concern, and nod. "He didn't give her a choice. One day last December, my mom, sister, and I came home to a note from my dad saying he couldn't do it anymore. He didn't want a family anymore. He didn't want us."

"Holy shit. Noor, I'm so sorry. That's—"

"Horrible? The worst? Yeah. That's my dad. And the killer thing is none of us saw it coming. He hid it all. He was actually an awesome dad. He seemed happy, but he wasn't. We weren't enough for him. Now he's living his best life in London. . . ." My voice fades.

Faiz's jaw is practically on the floor. Panic floods me. I blurted all this info, and what if…he can't handle it? What if it was too much? There's so much shame around this kind of thing in the desi community, and it's always on the woman. Patriarchy stays winning. It's so unfair. It's—

Faiz interrupts the runaway train of my thoughts by stepping closer to me and gently placing his hand on mine. My skin warms under his touch. And there's this brief, exquisite stillness where I can't even tell if I'm breathing.

"Do you ever see him? Talk to him?" he asks.

I shake my head, wiping away a few more tears. "Not really. A few texts. I honestly don't want to talk to him. And he seems fine with it. Apparently, that's a trait of men who abandon their wives."

"Abandon their *families*," Faiz says. My eyes meet his. "You deserve so much better, Noor. And you're totally enough exactly as you are. Sorry he didn't get that."

I give him a small, broken smile and clear my throat. My insides feel all wobbly, and I'm afraid I'll melt into a puddle on the floor if I let myself linger here too long. So I pivot. I shake my head like a reset. "So, dumb question, but where'd you learn to do all this." I move my hand from his and wave it around the kitchen.

This cute shy smile creeps up on his face, and I'm grateful he seems okay with the whiplash change of subject. "Well, I was obsessed with cooking shows. My parents and I would watch them together and then try out recipes. When I started watching YouTube tutorials on how to sous vide, my parents signed me up for summer camp at a cooking school nearby. Then, last summer, I spent a month in Chicago interning at Bombay Talkie—"

"No way! That's, like, one of the best Indian restaurants in the city. The chef is famous."

Faiz chuckles. "Yeah, she's a cousin of my mom's friend from college. She wrote me a rec for cooking school."

"Pretty badass, dude," I say as I move closer to Faiz, the atmosphere around us rippling with possibility. I'm also embarrassed to realize I've barely ever asked him about himself because I've been so caught up in my own life.

"Thanks." He looks down shyly but leans a shoulder into me.

Amal comes bounding down the stairs. Faiz and I jump away from each other. The possibility of Faiz feels so much more complicated than liking Andrew. There's a weight of expectation when a desi Muslim boy enters your orbit. So many unsaid things, a sense of potential in the extremely distant, post–grad school future. Sometimes that can feel like a lot for something so new. Like a lead weight trying to balance on a feather.

My sister eyes us. I can tell she wants to say something to embarrass me, but she stops herself and I appreciate it. "Please tell me it's time to eat, because I am starving!"

The three of us sit on stools at the kitchen counter happily shoveling food into our mouths. We talk and laugh about aunties at parties who always tell us that we need to eat more or that we look a little too tired, or uncles who ask if we're going to be premed once SAT season hits, then suggest law or engineering as other equally acceptable pursuits. For the record: no, no, and no. Faiz asks Amal about the book she brought downstairs with her: *All My Rage*, by Sabaa Tahir. Another one of the books on the challenged list.

Amal excitedly gives him a synopsis and talks with her hands about how sad but also hopeful the story is. How it deals with actual problems in our community that adults always want to pretend don't exist. "I'm not done with it yet, but I know it's going to completely wreck me," Amal says. "You can borrow it when I'm done."

"Sold." Faiz picks up the book to read the jacket. "Have you read her fantasy series?"

"Twice. She's so good at destroying her readers and I loooove it," Amal says. "I can give you other recs, too, if you want."

"Amal is the best book reviewer and reads, like, fifty books a year," I say proudly.

"Probably going to hit seventy-five this year."

"Impressive," Faiz says. "So books are, like, a family obsession?"

Amal and I exchange a glance. "Yeah, they kinda are. We used to read novels out loud together in the evenings, before..." Amal trails off and rounds her shoulders a little. I feel like someone's reached into my chest and is pressing my lungs till I can't breathe.

"Anyone for seconds?" I quickly ask, trying to fill the silence of our lost thoughts.

Faiz glances at me, understanding in his eyes. "My eating habits are pretty much Hobbit-like, but I've already had thirds, so I'm good." He stands up and takes his plate over to the sink. "Shall I load the dishwasher?"

"I got it!" Amal chirps, too cheerfully.

"Who are you, and what have you done with my cleanup-averse little sister?" I joke, and give her a little side hug.

"Ha ha. Do we need to compare closets? You know I can out-Kondo you anytime, anywhere. Seriously, I got this."

Faiz rinses off his dishes and puts them into the dishwasher anyway, and starts gathering the spices he brought over. He is truly a desi mom's dream. Amal and I clear the kitchen island, but she shoos me away so she can finish the cleanup.

"Actually, if you have a few minutes, I'd like to take you someplace," he says rather cryptically.

I'd promised to drive him home, so I nod. "Sure. As long as it's not to your secret murder cabin." I cringe when the words come out of my mouth because it's a repeat of something I said to Andrew, not that Faiz would know this, but it still gives me a vaguely queasy feeling, like I'm cheating on someone. But who? To cheat is to deceive, and I wonder if maybe the person I'm actually lying to is me.

"Who told?" Faiz smirks, finishes gathering his things, and goes to put his shoes on.

I sidle up next to Amal. "You good? Okay with me heading out for a bit?"

She makes a face. "Oh my God. I've told you a million times to stop babying me. Besides, Mom should be back any minute. I'm going to make a plate for her and take full credit for cooking *and* cleaning."

"Of course you are." I laugh and turn to Faiz. "Murder lair, here we come!"

CHAPTER 29

Faiz and I step out into the crisp night air. The sky is clear, and there are so many stars. There's a freshly mown grass smell and I inhale deeply. We silently settle into my car, pulling on our seat belts. I look at Faiz, my right hand upturned in a typical desi question gesture.

"Drive toward downtown, and then turn left on Jefferson Street right after the Abbey Farms sign."

I laugh.

"What?"

"This town . . . I love how all the directions are like, turn right at the large maple, then look for Mrs. O'Leary's barn, and you'll be at your cow-tipping destination."

Faiz reaches down to turn on the car radio. "Isn't she the one responsible for the Great Chicago Fire?"

"That's a myth."

"So is cow tipping. We would never do that in our town." He

pauses a beat, then presses the eject button on the radio and holds up the cassette that pops out. "We tip cows two towns over. Also, is this car a time machine?" He twirls the cassette around and raises his eyebrows.

"Yes. But that is *Purple Rain*, by Prince, and it may be a million years old, but every song on it is an absolute banger." I take the cassette from his hand, our fingertips brushing. Keeping my eyes on the road, I slip it back into the stereo and hit play. The notes of "Let's Go Crazy" ricochet against the car's interior as I turn up the volume. This was one of a handful of cassettes that my dad kept in this car that were actually worth listening to. In the days and weeks right after he left, I aimlessly drove up and down Lake Shore Drive, blasting this album, thinking about Dad, wondering when he'd come home. In the beginning, I was so sure he would be back. He couldn't leave us forever, could he? The thing is, when you ask a question, you have to prepare yourself for the answer.

Jefferson Street appears before "Take Me with U" ends. I make the turn and slow down. It's a dimly lit street with a few darkened office buildings and a florist shop that is also closed.

"You can park anywhere," Faiz says as I pull over to the side of the street.

We get out of the car. I look around. The main strip of downtown is a couple of blocks away, and there is actually some activity. By that I mean some people going to the pizza place and popping into the coffee shop. There's also a bar that seems popular. But the block we're on is dead.

"So you *are* taking me to your murder cabin."

"Technically it's a lodge." Faiz points to a small single-story building at the end of the block. Honestly, it looks as if it's made of Lincoln Logs.

"Why does everyone keep taking me to serial killer lairs?" I mumble, thinking back again to Andrew and the pond in the woods.

"Hey! We cultivate that vibe. You should see this place at Halloween." Faiz laughs.

I fake chuckle. "Haunted small-town charm. Gotta love it."

We stop at a green door with a small lamp above that illuminates a worn wooden sign: VETERANS OF FOREIGN WARS LODGE 2712. I raise my eyebrows at Faiz. "C'mon," he says, stepping up to the door.

"Hang on...should we be..."

He turns the knob, pushes the door open, and steps inside, swallowed up by a musty darkness. People always bad-mouth Chicago— especially the South Side, as if we are walking around in a war zone, each of us with a gun and a death wish. But I swear to God, I don't know a single person from my old neighborhood who would willingly walk into dark woods or a creepy unlit lodge.

I hover at the threshold. Faiz has walked in, and all I can hear are the quiet shuffles of his shoes and some kind of faint scratching, which I'm afraid might be mice. I shudder. Rodents are the absolute worst.

"You can come in," Faiz's voice calls from the dark. "Unless you're a vampire and I need to invite you to enter."

"You bring me to a creepy old cabin and you think I'm the one giving off killer vibes?"

Faiz laughs. I hear him flip a switch; the space fills with a faint buzzing, and then a row of old track lights flickers on. I let out my breath and look around the room. It's one large space with a stage at the end. Scattered around the perimeter are old metal folding chairs, some tables. Next to the stage are three flagpoles. An American flag hangs limply on one. The other two are bare. I step all the way inside. With the lights on, this place is not so much creepy as dusty and slightly run-down.

"Ta-da," he says, waving his arms around the place.

I look around at the cobwebs and mice droppings. "I'm clearly missing something."

Faiz smiles proudly. "You said you wanted to double down, right? The board wants to ban us from reading books. Carter wants to prevent us from gathering at the park during lunch. But they can't stop us from doing anything outside of school time and off school grounds."

I walk into the center of the large room and bite my lip, the realization of what Faiz is suggesting dawning on me. "So we find a place off campus to meet and read whatever the hell we want. You're brilliant!" I say, and then give him a hug that catches both of us by surprise.

Faiz clears his throat and turns away when I step out of the hug. I look away, too. It's as if we're both expecting an auntie to walk in and catch us alone.

He begins walking around. "This place hasn't been used regularly in years, but it's still owned by the VFW chapter in the area and my dad knows the president."

"Is your dad a veteran?"

"Yeah. A medic in the Gulf. He went to med school on a military scholarship; he served four years after he graduated."

His answer surprises me. I'm not sure why. There are totally Muslims who serve in the US military. I mean, my mom's cousin, Saleem, is a military lawyer, in the JAG Corps. "Oh. Wow. The Gulf, huh?"

Faiz scrapes through a layer of dust on the floor with the toe of his sneaker. "It's complicated for him. Being a Muslim in the US military that's fighting a war against other Muslims. He definitely had a lot of feelings about it, but he also did his duty. He doesn't talk about it much, though. Not with me, anyway."

A moment of silence passes. "You know," I offer, "I get it—parents hiding things from you. It's weird to think about how they had entire lives before you that they don't share with you." I watch as dust motes, unsettled by our movement, waft gently back to the ground. When my dad left, it wasn't just his life before me that I didn't know much about. I could almost accept that. It's that him abandoning us cast a shadow on *my* life, too. It made me wonder if I ever really knew my dad at all.

Faiz brushes away some dust from my shoulder with his fingertips and smiles softly. In that moment, I know he understands exactly what I'm thinking. And thankfully, he chooses now to shift the conversation before I fall down the dark pit of despair.

"Anyway, that's how I got permission for us to use this space. The president of the chapter was supportive. The way he sees it, he swore to uphold the Constitution. America is supposed to be about defeating fascism, he told me, not embodying it."

"No doubt," I say as I walk around the perimeter. The space could easily hold fifty, sixty people. Maybe more. It needs a good cleaning, but nothing some mops and gallons of soap can't handle.

And maybe some candles to demustify the place. My brain whirs, happy to have a distraction from the earlier onslaught of overflowing feelings and too many unanswerable questions. "We can let people know by word of mouth and on our socials. We can figure out a way to share the books. Maybe I can find someone to buy copies for us?" I'm literally spilling every thought that enters my head right now. "This is going to work!"

I walk back toward Faiz. "Thank you," I whisper as we edge closer to each other. His eyes are warm and bright. A gentle smile curves his lips as he reaches out a hand and cups my elbow, drawing me a tiny bit closer. The space between us heats up, and I'm suddenly deeply aware of my heart pulsing in every part of my body.

I've never kissed a boy.

I've never kissed anyone.

Faiz and I move ever so slightly nearer, in microsteps, as if we're feeling our way across a frozen pond. Faiz has listened to me, helped me, trusted me, offered me friendship when I was so convinced I was not looking to make new friends. Oh God, what if I totally mess this up? For the first time I truly understand how much Faiz's and Juniper's friendship means to me, how all the crap I've been dealing with since I got to the school would've been so much worse if they hadn't stood by me. I close my eyes and the earthy, warm smell of sandalwood surrounds me. I suck in my breath, suddenly shivering.

A hesitation creeps into my body.

A seed of doubt worms its way into my mind.

I want this.

I don't know what to do.

I shouldn't want this.

I—

Dammit. I suck in my breath and blurt, "So...uh...what mosque do you go to?" Oh my God. I'm asking him about a mosque when we might've, maybe been about to kiss? *Heathening much, Noor?*

"Huh?" Faiz straightens his shoulders. Wait, he'd been leaning, tilting, down toward me. I wasn't imagining that space between us narrowing to an almost kiss. "Oh, um, yeah, we go to one a couple towns over."

I take a dizzying step back, the claws of guilt bursting the magic bubble we'd been standing in.

CHAPTER 30

A friendly bell jingles as I enter Idle Hour, the quaint little bookshop downtown, not far from Common Grounds. Afternoon sun pours into the bookstore through the two huge picture windows that take up the storefront. There are three tables as you enter, bookshelves that line the walls, along with some freestanding bookcases in the back of the rectangular shop that designate the children's book area. There's an overstuffed worn dark red couch in the center of the store with a small oval coffee table in front of it and two blue velvet high-back wing chairs rounding out the conversation nook. It looks like the front parlor of an old Victorian home that's been renovated by millennial hipsters. I take a deep whiff of new-book smell and immediately feel at home.

I stop in my tracks when I see a mom and her kid talking to a woman. It's Ms. Clayton. "*New Kid* is a wonderful graphic novel," she says to them. "It's the start of a trilogy by Jerry Craft, and if you're looking for a funny adventure, I'd recommend the Alston

Boys series by Lamar Giles." She points to a back shelf marked MID-DLE GRADE, and the boy hurries off, his mom in tow.

"Ms. Clayton?" I squeak.

She puts a book back on the shelf and turns to see me, a huge smile crossing her face. "Noor. I was hoping you'd wander in here."

My mouth drops open. "Someone left a bookmark for the store in my locker. Was that—"

She nods. "I still have a few friends in the school but didn't want to get anyone in trouble for being too direct."

I gulp and walk toward the register. "Ms. Clayton. I am so, so, so sorry. I wish—"

"I'm going to stop you right there, dear. You cannot blame yourself for me getting disciplined. Got it? I chose to share that QR code, and the board chose to put me on leave for it."

"But it's your career. Working here can't make up for—"

Ms. Clayton sighs and nods. "No. But I'm fighting them. I'm entitled to due process, and the union and our lawyers aren't going to let this slide. Don't worry. One way or another, I'm going to land on my feet."

My eyes widen. If my dad were here, I'm a hundred-percent sure he'd offer Ms. Clayton and the union his pro bono services. At first that makes me feel a little twinge in my chest, but you know what? He's not here, and it doesn't matter what he would or wouldn't do. I take another step toward Ms. Clayton. "I hope the union makes the district regret their decision."

She smiles. "Now, how about a little tea? I think we have a few things to catch up on."

I twirl around but don't see a café in this tiny store. "Sure, but..."

"I have a kettle in the back. Thoughts on genmaicha?"

I shrug. "Don't know what that is."

"A delightful Japanese green tea, a bit nutty with roasted popped brown rice. It's my favorite for the afternoon."

"Sold," I say as I step over to the shelves marked YOUNG ADULT, and Ms. Clayton heads into the back room.

I run my fingers over the spines of the gleaming hardcovers. I want to get a new book for Amal. She's practically through her entire to-be-read stack. I pull the list of challenged books from my back pocket and search for the titles. I pull three books from the shelves: *All Boys Aren't Blue*, a memoir by George M. Johnson that's supposed to be amazing; an anthology of vampire stories called *Vampires Never Get Old* (I chuckle at that title); and *Shout*, a memoir in verse by Laurie Halse Anderson. In seventh-grade Humanities, we read a book by her called *Chains*. I can't decide which one to get for Amal, so I figure I'll get all three. She and I share all our books anyway, so it's like a gift for myself, too.

I haul my small stack over to the coffee table and take a seat, sinking into the comfy couch. I grab *Shout* and put the other two on the table. I read a quote from the back cover: *We should teach our girls that snapping is okay, instead of waiting for someone else to break them.* I feel that deep in my bones.

"Here we go!" Ms. Clayton reemerges, places two steaming cups of green tea on the table, and nestles into a chair across from me.

I decide to go ahead and address the elephant in the room. "Thanks for being my book fairy."

She smiles wide. "Absolutely. And *book fairy* is an excellent honorific. I'll take it."

"But why? Did you know..." I trail off, my mind spinning.

"Honestly, I heard you and Juniper talking about your broken lock and hoped you wouldn't mind if I slipped a few books into it. I figured you'd read them, share them. I couldn't stand having all those books boxed up in the back room. I didn't expect anything, definitely not this brilliant idea of Bulldog Banned Camp that you and your friends came up with. I absolutely did not want you to get into trouble. I'm sorry that happened. But truly, you've inspired me."

"But you got suspended; you're probably going to lose your job," I whisper.

"My job is to get kids the books they want to read. Period. I'm a librarian, not a book cop. That's why I passed out the Brooklyn Public Library QR code, so kids could have the freedom to read what they want."

Oh my God, I love her. Ms. Clayton looks at the surprise on my face and then says, "We're not in school. I am free to express my very correct opinions." She takes a sip of her tea.

I raise my mug to her. "Thanks for standing up for us when most adults in this town seem glued to their seats."

She nods and pauses, thinking for a second. "You know, I bet there are more people that agree with us than you think. The other side has the loudest voices, and unfortunately, the system is built for them."

I take a sip of tea but it's still scalding, so I quickly put my mug down. "So we have to figure out a way to make our voices louder?" I think about the conversation I had with Faiz.

"Mm-hmm. Have you ever seen one of those neighborhood

libraries? The take a book, leave a book ones in people's yards?" She crosses her legs and picks up her tea. Unlike her usual school uniform of pencil skirts and blouses, Ms. Clayton rocks ripped jeans and a T-shirt that reads BAN GUNS, NOT BOOKS. Bright blue reading glasses sit atop her head, and her cranberry-red lips pop against her brown skin.

"Yeah. There was one on my old block," I say, recollecting my neighbor's little green library. It looked like a dollhouse, with a large glass door so you could see the books inside. One row for adult titles. Another for kids.

"I have one in my yard," Ms. Clayton says. "I've been filling it with books that are on the challenged list."

"Love that!"

She puts her half-empty cup down, and I realize I'm still neglecting mine. I take a hesitant sip. It's cooled a bit, but I've never been one to be able to drink hot beverages. Much to my parents' chagrin when they see my chai sitting on the counter, abandoned for ten minutes.

"You know those little neighborhood libraries are privately owned. Even if you're a school employee or student, district policy doesn't apply."

Like the VFW Lodge—a way to get around the book bans. My eyes spark with the full understanding of what Ms. Clayton is saying, and I'm reminded of the first day I met her. "Approaching the problem by a side angle." I grin. "I could try to put one up at my house, if my mom lets me."

"I think you could get others to join in, maybe? Perhaps with the help of the store or others in the community?"

"You'd help? Won't that take away from the business?"

She chuckles. "Not at all. Anyway, I'm good friends with Sylvia, the owner, who also has one up in their yard. Remember how I said there are more allies than you think?"

I frown. "I don't have the money to buy dozens of challenged books and stock them, though. I mean, I have a few, but it would be, like, a teeny-tiny library."

"Hang on." Ms. Clayton goes to the back room again.

I take a few more sips of my genmaicha. Tea always feels soothing, like the mere act of drinking it relaxes me. That's one small way I'm like my mom, I guess. Ms. Clayton returns with a small copy-paper box—the kind with a lid that my mom hoarded from the Xerox room at work to pack books in when we moved.

I give Ms. Clayton an expectant smile as she places the box on the table in front of me and gestures for me to open it. I take off the lid and it's filled with paperbacks—some used, some new. Titles that have been pulled from the shelves at school. My eyes grow wide as I take one of the books out of the box.

"Don't worry," she says with a laugh. "I didn't abscond with the books from the school library. Sylvia and I have been collecting some of the challenged books from used bookshops and also scouring sales at other indies. We're encouraging folks in our book club to join in and build small libraries in their yards, too. I *was* going to put these in my library."

I look up at her. "You're giving these to me?" My heart feels so full. It's been so long since it's felt like there was an adult totally on my side.

"Of course. Even if you can't convince your mom to let you put up a sharing library on your lawn, maybe you can lend these to your friends."

"We have this idea of pulling together Banned Camp outside of school. We even have a space for it."

Ms. Clayton smiles. "These are yours to read and share as you like."

I finish my tea and place the cup back on the table. "Don't you ever get tired of it?"

She raises an eyebrow. "Of…"

"Of fighting the good fight constantly? Of *needing* to be strong, looking for that side angle?"

Ms. Clayton sighs. "All the time. You have to pay attention to that. You don't want to run yourself ragged. But for me, at least, hope keeps me going. Hope is an act, not just a feeling. Hope is a choice. So are hate and cynicism and silence. Every day I have to think about what I'm going to choose. And so do you."

CHAPTER 31

I've barely talked to Andrew since that moment at my locker a few days ago. I mean, it felt like a *moment*. A time-slowing, heart-thumping, eyes-connecting, gazes-held moment. I flush a little, remembering. Yup, definitely a moment. Of course, that made me absolutely avoid him in the immediate aftermath of that butterflies-in-my-belly situation. Totally normal. Nothing to see here.

I'm not exactly sure why I'm shying away from him.... Well, that's not true. I'm actually somewhat sure. Because I also had a moment like that with Faiz in the VFW Lodge, where I got all cotton-mouthed and weird and then guilt swelled up in me, taking over every cell in my body. It's like my guilt has layers because I definitely feel conflicted about almost kissing Faiz and I also feel guilty because I'm kinda hanging out with Andrew. My thoughts waffle between Andrew and Faiz like a tennis match where I'm my own opponent. Feelings are bullshit.

I turn back to my laptop screen. For the last hour, I've been researching how to build one of those sharing libraries. There's an entire subculture of people who build and maintain them in their neighborhoods, and they even have free plans online for DIY ones. I know putting one up in my yard isn't enough to counteract the bans, but between that and Banned Camp, I love that we're creating sort of a renegade system to share banned books.

But building one requires knowledge of wood and tools and general handiness. Unless one of my hidden talents suddenly reveals itself to be constructing stuff, I'm going to need help.

I pick up my phone and swipe my finger over the screen until it hovers over Andrew's number. I take a deep breath. It's a text. Easy. So why am I frozen? Like, my mind is saying to text, but my fingers won't listen. *Get over yourself, Noor. Do it.*

Oh no.

No. No. No.

What did I do?

I didn't hit the message button. I hit the call button. Oh God. My phone is calling him. I'm calling him. Phone calls are strictly for medical emergencies and parents checking up on you.

There's a ring.

And another.

I've heard stories about this ancient, magical time where phones did not exist in pockets but were connected to walls. A time when callers couldn't see who was calling. A time when you could hang up on someone without them knowing it was you. I could hang up and blame it on a butt dial. But a part of me wants to hear Andrew's voice, and while I'm still waffling, he picks up.

"Noor?" Andrew's voice is husky with sleep. I glance at the time on my laptop. Nine a.m. on a Sunday. A time when most normal teenagers are still dead to the world and definitely not researching lumber.

My mouth is open but there are no words coming out of it.

"Is everything okay?"

Speak, Noor.

"Heyyyy. Uh...I'm so sorry. I meant to text you, and then I... inadvertently, um, pressed the wrong button. So here I am calling you like it's the eighties." The words tumble out of my mouth.

He lets out a gravelly chuckle. "It's okay."

I don't come up for air. "I've obviously woken you up because it's a Sunday, and of course you're sleeping because you're not a weirdo like me who has been awake for a couple hours."

"And who's already had two cups of coffee?"

"Three," I say sheepishly. "I think I need a refill and you should go back to bed—"

He laughs again. "Seriously. It's okay." There's a rustling sound from his end of the line. "I've been lying around in bed awake. My mom and Steve are at church, so there's no one to force me to get up and make myself useful." There's a bit of an edge in his voice as he utters that last sentence.

"Oh. You don't go to church with them?"

"Nah. Used to go with my dad sometimes to Bethany Lutheran. But when my mom got remarried, she started going to Steve's megachurch, like, an hour away. Not exactly my speed."

I nod. Not that he can see it.

"Anyway, what's up?" he asks.

"Uh... well, it's sort of silly, but do you have tools?"

"Tools?" he asks, amusement in his voice.

"Yeah. Like, to build stuff."

"Tools to build stuff," he repeats. "Can you be more specific? Like, tools to build a medieval torture chamber or something more like a cutting board?"

"Are those the only two options?" I chuckle.

"No. That's my range," he says.

"If you do say so yourself."

He laughs. "You're talking to the fourth-place finisher in the Bayberry soapbox derby relay. I built the car myself... with help from my dad."

"Wow. Fourth place. Did you get a ribbon and everything?"

"Of course, everyone gets a ribbon; otherwise, the organizers would be risking a riot from a bunch of helicopter parents."

A lot of my conversations with Andrew—like this one—are easy, funny. Like, I don't have to think of anything else and can just be in the moment. He has a natural charm that wins people over. I see it when he's talking to teachers and other kids. People want to smile around him. They want him to like them. That's a superpower I don't think I'll ever have.

"I need help building a library," I rush out.

"A library?"

"Yeah. You know, like, those small sharing libraries people have in their front yards, where anyone can leave a book or take a book? They look like tiny houses?"

There's a pause on his end of the line. I hear him take a long breath. I wonder if this was a big mistake. However nice he seems, his stepdad is the school board president, running for office on a censorship and morality and take-back-America platform.

"I love a weekend project," he finally says. "Do you have, like, instructions or pictures?"

I'm smiling so wide, he must be able to sense it over the phone. "Totally. Texting you now."

We make plans to meet in a couple of hours before we say good-bye. He's coming over. I'm building this little library in our yard. And I'm going to have to tell my mom about it.

———————

It went fine. Apparently, telling your checked-out mom while she's bleary-eyed and sipping her second chai is the best time to ask permission for virtually anything. "That seems nice," she'd said. "You always loved to read."

Past tense. *Loved.* At first I was confused by that. I mean, I obviously still read.

You. Loved. Always.

Then I realized the *you* wasn't me.

She was talking to me. But it wasn't me she was talking *about.* It's my dad. He is the *you.* He is the past tense.

I'm waiting outside when Andrew pulls up in a small pickup truck. It's not his regular car but I guess he has access to more than one. No surprise. He hops out of the driver's side. He's wearing his usual Sambas. But this time he's sporting slightly trashed jeans and a dark blue tee with splotches of paint on it. A huge smile is plastered across his face.

"Help me?" he says, and nods toward the back of the red truck as he walks around and pops down the tailgate.

I saunter over. "You are dressed very Carhartt catalog model."

"So you think I look like a model?" He smirks, his eyes dancing.

"Oh my God. You're so full of yourself."

"And you're dressed like—"

"Nineties grunge never ended?" I gaze down at my ripped jeans, the ancient Pearl Jam T-shirt I found at Village Thrift in Chicago, and the red-and-black plaid flannel I threw on top.

He shakes his head. "I was going to say, you look way too cool to live in this tiny town."

A soft, embarrassed smile crosses my lips, and I internally berate myself for the nervous giddiness that's apparently taking over my body. He pulls out a wooden post from the back of the truck that is maybe four or five feet tall. I grab a few other pieces of wood. There's a toolbox and a few small cans of paint and some brushes.

The pieces of wood are already cut into the shape of a small house. "You cut everything already?"

"Yeah, at the store, according to the plan you sent me. I assumed you didn't have a band saw in your garage."

"Have no idea what that is."

Andrew lays down a tarp on the driveway and we place the wood and other stuff on it. He quickly organizes all the items. Then he pulls out the plans from his back pocket and proceeds to tell me what we need to do. It's honestly not as hard as I thought it was going to be. It's basically a lot of gluing and clamping and waiting for the glue to dry.

Amal comes out with *All Boys Aren't Blue* in hand and takes a seat on the small porch swing and starts reading.

"We're almost ready to paint. Want to join us?" Andrew asks after she's been reading for a bit. I'm happy that he wants to make her feel included.

Amal looks up from the book, nods enthusiastically, and hops over to join us as we sit cross-legged on the tarp. "I thought you'd never ask." She smiles sweetly at Andrew. I watch her and Andrew chat about the book she's reading. Then she shares that my mom finally let her watch *Stranger Things*, only a few years after everyone else did. That flows into a discussion about villains. Their conversation is genuine and light. She smiles and laughs as she paints one side of the library a bright blue and Andrew paints another a sunshiny yellow.

"People aren't born evil," Amal says. "That's the most boring kind of villain. The interesting villains are the ones with a backstory. The ones who get more evil over time."

"So we're talking Darth Vader. Kylo Ren. That sort of thing," Andrew suggests.

Amal sighs. "Yeah...but I also am not a huge fan of easy villain redemption. I mean, a good redemption arc can be awesome, like, Zuko's. Best. Arc. Ever."

"Zuko?" Andrew looks up.

Oh no. I can see Amal's face transform into a mask of disbelief. She's readying a lecture. I can feel it in my bones. "You've never seen *Avatar: The Last Airbender*?"

"Isn't that, like, super old?"

Amal audibly gasps. "It's a classic. One of the greatest animations of all time." She shakes her head. "Don't worry, young padawan, I will set you on the right path." Amal puts her hand on Andrew's shoulder, and when she pulls it away, there are streaks of blue paint on his shirt.

I start laughing. Andrew gazes up from his shoulder, and his smiling eyes slide over to mine. He looks at the brush in his hand, dripping yellow paint, then smirks and stands up. Amal yelps and makes a dash for the porch.

I begin edging away from him and onto our front lawn. "No. Absolutely not. Do not even think about it. I swear I'll—"

I don't finish my statement because Andrew hurries toward me, raising the paintbrush above his head and flicking it at me. A drizzle of yellow paint arcs through the air. I dodge most of it, but some splats onto my cheek and nose. Amal howls with laughter. I set off running, and Andrew chases me as I seek refuge behind the trunk of the single large elm in the front yard.

"Don't! My mom will kill me if you get paint on this tree. Don't be anti-tree!"

Andrew pauses and throws his head back and laughs. "You're using the tree as an arboreal shield! *You're* the one who's anti-tree."

I wrap my arms around the scratchy bark. The trunk is too wide for my fingers to meet. "How dare you? I'm a total tree hugger."

"Dad joke!" Amal yells from the porch. I see a pained look on her face as she hears the word *dad* come out of her mouth, but it passes.

Andrew shoots a quick glance from Amal to me and then puts his hands up. "Okay, truce."

"I don't accept truces," I say. "Only total capitulation."

"Ruthless. Okay, fine. I surrender even though I clearly have the high ground here."

I inch out from behind the tree. "I'm glad to see you're reasonable and willing to accept your inferiority." I step closer to him.

He cocks his head and raises an eyebrow and in a flash traces his dipped-in-yellow-paint index finger across my cheek. He pauses for a second when he reaches the slight indentation on my chin. My eyes flicker toward him, and I feel a rush of heat from my head to my toes. In my peripheral vision, I clock Amal looking at me and take a small step back. Andrew withdraws his hand.

"I'll get you for that," I whisper.

He winks at me and then says loudly, "Let's get this library up and running!"

We work together to dig a hole about two feet deep in the ground, positioning the post and fastening the cheery blue-and-yellow house onto it with the hardware Andrew installed. The door of the little library, with its plexiglass window, is open on its hinges. I run inside and return a couple of minutes later.

I show Andrew and Amal the books Ms. Clayton gave me. I almost tell Andrew where I got them from, but I stop myself because of his stepdad. I hate that I'm censoring myself, but I want to protect Ms. Clayton. I guess it's unlikely, but what if Andrew tells his stepdad she's still helping me?

The library has two shelves, and we quickly fill them up with the books, arranged in rainbow color order. Andrew gestures at me and I close the door of the library with a satisfying click. The three of us step back to admire our handiwork.

"This looks amazing," Amal says, pauses, then adds, "largely due to my brilliant painting skills."

"Ha ha ha ha. You're hilarious, little sister."

Andrew walks around the post, pushing against the braces of wood underneath the library, making sure we've secured everything properly. "She's right. It's pretty incredible," he says. "Thanks to

Amal's artistic flair." He points to a few pink flowers Amal added to the sides of the library.

"And to you," I say. "Thanks to you."

Amal catches my eye and says, "I'm going in. Building a library is making me want to finish my book."

"See ya," Andrew says. She waves and jogs back inside.

The sharp late-morning sun has mellowed into the afternoon, a golden pink light reflecting on a few fluffy white clouds. I stare down at my Docs, digging the toe of one into the freshly upturned dirt at the base of the library. Andrew takes a step toward me, closing the distance between us. I hear him breathing but I keep my gaze locked on my boots. I can't help it. There's a commotion in my head, a riot in my heart. I'm afraid that if I look up at him, the earth will tilt and I'll slide right off.

"Noor," he whispers.

I tilt my chin up; our eyes meet. "Andrew," I whisper back, trying to pinch back my too-wide grin.

The world around us slows. Tender green leaves rustle in the slightest breeze. The smell of new paint floats off the library. The ground beneath my feet pulses in rhythm with the loud *thud-thud-thud* of my heart thumping against my rib cage. He takes one more step, the light between our bodies fading as the distance between us narrows. *Thud-thud-thud.* I am pretty sure he's going to kiss me. Wants to kiss me. Is that what I want? I think it is. It's what my body wants. But there's a tiny contrary voice in my head clamoring for attention. A word of reason, logic. A reminder of painful lessons I've learned—that trust is too easily broken. Faiz's smiling face flashes through my mind. *Thud-thud-thud.* Apparently my heart and head have chosen this exact moment, this broken soil as their battleground. May the best body part win.

The toe of my right boot lifts and inches closer to Andrew, as if part of me is puppet-mastering the other part. I breathe. Oh my—

"Noor, beta, can you run to the store?" I step back from Andrew so quickly I almost trip over my feet. Of course my mom chose this second to thrust open the front door and ask me to run an errand. Parental timing is uncanny.

Andrew gives me a shy, awkward grin, then turns around and waves to my mom. "Hi, Mrs. Khan. Uh...Ms. Khan. I—"

"It's Ms. Razvi," I whisper to Andrew. My mom kept her last name.

"Oh...I'm sorry. Hi. Ms. Razvi." Andrew stumbles over his words, embarrassed.

"This is Andrew, Mom," I say, stepping up to rescue him. "He helped me build the library." I point to our handiwork.

My mom looks at it, squinting. "Oh, good job, you two. It looks great," she manages. "Noor, you probably need a few things for your lunches. Can you run to the store? Maybe grab some tea, too. You can take Amal with you."

"Sure. On it, Mom." I sigh as she closes the door. "Duty calls," I say, turning to Andrew and shrugging. "Let me help load up your truck."

We hurry to clean up the tools, paint, and tarp, and dump everything into the back of the truck. "Thanks, again," I say as he slams the tailgate shut. "I literally couldn't have done it without you."

"Of course. It was fun."

We walk toward the driver's-side door.

"So," I say.

"So," he responds. "I'll see you at school tomorrow?"

"Unfortunately, yes."

"I know school sucks, especially lately. But I hope there are one or two things you like about it." He toys with the key ring in his right hand.

"Maybe one or two things are okay." I press my lips together, trying to hide a smile.

He closes the door and backs out of the driveway. I watch as he drives off, then walk over to the small library we built today, with our own hands. I snap a few photos and send them to Faiz and Juniper. Then I post one to our social media account, tagging it *fREADom Library*—an idea I got from that hashtag made up by librarians—and list the books I've stocked it with so far, inviting people to take a book, to leave a book.

It's a tiny stand against censorship. One little library filled with banned books might not turn the tide, but it could cause a ripple. And that's a start. I think of what Ms. Clayton said—it's a choice to be silent as much as it's a choice to speak out. To roar.

CHAPTER 32

My alarm goes off to the chorus from "Manic Monday," an old eighties song that my dad thought was hilarious to play when Amal and I would trudge down the stairs for breakfast before school on...yup, Mondays! My mom would be at the table or the counter, sipping her chai, smiling as if he was so clever and funny. I don't know why I kept it as my alarm. I guess maybe I did it ironically, at first, to joke with my dad about it. After he left, well, I didn't want to change another thing because of him. Even though it reminds me of him. It's like picking at a scab. It's a bad idea. It doesn't make sense, but I keep doing it anyway. I don't want my dad's voice in my head telling me I shouldn't.

I reach over to grab my phone, ready to snooze away to within an inch of my life, when I see a notification from the newspaper. Yes, I get alerts from the local news and the school paper because (1) I'm a nerd, and (2) it's the easiest way to keep track of people bad-mouthing me before I have to run the gauntlet of senior hall at school. *Forewarned is forearmed*, my mom loves to say. But I don't think you're ever ready to be barraged by hate, no matter how much you expect it.

The clickbait headline in the *Gazette* shouts, TALKING ABOUT A REVOLUTION? BOOK BOUNDARIES AT BAYBERRY HIGH. "Boundaries" is a euphemism they're using because they're afraid to say "bans." The article reads like a puff piece supporting Andrew's father and Principal Carter, who give their spin on Banned Camp.

> Unfortunately, a handful of students decided to flout the new district-wide policy that has put some harmful books under review—a policy, mind you, to protect our students. Their rabble-rousing resulted in a change to the off-campus lunch privileges. Naturally, many upperclassmen are upset at this.

I read a bit further and almost gag at this gem:

> School board president and candidate for state representative Steve Hawley believes that there is no rebellion fomenting at the school. "It's a few youths playing at being radicals," says Hawley. "Typical rebellious teen behavior. The instigator is an outsider to this community, a transplant from Chicago's South Side, who I'm sure is a wonderful young lady but needs to learn about our local values and culture. The policy that I shepherded through the school board, and hope to take statewide once I make it to Springfield, is for the

protection of our children. There is absolutely no book banning going on in our district; this is a commonsense process of reviewing and removing books with objectionable and obscene material. This is about local control and parental rights."

Fantastic. He doesn't name who he's talking about, but it's obvious it's me. Everyone needs to save their precious snowflakes from me, the scary outsider from the big city. I sigh. This is a lot for only 6:30 a.m.

Amal is already downstairs toasting a waffle. She gives me a meaningful look and then tilts her head toward my mom, who is furiously scrolling through her phone. *Oh no.* Guess I'm not going to be able to hide this from her.

She looks up at me as I hop down the last step. She doesn't seem mad. I'm sure she *is* furious, but mostly she looks tired. Disappointed. More gray hairs seem to have sprouted along her hairline, almost overnight.

"I don't know how to get through to you." She shakes her head. "We've discussed this. I made it clear that I wanted you to focus, follow the rules, graduate."

My jaw clenches. I'd expected yelling, but her voice is heavy and low, and that's somehow worse. "I thought you and Dad raised us to speak out when rules are wrong, or was that someone else dragging their kids to political protests?"

She stands up from her stool. "There is a time and a place for speaking out. This is not it. In the short while we've been here, you've managed to make enemies of the principal and the school board president." She sighs deeply. "We're supposed to be making a fresh start. What must these people think of us? You have an obligation to this family, to—"

I explode. "*I* have an obligation? Me? What about you? Maybe if you stopped worrying about saving face or shame or whatever you're talking about, you'd realize that moving to this crappy town made everything worse. We're alone here!" My voice is on the edge of a sob. "Mom, I'm trying to do my best. I'm sorry you couldn't stand being in our old home, in our old city where your husband left you, but..."

From behind my mom's back, Amal's eyes go wide and she shakes her head, an angry expression on her face. I've gone too far. I see it in the way my mom's mouth quivers and draws down at the corner, at the glistening in her eyes. I feel a sting behind my eyes, too. My mom gathers up her things, moving so slowly, like she's trying to catch her breath. She walks past me, pausing to say, "I'm trying to protect you, keep you safe. You seem to have forgotten that I'm not the one who abandoned this family. I'm the one who stayed."

CHAPTER 33

After we traded text-pletives about the article this morning, Juniper, Faiz, and I picked today for our first VFW Banned Camp meeting. Kids were bound to be talking about the article, so we figured no time like the present. As soon as the last bell rang at school, we took off to get the space readyish.

"I wrote a letter to the editor," Juniper says while stringing fairy lights across the VFW hall. "Doubt they'll print it. But still, I had to."

"You what?" I ask as Faiz and I sweep the dusty floor and set some folding chairs in a U shape around the podium. Her parents went in to talk to Carter about the homophobic graffiti and notes Juniper got, and he promised he'd look into it. *Yeah, right.* Juniper found another one in her locker today, but she's still here, doing the work, helping me, making a choice, even if it isn't easy.

"Not that I expect the *Bayberry Gazette* to have high journalistic standards," Juniper fumes. "But that reporter let Hawley spew a bunch of hate totally unchecked."

"Oh, you mean, the whole *we're trying to preserve our culture from this outsider* thing?" I pretend to puke.

Faiz nods. "Classic white supremacist dog whistling never goes out of style."

Juniper gingerly steps onto a windowsill to string some lights across the top of the frame, and dust motes waft to the ground. She sneezes and loses her balance. Faiz takes two long strides toward her, his arms wide, but Juniper artfully rights herself and jumps to the ground, landing on both feet, then does a little flourish with her hands as if to say *voilà*.

"Impressive," I say.

"In my other life I was a parkour champion." She grins, then, turning to Faiz, adds, "Were you about to go full-on chevalier and catch this damsel in your arms?"

Faiz clears his throat. "I would never, ever presume, milady, that you need rescuing. Only an occasional soft place to land." He Regency-bows to her, and she curtsies.

"Okay, you two are all over the place. You mashed up Arthurian chivalry with Jane Austen."

"Nerd!" Juniper laughs.

"Takes one to know one," I say with a wink. I lean my broom against the wall so I can survey the room. "Not bad."

"Hang on." Juniper plugs in the connected strings of lights. "Instant vibes." She scans the room approvingly.

"And bonus, the low lighting hides the mouse droppings."

"You're such a romantic, Faiz." Juniper walks over and nudges him. "Shocker that you haven't snagged a date to prom yet."

Faiz makes eye contact with me and then quickly turns away, nudging Juniper back. "Like you've asked Hanna?"

"I thought dates weren't allowed at prom," I say.

"They're not." Juniper shrugs. "But most people have dates for dinner and post-prom even if they go to the dance in a big group." She pauses and a huge smile spreads across her face. "And FYI, I may be working on a little promposal."

I squeal and clap my hands. "Ah! Let me know if you need any help planning or getting Hanna to a specific spot or whatever."

The ancient clock on the wall emits an annoying buzz as the hour hand moves and hits 7:00 p.m. People should be here by now—if anyone is coming, that is. I glance nervously at Juniper and Faiz. I pick up the box of books I brought—thank you, Ms. Clayton—and grab the book I was planning on reading from tonight—*When the Moon Was Ours*, by Anna-Marie McLemore—and thumb through it, trying hard not to peek at the clock. Juniper and Faiz walk up to me. They don't say anything. Juniper digs through the box and snags a book, then hands one to Faiz. They take seats and read silently.

It's 7:04 p.m.

I should've known better. Should've guessed that the article today would scare people off. There were, what, forty people who showed the last time we read in the park at lunch before getting busted? A good turnout, but not exactly enough to start the rebellion the newspaper implied. I slip into the chair next to Juniper, who gives me a sympathetic smile.

"Fifteen-minute rule applies," she says.

"That's an urban legend."

"Good thing I believe in magic."

On cue, the word *magic* still lingering in the air, the door to the hall creaks open a bit and Andrew's head appears. "Is this where the party's at?" He smiles and pushes the door open. Fifteen kids behind him clatter into the room, bringing the space to life.

Juniper pops up and grabs the box of donuts that Andrew is holding. A few other students have also brought treats. Our social media posts said tonight was BYOSnacks. Juniper points to a table along the wall and leads people over to set down the various baked goods and chips they brought.

"We are big on snacks downstate." Andrew grins as I approach him.

"So it seems." I tug at the lapel of his coat and then quickly step away, needled by guilt, remembering that Faiz is at the other end of the room. "Thanks for showing up and bringing friends," I whisper.

"Of course," he whispers back. "There's literally nothing else to do in town tonight."

I give him a tiny shove. "Ha ha."

As we laugh, a few others enter the room, including Hanna. I peep over at Juniper, who has the hugest smile on her face as she hugs Hanna hello. Then Amal walks in with her friends Cecily and Blaine, all of them holding coffee cups in their hands. She waves shyly at me. I don't hide the surprise on my face.

"How'd she get..." I turn back to Andrew. "Did you give her and her friends a ride over?"

He shrugs. "She asked."

I hadn't told Amal about tonight, but it's not as if I hid it. I mean, she has a phone. But after the fight with my mom this morning, I didn't want her to get in trouble, too. "Wait. How'd she get your number?"

"I will take that to the grave," he says. I make a face. "She was worried you'd be mad."

"She'd be right."

"Look, I don't have siblings, but I think she wanted to be here for you. I couldn't argue with that."

I can't argue with that, either.

"Hey, man." Faiz walks up to us. I immediately tense. I haven't been alone with Faiz since the day we cooked at my house, and we haven't talked about that near kiss between us, because, no, I don't want to invite more awkward into my life. But I've been replaying that moment every time I make eye contact with Faiz. He's been tiptoeing around me since that evening, so, I dunno, maybe he got weirded out? Maybe I'm weirded out? Maybe it's too much weird for us to handle so we've silently agreed to say nothing.

Then there's Andrew. Things are, uh, weird with him, too.

And they're both right here. Right now. Next to me. This moment is about as cringe as it can get. I honestly wouldn't mind if a crack appeared in the floor right now and wormholed me to another dimension. Maybe I'd even welcome it. Because we're all standing here, suffocating in awkwardness.

"Listen," Andrew finally says, "I know we've had issues in the past."

"You think?" Faiz raises his eyebrows and folds his arms over his chest.

"Okay, yeah, I was a dick in fourth grade and—"

"It wasn't just fourth grade." Faiz grits his teeth and straightens his shoulders.

"Fine, I've been a shit. I'm sorry. Seriously, man. I'm trying to do better," Andrew says, and extends a hand. I don't exactly understand this weird boy code of half-spoken thoughts, but I suppose that doesn't matter.

Faiz glances down at Andrew's hand that's awaiting his, scoffs, then looks at me. Eventually, he shakes hands. "Cool," he says.

"Cool," Andrew responds. They nod at one another, and then Faiz walks over to the overflowing refreshment table.

I scrunch my eyebrows at Andrew. "That was both somewhat mature but also weirdly dysfunctional and devoid of any discussion of feelings."

"It's a truce, I guess? Isn't that what you wanted?" Andrew shrugs and then heads off to get a cookie, leaving me a bit confused because it's not about what I want, it's about what's right. Doesn't he get that?

"What exactly was that?" Juniper asks as she and Hanna sidle up to me. I notice they're holding hands, and I have to try very hard not to make embarrassing kissy noises at Juniper.

"One small step for *non*toxic masculinity?" I suggest, playing it cool.

"Dudes are bizarre," Hanna says.

"Facts," Juniper adds, then turns to me. "Your podium awaits. Let's goooooo!"

All eyes in the room follow me as I walk to the podium and people find their seats. But it doesn't feel right to be standing in front of everyone. Like I'm the leader. I might be the one who started reading the challenged books out loud during lunch, and I'm definitely the person everyone blames for our off-campus privileges being pulled—Carter made sure of that. But this feels too formal. Too hierarchical. Too *look at me!*

"Do you guys mind if we move the chairs into a big circle?" I ask.

"Like group therapy!" Blaine shouts.

Scattered laughter erupts around the room. I nod. "Something like that."

Chairs screech and clatter against the floor as we drag and shift them into place. I position the box of contraband books in the center of the circle before taking a seat.

"Hi, I'm Noor." I smile. "And I read banned books," I say, starting this meeting as we have the others.

There's a chorus of "Hi, Noor!" amid a few whoops and claps.

I take a breath, catch Andrew's eye. He holds my gaze and grins. I continue, looking around at the thirty or so people who've joined. Most of them are juniors and seniors, but Amal brought a few other ninth graders, and there are a few sophomores, too. We're probably more diverse than the general school or town population, percentagewise, but that's not a surprise. When the powers that be are literally trying to erase you, you don't have the luxury of pretending not to notice what's happening.

"Thanks for turning out, everyone. I think a lot of you were at the park during lunch when we started reading these banned novels that Liberty Moms and Dads think are pornography—"

"They have to protect us from all the scary books." Hanna snickers.

"Such bullshit," a senior named Kamal adds. He's one of the few Black students in the school. This has got to suck ten times harder for him. "They don't care about kids. Definitely not Black kids. One of the parents in that group said something to me after a basketball game about how lucky I was that 'my people' were naturally good at sports. How I would be able to write my ticket to college with it."

"What an asshole! Did you say something to her or tell Coach about it?" Hanna asks.

Kamal scoffs. "Say something? Like what? *Lady, I'm on honor roll, and you're a racist?* She's one of the Athletic Boosters and donates money for uniforms. Coach probably would've benched me if I complained, and if I'd gotten mad, I'd be the 'thug' who yelled at the nice white lady. So I fake smiled and headed into the locker room."

There's a moment of silence in the room. Then Andrew pipes up. "I'm sorry, Kamal. That sucks."

Kamal shrugs.

Amelie, a petite blond girl with pale blue eyes next to him, scoffs. "Andrew, spare us your *I'm a woke ally* act. Your dad is the reason we're here. Censorship and MAGA garbage is literally his entire platform."

"He's my stepdad." Andrew winces as he responds.

I jump in. "It's not right to hold one person accountable for another person's actions. Andrew's not his stepdad." I don't know why I feel so defensive on Andrew's behalf. He wears big-boy pants and can defend himself. But I understand not wanting to feel as if your dad's behavior reflects on you.

"Aaaaanyway," Juniper segues, "Mr. Carter and Mr. Hawley don't get to shut us up. Thanks to Faiz, we found this place and figured we could meet here, share books, and rage against the machine together."

I nod at Juniper and mouth a thank-you at her masterful transition. "Also, I have a bunch of books"—I point to the box—"that have all been pulled from the school library or curriculum, so feel free to grab one and take it home if you want."

Amal's friend Cecily nervously shifts in her seat. "I like the fREADom Library you put up in your yard."

Amal beams. "I helped make it. So did Andrew! Other people should build them, too. It's easy."

"I can help get you plans, cut wood, whatever," Andrew adds when he sees people nodding. I see he's trying, and I appreciate it.

Juniper practically jumps out of her seat. "That would be amazing. A whole bunch of fREADom Libraries spread around town filled with books the school doesn't want us to read." She mimics a chef's kiss. It's like what Ms. Clayton and I talked about. If she can get some of her book club friends to build some and some kids do, too, it would be another way to speak out.

Everyone starts talking at once. Juniper drags over an old chalkboard that's on wheels and starts jotting down ideas that people are brainstorming about the fREADom Libraries—where they can go, how to use recycled materials to build them, where we can get more books to fill them. There's a buzz of excitement in the room, and it makes me so happy I'm practically floating.

After action plans are made, we decide to end with a reading from one of our challenged books. I hold up Anna-Marie McLemore's *When the Moon Was Ours*. It's so gorgeously written. Every line of their prose is like a song, and it reads like a kind of magical realism fairy tale with a girl who has roses blooming from her wrists and a love that seems impossible. It's about vulnerability and strength. It's a story about being who you are even when society doesn't want you to be. The author imagines a world for readers who have to live in the in-between spaces. My voice starts to get choked up when I read the dedication out loud:

To the boys who get called girls,
the girls who get called boys,
and those who live outside these words.
To those called names,
and those searching for names of their own.
To those who live on the edges,
and in the spaces in between.
I wish for you every light in the sky.

CHAPTER 34

Three days later and I'm still hyped from the meetup at the VFW. It felt good to do something. To put my rage into action. I imagine my dad saying, *See, I told you anger can be a powerful tool.* It's the whole reason he became a lawyer. The reason he took on pro bono cases and tried to fight against injustices. I know I'm like my dad in a lot of ways—my two loves who love to argue, my mom always joked. I liked that. When I was little, my dad felt like the sun I was orbiting around. He was my hero. Now I'm afraid of all the selfish ways I might take after him. What that means about who I am and how I could hurt people I love.

"Why are we taking this way to school?" Amal asks. She's shuffling through Conan Gray songs on her phone and briefly stops at "Family Line," but quickly switches to "Disaster" because she sees me physically recoil at the lyrics about a terrible father and whether you can escape your family's fate.

"Huh?"

"This isn't the usual way we drive."

"Oh. Yeah. Uh, Andrew texted me this morning and asked me to take this street." It's only slightly out of the way, and he said it was a surprise, told me to trust him. He didn't understand that I didn't want to be surprised anymore by people I trust. But he promised I'd like it, and I'm still in a good mood from the meeting, so I thought I'd take the chance.

"Ooh, Aaandreeew." Amal draws out the syllables of his name. "You like him. *Like* like him."

"Ugh. Shut uuuuuup. We're friends, that's all," I say. What I don't say: Maybe I do *like* like him, but I think I also *like* like Faiz, and that feels like a ginormous, messy problem. It feels like drama. I came to Bayberry hoping to cruise through with zero drama, and instead I floored it to a hundred. Take away my driver's license.

Amal ignores me. "That's why you get all heart-eyes emoji whenever you say his name." I shake my head but it doesn't stop her. "You like him. You love him. You want him," she starts singing.

"I have no idea what you're talking about!" My protest is pretty unconvincing since I'm smiling so hard right now that my jaw hurts.

Amal heaves a dramatic sigh and traces an invisible heart on the passenger-side window with the tip of her finger. "You know... it's okay to like someone. You don't have to act like you don't have feelings."

I steal a quick glimpse at her. "Hey, I have feelings, okay." The problem is not that I don't have feelings; it's that I have too many. For Andrew. For Faiz, too, even though it feels as if he's avoiding being alone with me. "But... I don't know how to trust them." My throat tightens as I say this—I never explained it that way to myself before, let alone out loud.

She nods. "My therapist says that's normal, especially after, like, trauma."

We're silent for a few moments. The repetitive thud of the tires over the bumpy road reverberates in my body, almost meditatively.

I clear my throat. "What about you? Anyone you're crushing on?"

"Nah. Honestly? I like flirting, a little, maybe? But having a boyfriend or girlfriend... I'm not sure if that's really my thing."

"That's cool." I hesitantly slip one hand over hers and squeeze for a second. "You do you. Everyone's mileage varies."

"Yeah. Tell that to the first auntie who asks for my biodata when I'm about to graduate from college."

"That's, like, eight years away. But yes, you have my sword." We laugh.

"Whoa. Slow down!" Amal yelps.

I pump the brake and look out the window to where Amal is pointing. She's practically jumping in her seat. I slow down and pull over onto the gravelly right shoulder. Right in front of me, close to one of the main intersections on the way to school, where cars and school buses pass every morning, stands a little library like the one Andrew helped us build in our yard. Shaped like a tiny house, its cheery egg-yolk yellow exterior pops against the green fields and bright blue morning sky.

Amal hops out of the car and I follow, my mouth agape, as I see the blue letters painted across the front: *fREADom*. This is why Andrew asked me to go this way. This is what he wanted me to see.

"There's a letter for you!" Amal squeals as she plucks an envelope from the side of the little house, pulling tape off the back before she hands it to me.

My pulse quickens when I see Andrew's squiggly handwriting spelling out my name, confirming my guess that he did this. For me.

"It's from him, isn't it?" Amal waggles her eyebrows and does the desi head bobble.

I open the envelope with trembly fingers. Why am I so nervous? It's not like this is going to be some declaration. Amal repeats a version of her irritating lyric, "He likes you. He loves you. He wants you." I give her a look as I unfold the piece of paper that was inside. It's a map of the town with five gold-star stickers scattered in a constellation across it, including the spot I'm standing in now. There's a pink Post-it note stuck to the top: *After-school treasure hunt?*

I move closer to the door of the fREADom Library, my heart growing two sizes with each step. There are two shelves of books—all titles we've read in Banned Camp.

Amal snatches the paper from my hands and quickly scans it. Then she looks up, gazes at me, her dark brown eyes twinkling with mischief. "Oh. My. God. Look, I know you're not a rom-com fan like me and Mom, but this is definitely Big Gesture territory." For the third time on the way to school, she starts up with that annoyingly catchy tune: "He likes you. He loves you. He wants you."

I wave my hand at her dismissively, pretending I don't care even though my heart is racing. I snap a picture of the library to post to the Bulldog Banned Camp socials. Who knew rebellion could have so many clammy-palmed, heart-fluttering, head-spinning moments? A couple of buses and a bunch of cars pass us, some slowing down to check out why two girls are standing next to a bright yellow little house stuck on a wooden post.

As I approach the driver's side of the Karmann Ghia, a silver car heads toward us. For a second I think it's Andrew's car so I wave, but as it gets closer, something feels wrong. It's still in the distance, but I swear to God, the silver car is speeding up as it approaches. You're supposed to slow down when you see people on the side of the road, not gun it. No way he doesn't see us.

I fumble with my door handle. Amal is already inside, her door shut, her face buried in her phone, so she's oblivious to my panic. For a second, everything slows down. I hear the ragged echo of my breathing. I feel a chill snaking up my spine, the shadows of clouds passing over me, and the furious scratch of accelerating wheels on pavement. That silver car is too close to the shoulder. Too close to me. There's a screech, and when it passes, a few bits of gravel kick up and pelt me. I open my eyes and whip my head around, but the car has already sped off. I only get a glimpse of the driver. I can't be certain. It happened so fast, but I swear it kinda looked like Andrew's stepdad.

CHAPTER 35

"I haven't stopped smiling all day. I can't believe you did this," I say as Andrew drives me to the third gold-star location on the fREADom Library map he made for me. Even as I'm saying the words, though, I know it's a lie because my head has been filled with the few seconds of terror from when that silver car seemed to swerve toward me this morning. A car that I think, maybe, was driven by Andrew's stepdad. I want to ask him about it, but I don't want to burst this little bubble we're in. Pretending everything is awesome is easier, and I can almost make myself believe that it is. It spares me from today's emotional whiplash, anyway.

Andrew keeps his eyes on the road but I see them brighten with a smile. He's wearing a dark blue Henley with the sleeves rolled up and smells faintly like freshly mowed grass and citrus. "I didn't do it all myself. I worked with some of the kids who were at the VFW, and we made an assembly line. Expect some more to go up in people's yards. The books were the easy part—thank you, stepdad's credit card."

I grimace. "Isn't he going to be pissed?"

"Probably. But if there's one thing I learned from my politician stepdad, it's ask forgiveness, not permission."

I lean toward him and part of me wants to reach out and touch his hand, say something that is probably too cheesy to bear. I stop myself.

Andrew pulls over to the third fREADom Library so I can take pictures to upload onto the Banned Camp socials. Like the other ones, it's also painted lively yellow with blue letters. This one has the distinction of being next to Scoopers, an old-timey ice-cream shop.

"Did you ask permission? Isn't this the store's property?"

"It definitely is, and yes, I did. I've known the owner, Phyllis, since grade school. When my dad died, she gave me free ice cream every time I went in. My mom asked her to stop when I started frequenting the place a lot and ended up with a cavity."

I laugh. "She sounds like a good person."

"She's the best. She also paid for the books in this one."

"Amazing."

"Didn't even ask her to. But when I told her what it was, she was super into it and offered."

I snap a few selfies with the door of the library open and Andrew takes a shot of me reaching in to grab a book with Scoopers prominent in the background. This is the first photo I've posted with me in it—Faiz, Juniper, and I have mostly only been writing posts with quotes from the books we've read or about censorship, but it's not like everyone in this town doesn't know who started all this.

I take a deep breath and work up my courage because I can't

fight the urge to ask any longer. "Hey, so does your stepdad drive a silver car, kinda like yours?" I ask, trying to act casual.

"Silver BMW? Yeah. He thought it would be cool for us to have the same car." He rolls his eyes. "Why?"

"Oh...uh...I thought I saw him this morning when I stopped at the first fREADom Library."

"Before school?" Andrew sounds confused. "Nah. I don't think so. He left the house pretty early because he said he had a breakfast meeting in Urbana. Maybe it was someone else?"

"Oh, yeah, probably," I mutter. I don't know if I should believe him. But why would he lie? It's not as though he defends his stepdad. I guess I could be wrong. Sometimes your mind can play tricks on you; maybe I imagined the driver was him? Andrew seems pretty certain his stepdad was out of town. Then again, how many silver BMW drivers want to scare the crap out of me? I try to refocus, not let my head linger in this confused space, because I'll probably never learn the truth. Not like Mr. Hawley would admit to it. I try to sit in the present moment. To be here, in the now, with a boy who did something very cool for me who happens to have a terrifying, racist stepdad.

Evening descends and we're losing the light, so we only do a quick drive by the fourth library. I grab a few shots for a photo dump I'll add later on social. We hurry to the fifth and final star on the map. The insects are out and chirping and I'm not sure I'll be able to get any decent photos, but I don't tell Andrew to take me home. I want to see the last library he put up. I want to be here, with him.

"I love this time of evening, with the light fading and the random insects taking over the day. It's sort of romantic but in a way that can turn creepy pretty fast."

Andrew turns to me for a brief moment, his hazel eyes twinkling. "We'll try to avoid the creepy."

I chuckle nervously. I melt a little when he smiles at me, so I fumble around with my bag, pulling out a lip balm and swiping it across my mouth because when I'm nervous, I fidget. "*Dusk* is such a weird word, right? I looked it up once. It comes from Middle English: *dosc*, meaning 'a tendency toward darkness or shadow.' But some scholars say it could be Old English. There is even a possible Sanskrit root, *dhusarah*, or dust colored. Isn't that interesting?" When I'm nervous, I also blather.

"Thank you for en-*liiight*-ening me," Andrew says, stretching out the word. "See what I did there? Light, dusk, get it?"

I give him a jokey groan. Andrew's not too cool to go for the cheap pun, which makes me like him more.

"Here we are." Andrew pulls into the town square next to the gazebo that is always strung with lights. Yes, there are gazebos all over this town, but when folks here say, "the gazebo," this is the one. It's where the fifth fREADom Library is. There are fairy lights running up the wooden post holding up the tiny house; colorful fake flowers adorn the roof. It's gorgeous.

I hop out of the car and hurry toward the gazebo. The town square is always done up like it's movie-set ready. Apparently there's even a town committee that ensures the square is properly decked out for every season and holiday. In winter, it probably looks like a Hallmark holiday special.

This fREADom Library is a bit larger than the other ones. As I approach, I see a bouquet of dead flowers inside. But when I get closer, I see that's not what they are at all. They're roses made from pages of books. I open the plexiglass door and pull them out. They're so pretty, but I immediately panic thinking about the sacrilege of ripping up a book to make this.

"They're from books that were damaged and were going to be thrown away or recycled."

I turn to Andrew's voice. He's slowly walked up behind me. "Wait. You made these?"

"Shocking, I know. Thank you, YouTube. I figured they were on point."

"They're for me? You made them for me?" My heart hammers in my chest. I look down at the bouquet I'm holding tightly in my hands and raise my eyes to Andrew. I want to melt into the moment because it doesn't feel real and I'd like to be stuck here forever, thank you very much.

"Yeah, New Girl. For you." His voice is soft and he steps closer to me. "You probably think it's a corny, patriarchal tradition, but whaddya say, want to go to prom?" His smile is warm and he has this incredibly sincere look in his eyes.

Prom is undeniably clichéd and rooted in sexism. And I'll probably have to sneak out because my mom won't let me go. I think of that brief heart-pounding moment I shared with Faiz that turned weird. I think of how the school stopped selling couples tickets because they wanted to dissuade queer kids from going. I bite my lip; my face twists before I meet Andrew's gaze.

"Noor? You okay? Is this the part where I slink away to my car in humiliation or—"

"Yes. No! I mean. Yes, I'm okay, and no, please stay right here. Exactly where you are."

Andrew smiles, a look of relief washing over his face.

"This is the sweetest thing ever, and I would totally love to go with you. . . ."

"But? Sounds like there's a big *but* in there."

A nervous smile crosses my face. "*But* I think it's wrong that the school is trying to stop queer couples from going to prom."

Andrew nods as if he's thinking for a moment, coming up with a plan. "What if . . . what if we go as a group? If Juniper wants to go with Hanna or by herself or whatever. Faiz, too, if he'll deign to be in the same car as me. We'll rent a party limo. It'll be fun."

Is it wrong to love the Big Gesture even when your feelings are chaos? I hesitate for a second, then wrap my arms around him in a huge hug, our bodies colliding from the force of it. "That sounds brilliant," I whisper in his ear, and hold on a little longer, pressed against him in the descending darkness, our faces lit by the fairy lights, in a single moment of life's perfection.

BAYBERRY GAZETTE

Around Town by Stephanie Ludwig

No, those aren't fairy houses popping up in people's yards, at various intersections, and in the town square. Those cheery yellow structures are what their builders refer to as fREADom Libraries. No, that's not a typo.

Students at Bayberry High, led by senior and new transfer Noor Khan, have taken to building and stocking these so-called fREADom Libraries in a kind of protest against the Bayberry School Board's policy on book challenges. Parents may raise an objection to a book in the curriculum or in the school library by filling out a form noting why the story is problematic, and the district will pull the book from shelves while it is under review. It is a policy that school board president and candidate for state representative Steve Hawley assures the community is aimed at "keeping pornography and obscene materials out of our schools." He continues, "It's simply a matter of parental rights. These are public schools. Paid for by taxpayer dollars. Of course, the curriculum should reflect the community's values. Parents should absolutely have a right to decide what their children are reading. It's our obligation as parents and as moral, upstanding citizens to protect our kids from indecent novels, from the far left agenda, from groomers."

The students, who refer to themselves as the Bulldog Banned Camp, have created social media accounts and are spreading the word of their dissatisfaction via posts decrying the policy and urging like-minded community members to build these fREADom Libraries and fill them with books from the challenged list that they've posted in full. Students, apparently, have also gathered at the local VFW hall to read these banned books off school property, in attempts to circumvent district policy.

"It's not right," Tom Webber, owner of Webber Hardware, says. "Those little blue-and-yellow houses are an eyesore. Not to mention that these kids are peddling pornography in our town. Their parents need to shut this down. If they won't, the community should."

While most of the over dozen or so libraries that sprouted up this week are on private property, a couple were erected in public spaces without formal permission, including next to the gazebo in the town square. The City Council will take up the issue at their regularly scheduled meeting next month. Meanwhile, you can keep track of our very own rebels with a cause via their Bulldog Banned Camp account.

Disclosure: The Bayberry Gazette is a wholly owned subsidiary of Hawley, LLC News coverage. Reporting is independent of ownership.

CHAPTER 36

Since Andrew asked me to prom last week, life had been kinda awesome. I'd been floating around, all heart eyes and good moods. Ugh. I couldn't help it. I had a prom date! I was all weird and bubbly inside, like a girl in one of the rom-coms my sister loves so much. And it was gross, but I'm barely even embarrassed about it. I instructed Amal to slap me if I started singing alongside cartoon birds like an animated princess.

But perfect moments never last. Joy is a scam. And the joke is always, always on me.

On this fine Monday morning, the town gossip pulled a name and shame on me in her daily column on the *Gazette* website. It's not exactly illegal since I'm eighteen and technically an adult, but it's definitely crappy. Walking into school, I was sure that Mr. Carter was going to pull me into his office to yell at me about...I don't know...the bad press, the school's reputation, *the rules*. But he didn't. In fact, when he passed me in the hallway a few minutes ago, he didn't say a word. But he gave me a knowing look, a grin that said, *Noor, you messed with the bull and now you're going to get the horns. Like I promised.*

Amal went to a friend's house after school, and I'm hurrying home so I can grab a couple of things and then meet up with Faiz and Juniper at the VFW to prep for our next meeting and also get some homework done. I even invited Andrew, and Faiz didn't object. Of course, I haven't told Faiz about prom yet, either, because I feel weird about it. Guilty, even? It's going to come out eventually, but maybe it won't matter by then. Maybe I'm the only one who imagines it as a tiny betrayal.

I make the turn onto our quiet, leafy street and immediately panic when I see a silver BMW parked in our driveway. My mind flashes back to the car—the one that wasn't Andrew's—that swerved toward me last week. My anxiety spikes and my suddenly sweaty palms grip the wheel so tightly, I'm white-knuckled as I slow down. *Breathe*, I remind myself. I'm safe. I'm okay.

My mom is out front talking to a bald, broad-shouldered man. His back is turned to me, but I recognize him immediately from when I saw him at school with Andrew. My heart rate shoots up and I have to talk myself through easing my car next to the curb and parking.

As I nearly tumble out the door, my mom turns to watch me. Her face is drawn, her eyes crinkled at the corners, full of worry.

"Well, my wife and I have been meaning to stop by and welcome you to Bayberry. We've been remiss in letting this much time pass," Steve Hawley, Andrew's stepdad, says in an unnecessarily loud voice to my mother.

As I get closer, my mouth goes dry and I shove my hands into my pockets so no one can see them shaking. I see that my mom is holding a bottle of wine. I roll my eyes behind Mr. Hawley's back. Of course, he brought us alcohol as a housewarming gift. He probably never even considered that we were Muslim and didn't drink. Even if that weren't the case, what if someone in the house were sober? My mom is too polite to refuse and will give it to a neighbor or someone at work.

"Hi, beta, this is Mr. Hawley, the school board president. Mr. Hawley, this is my daughter Noor. She's a senior."

Mr. Hawley turns to me, shoulders square, huge politician smile plastered across his face. "Well, hello there. We haven't had the pleasure of being formally introduced." He's acting as if he's never seen me before, as if he never sped past me trying to scare the crap out of me. "I believe you know my son, Andrew."

Stepson, I want to correct. But I keep my mouth shut and nod a hesitant hello. He pulls his hand out of his pocket and reaches out, not to shake my hand, but to give me a campaign button that reads *I Believe in Steve*. His grinning face is plastered across the button, and it makes me want to gag. Not a chance in hell I'm going to wear it, which I'm sure he knows.

"Now, Noor," he says after I take the button, not that I had a choice. "I was telling your mother that Bayberry is a welcoming place. Friendliest town in Illinois. We all get along here because we share the same *values* and *beliefs*." His voice is syrupy sweet, but with a hidden edge. Classic Midwestern Nice passive aggression.

I nod, realizing I've been holding my breath, fumbling around for what to say, what to do. Figuring out if I can get him away from my mom, from us.

My mom forces a smile on her face. "True. Such a friendly place. Thank you so much for coming by."

"Now, I know you're city folks." Mr. Hawley keeps talking, ignoring my mother's attempts to end the visit. "And our little town might seem quiet, provincial even. But that's how we like it here. Everyone getting along, doing their part. If nobody rocks the boat, the boat stays steady even in choppy waters. You get my drift?" He chuckles at his pathetic metaphor.

"Yes, Mr. Hawley, I moved my family here for the peace and quiet," my mom says through her forced smile. Damn, she's throwing a bit of Midwestern Nice back at him. It's giving hints of my fierce Before Mom. I look at her, her jaw tight, the muscles in her face taut, and it makes me feel less scared despite Hawley's dog whistles and low-key threatening energy.

"Well, that is music to my ears, Mrs. Khan."

I cringe when he calls her that. Her last name is Razvi, not Khan. She didn't change it when she got married. The house is registered in her name. She's obviously listed as my parent on all my school forms. Maybe Mr. Hawley didn't bother to check any of that, but still, I hate him for assuming that women automatically take their husbands' names. It's not the 1950s. Besides, I don't believe he hasn't done his homework. He must know we're Muslim, that we don't drink. He knows Andrew and I are friends. When he makes deliberate eye contact with me, I'm certain he knows I saw him in his car at the fREADom Library. I bet it's part of this whole act, this charade happening right now on our driveway. He's a giant, unyielding threat.

"A pleasure to meet you both." He nods and then starts walking down the driveway. I move closer to my mom, and it's only then that I notice her hands shaking a little. Mr. Hawley pauses at his car door. "You know what happens to people who rock the boat, don't you?" he asks, letting the answer to that rhetorical question linger like a stench in the space between us: *they drown.* "Y'all have a good day now." He grins at us, his smile a thousand sharp teeth.

As he drives away, I turn to my mother. The worry in her eyes has been replaced by fury.

"Can you believe him!" I shake my head, letting myself breathe normally again.

"What I can't believe is your absolutely reckless disregard for rules or safety. This little fiasco that played out in our driveway? This is on you."

Her words slam into my chest, and I blink back tears.

She continues, "I told you to keep your head down. Graduate. You'll be out of this place soon enough. But no. You have to cause a ruckus. Suddenly decide that you're an activist."

I brush the back of my hand across my eyes, willing myself not to cry. "I don't get why you're mad at me! If anything, you should be supportive of me trying to fight this stupid book ban. It's not like I'm selling drugs; I'm reading books. Besides, you're the one who taught me to be an activist. You and Dad told us we have to stand up for what's right!"

The tension in my mom's jaw eases and her shoulders slump slightly. "Beta," she says with a sigh, her voice softening. "You're right. The ban is ridiculous. But sometimes you have to stand down so you don't get hurt. Live to fight another day."

I hear my mother's words but don't believe she's saying them.

"Silence is complicity, Mom. You literally held a sign with those words during a protest at Daley Plaza over illegal detention of refugees at the border. *You* took me to that protest."

My mom takes a deep breath, steps closer to me, almost as if she's going to reach out to hug me, but I take a small step back.

I lower my voice to almost a whisper. "I thought you'd be proud of me for speaking out. Or did that all change because Dad left us?"

"Beta," she says in a trembly voice. "Everything has been so rocky, so hard. You've been hurt so much. We need to make things easy for ourselves right now, get our footing back. There will always be policies to protest, but now is not the time. It's okay to let others carry the banner for now."

"But, Mom..."

"Enough," she says, her voice almost pleading. "That's all I have to say." My mom shakes her head a little before heading back inside the house, leaving me in the driveway alone in a chaotic swirl of broken feelings.

CHAPTER 37

"I still can't believe Andrew's dad—"

I shush Juniper so the other people in the library don't hear us, but we're at the first table by the entrance and the only students close by have earbuds in and hoodies over their heads. Faiz, Juniper, and I all snagged passes from sixth period to the library. It sucks without Ms. Clayton here, but it's still better than class. Different subs have been in the library since she was suspended.

Juniper begins again, and Faiz and I lean closer to her. "I still can't believe our friendly neighborhood fascist went to your house. It's creepy AF." My friends only know about Mr. Hawley's driveway threats; I haven't told anyone about the incident with the silver BMW. Technically I don't have real proof, not that my friends would need it, they'd believe me, but I don't want them to freak out. I don't want them to see how freaked out I still am by it, either. I rub away the goose bumps that pop up on my arms.

"It's been *two* days, and my mom is still so mad at me, she's barely speaking to me at all. I don't get it."

"I'm surprised you didn't break that bottle of wine over his head." Faiz grimaces as he speaks.

"Yeah, but for some reason, assaulting the school board president seems like it could've landed me in a bit of trouble." I pinch my fingers together and laugh a little.

"Shhhh." The woman who is subbing today turns in our direction to quiet us.

Juniper says her name is Mrs. Rogerson—a middle-aged woman with a strawberry-blond mom-bob and blindingly bright teeth. She's wearing dark blue slacks and a white blouse with a big bow at the neck. She's the president of the local chapter of Liberty Moms and Dads, so it's pretty gross that she's subbing in the library.

Juniper gives her a fake smile and then lowers her voice even more. "Ugh. Even her clothes look homophobic."

"She needs a hobby besides fascism," Faiz deadpans. I'm glad I'm not drinking anything because I would've spewed it all over the table. I quickly glance at Mrs. Rogerson, but she's now packing more books into boxes and her back is to us.

"So what did Andrew say about his stepdad?" Juniper asks.

I shrug. "He was super apologetic, but it's not like he can get him to stop."

"Has he even bothered to try? Like, maybe tell your parents when they're being racist and homophobic," Faiz scoffs.

I tap my pen against my cheek, not sure how to respond. I haven't pushed Andrew about it; we try to avoid talking about his stepdad.

"Faiz has a point," Juniper says. "Andrew needs to push back. I mean, he actually seems okay with pissing off his stepdad. Like, he must be apoplectic about you going to prom together."

Faiz's face falls. "Wait. What? You're going to prom? With Andrew?"

I bite my lip as I'm caught in another little lie of omission. I'm the worst. I'd been meaning to tell Faiz for the last few days but kept finding excuses not to. Since that night he showed me the VFW for the first time, he seems to be avoiding being alone with me. It made me question whether I imagined the flirty moments that passed between us, so I tried to brush off any more-than-friends feelings about him when they threatened to show themselves. It's not as if I could straight up ask him about it. How nightmarishly cringey. *Do you like me?* It could've wrecked everything about our little trio, and Faiz and Juniper are my only lifeline in this town.

Juniper looks incredulous. I told her about Andrew asking me to prom right after he did it, and then she asked Hanna and we've been texting about plans ever since. But I never told her to keep my prom date a secret from Faiz.

I look at Faiz, a smile painted on my face. His brow crinkles in confusion. "Yeah," I finally say. "But it's not a big deal. We were thinking we'd make it, like, a big friend group kind of thing. Juniper and Hanna are going."

Juniper turns to Faiz and gives him a reassuring nod.

"It would be cool if you did, too." I try not to sound as if I'm making a pity offer, but I'm pretty sure that's how it's coming off.

"With Andrew? And probably James and Richard?" He looks away. "Hard pass."

I honestly hadn't given much thought to the possibility of them joining us because it would be impossibly dense for Andrew to think that would be okay with me.

"What did you just say about us?" It's Richard. He and James walked into the library while we were talking. I'm not sure what all they heard, but they definitely caught their names and Faiz's tone.

I sit up straighter in my seat, turning to look at James and Richard, who are wearing nearly identical scowls on their faces.

"I was saying I'd rather have flaming-hot needles stuck under my fingernails than be in a car with you two."

Oh crap. I catch Juniper's eye as she reaches out to put a hand on Faiz's forearm.

"Like we'd want your curry stink in one of our cars anyway." Richard laughs, and James high-fives him.

"Fuck you," I spit.

Faiz pushes his chair back and stands, his hands curled in fists at his sides. Juniper pops up, too, sticking right next to Faiz. I'm on the other side of the table from them, and when I stand, I'm closest to James and Richard.

"Ooh, defending your little boyfriend?" James mocks. "I'm sure Andrew would find that interesting."

"Shut up, dickbag." Juniper's face is getting red and blotchy from her anger, and next to her, Faiz is visibly seething. I'm afraid this could get so much uglier.

"You could probably use some dicks in your life," Richard sneers.

Juniper's mouth drops, and before I can say or do anything, Faiz has taken three long strides around the table and is in Richard's face. They're nearly the same height, and they're practically nose-to-nose, both of them breathing hard, staring at each other as though they can't see or hear anything else in the room. There's a crackling, angry energy that spreads from Richard and Faiz in waves.

I grab Faiz's elbow and try to tug him away, but he's anchored in place. James snarls to Richard, "They're not worth it, dude."

My heart pounds in my ears. I've never seen a fight—not in real life, not in school—and even if they're the same height, Richard is a lot bulkier than Faiz. And no doubt Carter would blame Faiz for starting it. He could get suspended. I can't let that happen, not when this entire messed-up situation is my fault.

When neither Faiz nor Richard moves, hot whips of panic lash my body, and without thinking, I wedge my shoe between their legs and slam my foot on top of Richard's foot.

He yelps, "What the hell?" and turns to me, face red with rage.

"Sorry, didn't see your foot there," I stutter. My heart races, but at least Richard and Faiz aren't in each other's faces anymore.

Richard's yelling finally gets Mrs. Rogerson's attention, and she calls out, "What is going on?" as she hurries toward the five of us.

"Richard, James, what's the meaning of this?" she says. "I expect better from you boys. I'm sure your moms will be disappointed to learn that you're not using your inside voices in the library." She's clearly known them and their moms for a long time, which is maybe why she's talking to them as though they're in grade school.

"Sorry, Mrs. Rogerson," they say in unison.

She nods. She's still ignoring me and my friends, and I can't figure out if that's good or really bad.

"So what were you all discussing so animatedly?" she asks.

We all hem and haw a bit until James speaks up. "It's nothing,

Mrs. Rogerson. We were goofing around, talking about physics homework." James flashes her a wide smile. "Promise it won't happen again."

I don't see how she could possibly believe that BS, but then I see her shake her head and chuckle. Must be nice to have even your most blatant lies believed without question. "Oh, you boys. I assume Mr. Carter sent you here to help me out?"

Juniper, Faiz, and I exchange curious looks, trying to figure out what's happening.

Richard and James nod in response to Mrs. Rogerson's question. "Good. Here are my keys." She fishes them out of her pocket. "I need you to take the four boxes I've packed up and put them in my trunk and then bring the keys right back. No joyriding." She laughs. "It's the red Audi. You know the one, right?"

"Sure thing, Mrs. Rogerson," Richard says, taking the keys. Then he taps James on the chest, and they head toward the boxes.

James sneers at me as he passes by, bending down to whisper in my ear: "Have fun at prom." What's that supposed to mean? Because it's definitely not sincere.

Mrs. Rogerson turns to face us. She either didn't hear James whisper to me or doesn't care. She clearly knows them—I mean, she trusts them with her keys. I swear to God those two can get away with anything in this school.

"Now," Mrs. Rogerson says, "I assume there will be no further issues?"

I scrunch my eyebrows together. "We weren't the ones who started it," I balk.

Juniper gently nudges me and clears her throat. Faiz has already taken a seat, his head in his hands. "We're fine. There won't be any other problems, Mrs. Rogerson," Juniper chirps, and pulls me toward our table.

"You're the new girl, aren't you?" Mrs. Rogerson asks. "Noor, is it?"

I nod, my mouth going dry as sawdust. I wish everyone didn't know me.

"The one causing the fuss about the sensitive materials challenges?" Mrs. Rogerson says this almost sweetly, innocently, which I could almost buy if I didn't know that Liberty Moms and Dads were totally toxic.

I sit down and Juniper shakes her head at me, clearly telling me not to talk back. I think of my mom lecturing me about living to fight another day. But this fight is right here, right now.

"I didn't realize reading books was *causing a fuss.*"

Mrs. Rogerson smiles. "Of course not. We all support reading and are so proud of the district's high literacy scores. I'm talking about books that are under review for obscene content. I'm sure your parents would not want you reading inappropriate materials."

I cringe when she mentions my parents, but I can't stop myself from adding, "My parents believe that you can tell your own kids what to read, but you don't have the right to decide what other people's kids can read."

Her smile falters. She takes another breath and regains her happy mask.

"Are more books being ban—I mean challenged?" Juniper asks. When I give her a look, she shrugs. Since I'm not keeping quiet, I guess she decided not to bother, either. "Is that why you're packing some up?"

"Yes. As it turns out, Ms. Clayton neglected to remove all the books under review, so I am finishing the job, and I thought why not take a look-see in case there are any other books of concern."

I have no idea how she can say any of this with a straight face. How she can believe her own fascist BS. I guess that's what makes people like her dangerous—they believe their opinions are facts that they get to impose on everyone else.

"Now I think I'll get back to it. Lots to do!" she adds cheerily, and starts heading to the circulation desk.

My brain is about to explode. If all the parents in Liberty Moms and Dads are like her, there's no hope of persuading them otherwise. No way of showing them how hypocritical it is that they talk about the importance of freedom while practicing censorship. Musing on their hypocrisy reminds me of a news story I reposted on the Banned Camp socials about a group of kids in Florida who are also fighting against book bans. They have it even worse because their governor is a total fascist and he's leading the charge, but they've found some creative ways to push back. A few weeks ago, some of those kids showed up to their local school board meeting to actually challenge a book—it was to make a point, not to really ban it. But their point was razor sharp and I'm about to borrow it.

"Oh, Mrs. Rogerson," I call in a sweet voice. She turns back toward us. "Do you know if there's a Bible in the library?" Juniper kicks me under the table. Faiz has finally looked up, his eyes wide. They know exactly where I'm going with this and the steaming pile of crap I'm about to step into.

"I'm sure there is. I can help you find it, if you'd like. Now, there's no religion section on the shelves, but perhaps in reference. Do you need it for class?"

"No," I say. "I was wondering if the Bible has been challenged yet?"

"Excuse me?" Her voice dips.

"I mean, books can be challenged for sensitive material? Right? Like incest, prostitution, sexual content, violence?"

Mrs. Rogerson takes two steps back toward me and I can see the tightness in her jaw, the strain of her neck muscles. "I'm not sure what point you're trying to make, young lady, but—"

"My point is the Bible has all those things."

"Bonus points for bestiality!" Faiz speaks up.

"Aren't there references to cannibalism, too?" Juniper adds.

"So will you be removing the Bible as well, Mrs. Rogerson?" I ask, trying to make my voice as syrupy sweet as I can to piss her off.

Mrs. Rogerson's cheeks turn pink as she sucks in her breath. "I think Mr. Carter will want to finish this conversation with you. Noor, pack up your things and head to the front office. Now."

CHAPTER 38

My mom is waiting for me in the driveway. She's in a statue-like stance: arms folded in front of her chest, lips a tight line, shoulders drawn back. Ready. She's a petite woman. I'm nearly four inches taller than her, and she's lost weight since Dad left, so she's practically waifish, but right now, she looks like a mountain. *An immovable object.*

I park the car and take my time gathering my things while Amal hops out and kisses my mom on the cheek. I know Amal is trying to defuse the bomb that's about to go off, but it's probably no use. I knew Carter was going to call Mom. My conversation with him after the library incident barely lasted two minutes, and it was a repeat of all his previous lectures: civility, values, community, blah, blah, blah.

For a moment, sitting there in the quiet of my car, feeling the unbearable weight of my mom's stare, of her judgment, I think this must be a dream. No. A delusion. A nightmare. One that began when my dad walked out the door. How did our normal, regular, boring lives suddenly become this...this painful, disconnected chaos? The move. Banned books. Andrew. The threats. Faiz. The shocked look on Mrs. Rogerson's face. The harsh tone in Carter's voice. The racist taunts. When I glance down at my scar, I notice I've rubbed it so much it's red and raw.

I open the car door and step out. Amal shoots me a quick, pleading look before heading inside. The air around my mom crackles with her anger. The muscles in her face and neck are taut. Like she's ready to pounce. *An unstoppable force.*

"Mom, I know what you're—"

"Not. A. Word." My mom fixes me with a gaze so fierce, it pins me in place. Her voice is low, a grave whisper. "No need to try to explain your little...what would you call it? Stunt? Provocation? Your principal gleefully shared it all with me. I had to practically beg him not to suspend you."

"But I didn't—"

"When I said not a word, I meant not one single word. You will stand there, in silence, and listen." I shove my hands into my pockets and rock back and forth slightly on my heels as my mom continues. "You have no idea what you've done. The position you've put us in. I distinctly remember telling you—oh, maybe a thousand times—that you were going to leave everything alone. That is all. But no. You decided to tell the head of Liberty Moms and Dads that you want to ban the Bible? After causing some kind of scene in the library?"

"That's not what happened!"

My mom snaps her fingers like I'm a pet she's commanding and continues her tirade.

"Your petulant, foolish choices could blow up in our faces. Did you consider the consequences at all? You're going to graduate and leave; Amal is still going to be here. Did you think about that? About her?"

I know I should keep my mouth shut, but I can't hold back anymore. "I *am* thinking about her! I've been the only one thinking about Amal since Dad left. You weren't there when she was depressed, or did you forget that I'm the one who got her help? It's like when Dad left, you left, too. She's so afraid things could get worse—that's why she tries to act perfect all the time, plays the peacemaker. Amal—"

The front door opens and my wide-eyed sister steps halfway out—she must've been listening at the window. A pained look crosses her face. I hate having her get caught up in everything, that's why I don't always tell her about what I'm doing. But here she is in the thick of it anyway, thanks to me. My entire body shakes in anger at myself, at my mom, at this whole stupid town. I suddenly feel so tired. Like, in my bones tired. I lower my voice, my throat sore and scratchy. "It's like we lost both parents at the same time," I whisper to my mom.

She recoils like I've punched her, and I guess, in a way, I have. Mom opens her mouth but quickly snaps it shut, then shakes her head as if reconsidering. She takes a deep, pronounced breath and says, "I'm not perfect. Sometimes I think you forget that I'm a human being, too. That I make mistakes. That I've made mistakes I'll regret for a long, long time to come. And you're right it's unfair that the two of you have had to deal with the fallout of what's happened. Don't you think I know how painful it is that your father left us? All the ways in which I've failed?"

I stand perfectly still while my mom speaks, my lower lip trembling. I will myself not to cry, to keep quiet because it's been so long since my mom really talked to me.

She continues, her voice shaky. "Sometimes I think you want to take on the whole world by yourself. Protest isn't simply confrontation. It's planned, purposeful, ideally with community. The way you rush headfirst into conflict without thinking, beta, it's foolish.... It reminds me of your father when he was young. And that scares me."

I feel those words like a slap. Like she's tightened a vise around my body and I have to gasp for air. "You know," I begin with a shuddery breath, "sometimes I get why Dad left."

Amal gasps. I know my words were daggers. I see the hurt on my mom's face. Amal narrows her eyes at me, hurries over to our mom, who she wraps in a hug. I want to walk up to them, apologize, join them, feel the warmth of my mother's arms around me, which I haven't felt in so long. But looking at the two of them, I'm not sure if there's room for me.

CHAPTER 39

I go straight to my room and don't go back downstairs at all—not to get something to eat or drink, not when Amal knocks on the door and pleads with me to talk to Mom, not when half of my brain screams at me to apologize, to smooth things over because, honestly, I don't know how many fractures this family can take before we're irreparably broken, and right now, I'm the one holding the hammer.

Respecting elders in our culture is supposed to be encoded in our DNA. One time, when my nani was still alive and I'd gotten into a disagreement with my mom, I overheard Nani saying in Urdu that I was "becoming too American." I was in eighth grade, and the argument was about going to a concert with some friends. My mom said I could only go if there was a parent with us, and it made me so mad that she didn't trust me. Of course, my dad sided with my mom.

Maybe I am "too American," except to people like Hawley, who have a specific definition of American that my family and I do not fit into. The thing is I am Indian and Muslim and American. I am one hundred percent all those things, but it's not always easy to be all of them at the exact same time. It was easier to know, to feel all those parts of myself when I was home in Chicago, where I didn't stick out like I do here. Where I wasn't the only one in my class. Here it's just me. And...Faiz. Even more reason not to let them erase us.

I waste time in my room doomscrolling, pacing, watching random TikToks until I feel almost physically ill from staring at my screen. I sit on the edge of my bed, gazing out the window while the night descends, eating a granola bar I found in my backpack as hunger gnaws at me. I finally hear my mom shut her bedroom door. I listen quietly for her white noise machine to go on. It's only 9:30, but recently I think she's been taking a sleeping pill and heading to bed early. Some evenings I hear her and Amal chatting downstairs, but I never join. I always seem to take the air out of the room when I enter.

I don't care if I'll get grounded for life. I need to get out of here. I don't care that maybe I'm totally irrational right now. *Foolish*, that's what she said. I peek outside my room. Light seeps from underneath the bottom of Amal's bedroom door. I tiptoe out of my room in my stocking feet. It's a newer house, so the wood doesn't creak as it did in our old house in Chicago. When I near the stairs, I hear the low sounds of dialogue from the TV, the downstairs bathed in a soft bluish glow. Dammit. I was hoping Amal was in her room. I pad down the steps and slip my shoes on by the door, grabbing my keys from the wicker basket I usually toss them in.

"Are you seriously not going to say a word to me? It's not like you're invisible." Amal turns her head from her perch on the sofa.

"I didn't want to bother you."

"Right."

"I'm going for a drive. Wanna clear my head."

"I'm not covering for you." Amal glares at me.

I sigh. "I didn't mean for you to see that fight with Mom. Are you okay? I'm sorry if it was triggering."

"God. Stop treating me like a baby. I don't need you to protect me."

"Actually, you do. Someone has to look out for you after . . . well, everything."

"You are never going to let that go, are you? Yes, I was depressed. You can say the word in front of me. But I'm taking my meds, seeing a therapist, paying attention to myself. I'm not made of porcelain, okay? And I'm sick of you using me as an excuse to be a jerk to everyone."

My jaw clenches, but I don't respond to her accusation. "Shhhh," I finally say. "You'll wake up Mom."

Amal shakes her head. "Whatever."

I squeeze my eyes shut. I don't have the energy to fight my sister and my mom. "You're right. I'm like a helicopter sister and I can be annoying, but—"

"Nope. Stop right there. Repeat the first part, again, a little bit louder this time."

I groan. "I said you're right, okay? Happy?"

"I wish I'd recorded that."

The thing about Amal is that she wants to forgive. Her forgiveness is not hard to earn. She's got the biggest heart of anyone in the family. "You won't say anything to Mom?"

"You'll stop looking at me like I'm going to break?"

"I'll try."

She sighs. "Okay. You owe me, though."

"Ugh. Fine." I roll my eyes and open the door. "I'll be back in a bit."

"Is your drive going to end up at Andrew's?"

I shrug. Guilty as charged. But I didn't even know I was going there until I texted him five minutes ago.

"Did you tell him about his friends being dicks to you?"

"Not yet," I mumble.

"As the smart younger sister, I'm going to say that maybe you should. Maybe it's screwed up that his friends treat you this way and he doesn't do anything about it. Isn't that what you'd say to me?"

Amal is right, again, but a wave of defensiveness rips through me. "I get it, but it's not like he's responsible for them."

"But if they're supposedly friends, shouldn't he call them out?"

Yes, he should, I think but don't say out loud. Instead I find myself explaining. "He's been friends with them forever, and James was there for him when his dad died and—"

"You never give Mom this many chances, you know," Amal interrupts. "Or anyone else, for that matter."

I suck in my breath. Amal is often quiet, keeping herself on the periphery of things, and I forget that it also means she sees everything from a bit of a distance. She's right—it's probably not the best idea to go over there, where there's a chance of running into his stepdad. I don't know how to explain it to Amal, but I feel like I want to drive and I feel like I want Andrew next to me. He's fun and he doesn't challenge me or ask me to think too much or pummel me with questions I don't want to worry about. He makes it easy to be in the moment. "I'll talk to him," I say, but it's a whispered half promise.

"Cool," Amal says. She's so trusting of me. I don't think I deserve it. "His friends are definitely problematic, but he's kinda hot and has a lap pool, so he's got that going for him," she adds, giving us a chance to laugh as I head out the door.

Stepping into the spring night, I take a long, slow breath, inhaling the light scent of blooming flowers and hay dried in sunshine that still lingers on the fresh air, but beneath all that there's a faint whiff of sickly sweet rot from the dead, lingering leaves of winter.

CHAPTER 40

Andrew's waiting for me on the edge of his front lawn next to a little statue of a jockey. I thought lawn ornaments in the shape of humans died out in, like, the 1950s, but apparently not. At least the jockey is white and not Black, at least it isn't one of those cigar store Indians that I'd seen once in Wisconsin Dells. I grimace at my depressingly low bar for "at least they're not overtly racist."

I pull up. Andrew hops into the car and I speed off. The windows of his house might've been dark, but I didn't want to risk being anywhere near his stepdad.

"Hey," I whisper, putting his house in my rearview.

"Hey," he says. "Are we going anywhere in particular?"

I shake my head. "Not sure."

He waits a beat, then says, "I heard about the library."

"Oh?" I grip my hands tighter around the steering wheel. "And what did James say?"

"Actually, I heard about it from Steve."

"Your stepdad?" I ask, confused about his role in the rumor mill.

"Mrs. Rogerson and her husband are besties with Steve and my mom."

Of course they are. Racists stick together.

Andrew explains, "She came by before dinner, and I saw her talking to my mom and Steve on the porch."

"And?"

"I dunno." Andrew shrugs. "Steve told me you confronted Mrs. Rogerson when she was subbing, and she was upset about it. And that Richard and Faiz got into it with each other."

"So she totally glossed over the racist and homophobic BS your friends were spewing."

From the corner of my eye, I see Andrew clench his jaw. He rubs his forehead. "Sometimes they don't think and say stupid shit and—"

I am suddenly overwhelmed with the desire to not talk. To be completely still and silent. I'm afraid I'll hear him say something unforgivable, and I just don't have the energy. I can't fight anymore tonight. I'm wrung out and I'm giving myself permission to thrive in denial.

"You know what? I think I want to drive, not talk."

Andrew nods and leans back, settling into the passenger seat. One thing I appreciate about him—he lets me have the silence. It's confusing, but I don't want to be alone. I also don't want to talk or even think about banned books, or threatening notes, or my dad, or my mom. So I drive past the darkened houses and the cornfields and I wind up at the road that dead-ends in the woods near the pond that Andrew brought me to weeks ago, a hundred years ago, yesterday. I don't know. Time feels so wonky right now—as if it's squished and stretched at the same time.

I park the car on the side of the road and look at Andrew, who smiles at me. A storm of emotions swirls inside me, even as I smile back.

We get out and walk around to the front of the car, leaning against the warm hood, our bodies close. I surprise myself by resting my head on his shoulder. I probably shouldn't be doing this. I'm not sure why I let myself be so comfortable around Andrew when his stepdad has it out for me. When his besties are mostly assholes. Maybe I'm in denial because being in this space right now feels so easy—he doesn't ask me to explain myself or to confront anything; he *wants* to be around me. I don't have to think all that much to be around him. I pause for a second, realizing that maybe this is what my mom meant when she talked about the path of least resistance. God, maybe I'm more like her than I realize.

We stand there in silence for a few minutes. In the dark quiet, the buzz and chirp of insects fills the air, and the only other things I can hear are Andrew's deep and steady breaths and the soft thud of my heart in my chest. I tilt my eyes upward at the velvet blanket of stars in the sky. Weird how a million tiny pinpricks of dying light can be so beautiful.

"When my dad first told me about how starlight traveled to get to us, I thought it was kind of sad that some of the stars that gave us that light were already dead and also sad that light pollution always got in the way of me seeing them," I say after some time passes.

Andrew chuckles. "My dad had a telescope set up on our roof so we could check out stars and planets. Don't have to worry much about light pollution out here."

"That's so cool."

"You know, I think we still have that old telescope—haven't used it in a while." Andrew pauses and clears his throat. "Maybe we could bring it out here sometime?"

"I'd love that," I breathe.

"After he died, that's where I'd imagine my dad when I talked to him." Andrew points to the sky. "On a planet, on a star, on some wild adventure."

I squeeze his hand and lift my head from Andrew's shoulder. "One thing I'll say for this town, you guys got stars."

"What do you mean, 'you guys'? Last I checked, you live here. You're one of us."

I scoff. "Yeah, right. Sure. Everyone's been real welcoming like."

Andrew turns to look at me. The space between us stills, and all I can hear is the soft intake of his breath. "Happy to increase the warmth of that welcome anytime." His eyes shine as he tilts his head closer to mine and brushes a stray hair from my cheek, tucking it behind my ear. Goose bumps pop up all over my arms, and I shiver for a second, wanting to move closer to him but also so uncertain of what I'm doing, if I should even be doing it.

I snort. Snort! Oh my God. Then I blurt, "Do those cheesy lines actually work on any girls?"

"You tell me," he whispers in my ear, his breath hot and feathery against my skin. He smells like lemons and mint, like he's just showered.

I let out a small sigh. I want to freeze this moment in time, let everything else fade away while I melt into the quiet now. A minute of no responsibilities, no burdens, no ghost of an absent father, no wondering about the right thing to do, no decision to make except to be exquisitely still while the earth spins and the light of impossibly distant stars burns in the shifting skies above us.

I tilt my head up. Andrew gently runs a knuckle across my jawline. I allow my eyes to close, soaking in this perfect, tiny moment.

Andrew's phone buzzes. He ignores it. A few seconds later, it buzzes again. And again. He groans and reaches for it. "Shit," he whispers. "It's Steve. I need to get home."

Dammit. This is why I can't believe in the promise of nice things. Something or someone is always there to tell me I don't deserve them.

———————

The floodlight in Andrew's driveway is on, sending a harsh fluorescent beam into the night. It's visible as soon as I turn onto his street. Andrew sits next to me, his hands clenched in fists on his lap. We didn't utter a word the whole ride back, but unlike on our quiet drive earlier tonight, it's not a companionable silence. It's fraught and weighted.

I pull up to the driveway, and Mr. Hawley is standing by the curb, his arms crossed in front of his chest. Andrew turns to me for a second and mouths a sorry, but his stepdad raps at the window. What the hell is wrong with this guy?

Andrew steps out of my car, his head down, shoulders slumped as if he's admitting he's guilty of something he hasn't even been accused of yet. I know I should drive away, but I don't. It doesn't feel right to leave Andrew alone. Without thinking, I swing open the car door and step out onto wobbly legs.

"What's this, Andrew? You said you were heading out with James, but it looks like you lied. I made my feelings very clear about who you're allowed to spend time with."

Wait. What the hell? Andrew is forbidden from seeing me? Since when? Hawley is literally pointing at me—guess he's given up the pretense of being nice.

"Ms. Khan," Mr. Hawley spits as I stagger up next to Andrew, "you have a lot of nerve showing up here after the ruckus you caused in the library today."

A queasiness grows inside me. I reach for words but I can't find any.

He continues, "What exactly are you pulling my son into here?"

I wait for Andrew to say something, to correct him, to say he's his *stepson* the same way he's always correcting everyone else. But there's a pinched grimace on Andrew's face, and he doesn't say a word.

"We...we were just hanging out," I stutter, and nudge Andrew. He glances up and gives a halfhearted nod in agreement. The space between us has grown ice cold, and I'm so confused by his change of personality and being caught out of sorts that I can't make sense of my fragmented thoughts. "I...didn't...wasn't causing a ruckus." I feel the fearful uncertainty in my voice, in my body.

Mr. Hawley lets out a sarcastic chuckle. "When you suggest the Bible is obscene...around here, we call that a problem. A big one. One you don't want to find yourself in."

His words have the force to shove me backward. I stuff my shaking hands into my pockets. Andrew squeezes his eyes shut as if he knows what's coming and doesn't want to see it.

Hawley keeps talking. "The fact of the matter is, I wasn't surprised to see you causing problems, but denigrating the Bible?" His forehead furrows. "Your mother assured me that you were making efforts to fit in. Around here, good God-fearing people don't take well to their faith being ridiculed."

I hesitate, then finally force air up from my diaphragm so I can speak. "I wasn't...I was just trying to say—"

"Oh, I know what point you were trying to make. Mrs. Rogerson filled me in on everything. She was in tears recollecting your nastiness."

I can't imagine the one-sided version of the story she shared. "But I wasn't questioning anyone's faith. Muslims actually believe in Jesus." My voice grows shakier. "I was saying the First Amendment—"

Hawley cuts me off again. "Ms. Khan, I assure you I wholeheartedly support the First Amendment and most definitely the Second, for that matter, especially when there are unwanted people trespassing on your property." He narrows his eyes at me.

I gasp, willing my knees not to buckle. My mouth grows dry, and cold sweat trickles down the back of my neck. I have no idea if Mr. Hawley owns guns, if he has a gun on him right now. All I know is that this is the second time he's threatened me, and Andrew...he's still standing here, totally silent. I struggle to calm my breath, to figure out what to do. Andrew glances at his stepdad, an inscrutable look on his face.

All my instincts scream at me to run, but I'm also frozen in place. Tears well in my eyes as my voice falters. "We just want to read what we want."

Mr. Hawley sneers. "Your woke values are neither wanted nor needed around here, young lady."

Andrew clears his throat and finally, *finally* speaks up. He cups my elbow and whispers, "I think you should head home."

Andrew's face is blank and ashen as he directs me back to my car without even glancing at me. I want to shake him and ask what's going on, but I'm afraid of the answer. I'm scared Hawley's 2A threat was real. I wonder if he bullies his family, if he threatens them, too. If that's why Andrew's retreated into his shell.

My whole body trembles, but I grit my teeth and yank my arm away from Andrew's grasp, walking the rest of the way to the driver's side by myself.

"Freedom isn't a woke value." I stumble over my words, trying to force something like courage into my faltering voice, but I can tell I'm barely speaking above a whisper. "Last time I checked, it was an American one." I open the car door and fall inside. My hands are shaking so bad I can barely pull the keys out of my pocket. I can feel Hawley's eyes shooting daggers at me through the car windows, but I don't look up at him or Andrew. I manage to shove the keys in the ignition and drive off, my heart pounding in my chest. I glance in my rearview mirror as I pull away. Mr. Hawley grips Andrew's shoulder, glowering down at him, shaking a finger furiously in his face.

CHAPTER 41

I wake up to zero text messages from Andrew. When I returned home last night, I'd texted him, *You okay?* but he never responded. Not sure what I was expecting, and now I'm angry at myself for texting him in the first place. He didn't even try to stand up for me. God, how have I been so clueless?

I brace myself for a volcano of leftover parental rage from the fight with my mom last night as I force my feet down the stairs for breakfast. Not ready to face my mom, the other kids at school, or any part of this day. In fact, this morning feels like the perfect time to run away from my life. Maybe Mom was right. Like father, like daughter. Except Dad had the means to leave his life behind and I don't.

But Mom is not in the kitchen. I expected to see her perched at the counter, her hands wrapped around her usual cup of chai, steamy tendrils scented of cardamom, fennel, and loose-leaf Assam rising from her cup and swirling around the room. Amal, who is alone at the counter, pouring too much maple syrup on her waffle, looks up at me.

"Did Mom leave already?" I ask, surprised that she'd want to miss out on yelling at me, at grounding me for the rest of my life. But I think this might be worse. She's too mad to even be under the same roof, apparently.

Amal nods, giving me a half-cocked, pitying smile. "She printed that out for you." She points to a sheet of paper, a corner of it pinned under the fruit bowl.

"Do I even want to know?"

"Seriously doubt it." Amal cuts into her waffle and takes a huge bite, watching me.

I grab the paper—a printout from the *Gazette*'s website. It's an op-ed written by Andrew's stepdad. Posted at 5:00 a.m. Fascists never sleep, I guess. I scan the headline and groan, the piece of paper like a lead weight in my hand.

BAYBERRY GAZETTE

Protecting Our Values by Steve Hawley

Here in Bayberry, we hold this truth to be self-evident: It is the duty of every parent, of every good citizen of our town, to protect our children from the insidious agenda of the radical left. That's been my mission as your school board president, and it is one I promise to take to Springfield should I be elected.

The fight for freedom is at our doorstep and it is more important than ever that we parents become warriors for liberty. Over the last few years, I've watched with increasing concern the radicalization of our schools, influenced by critical race theory, that seeks to lay the blame for all society's ills at the feet of some of our children. This leftist philosophy, this union-backed indoctrination, has seeped into our curriculum and onto our school library shelves, including texts supporting perverse ideologies and lifestyles, books that intend to make some children feel bad for alleged inequities in the United States, books containing graphic depictions of sexuality, stories encouraging our youth to question their gender.

Earlier this year, alongside two other members of the board and in cooperation with a committee of concerned parents, we enacted a full review of the curriculum that put decision-making powers where they belong— with parents. We worked to create a streamlined process for parents to raise questions about inappropriate texts, and thanks to the cooperation of many in our community, we have identified five hundred titles that promoted, among other things, grooming, gay lifestyles, racial guilt, animosity toward law enforcement, and a rewriting of this nation's history. After some setbacks in the state, many districts are only now putting such measures into place and are using Bayberry as a model. We are on the right track, but we cannot give an inch nor sway from our moral duty.

Unfortunately, in direct challenge to school board regulations, a small group of radicalized young people, led by eighteen-year-old Noor Khan, have formed the so-called Bulldog Banned Camp, which is reading profligate materials with the express purpose to indoctrinate our children to their cause in an almost cultlike fashion. This group is now meeting at an off-campus location—the old VFW hall on Jefferson Street—in attempts to circumvent the school's policy. I am told that children as young as thirteen years old are attending without parental knowledge or supervision.

Now more than ever, we must stand together. We will not allow this woke progressivism gone wild to invade our town, our schools, our homes.

I'm urging all patriots to join me tonight at the gazebo in the town square at 7:00 p.m. We will rally for our parental rights, for our values, for nothing short of the survival of America by unifying, educating, and uplifting true American voices.

CHAPTER 42

Aside from a halfhearted wave as he walked down the hall with James this morning, Andrew's avoided me. He hasn't come by my locker or responded to my text from last night and was not in the cafeteria at lunch.

"He's a dick," Juniper says as we walk to seventh period. "A whole bag of dicks."

Faiz, who we picked up along the way, doesn't say a word. He doesn't have to say *I told you so*; it's written all over his face. To his credit, he doesn't look smug, more like he feels bad for me.

"Blow him off," Juniper says. "He doesn't deserve the pleasure of your sparkling company."

"Never did," Faiz whispers, so quietly I almost don't hear him.

I smile. "I wish Andrew would say *something*. Anything."

Juniper pulls a face. "Yeah, like, 'Sorry my stepdad is a fascist and threatened you. Sorry I didn't say or do anything about it.'"

Faiz adds, "Seconded." He pauses. "Don't you think he should've been the one checking up on you, not the other way around?"

Faiz putting things so starkly makes me realize how foolish I've been. How I failed to read the situation that was unfolding right in front of my face because I trusted the wrong person. Maybe because I didn't want to believe what I was seeing. But now I can't pretend that nothing happened. I deserve answers, not the silent treatment.

———————

After school I hurry to grab my books, shoving things into my backpack while keeping my eyes peeled for any sign of Andrew at his locker. Maybe I'm being rash, but I don't care. It's not as if I have anything to lose. I want answers even if I have to corner him. Yesterday, standing by my car under that blanket of stars, we had a moment. I know we did. I know he felt it, too. Now Andrew's done a one-eighty overnight. I want to know why.

My heart clenches as if someone is reaching into my chest to squeeze it. I don't want to consider the possibility that I've been played. That trusting Andrew was stupid. That trusting anyone leaves you open to hurt. After my dad left, I swore I wouldn't let anyone hurt me again. Yet here I am, my chest cracked open, inviting everyone to tear out pieces of my heart.

I hear James's cruel laugh behind me and am sure that Andrew is with him. I turn to see him heading to his locker, half hidden by Richard and James, who are apparently his human shields. "See you tonight," Richard says with a nod, before they part ways. James catches my eye, a smug sneer on his face. God. I can't believe how full of himself he is. I hustle toward Andrew so when he shuts his locker, I'm standing right there. His eyes practically pop out of his head in surprise, and he jerks back a little, startled.

"Oh...uh...hey...Noor." He reaches for my name as if I'm a stranger he met once a long time ago. "I didn't see you there."

"That's what it seemed like, all day." I try not to sound petulant, but I'm pretty sure I'm failing at that.

He furrows his brow in confusion. "What do you mean?"

"I mean you've been ignoring me."

He opens his mouth to speak, but at first no words come out. He's standing there, slack-jawed. Then he mutters, "Oh, um, yeah... sorry. I was distracted. Had to make up a calculus quiz."

I laugh as if he's told the most hilarious joke, and in a way he has, only it's on me. "You couldn't be bothered to text me last night after your stepdad went psycho, then blew me off all day because you were deeply focused on passing a *quiz*?" Even saying that last part out loud feels comical. It's practically insulting that he can't come up with a halfway believable lie.

I pause, waiting for him to respond, but he stares at me, a sheepish look on his face. He leans into his locker.

I keep going because there's empty air between us and I might as well fill it and make this situation even more awkward. "Was that what you and James were laughing about a minute ago? The high-stakes quiz that made you forget I exist?" He's gone statue still while I rise on my toes and rock back on my heels, in constant nervous motion. "Are you seriously going to pretend last night didn't happen? That we..." I suck in a breath, I can't go there, so I redirect.

"That your stepdad didn't threaten me and print a bunch of lies about me in his own paper?"

Andrew briefly closes his eyes and then opens them and finally looks at me directly. "Look, Noor, I'm sorry. I swear. But I think *threaten* is a bit of a reach. My stepdad is on some kind of crusade. That's why he was so pissed...."

I scowl at his use of the word *crusade*.

"You know he's running for office. Politicians all have platforms. We have to stay on message. Focus on my family," Andrew finishes meekly, as if he's reading from a script Hawley gave him.

A tidal wave of rage builds in my body. I take a deep, raspy breath and lean into Andrew's face, my voice a low growl. "His message is hate. Words matter. It's not okay for him to say anything to get elected. People get hurt that way. And you're fine going along with it? What the hell is wrong with you?"

Andrew glances nervously around the hall. I watch as he turns and makes eye contact with James and Richard, who are gawking at us. "You don't understand. I don't know how things are in your family, but with Steve...he runs the house with a tight fist. My mom doesn't work. Steve bought our house, my car. He doesn't have to, but he's gonna pay my college tuition. He said—"

I explode. "So he bought you off. He pays for you and that makes his homophobia okay? Excuses his racism? Jesus, grow a spine!"

Heads turn toward us as I raise my voice, and I do not care. I vibrate with fury. "What I don't get is why you helped me with the fREADom Libraries and came to Banned Camp. I thought you were in this, with me," I say, a dull realization washing over me.

Andrew's voice is low and flat when he responds to my plea. "I know. I...I'm sorry if I gave you the wrong idea. I wish..." His voice trails off when he locks eyes with me.

The wrong idea. Holding hands and eating ice cream at a hidden pond, gazing out at the stars, asking me to prom. All of it was signals crossed? I'm too stunned to respond.

"The truth is, I've never been political," he continues, like it's a confession instead of a crappy excuse. "We're so close to graduation and, well...you were new, and, uh...and interesting, and I wanted to be nice—"

"Nice? Are you freaking kidding me?" My face burns. "You asked me to prom. Was that you being *nice*, too?"

Andrew bites his lower lip. He looks as if he's been sucker-punched. Good. A moment of silence passes and then another, the awkwardness building with all the words left unspoken. But I'm not letting him off the hook, so I stand here, expectantly, waiting for him to say what I know he doesn't want to say out loud.

"Noor. I...I am so sorry, but I..." He trails off, trying to find his footing, trying to figure out what he can possibly say to get out of this mess.

"Go ahead. Say it," I push. I hear James and Richard snickering. And out of the corner of my eye, I see Juniper and Hanna walking fast down the hall toward us.

"It's that, um, before you moved here, I went to Sadie Hawkins with Leigh—she's best friends with James's girlfriend, Sloane—and that night, I sort of promised I'd take her to prom. We're going in a big group, James, Sloane, Richard and his date, a couple other people. James already rented the limo. I'd sort of forgotten about it until James reminded me."

My face flushes and my heart twists. "You forgot?"

He nods.

"You. Forgot," I repeat, in disbelief that this is the excuse he's going with instead of telling me the truth. "It slipped your mind that you'd already asked someone else to the biggest social event of high school? God, did James and Richard put you up to this? Your stepdad?"

My eyes start to sting, and I will back tears. He doesn't deserve them. Andrew turns to me, his gaze lingering on my face, his watery hazel eyes searching. "Noor," he whispers, and reaches out a hand to take mine, but I step back. "I can't—I'm sorry. For everything."

Juniper and Hanna approach, and I gesture with my hand, and they stop a few steps away from us. The tightness in my chest loosens knowing they have my back, but I want to finish this on my own.

"I don't accept your shitty apology, Andrew." My voice cracks as I speak. "I guess you also have other plans for tonight that you forgot about?" Not sure why I'm asking about the study date we'd planned, not like I would go anyway. But I want to force him to own all his lies. If nothing else, I want to make him feel as uncomfortable as he's made me.

He rubs the toe of his shoe back and forth across the carpet. "I got in trouble after last night, so I'm grounded."

"God. You're pathetic! I literally just heard Richard say he'd see you tonight."

From behind me I hear James scoff. Andrew's face falls, and when he finally speaks, I have to lean in a little to hear him. "We're going to the rally in the town square. I promised Steve I'd help him out. He wants our family to be there together in a united front."

"What!" Juniper yells. She and Hanna step up and flank me, a little wall of protection. "You are seriously damaged, dude."

I'm about to say something else when Juniper gently tugs on my elbow, and I understand that there is nothing else worth saying. My friends and I begin to walk away from Andrew. My throat tight, my eyes burning. From the blurry edge of my vision, I see James and Richard slouching against some lockers, laughing.

"Noor," Andrew calls. "Noor, I—"

"Leave it alone, man. She's not worth it," James says. Andrew doesn't respond. I guess he agrees.

Juniper pauses and glares at James. "You're such a tiny manbaby."

James gives Richard a knowing look, and they both start chuckling. Then he straightens, stepping closer to Juniper and Hanna, his gaze dropping to their hands as they interlace their fingers, drawing closer to each other. "Nothing tiny about me; happy to show you both, if you'd like."

"You're disgusting," Hanna says. Juniper's eyes narrow and she balls her free hand into a fist. For a moment, my brain short-circuits and my pulse thunders in my ears. Then I grab Hanna and Juniper and drag them away before things escalate.

When we're safely in the main hall, I watch as Juniper places her hand on the small of Hanna's back and kisses her on the cheek as we walk toward the doors. It's such a sweet contrast to the toxic mess that just went down, and I realize I'm blinking back tears.

I demanded answers from Andrew and I got them. The problem with relentlessly pursuing the truth like my dad pushed me to do is that sometimes you learn things you never wanted to know.

CHAPTER 43

"Are you sure you should still do this?" Amal asks as we sit in my car parked near the VFW.

There's a soft purple haze as the evening descends into night, almost like a promise of something romantic in the air. But I know better. Gorgeous sunsets and starry nights might help you tell stories to yourself, but those are sugar-spun fairy tales, not reality.

"It's going to be fine." I turn to look at Amal, hoping she'll buy the lie. There's worry in her eyes, so I try to mask my own concerns with a smile. But the truth is I *am* worried, at least that's what my unsettled gut is telling me.

She looks at me, the straight line of her lips slowly turning up at the corners. "Primal scream?"

I nod and count down from three, and we scream at the top of our lungs. I can almost feel a few pounds of weight lifting off my shoulders.

It's been two days since Andrew canceled on prom and since

Hawley's well-attended, borderline Nazi rally was the talk of the town. Since then, the Bulldog Banned Camp account has been assaulted by trolls. Forty-eight hours of nonstop vitriol—most of it directed at me. It's been nasty slurs and threats from Islamophobes and racists and people with "patriot" and "Liberty Moms and Dads" and "1776 project" in their bios. Over the years, I've grown a thick skin, but it's not armor. I still bruise and feel the sting of every burn.

Amal still looks a little worried as she attempts a reassuring smile.

"Seriously, it's okay. You know trolls are all bark and no bite," I say as we get out of the car and walk toward the VFW. "Besides, so much crap has gone down"—I push open the door—"it'll probably only be us and our friends."

We step inside. The hall looks bright and cheery, there's the smell of coffee in the room, and music is thumping from a wireless speaker. Faiz told me he and Juniper were heading over early to set up, so I expected to see them here. What I didn't expect are the thirty or so other people who are milling around, moving chairs, chatting and laughing. It's not just students, either.

Juniper grins when she sees me and skips over to give me a tight hug.

"Who are all these people?"

"Have you not checked socials in the last hour or two?"

"Been avoiding it—didn't think the hate was going to get any more creative or interesting."

Amal waves to Cecily, who is setting up refreshments at a table under the windows at the back of the room, alongside a few adults, including one who looks vaguely familiar. "That's my English teacher," Amal says, astonishment in her voice. She squeezes my hand and then hurries over to help them.

"There are teachers here?"

"Yup."

"And parents?"

"Yup. And more are coming." Juniper beams.

"Did you set all this up? Your group chats must be on fire," I joke.

"It wasn't me. Or Faiz." Juniper loops her arm through mine. "It was Ms. Clayton. She saw the Liberty Moms and Dads going after you, so she and a few other reasonable, non-fashy adults dragged them in the comments for attacking kids, and I guess she called people and told them about tonight, and someone put up a post on the parents association Facebook page and told everyone to show up here in solidarity."

I turn to her, my mouth agape, as we step toward the center of the room, waving and saying hi to people. "Middle-aged parent power activate," I say. A huge smile spreads across my face. I see Ms. Clayton moving chairs into rows and wave at her. She nods at me and raises a fist.

———————

By the time we're ready to start, the room is packed—there aren't nearly enough chairs. The owner of Common Grounds came with coffee and pastries. Ms. Clayton and her friend Sylvia, the owner of Idle Hour, brought more books to donate to Banned Camp. There are other faculty members and a bunch of parents with their kids. I keep rubbing my eyes to see if I'm awake and not caught in a hazy dream.

I take a deep breath and walk up to the podium. It's weird, because in the past, we'd been sitting or standing in circles, and this feels so much more, I dunno, formal? Official? My hands shake a little. I pull out my phone and place it on the podium so I can see my notes. I study the room for a moment, and people smile back, a warmth growing inside me. There have been so many ugly surprises since we moved here, so I'm extra grateful for this moment, at being surprised in a good way. In a restore-your-faith-in-humanity way. God knows I need it.

I grip the sides of the podium. There's no microphone, so I remind myself to project. As I scan the room, I'm struck by my mom's absence. I hadn't even thought about her until I looked at this sea of parents who came here to support their kids. Now her face feels conspicuously absent. No surprise. She wasn't even upset when I told her Amal and I were coming here. She shook her head, totally resigned. I think, maybe, her disinterest hurts most of all. I might not always get along with her, but I didn't want my mom to give up on me, not after my dad already did.

I shake away the disappointment because right here, right now, there are people who care, and their presence inspires me to feel genuinely hopeful about what I've been doing.

"Hi. My name is Noor, and I read banned books," I say.

Chuckles spread across the room, along with some whoops and "Hi, Noors."

I look down at my screen and continue. "You may have heard some people call me an *outsider* who has messed-up, perverse values." The crowd boos at that. "I want to start by saying thank you for showing up tonight." My voice falters as I gaze out at receptive smiles and kind faces. When we moved here, I was convinced I didn't need or want any friends, but by cracking myself open a tiny bit and letting them in, I found my people.

"We got you, Noor!" someone yells out, and there's a chorus of yeses in agreement and scattered applause, and I feel this incredible lightness in my chest. I stare at the worn grain of the podium, knowing that if I make eye contact with my sister, I'll choke up. I can sense waves of pride emanating off her all the way from the back of the room, where she's standing, leaning against a windowsill.

I glance up with an embarrassed smile. "Ugh. Stop, you guys, or you're going to make me have feelings." A few awws spread across the room.

"When I found out five hundred books had been pulled from the library, my friends and I decided to start reading bits of these supposedly obscene books out loud during lunch." I pause to gesture toward Faiz and Juniper, who is holding hands with Hanna. Faiz gazes at me, smiling warmly, his eyes twinkling, sending me silent encouragement. "Honestly, I didn't think anyone would even be interested in listening. Then the administration shut us down because it turned out some of you *did* want to listen." More cheers and shouts of "Hell, yeah" and "Yes, we did" from the group.

"So we moved here, and honestly, we didn't plan any of this and didn't really know what we were doing. Still kinda don't. But we know book bans are wrong. Mr. Hawley and Mr. Carter and a bunch of parents and elected officials claim that they aren't banning books, only advocating for parent rights. They say they aren't being racist or homophobic or transphobic even though pretty much all the books they've banned are by Black, brown, and queer authors or supposedly have *content* that they don't want us to read, like we don't live in this world where men accused of sexual assault get to be Supreme Court justices."

"That part!" someone yells out to murmurs of agreement.

There's something about knowing everyone in this group is with me, the feeling of support—of belonging—that I haven't felt in such a long time. "Liberty Moms and Dads say they're trying to protect students. But we don't need protection from ideas in books, from stories of love or rebellion or the brutal realities of American history. We need protection from fascism and censorship and bigotry."

"Ban guns, not books!" another person yells, to a burst of applause.

I look up from the podium, my face beaming. I've gone through all the bullet points on my phone and, fueled by this buoyant feeling inside of me, ad-libbed a whole lot. The room bursts into applause and cheers. I spy Amal at the back of the room applauding wildly, a giant smile on her face. I gesture to Faiz, who makes his way to the podium with a book in hand. It's *Fahrenheit 451*, by Ray Bradbury. It's considered a classic and is taught in tenth-grade English, but this year two parents objected, so it was removed. Ray Bradbury was a white guy, and his book doesn't have a queer storyline or even any sex, if I remember it right. But it's a story about censorship and ignorance and books being burned. It's a book that tells you to open your eyes. It might have been written a long time ago, but it feels like now. Faiz said there was a paragraph from it he wanted to read out loud.

When he gets to the podium, I reach up to give him a quick hug.

I'm proud of him for stepping up to read. He wraps his arms around me and it feels so good that I let myself melt into him for a second before I let go and smile at him. Faiz smells like that sandalwood soap, and for the first time, it doesn't make me flinch.

I turn back to the podium to introduce him, but when I gaze up and out toward the back of the room, I see headlights beam through the window that Amal is standing near. The window looks onto the street, so it's not a surprise to see cars passing, but these lights don't move. They seem too close, too bright. In that flood of light, I swear I see a figure rushing toward the window, their arm raised as if they're about to throw something.

I scream.

Then my vision fragments, and the room moves in juddery slow motion, all sounds muffled.

Glass shatters.

Shouts fill the room.

Fire.

Smoke.

All I can think is that Amal was standing by that window. Everyone is on their feet, screaming, scattering, panicky, rushing to the exit.

Faiz grabs my hand and pulls me toward the door. But I yank it free. I need to get to Amal. I don't see her anymore. Where is my sister?

A couple of parents run toward a fire extinguisher. Some of the teachers are yelling at people to stay calm, not to run. "Slow is smooth, smooth is fast," I hear someone shout above the noise of the crowd.

I push against people to get to the back. Ms. Clayton is there and she yells, "Move back," as she aims the extinguisher at the curtains that have caught fire and douses them with foam. There's a teacher a few feet away with a second extinguisher putting out another fire. How did the fire leap like that?

"Amal!" I scream into chaos.

"She's here!" Faiz yells from one side of the now overturned refreshment table.

Oh no. No. No. Amal is on the floor, face down. I hurry over to her. I can't tell if I'm yelling her name or saying any words at all. Panic floods me. My heart stops.

I hold my breath as Faiz helps me turn her over.

"Noor?" Amal coughs. A trickle of blood runs down the side of her face.

I let out a breath and pull her close to me. "I'm here. I got you."

"We need to get her outside," Faiz says.

I nod and we lift her up, and she groans. I can't tell how badly hurt she is. Letting her lean on us for support, we start walking toward the door. Everyone is pretty much outside, and it looks as if the fires have been put out, but the room is still smoky and the sharp smell of alcohol and chemicals swirls around us.

Amal stumbles as we near the door, her knees giving out a little. I try to steady her, but Faiz lifts her into his arms and walks out. Before I join them, I hear one of the adults say, "I think it was a Molotov cocktail."

I step out into the crowd of confused and crying students and adults. Faiz has Amal propped up against a tree; her face is bloody and smudged with soot. I kneel next to her, gingerly taking her hand in mine, whispering that it's going to be okay as I press my cuff to her bloody temple.

The sounds of sirens fill the night.

CHAPTER 44

The local hospital isn't anything like the sprawling medical center campus at the University of Chicago. Here, it's only one big building with a side entrance for the ER. It's small, only four or five triage rooms. There must be fifty people crowded in here, so it's fair to say the doctors and nurses—there were only four when we got here—were a little overwhelmed until they called in help. Fortunately, no one was too badly hurt. Amal bore the brunt of the injuries.

She'd been standing right by the window that the Molotov cocktail had been thrown through, and that's why she was bleeding from the side of her head—cuts from the broken glass. Luckily, she'd fallen away from the window as the fire spread to the curtains. But Amal has been coughing since we pulled her out of the lodge.

Looking at her, I keep thinking about how it could've been so much worse. How badly she could've been hurt. How she might've been hit in the head with that glass milk bottle that had been filled with alcohol, stuffed with a flaming rag, and thrown through the VFW window. God, she could've caught on fire. Every inch of me is aware that she is here, in the hospital, because of me. And, I hate myself for it.

I stand next to the side of her bed, numb, watching everything as if I'm outside my body. I hold her left hand as the ER doc finishes a small row of neat stitches by her right temple. Faiz, Juniper, Hanna, and a couple adults who were at the meeting are standing around by the foot of the bed, and others keep checking in.

"I'm okay," Amal whispers to me, squeezing my hand. She shouldn't be the one reassuring me.

"Excuse me. Excuse me." I hear the frantic high-pitched tone of my mom's voice. People move aside to let her in. The doctor asks everyone to move to the waiting room as she steps toward my mom with her hand outstretched.

My mom walks right by her and rushes to Amal's bed on the opposite side of me. "Oh my God, beta. I can't believe this. What happened?" My mom's panicky eyes look over Amal's entire body, presumably scanning for injuries she didn't immediately notice. Her gaze comes to rest on my sister's face and the stitches and small red scratches that constellate her forehead and cheeks. There are bandages on Amal's right arm, too, and my mom gingerly rests her hand on my sister's fingers. She still hasn't looked at me.

"It's okay, Mom. I'm all right." Amal coughs a little and shivers. "Just a little cold." My mom yanks off the scarf from around her neck and covers my sister with it.

The doctor, a woman with chestnut-brown hair pulled back into a loose ponytail, steps up closer to my mom. "I'm Dr. Kent," she says.

My mom looks at her blankly for a moment, then shakes her

head as if realizing where she is. She reaches out with a trembling hand to greet the doctor.

"Amal is right. She's going to be fine," Dr. Kent says. "Luckily, none of her cuts were too deep. Some contusions but no broken bones. I'm going to have you come back in seven days so I can check on those stitches. The nurse will give you care instructions before you leave. Happy to answer any questions." She smiles, and small wrinkles appear at the corner of her eyes. She has a kind, reassuring face, but I don't think it's enough to calm down my mom.

My mom's normally tidy bun has pieces of hair sticking out, and her mascara is smeared. She must've been terrified when the hospital called her. It should be me in the hospital bed, not my sister. I wonder if that's what my mom thinks, too—that the wrong kid got hurt. Guilt is a parasite consuming my insides. I deserve it.

"Thank you, Doctor. I'll call with any questions," my mom says gravely, and then turns back to Amal.

Dr. Kent gives me a soft smile before heading out.

"It's only four stitches, Mom. It's fine," Amal says as my mom strokes her hair. "You should see the other guy." My sister attempts a grin, then winces in pain.

"You are my brave, sweet girl," my mom says to my sister. Then her eyes flash to me. "How could you let this happen?"

I didn't think about how my actions could hurt my family. I should've kept my big mouth shut. I should've listened to you. AITA: yes.

"I...I...I'm sorry. I shouldn't have taken Amal with me," I whisper as I trace a finger around my burn scar over and over.

"You're right on that account, at least. Your behavior is unacceptable."

"Hold up. I wanted to go. It's not like she forced me, Mom. Please don't blame Noor for this." Amal gestures to her injuries, then looks at me. "She was attacked, too."

My mom gazes at my sister, eyes brimming with tears.

"I'm going to go check to see if everyone else is okay," I say, and leave my sister's bedside after giving her hand another squeeze. I don't think my mom wants to deal with me right now. Besides, I can't take another minute of her deep disappointment in me—it's resting on my chest like a boulder.

The crowd in the ER has started to thin out. When I step into the waiting room, Faiz looks up, then nudges Juniper and Hanna, who walk over to me.

"Is Amal okay?" Faiz asks.

"She will be." I turn to Faiz and put my hand on his forearm. "Thank you...for everything. I couldn't have carried her out of there by myself."

"It's nothing. Glad she's going to be okay. Glad everyone is okay." Faiz locks eyes with me and gives me a soft, assuring smile reminding me that he's here. He's not leaving.

"How are *you*?" Hanna asks me. "Your mom looked..."

"Like she wanted to murder me? Yup. I don't blame her, though. This whole mess is my fault."

Juniper's jaw drops. "You are not the person who threw a literal bomb. A Molotov cocktail is a bomb, right? Anyway, you are not the person who threw an incendiary device into the meeting. I forbid you from feeling guilty, okay?"

I sigh, my shoulders slump a little, and Juniper hugs me. "Listen, are you hungry? Can we get you some highly salty snacks from the vending machine?"

"Junk food is an excellent stress reducer," Hanna says, and we all laugh a little.

My phone dings, and I fish it out of my back pocket. My body goes rigid when I see the name: *Andrew*. I show the text to my friends: *I heard what happened. Are you okay?*

"Is he serious? He has zero right to talk to you." Juniper twists her lips in disgust.

Faiz looks at me, then turns away, subtly shaking his head.

A low-voltage rage builds under my skin as I stare at Andrew's name, his words.

"He didn't even have the balls to show up here in person," Juniper says.

"Probably because he knows you'd rip his throat out." Hanna slips her hand into Juniper's and squeezes. "And I'd help."

My phone dings again.

Andrew: I'm sorry. Let me know if there's anything I can do.

I am frozen with anger, my hand wrapped so tightly around the phone it feels as if I could crush it.

"I told you he was a selfish asshole," Faiz says.

Juniper looks at him. "Not now, dude."

Faiz opens his mouth and then shuts it, walking away as he clenches and unclenches his fists.

I move to text something back, but I'm not sure what to say. I feel so hollow right now, like my insides have been scooped out and dumped on the floor.

Juniper moves closer to me. "You don't have to respond. You don't owe him anything."

I look at my friend, her kind eyes filled with sympathy. "I know," I say. "You're right."

I rub my thumbs over my phone screen as if I can erase his name. As if I can erase him and everything that's happened. I messed up everything, gave away my trust to people who didn't deserve it, misjudged so many situations, put my sister in danger. I want to scream. Smash my phone into the ground. Punch the wall. I want to curl up on my bed and let myself bawl my eyes out. I want my mom to walk out of the ER doors and wrap me in a giant hug and say, *Everything is going to be okay*, like when I was a little kid and fell off my bike and came in the door crying with bloody knees. I want my dad to have loved me enough to still be here.

I want all the things I've lost forever.

CHAPTER 45

Mom has doubled down on giving me the silent treatment. I get it. I'm still pissed at myself, too. Everything is the Worst, and it's mostly my fault.

It's Sunday, and normally I'd still be sleeping or slouched on the couch watching ridiculous early 2000s TV with Amal. But I couldn't sleep at all last night, and after tossing and turning, I forced myself out of bed at 6:00 a.m., went out to grab a giant latte and donuts, and then holed up in my room to doomscroll and break the do-not-eat-in-your-bed rule my parents have drilled into us since we were toddlers. There's a tentative knock on my bedroom door.

"Come in."

Amal hesitantly opens the door. I suck in my breath when I see her face. A small bandage covers the row of stitches near her temple. The nurse in the ER told us to keep the stitches dry for twenty-four hours and then gave Amal an instruction sheet for follow-up care, how to clean the area and make sure it doesn't get infected.

There's also an array of tiny cuts across her neck and face. I can tell she's applied a thin layer of Vaseline over them from the sheen on her skin. The doctor said the cuts would hopefully not leave scars, but keeping the wound moist could assure that. Amal and I both flinched when she said the word *moist*. Worst word ever. Blech.

"Do you think it's going to leave a mark?" She points to her bandage. I gently run a finger across my own scar, thinking of the lessons I'm reminded of when I touch it, of the memories it holds, of the pain.

"I don't know," I answer honestly. "All wounds heal differently, but you're beautiful no matter what."

Amal smiles and shuts the door. She plops down on the bed, eyeing the detritus of my café run. "I assume you brought something for me?" She raises an eyebrow. "Also, you know, crumbs in the bed—"

"Lead to ants on your head." I repeat the rhyme my parents used on us.

I shove the waxy paper bag toward her, and she peeks in and claps gleefully before removing a chocolate glazed donut with sprinkles.

"Thank you," she says, taking a huge bite, making sure any crumbs fall into a napkin.

"It's the least I could do after my event ended up with you getting stitches."

"Shut up." Amal looks at me and holds my gaze, suddenly serious. "I mean it. It's not your fault and I don't blame you."

I sigh. "I know. I know, but—"

"No *buts* allowed!" Amal giggles at the phrase—a habit she began in nursery school and that's stuck with her ever since.

"Seriously, though. Don't lock yourself in here all emo-like, feeling sorry for yourself."

"Ouch. Harsh."

"The truth hurts sometimes." She winks at me and takes another giant bite of the donut.

"Fine. I'm—"

"If you say 'I'm sorry' one more time, I will smash this donut in your face."

"Asphyxiation by donut?" I shrug. "There are worse ways to go."

"On second thought, nah. Don't want to waste a good donut!"

"Ha ha ha. You're hilarious, little sister."

Amal smirks. "Is your phone on fire?" She nods at my hand. My fingers are wrapped in a death grip around the screen.

I sigh. "Yeah. Some people last night posted video of the aftermath, and it's gone viral along with the tag #Bayberryblowup."

Amal grimaces. "Annoying, but the hashtag kinda works."

I roll my eyes and grab my third donut of the day from the sack. Pistachio buttermilk. Truly a gift from the pastry gods. "Unfortunately, it's also caught the eye of the local news—WSPL. The producer has DM'd me, like, five times asking to interview me this afternoon."

"Oh my God. You're going to be famous?"

"It's local news from Springfield, not MSNBC. They're interviewing a bunch of people at the gazebo in the town square, apparently, and they wanted to get my perspective."

Amal sits up straight. "You're going to do it, right? You have to do it."

"What? No. No way. Not after what happened last night." I

point to her stitches. "It could've been a lot worse if some of the adults hadn't put out the fire."

Amal shakes her head. "I'm not asking you to stop fighting these bans. More like the opposite. You have to do the interview *because* of what happened last night. You can't let the book banners and haters win. Or scare us into quitting."

I nod, letting Amal's words sink in. "Mom will kill me, though," I joke.

"She's going to anyway. And she can't murder you twice."

"Never underestimate an angry desi mom's ability to vanquish you, then raise you from the dead only to kill you again because once wasn't enough." Both of us laugh. "But you're right. I should do the interview. I'm scared, but I know—"

"A lot of people got your back." Amal smiles.

There's a moment of silence as we both pause to think about things.

"Mom loves you. She's just afraid," Amal says gently.

"I wish it wasn't always tough love, though. And I'm tired of her fear running our lives."

"I get it, but Dad didn't just leave *us*." Amal gestures to me, then herself. "He left her, too. Sometimes you act like what he did was Mom's fault. It's like you don't see how much Dad going away destroyed her." Amal's voice is soft, but her words explode like a grenade in my chest.

CHAPTER 46

I tried to convince Amal to stay home. I was afraid my interview would be triggering, but she refused to listen. She also worked the guilt angle: *I literally bled for the cause. You have to take me.* She already has the makings of a fabulously tyrannical desi auntie. I'm so proud.

When we drive up to the town square, there are two news vans and a crowd of people. My stomach flips. I hadn't planned on having an IRL audience—or at least I was too distracted being nervous about being on camera to let it register that, of course, where there's a camera crew, there would be gapers.

I park the car and sit there for a moment. Amal waits patiently for a few breaths before her sarcasm kicks in. "Are we going to get out of the car, maybe, or..."

"Remind me why I'm doing this again?"

A knock on my window startles me. Juniper sticks her face right up to it, making a goofy grin. Hanna and Faiz stand behind her.

"You called in the home team. Nice," Amal says, and hops out of the car.

The five of us meander over to the white gazebo. The day is overcast and a bit chilly, and I'm wearing my I READ BANNED BOOKS T-shirt with a zip-up hoodie and jeans. The reporter is in the gazebo with Mr. Hawley. *Dammit.* Literally the last person I want to see. I can't hear what he's saying, but he seems to be making jokes. He's vile. He's wearing a suit with a big VOTE FOR VALUES, VOTE FOR HAWLEY button on his lapel, and on the other lapel, he has an American flag pin, and right below that a pin that says 2A. I physically reel back, stumbling, thinking of his threatening words in his driveway. My body begins to vibrate with nerves, with fear. I force myself to take a few deep breaths.

For a second I wonder if I could expose him, tell the interviewer about his visit to our driveway and his threats and his car swerving to scare me. But I stop that line of thought. It would be my word against his, and it doesn't take much imagination to know who would be believed.

I walk over to a woman holding a clipboard and wearing a shirt with the news station logo on it. "Excuse me?" She eyes me up and down. I glance at my scuffed boots and make a face at my sartorial choices. It sucks that you have to dress as if you walked out of an old men's clothing catalog to be taken seriously. "I'm Noor Khan," I say, trying to make my voice sound steady and confident but pretty sure I'm failing spectacularly. "A producer contacted me to be interviewed?"

"Oh!" The woman's face brightens. "Yeah, that's me, Emily Coates." She extends a hand, and when I offer mine, she shakes it firmly. "Thanks so much for showing up." She tilts her head toward the reporter. "Karen is going to interview the school board president, and then you'll be up. Did you get my email with what we're looking for?"

"Umm, yeah. She's going to talk to me for, like, a minute or two about what happened at the VFW last night—"

"Yes, and about your lead role in opposing the book bans in the district. Why you decided to do it. What your plans are, that kind of thing."

"Oh, well, I'm not really—"

She interrupts me with a smile still on her face. "Sorry, we're about to roll tape. Can you hang back for a second? We'll come get you when we're ready."

She doesn't wait for me to answer. I pull a face and take a couple steps backward. A hand on my shoulder startles me.

"Whoa. You are jumpy today," Juniper says.

"Yeah, well..." I trail off when I notice the homemade T-shirts that she, Faiz, Hanna, and my sister have slipped on over their clothes. They're plain white tees with BULLDOG BANNED CAMP printed in blue and yellow puffy ink on the front. I smile broadly.

"You like?" Juniper asks.

I nod. "I love. When did you make these?"

"Right after you texted about the interview. Juniper and I are both so crafty we already had the supplies." Hanna kisses Juniper on the cheek and then takes her hand. Juniper blushes a little, which is adorable and makes me grin so hard.

There's shushing around us, and we quiet down and step closer to the gazebo to listen to the stream of lies Hawley is vomiting. I'm jumpy watching him, that fake politician smile plastered on his face giving way to a bogus look of concern. My breath goes shallow and my brain is screaming at me to run. I pinch my scar between two fingers. It smarts, but it brings me back to now. I'm here with my friends, in public. He can't hurt me. I'm safe. I take a breath and listen in even though his voice feels like nails on a chalkboard.

> **Karen McManus:** I'm here today in Bayberry, Illinois. A small town like so many others in central Illinois that prides itself on its high school football team, Fourth of July parade, and neighborliness. But that friendliness has been tested over the past few weeks as locals have found themselves at odds with one another over recent book bans enacted by the school district, a conflict that erupted in violence last night. I'm joined by Steve Hawley, school board president, who is also running unopposed in the special election to replace Republican state representative Joe Meese, who resigned under a cloud of multiple malfeasance accusations. Mr. Hawley, thanks for joining us.
>
> **Hawley:** Of course, happy to be here and always happy to show off Bayberry's beautiful town square, Karen. But I must say I take issue with your characterization of recent goings-on.
>
> **McManus:** How so?
>
> **Hawley:** Well, we are certainly not at odds with one another. And we are absolutely not banning books. A few months ago the school board instituted a more streamlined procedure for parents to raise questions

and concerns over objectionable material in our schools. It's every parent's right to choose what their child reads, after all.

McManus: But is it the right of one parent to decide what other people's children read? Isn't that what these challenges allow? There are five hundred books in the high school library that students no longer have access to.

Hawley: Those books are merely under review for pedagogical value and to ensure the texts are free from pornography or obscenity. Who could have a problem with that?

McManus: Opponents, including those supporting a statewide anti–book banning proposal, say that the challenged books are being wrongly slapped with those labels. They point out that ninety percent of the books being pulled are written by marginalized authors. Is that correct?

Hawley: I would have to check my records. I'm not aware of the statistics. But I resent the accusation of bias. Final decisions will be based on rigorous criteria.

McManus: And what is that criteria?

Hawley: We have a committee of parents and school board members who will read and review each challenged book for literary merit and curricular alignment before determining if the book is to be permanently deshelved.

McManus: How many books have completed that review process?

Hawley: I'd have to check on that.

McManus: According to the district office, it's zero.

Hawley: Like I said, I'd have to check on that.

McManus: What do you make of the bombing at the VFW hall last night when a group of students and adults were meeting as part of the Bulldog Banned Camp?

Hawley: Well, I think calling it a bombing is quite an exaggeration. Some might even consider that phrasing left-wing fear mongering.

McManus: The police report indicated that a Molotov cocktail was thrown through a window, so how would you characterize that?

Hawley: I'll leave that up to our excellent police department. I'm certain they will find the vandal.

McManus: You've called opponents to the book challenges "un-American," "outsiders," "perverts," "groomers," and even named a student in a recent op-ed you published in a paper you own. Would you say those were incendiary comments?

Hawley: I'd say they were the truth. Those are all the questions I have time for. Thank you.

My friends and I look at each other, stunned by Hawley abruptly ending the interview. I guess we're so used to the local newspaper doing his bidding that we thought this interview would be all soft-ball questions. I guess that's what Hawley was expecting, too.

"Damn," Faiz says as Hawley storms off to loud applause from some onlookers. "Look at Springfield News going hardcore on his ass. That was awesome."

"Did you see how red his face was getting?" Amal laughs. "I thought it was going to pop off the top of his neck."

From the corner of my eye, I see the producer jogging toward me. "You're up. You ready?" she asks as she nears me.

No. I want to say no. I'm not ready. I haven't been ready for a single thing that has happened to me since I moved to this town. Watching that interview, I'm afraid the reporter will press me the same way she did Hawley. What if I don't have good answers? My heart thumps against my chest like a trapped butterfly. My palms are clammy, and there's a faint taste of sawdust in my mouth.

"I guess," I mumble.

The producer nods and I follow her to the gazebo. "We'll be running a special segment on Bayberry on tonight's evening news. We're so glad you could do this." She gives me a wide smile as she introduces me to the reporter. "Karen, this is Noor Khan. Noor, Karen McManus."

Karen has the most blindingly white, perfect teeth I've ever seen. She takes my hand in both of hers, one of those strange handshake sandwiches that indicate sincerity. "Noor, I can't tell you how happy I am that you decided to tell your side of the story. You're so brave, standing up to the establishment. Very Gen Z for Change, am I right?" Her voice has this singsong quality to it and sounds different from the polished, crisp tones she uses when she's speaking on camera.

"Oh, um...yeah," I sputter. I'm suddenly incapable of complete sentences, and I need to get over that, fast.

"It's okay to be nervous." Karen steps closer to me and whispers conspiratorially, "I am nervous every time I go on camera. Use that energy. Channel it."

I nod. This is one of those adults-giving-advice moments that never make sense. Use the nerves in the pit of my stomach? How? The only thing I can imagine channeling my nervous energy into right now is puke. *Dammit.* Now I'm thinking of vomit. *Excellent.* Oh God, this is going to be one of those times when you keep telling yourself not to think of something but then that's literally the only thing you *can* think about. Why do human brains work this way? I can't mention puke on air. Or vomit on the reporter's shiny high heels. Bury me now.

The producer positions me, says something about the microphone that I don't exactly hear, and then says, "You good to go?"

"I'm not going to puke," I mumble, then realize with horror that I've said it out loud.

"Excuse me?"

"Uh, nothing. I'm all set." I give her two thumbs. *So smooth, Noor. So cool.*

Karen smiles at me. "Speak from the heart. You're going to be great."

Don't vomit on her shoes. Don't vomit on her shoes. I look out at the crowd and see my friends and sister in their homemade T-shirts. Amal smiles and nods and mouths, "You got this."

McManus: Now I'm joined by Bayberry High School
      senior Noor Khan, one of the student leaders who have
      been fighting the book challenges. Tell me, Noor, what

was your motivation to step outside of the school and begin reading the books that had been pulled from your library's shelves?

Noor: [*pause*] I . . . uh . . . I really like books.

Oh my God. Did I just say that on camera? Duh. Of course I like books. I hope they edit that out. Please, let them edit that out. Calm down, Noor.

McManus: [*chuckles*] Well, I should say so considering you launched a movement in your town opposing the book ban. Can you tell us how this Bulldog Banned Camp that you're a part of got started? Clever play on words, by the way.

I look out at the crowd and see Amal, that bandage on her face and the scattered cuts and scrapes clearly visible even at this distance. I clench my fists at my sides and take a huge breath, remembering why I'm doing this.

Noor: Banning books is un-American. Aren't we supposed to be all about freedom? When I saw the books being pulled from our school and that most of the authors were queer or authors of color, I knew I couldn't stand by silently. Silence is complicity. So that's why my friends and I decided to do something about it.

McManus: Your efforts included building fREADom Libraries around town, correct? In addition to holding gatherings where students read from the challenged books out loud.

Noor: An anonymous donor gave us copies of some of the banned books, and the fREADom Libraries were one way to share them with the community. People should read these books for themselves. It's obvious that some parents aren't. I mean, I saw one parent say Amanda Gorman's inauguration poem was filled with hate messages. Like, what? No one who's actually read "The Hill We Climb" could ever think that.

McManus: Now tell us what happened last night at the VFW during your group's gathering.

Noor: Well, it was our biggest crowd yet—students and parents, too. We were getting started, then someone threw a Molotov cocktail through the window. I thought it was a bomb. I thought...I thought...I was so afraid of what was happening. There was so much smoke. Fire. I couldn't hear anything but people screaming.

McManus: The perpetrators are still at large, and the police think it was unrelated to the book challenges but a random act of vandalism.

Noor: Vandalism? That's what they're saying? No. No way. They wanted to burn the place down. That's not random. Not after Mr. Haw—um—not after some people attacked us in the press, calling us subversive. Saying we support groomers and perverts. The attack wasn't random, it was...terrorism.

McManus: Do you think Mr. Hawley's words or the statements from Liberty Moms and Dads were incitements to violence?

Noor: Words incite violence all the time. It's one of the things you can learn when you can check a book out from the library. In history, we learned how Nazis used the power of words to spread hate and violence.

McManus: Are you comparing the school board members to Nazis?

Noor: No, I'm not saying that.... What I mean is that Nazis banned books, too. Then they burned them. They preached hate against the Jewish people, against queer people, disabled people, Roma. They used words to target them as outsiders. People who weren't Aryan, who didn't hold supposedly good Aryan values.

Hate speech, banning books, those were the first steps the Nazis took before murdering millions and millions of people. And why would you ever want to imitate a single thing the Nazis did? I guess what I'm saying is that no one who's banned books has ever, ever turned out to be one of the good guys.

CHAPTER 47

My interview clip actually turned out okay. The news station cut out my embarrassing *I like books* opener and kept what I said about Nazis and book banning being anti-American. I'm sure that will win me a lot of friends. They edited the piece so it seems like I'm responding to Mr. Hawley and added interviews from Sylvia, the bookstore owner, who was amazing. Unfortunately, they also spoke with Mrs. Rogerson and another parent from Liberty Moms and Dads, who made it seem as if trans adults were forcing kids to transition. They kept using the word *groomer* about queer authors, even when the reporter challenged them. They claimed books that even mentioned police brutality were promoting anarchy and were against democracy. It was gross to watch.

Juniper, Hanna, and Faiz came over to hang out, scarf pizza, watch the news, and simultaneously doomscroll the Banned Camp socials, which are currently full of trolls attacking us. No surprise.

"They call themselves Liberty Moms and Dads?" Juniper scoffs after the segment ends. "More like Bigotry Moms and Dads. They are totally unhinged."

"Yeah, but the thing is, by comparison they made Mr. Hawley sound reasonable," Faiz notes.

"He's gaslighting the whole town, though!" I slump back on the sofa. "He says they aren't banning books, but that's literally what they're doing!"

"The Party told you to reject the evidence of your eyes and ears. It was their final, most essential command." I turn to the soft voice behind me and see my mom. But it takes me a second to register that it's really her. Her voice. Here. With us. With me.

"It's from *Nineteen Eighty-Four*, by George Orwell," she says as we all turn to look at her. "Fascism wins when we let others manipulate the truth. When we accommodate their lies. When we are silent."

Amal leaps up from her spot on the sofa and sidles up to my mom, who runs a hand down the back of Amal's long, silky hair like she always used to do when we were little. "Noor was interviewed on the news and she was amazing," my sister says.

"Of course she was." My mom looks at me and holds my gaze. We haven't made up exactly. But her being here, looking at me with something like pride in her eyes, makes my heart feel like bursting.

CHAPTER 48

I wake with a start to muffled sounds. For a second, I'm sure someone is in the room with me. Glancing around in the dark, my eyes grasp for something to focus on. But there's no one here. I let out a breath and grab my water bottle to take a swig as my heartbeat slows down.

Then I hear it again. Shouts from somewhere outside my window. I sit straight up in bed, straining to hear over the rush of blood in my ears. At first it was weird sleeping in this house—in the unnatural quiet. No rumbling from the nearby tracks. Virtually no cars passing in the middle of the night. Barely ever any ambulances. The usual quiet I've grown used to makes the *unusual* noises and loud voices outside feel all the more wrong.

I force myself from my comfy bed, my heart thundering, glancing at the clock as I do: 3:00 a.m. I don't want to look outside. But I have to look. There are more sounds: laughter, a door slamming shut, a car screeching away. I suck in my breath and peek around my worn dark green velvet curtains.

My jaw drops. The blood in my veins freezes.

Our fREADom Library is on fire.

I scream, but I only realize I'm screaming when my mom comes rushing into my room, followed by my sister.

I've pulled the curtains completely aside so my mom can see the front yard as soon as she steps into my room. "My God! Call 911," she yells at us, and then turns and starts to run out of my room. "Do it! Now!"

I'm stuck, like I stepped in wet concrete. The whole scene unfolding around me has the viscous quality of a dream state. My brain is commanding me to move, but my body won't listen. Each step feels as if I'm pushing my body through liquid amber, trying to escape before I'm trapped.

"Stay inside!" Mom yells up the stairs at us before she slams the front door. The noise jerks me back into the moment. I stumble to my nightstand, fumble with my phone, but manage to dial 911 to get help. Amal stares bleary-eyed and scared as I give the operator the information.

"Come on." I grab her hand. "Mom needs help."

We hurl ourselves down the stairs and wrench the door open. I stop short on the front porch. The entire library is ablaze. The fire reaches so high and burns so hot, I can feel my cheeks heat up even from this distance. My mom has the garden hose on and aimed at the fire, but I can't tell if it's helping. She turns her head and sees us, sweat pouring down her face, the belt of her blue fluffy robe dragging on the ground behind her. "Stay back," she orders.

Moments later, the sounds of a fire truck race down the street, along with an ambulance and two police cars. Neighbors begin to pour out of their homes, everyone in a state of middle-of-the-night confusion and disarray.

A fireman gently pulls the garden hose from my mother's hands and gestures to her to stand by me and my sister at a safe distance. I glance at Amal, and her face is ashen, her mouth wide open at the scene unfolding in front of us. She hugs my mom when she joins us. Together, we watch the fire department get to work, quickly putting out the flames.

An EMT approaches and asks my mom to step to the ambulance so they can make sure she's okay. "I'm absolutely fine," my mom says, trying to defy the EMT's request. But she coughs a couple times, and when Amal takes her hand and pulls her down from the porch, she doesn't resist. They walk over to the ambulance, and I follow behind them, stopping in the middle of the driveway to watch the firefighters wrapping things up. A neighbor shuffles over in their slippers to check on my mom. The more drama-thirsty neighbors gossip in the middle of the street.

"Excuse me, miss?" A youngish police officer comes up to me. I notice a couple other officers speaking to my mom and sister. "Your mother says you're the first one who noticed the fire?"

"Yeah," I say, clearing the sleep from my voice. "I heard a noise— some noises outside. When I looked out, I saw the fire."

The cop nods. He has dark blond hair that peeks out from under his cap. His sharp blue eyes study my face. "Could you describe the noises?"

"Oh... um... it was, like, laughing, a car door slamming. Maybe someone yelled something?"

"Okay. What about the vehicle? Were you able to catch a glimpse of it?"

I shake my head, feeling as if I'm failing a test. "No. Sorry. By the time I got to the window the car had already driven away. I think I heard a guy's voice."

"Good. Okay. That's helpful. Did you hear any glass breaking?"

I give him a quizzical look. He gestures to our garage, behind me. I turn and inhale sharply. A couple of the garage door windows have been broken, but even worse, the words *Go home!* and *terrorist* are spray-painted in red. There's a large swastika, wet paint dripping like blood against the white door. I was so focused on the fire in front of me, I didn't notice the garage behind me. That's how trolls win—they keep your gaze fixed on one horrible act and they commit others while you're distracted.

"Oh my God," I whisper, my voice, my entire body trembling, terrified of the hate I've brought to our door.

The cop clears his throat. "Any idea who could've done this? Any enemies?"

I scoff. "Enemies? Well, the school board president hates me. Plus all the book-banning parents he's riled up against me."

Another man walks up while I'm speaking. He's older, looks more in charge. The younger cop nods at him and says, "Captain, I was asking Miss Khan here about who she thought might be behind this."

The captain is not in uniform—he's wearing jeans and a Bayberry Athletic Boosters sweatshirt. The Athletic Boosters are mostly alumni and football and basketball parents. His sweatshirt makes me think of the woman who made that racist comment to Kamal.

It reminds me of Mrs. Rogerson, who's a booster, too. He brings his hands to his hips, and that's when my eyes fall on the gun holstered there. I flinch. Stumble backward a little.

The captain signals for his deputy to go speak to my mom and sister, who are still sitting in the ambulance. I begin to move in that direction, too, closer to my mom.

"Hang on a moment, Miss Khan."

"I ... uh ... wanted to check on my mom," I stammer.

"She's being taken care of. I heard part of your conversation. You've built quite a reputation for yourself in the short time you've been a resident here," the captain says, and rubs the stubble on his jawline. I grimace at how his words echo Hawley's like a giant racist mind meld.

"I wouldn't know since I don't listen to rumors about myself," I say. Dread sinks into my tired bones. "I'm not sure what that has to do with this hate crime." I point to my garage and the burnt remains of the library.

"What makes you believe this qualifies as a hate crime, Miss Khan? This state has quite specific parameters around that designation."

I look around and laugh. "Are you serious? The word *terrorist* is right there. Plus that giant red swastika."

"But you're Muslim, not Jewish, correct?"

My jaw drops. I obviously know we're not Jewish, duh, but swastikas show up on mosques, too, especially recently. Bigots aren't exactly discerning about symbols of hate.

"I can assure you we will be investigating this incident. We'd like to question anyone who might know something. So it would be extremely helpful if you could get us a list of the people who were at your meeting at the VFW—"

A chill sweeps up my spine, and I cross my arms in front of my chest, tucking away my trembling fingers. "A list?" I suck in my breath. "I'm not giving you a list of names. No one fighting book bans would burn books. We're not Nazis." I clench my jaw, thinking of all the times in history class we learned about how governments used lists of people's names to hurt them, ban them, murder them.

Another man in plain clothes comes up to the captain. They both turn their backs to me. *Rude.* They speak in hushed tones, and I only pick up a few words from the conversation: *other fREADom Libraries... multiple fires...*

"Excuse me," I say, praying I'm hearing them wrong. "Excuse me," I repeat, louder. The captain turns to me, a grim look on his face. "Is something else going on?"

"At least five other of your so-called fREADom Libraries have also been set on fire. Looks like you've inspired a little hometown arson ring, Miss Khan."

His words stab me in the chest. He blames me for all of this? Like Hawley. Like half this crappy town. "We're the victims here," I croak, pointing to the garage.

The captain arches an eyebrow. "Maybe your words incited people. The whole town heard you say something about that on TV yesterday evening."

I freeze. My blood runs cold as I stare at this police captain who is supposedly here to serve and protect us.

Before I can respond, one of the other officers calls his name.

I follow him down the driveway so I can check on my mom. Our neighbor from across the street is standing there in her robe and sneakers. She's one of the few neighbors who has been overtly friendly. Brought us cookies when we moved in. She's gesturing to her phone. "I think my NeighborRING camera caught them," she says, almost breathless. "The ones who started the fire."

CHANNEL 12 WSPL, BREAKING NEWS

Karen McManus: Good afternoon. I'm standing in front
of the Bayberry Police Department. Two persons of
interest were just brought in for questioning in the
arsons of six fREADom Libraries in the early hours of
the morning. These are the latest attacks in a surge of
vandalism and violence that has recently rocked this
otherwise quiet community.

What began as online vitriol against students
protesting the widespread book challenges in the
district quickly escalated into online threats and then
into this weekend's attack on a VFW hall, arsons, and
vandalism of private property, which included painting
swastikas on a residence and at the gazebo in the town
square.

Right now, it looks like local school board president
Steve Hawley, who is running unopposed for the
vacant state representative seat, is about to enter the
building.

Mr. Hawley. Mr. Hawley, can I get a quick word?

Hawley: Morning, Karen.

McManus: What can you tell us about the young men
who are being questioned? James Green and Richard
Spence, both seniors at Bayberry High School.

Hawley: You know as well as I do that you cannot use the
names of minors on television. It's a violation of their
privacy.

McManus: Both young men are eighteen years old.

Hawley: Yes, well... these boys are fine, upstanding citizens. They play varsity sports. On the honor roll. Their families have been part of this community for a long, long time. Share our values, our faith. I'm sure this mistake will be cleared up in no time.

McManus: What about the videos allegedly showing them setting fire to at least two of the libraries?

Hawley: Those NeighborRING videos are so grainy. It was dark. Doubt they could see a thing.

McManus: There's also purportedly surveillance video from cameras the town recently installed in the town square.

Hawley: I have no further comment. Good day.

BAYBERRY BULLDOGS PARENTS ASSOCIATION FACEBOOK PAGE

POST: See link below. Two students are persons of interest in the arsons of the so-called fREADom Libraries.

Sherry "Liberty Mom" Arnold: Absurd. No way those 2 boys did this.

Stephanie Rogers: There is literally video of them doing it.

Sherry "Liberty Mom" Arnold: FAKE NEWS

R. Volt: LOL

Eva Harris: Are you children? These 2 set 6 fires. They're probably the ones who threw that Molotov cocktail into the VFW, too.

S. T. Beck: You're hurling false accusations at children. Typical libs.

Eva Harris: I said "probably" and they're 18 years old. According to the law, they're adults. FACTS.

Morris Cassidy: Hope they're arrested and charged as adults.

Stephanie Rogers: No chance. Probably wouldn't even get to trial. Not with who their daddies are.

Ryan Holloway: Of course. Fascists.

K. Brooks: There's no reason to call names. There are content rules.

Ryan Holloway: Are you serious? These "kids" literally could've killed someone and you're worried about name-calling. Get your priorities in order.

Sherry "Liberty Mom" Arnold: This all started because of that girl, Noor, causing trouble.

K Brooks: Bunch of woke BS.

S. T. Beck: She and her family aren't from here. We didn't have any problems till they moved in.

K Brooks: Agree. They don't belong here. They don't understand our community.

Eva Harris: Racist much?

Sherry "Liberty Mom" Arnold: How dare you call us racists. We're stating facts you worthless snowflake. Are you going to try and cancel me next?

Morris Cassidy: Racists are always mad about being called racist but don't have a problem with actually *being* racist.

Sherry "Liberty Mom" Arnold: That Noor girl is the one who put the book burning idea in their heads.

Ryan Holloway: You right-wing nuts love yelling about accountability except when it comes to your own actions.

LIBERTY MOMS & DADS INSTAGRAM POST

EMERGENCY SCHOOL BOARD MEETING TONIGHT

5:30 p.m. Please show up if you believe in freedom and want to protect our children! Protect them from groomers and the woke agenda!

Layla_80_: Only thing they need protection from is people like you.

2ARights: We won't let groomers into our schools.

Mira_Gray22: You are a cult.

M. Monroe: No CRT in Bayberry!

AVidlak88: You have no idea what CRT even is, do you?

BayberryBellow: It's been five days since those fires. About time the Board did something!

T_Clauser: Parents, if you believe in *actual* liberty, show up tonight. Censorship is unAmerican, and this school board is wrapping their racism and bigotry in the flag.

CHAPTER 49

I'm standing outside the school district office—next to a tree, a little out of the way but in clear sight of the door. Since last weekend's shit show, my mom's come home early from work most days this week to be with us, but she had a big division event tonight that she couldn't miss. So Amal and I came to the meeting without her, but I promised her we'd be okay. I hope I'm right.

My sister and I stand close together as people pour into the building. Emergency school board meetings can be called as long as two members of the board declare the need. It seems that no one can remember when the last one even was, so I figure some people might be here for the drama. Two teachers I recognize from the high school pass by without noticing me, and I hear one of them say, "Never thought someone on this board would call an audible for the nuclear option."

It's been five days, and they still haven't officially arrested James or Richard. But the news found comments made to a white supremacist website under the same handle that Richard uses for his Insta. Yeah, a real genius move. They must've figured they'd never get caught. They were almost right. The comments were about foreign invaders spreading lies in their town, about needing to kill a virus with fire.

"You ready?" Amal asks. "Or are we going to stand here waiting for a slo-mo preparing-for-battle film sequence with rousing music in the background?"

"Obviously, I'm hoping Aragorn shows up with his sword to give a heartfelt speech as we stand in front of the Black Gate."

"I'd lean toward Shakespeare myself," Juniper says. I hadn't noticed her, Hanna, and Faiz approaching us, a few steps away. "Comparing Hawley to Sauron is giving him too much credit."

"This is definitely a more 'out, damned spot' situation," Faiz suggests, coming to stand next to me, his arm brushing mine.

"Hawley for sure is a human stain." Hanna laughs.

I look at my friends, my sister, gathered here around me, and smile. "We few, we happy few," I recite from *Henry V.* "We band of brothers—"

"Let's make it 'siblings' to be more inclusive," Juniper suggests.

I nod. "That's right. Family."

"This is as much sappiness as I can handle," Faiz says. "Let's go."

We walk through the doors. The hallway outside the board room is full. There are two camera crews and reporters asking questions of some of the folks milling around. The four of us nudge our way forward. A middle-aged woman with a salt-and-pepper bun makes eye contact with me and nods, patting my shoulder as I pass by and whispering, "Thank you." Others notice us, and a few adults help clear a path so we can enter the room. There are lots of smiles but plenty of scowling, unfriendly faces, too.

The board room is absolutely packed. It's hot and stuffy. Some people are fanning themselves with books and magazines; others are opening windows to let in some air. I spot Hawley yelling at a custodian, who walks out and returns with a large standing fan, plugging it in close to the table where the board members sit. All five of them are here, and there are other administrators milling around, talking to the board members in hushed tones. The room buzzes with conversation, with the kind of charged, staticky energy you feel right before a thunderstorm.

"Noor." I turn in the direction of my name, and I see Ms. Clayton beckoning me. She's sitting in the third row, and there's an empty seat with a tote bag on it that says I READ BANNED BOOKS. My heart swells a little. "I saved you a seat," she says, smiling at me, her dark eyes twinkling.

"That's so nice of you, but how did you know I was coming?"

"Call it librarian intuition."

"Thank you, but I'll stand in the back with my friends—"

"She'll take that seat," Juniper says.

"Yeah," Amal adds. "Take it." She pushes me over.

"But will you be—"

Amal groans. "I'll be fine."

"We'll keep an eye on her," Faiz adds. "Don't worry. You should definitely have a front-row seat. Or at least a third-row seat."

Amal, Juniper, and Hanna head to an empty spot against an open window at the back of the room. Faiz dawdles a bit and bends down. "You okay?" he whispers in my ear, his breath soft against my cheek.

"Yeah. Sort of. I will be."

He smiles, his deep brown eyes full of concern. Then he gently squeezes my elbow and heads back. I turn to wave at Amal, who is now seated cross-legged on the floor next to Juniper and a few other students who've joined them.

"A lot of chaotic energy in here," I say to Ms. Clayton as I settle into the seat next to her.

Ms. Clayton laughs. "You could say that. But the good kind. The best kind. The kind that leads to change."

"I hope so."

"*Hope* is a verb. You've shown everyone in this town that."

"How do you mean?"

"I mean, you saw something—"

"And said something." I chuckle. More nervous blurting.

"Indeed," Ms. Clayton says. "You showed real courage. All of you did. You didn't let hate silence you. Remember what Toni Morrison said: 'The very serious function of racism—'"

"'—is distraction,'" I say, reciting the last two words of the Toni Morrison quote—the one Ms. Clayton placed in my locker with a banned book. She nods with a knowing smile.

Ms. Gaetz, the board secretary, bangs the gavel, bringing the meeting to order. The room quiets down. There's a scowl on her face that she doesn't bother hiding.

"This meeting has been called under Section Five-Six Emergency Meetings of the Bayberry Community School District Board bylaws. The regulation states that an emergency meeting of the board may be called if two or more members in good standing find a pressing need that meets the standards outlined in the bylaws. For the record, the three members who have requested this meeting are Romina Jensen, Tom Russo, and Kristy Roberts."

Murmurs spread around the room. No one was expecting three members to call for this meeting—especially not Ms. Roberts, who, according to Ms. Clayton, tended to keep quiet in meetings and vote with Hawley. I nervously rub the small burn scar on my thumb, not sure what to expect, not wanting to get my hopes up.

"Thank you, Gloria," Ms. Jensen flatly states into the microphone in front of her. "Speaking on behalf of Tom and Kristy, we felt compelled to call this emergency meeting of the board in light of the deeply disturbing acts of bigotry and violence we've seen in our town these last weeks, including throwing an incendiary device into a book club meeting that injured high school students, and culminating in the *burning of books* by other high school students," she says, a rumble of anger in her voice.

"*Alleged.* It's alleged that high school students committed those acts," Hawley interrupts. "You can't just throw around accusations like that, especially against kids. Especially when it's our job, our sworn duty to protect them!" Applause erupts from a section of the audience, and when I glance across the aisle, I see a group wearing red LIBERTY MOMS & DADS shirts that read THE GOVERNMENT IS NOT MY CO-PARENT on the back. Mrs. Rogerson leads the cheers. As I turn my head back to the front of the room, I spot Andrew. He's sitting next to a woman who I guess is his mom. They both wear tight smiles on their faces. He catches me looking at him and holds my gaze for a second before we both turn away.

"You're speaking out of order, Steve," Ms. Jensen says, then turns to look at the board secretary. "Isn't that correct, Gloria?

Can you please call this meeting back to order?" There's a definite no-f's-left-to-give tone in Ms. Jensen's voice. The air grows thick with tension as there's a brief silence.

The secretary sighs and weakly bangs her gavel. "Romina is right, Steve. I'm sorry, you'll have to wait your turn." A flash of anger passes over Hawley's face, but it quickly vanishes into his politician's smile as he leans back in his chair, crosses his arms over his chest, and nods at Ms. Jensen as if he's magnanimously giving her permission to speak.

Ms. Jensen narrows her eyes. "As I was saying, the purpose of this meeting is simple, and we have but one agenda item. For the last year, too many of us have sat on the sidelines watching as some very vocal individuals successfully instituted board policy changes that have allowed bigotry to be codified. It was wrong then. It's wrong now. We've had enough of these blatant attempts to politicize books, to virtually criminalize authors, and even, in some cases, the act of reading. This wrongheaded policy has led this community down a bleak path. I move to eliminate, by board action, Policy 111.5 Challenged Materials."

The uproar in the room is immediate. There are boos and cheers, some indiscernible shouting. A sneer passes across Hawley's face. While Ms. Gaetz, the secretary, bangs the gavel and tries to call things back to order, Mr. Carter, our school principal, walks up to Hawley, who puts his hand over the microphone as they exchange words. Hawley then gestures to a staff member, who escorts Carter to the microphone in the center of the room.

"Is there public comment during emergency meetings?" I ask Ms. Clayton.

"I checked, but there wasn't an online form to sign up like there usually is, so I'm not sure."

People finally start to quiet down, though there's a low-key, rumbly buzz in the room. "Is there a second?" the secretary asks.

"I second the motion," Mr. Russo says into his microphone.

"Motion to enter into immediate roll-call vote," Ms. Jensen says quickly into the microphone.

"Motion to allow fifteen-minute period of public comment," Hawley says with a smile.

I spy Carter, who is standing ready and waiting. I'm not sure what's going on, but it looks as if they're trying to out-bureaucratic-procedure one another?

"Second the motion for public comment," the secretary says, and before anyone else can say anything, quickly adds, "All in favor, say 'aye.'" Hawley quickly joins in, and then there's a moment of absolute quiet. There are five board members. They need three votes to pass anything, even the public comment period.

"Oh, this is all unnecessary," Ms. Jensen states. "We've already had hours and hours of public commentary on this policy when it was first passed. Much of which you disregarded. There is no language in the emergency board meeting regulations that requires more."

"Are you trying to suppress public opinion? Prevent parents—taxpayers—from having their say in their child's education?" Hawley twists the meaning of her words.

The crowd watches the two of them go back and forth like a tennis match. Who knew there could be so much drama in a small-town school board meeting?

"Don't be ridiculous." Ms. Jensen doesn't hide the vitriol in her voice. "We aren't impinging on parental rights. There is still *another* policy in place for parents to object to their *own* child's reading material if they so wish. Though, personally, I believe we should remove the opt-out option as well. But we are so far beyond the pale in this district that some parents believe they have the right to decide not merely what their own child reads, but what *all* children can read. This is antithetical to the mission of a school district, which is to educate our children, not create breeding grounds of ignorance!"

"Groomer!" one of the Liberty parents yells out, and some in the crowd clap while others try to shut them down. The secretary bangs her gavel but doesn't give a lecture about "civility." That low-level rumble in the room from before is now a full-blown tornado of emotional energy.

"All those in favor of allowing a fifteen-minute public comment period, say 'aye,'" the secretary asks again, louder this time.

"We have the votes, Steve," Ms. Jensen says, almost as an aside to Hawley.

"We'll see," he responds, and then raises his hand while pointedly nodding at Kristy Roberts. "Aye," he booms into the microphone to cheers.

"Aye," the secretary adds.

Kristy Roberts leans into the microphone after glancing back and forth at the other four board members at the table. "Aye," she whispers into the microphone.

"The ayes have it," the secretary says. "A fifteen-minute public comment period begins now. Principal Carter will be our first speaker." Rogerson rushes up to the microphone with a smug smile and gets in line. Two other Liberty parents follow suit. Like it's all going according to their plan.

Ms. Clayton rushes to grab a spot behind the microphone, but with such limited time, there's probably no chance she'll even get to speak.

I watch Hawley nod at Ms. Roberts. Oh my God. He's doing this all for her. She's the swing vote. He's trying to show her he has the power, the parents, the votes. Ms. Roberts looks nervous, and I wonder if Hawley low-key threatened her before the meeting—I would not put it past him. When I glance back, Juniper and Faiz are gesticulating wildly at me, and Amal marches up to my seat, grabs my hand, and drags me into the line. There are already so many adults in front of me, there's no way I'll get to speak. I'm not even sure what I would say exactly. A few other people join, and then Faiz, Juniper, and Hanna pull some other kids into the line, which now snakes through the packed room.

"This is sorta pointless, right?" Amal says. "But also . . . kinda not."

"Demanding to be heard is never pointless, but Hawley fixed it so only his side would get to speak."

"What's Kristy playing at?" one of the Liberty Moms ahead of us in line says to another.

Mrs. Rogerson leans toward her and says, "I wouldn't worry about it. I'm sure Steve has used all his powers of persuasion to get Kristy to do the right thing."

I scoff loudly. I know exactly how Hawley likes to persuade people—through bullying and threats. Mrs. Rogerson glares at me. I glare back. Amal sticks her tongue out at her, which makes me laugh. Mrs. Rogerson and the other mom shake their heads disapprovingly and turn back to the front to listen to Mr. Carter, who has already been droning on for a couple minutes.

I start paying attention to his monologue. "Let's be clear. Outside agitators have infiltrated our schools to sow the seeds of dissent. To distill woke values like so many dandelion seeds, to defile our soil."

I roll my eyes at the drama. Some hisses go up from the crowd. But Carter isn't deterred. "As principal I am charged with the education, care, and protection of our young people. These are formative years, and we cannot let their impressionable young minds be shaped by the pornographic and the profane, by so-called young adult novels that are merely doorways to delinquency and perverse, unnatural behaviors."

More boos go up from the crowd. Carter is even more disgusting than I thought he was.

"Sit down, Carter!" a man from the audience yells.

"You sit down, Brian," another man shouts at the heckler.

"I am sitting, dumbass," Brian yells back.

"You want to say that to my face?"

"I am saying it to your face." Brian and the people around him laugh.

The man he was yelling at stands up and starts to walk over. He is big. Tall. Very thick arms. Brian, who is also a pretty big guy, gets up, too. People begin yelling at them to calm down as they stare at each other, chests puffed up, shoulders squared.

Holy crap, there's going to be a middle-aged parent fistfight at a school board meeting. About books. And they complain about kids being immature and overly emotional.

The secretary bangs the gavel. "That is enough. Gentlemen, be seated. You will conduct yourselves with decorum or be removed from this room."

More people start yelling. Others stand up. There's some jostling. A few of the Liberty Moms put their hands up and step out of line, trying to avoid the scuffle. The banging of the gavel is barely audible amid the chaos in the room. A cop starts walking toward the commotion. Mr. Carter steps away, helping one of the moms to a seat.

Mr. Hawley bellows into his microphone. "Calm down, people. Take a seat, Brian. Take a seat, Nate."

With people distracted and the line in disarray, I grab Amal's hand and rush toward the microphone. I snatch it from the stand, and high-pitched feedback booms out of the speaker, drawing people's attention to the front of the room. To me.

Hawley stands up and points at me. "You are out of line and out of order, Ms. Khan."

"There is no line anymore," Amal says, leaning into the microphone that I'm holding. "Besides, possession is nine-tenths of the law." There's laughter around the room. No one's taken a seat and even more people are standing now.

The secretary bangs the gavel. That gavel is getting more floor time than anyone, at this point.

"Step away, ladies." Hawley makes a sour face. "Neither of you have a right to speak. It's not your turn."

"You made it so it would never be our turn," I volley back, my face growing hot.

Hawley leans over and places his fists on the table in front of him. "I said sit down."

There's jostling near the door and a few people move aside. "Let her speak!" a familiar voice yells out, loud enough to be heard over the buzz. Loud enough to silence everyone.

My mom steps through the crowd, marches to the front of the room, and comes to stand a few feet from Hawley. "You need to be the one to take a seat, Mr. Hawley. You will not speak to my daughters that way." My heart beats like a drum. My mom is here. For me. All five feet of blazing fire. Mama Bear mode engaged.

Hawley lets out a cruel laugh; he's trying to control his anger, I think, but his beet-red face and taut, veiny neck muscles betray him. "Or what? You gonna have one of your monkey gods put a hex on me?" Gasps go up from around the room. But Hawley doesn't notice. "You people are never going to be satisfied until you control everything, huh?" People start shouting at him.

Amal leans over to me and whispers, "Does he think we're Hindu?"

My face twists in disgust. "Racists aren't exactly big-brained."

"Mr. Hawley, you are so far out of order," Ms. Jensen says. "You need to apologize immediately."

"Resign!" someone yells from the back of the room. Others join in. "Resign, racist!"

The secretary bangs the gavel furiously.

My face burns with fury. I feel sick hearing him talk to my mom like that. She's standing there in front of him, her fists clenched, her back straight, her chin jutting out. Then she turns around, her back to him, and speaks to the audience. Our gazes meet and she smiles at me, a fierce pride in her eyes. And it makes me feel like I can do anything. "Two things you can always count on with racists is that they're ignorant and they eventually show you exactly who they are." The room starts to quiet down. "Mr. Hawley paid me a visit a couple weeks ago to *suggest* that I keep my daughter quiet if we wanted to fit in, if we didn't want any trouble in this town. It was a subtle threat, and so I tried to silence Noor. That was the wrong thing to do. That's not how you stand up to bullies. Now I'm here to say, let her speak."

I hand Amal the microphone and walk up to my mom and give her the tightest hug I've given her in years. Chants of "Let her speak, let her speak, let her speak" drown out the people who are boo-ing. Drown out an increasingly red-faced Hawley, who is yelling at people and beckoning the police officer. The wooden gavel pounds furiously, and my heart thuds in concert with it.

"Go on, beta. Say what you need to say." My mom cups my cheek with her hand, and I lean my face into it for a second before I move back toward Amal, who is holding out the microphone to me. I take a cue from my mom and turn my back to Hawley and the other board members. They're not who I want to talk to.

"I'm eighteen," I say, my voice soft and low at first. The crowd settles, some take their seats again, others stay standing, but it's quieter now. "I shouldn't have to be here begging you to let me read. None of us should." I gesture toward some of the other students. Faiz raises a fist. "We shouldn't have to fight for the right to read. We shouldn't have to convince adults who are supposed to know better that banning books isn't about protection. It's fascism." Heads nod, some people applaud.

"We've heard enough of this woke nonsense," Hawley's voice booms from behind me. I don't turn around.

"Shut up, Steve," a woman in the row next to me yells, and then winks at me. "Let her speak. We've all heard more than enough from you."

I ignore Mr. Hawley and continue. "You are actively hurting kids by banning books. You're telling queer kids and trans kids and Black kids and brown kids that our stories don't belong in school. That *we* don't belong. But that's so wrong. When you see it, you can be it, my seventh-grade literature teacher used to say, and you're denying us the right to see ourselves. To imagine all we could be.

"My parents have been taking me and my sister to the public library ever since we were little kids. We did the summer reading club and story hours. That library had a sign that read ALL ARE WELCOME. That's what a library should be—a welcoming place, a place where every kid can feel at home. That library is where I first learned how you could get lost in a good book, how a book could be a portal to different worlds, a time machine, a rocket ship, a source of comfort."

My voice cracks with emotion. It's sadness and anger, too, but also more than that. Looking around as the group of Liberty Moms and Dads stand up and walk out en masse, hearing the gavel banging behind me, hearing so many students and adults cheer, there's a kind of lightness that spreads through my body, something in the core of my being that feels unleashed. A feeling of rightness. Of pride. Of belonging.

I turn back toward the school board members. There's a huge smile on Ms. Jensen's face. Mr. Russo is nodding, and even Ms. Roberts, the vote we need, is paying attention. "Books help us see ourselves but they're supposed to challenge us, too, show us worlds and experiences that are different from our own. Books help us open doors. We're here asking you not to slam those doors in our faces. Let us read."

The moment around me slows and blurs. Ms. Jensen stands and claps. Others join her. A few people shout, "Let them read!" Hawley's face turns bright red. Ms. Jensen reiterates her motion. There's a second. Then a cacophony of angry, overlapping voices. Some people are calling my name, but I can't see who. All I see is my mom moving toward me, holding her arms out and pulling me into her. I breathe into her shoulder, the softness of her sweater soaking up some of my tears. It feels so good to be held this way. I've missed her so much.

My mom pulls away with a sniffle and then takes my sister and me by our hands and moves us toward the exit through the chaos around us. People nod at us, others glare in anger. I get some pats on the back. Andrew catches my eye and gives me a small smile and a nod. I turn away from him.

We step outside into the cool night air. Other students pile out after us, and the front yard of the school board building takes on the air of a party.

"You were amazing, beta," my mom says, squeezing my hand. "I'm so proud of this fierce warrior you've become." Her eyes glisten with unshed tears. "I'm sorry I wasn't hearing what you were trying to say to me. I haven't been there for you or your sister. That changes now."

I bite my lip. My heart clenches. "Mom, I'm sorry I blamed you—" I choke back a sob.

"Shhhh, I know, beta." My mom puts one arm around me and another around Amal. "It's going to be okay. *We're* going to be okay."

I close my eyes, and for the first time in forever, I believe her.

CHAPTER 50

We won. In a way.

The school board voted 3–2 to cancel the policy that pulled over five hundred books from our shelves. But it's a small victory in a much bigger and longer fight. Those Liberty Moms and Dads vowed to run candidates against all three school board members who voted for democracy. "We will never stop fighting to protect our kids from groomers. From the leftist woke agenda. We will protect our freedom of speech," Mrs. Rogerson said in the *Gazette* article I'm skimming on my phone. Weird to think that freedom of speech means banning books, but like my mom said, bigots are ignorant and definitely don't understand irony.

"Did they get your good side?" Amal asks as I stumble over to the kitchen counter, ready to drink the chai that is waiting for me. I feel as if all I've done is sleep since Friday night. It's noon, and I'm still tired.

"Every side is her good side." My mom winks at me as she makes what I like to call a desi omelet. It's a super simple dish that

I love—egg with sauteed onions, cilantro, garam masala, cayenne, and sometimes a bit of cumin—to be eaten on a fresh paratha with mango pickle on the side. Okay, she didn't make fresh paratha this morning; there were premade ones in the freezer that she heated up, but I'll take it. She slides a plate in front of me and I dig in.

Amal takes my phone and scrolls down the article. "There are no pictures of you. Not even a quote." She frowns. "Of course, they quote Hawley saying he will never bow down to a woke mob."

"What did you expect? Hawley owns that paper. Rich dudes never really seem to lose."

"Well, maybe sometimes they do," Mom says. "Someone posted a video of those terrible things he said at the board meeting on the parent Facebook page, and people started sharing it, and, well, a reporter from the *Tribune* called me this morning for a comment."

"Oh my God. If Chicago media picks up the story, it could go totally viral." I grin. "What did you tell them?"

"I said they should talk to my brilliant daughter who was *still* sleeping but would get back to them as soon as she ate." She hands me a sticky note with the reporter's name and number.

I scarf down the egg and paratha, grab my phone from Amal, and head upstairs to call the reporter.

We talk for a few minutes, and I try to sound smart and not blurt out anything that might get me in trouble. The reporter tells me that she spoke with other community members, including a parent who wanted to start a recall petition to remove Hawley from his board seat. Don't know if they can get the signatures, but I so wish I could see his face when he finds out it's happening. But also, if I never see Hawley's face again, it will be too soon.

I plop back on my bed. My curtains are pulled open and the bright sun streams into my room. I bask in a slant of light on my comforter, staring at my ceiling, thinking of how weird life is. How it can feel so bleak and horrible, like you're getting sucked into a black hole, and then you blink and the warm sun is on your face again, and you let yourself believe that things could be good, that people aren't all terrible. And a feeling a lot like hope fills you up but you don't say a word to anyone because it's fragile, like a bubble floating above grass. Also you don't want anyone to know what a sap you are.

I hear hammering from outside my window. I cautiously step toward the glass to see what's happening. Andrew's truck is parked on the street in front of our house, and he's putting in a new fREADom Library on the spot where the old one was burned down. My breath catches. I wasn't sure what I was expecting, but it's not this.

I pull on a pair of jeans and a maroon UChicago T-shirt, and race down the stairs and outside. My stomach is in knots, my palms clammy. It's the first truly warm day of the spring. Andrew is wearing workman's gloves and a charcoal-gray tee with dark jeans and a beat-up Illini baseball hat. He looks good, and I'm immediately mad at myself for noticing. He's still factually hot even if I can never be attracted to him in the same way I once was.

"Hey, what are you doing?" That came out more accusatory than I meant it to, but I don't apologize.

"Hi," he says, then takes his hat off and runs a gloved hand through his tousled hair. "I figured I owed you one of these." He points to the library that he's installed, nearly identical to the one we'd put up before.

"You don't owe me anything."

"I definitely owe you an apology."

"Is that what this is? An apology?"

"I guess...it's a start. I'm sorry. I know I messed up. A lot."

"Yeah. You did." I can feel myself start to soften but I'm not sure he deserves that, so I check myself. Even still, my brain and heart do not feel as if they're on the same side.

Andrew takes off his gloves and steps closer to me, but still keeps space between us. "Guess you heard that James and Rich were arrested and charged?"

I nod.

He shakes his head. "What assholes. I should've seen who they really were, or what they've become, I guess. Maybe a part of me did see it, but I decided to look away because it was easier or because we've been friends so long."

I know he's trying. I know he's maybe realizing a few things for the first time. That's great for him, but I don't think you deserve cookies for finally seeing the truth about your racist friends. I don't think I should bury Andrew, either, though, because I want to believe, to hope that people—some of them, anyway—can learn, can change.

He walks over to his truck and pulls out a box and heads back to me.

I take the box from him—it's full of books. "Thanks," I whisper.

"It's the least I could do since my once best friends attacked your meeting, hurt your sister, set your library on fire, and painted a swastika on your garage. And since my stepdad is a monster." He lets out a nervous, choked laugh.

"They've definitely been busy." I give him a half smile and step closer to the new little fREADom Library. "Is that a phoenix?" I point to a small bird painted on the back, rising from red-orange flames.

He nods. "Not exactly subtle, huh?"

"I like it. Sometimes it's important to be grateful for the obvious."

He's been staring down at his shoes, shuffling in place, running the toe of one boot over the other. Now he looks up at me, a softness in his eyes. "I lied to you. You were right about so many things and I should've—"

"Believed me?"

"Yeah, but not just that. I should've believed *in* you."

"You should've maybe believed in yourself, too."

Andrew gives me a half-cocked smile and begins to back up, returning to his truck. "See ya around?"

"Sure. Around." I lift my hand up, a half-assed wave. There's a whirlwind of mixed-up emotions inside me. Anger, sadness, confusion. And questions, so many questions. It wasn't epic, but this felt like a sort of goodbye. The realization that there would definitely be finality, if not closure, to whatever relationship Andrew and I had, whatever one we were trying to build.

I stand outside for a long time after Andrew leaves, after the gravel and dust kicked up by his truck tires settles. Puffy white clouds float past in the bright blue sky above me. A tear falls down my cheek, surprising me, then another. I lick away a salty drop as one of my tears slips to the corner of my mouth. I'm not sure why I'm crying, exactly. For no reason. For all the reasons. For my dad leaving us. For doors closing. For endings that are expected and the ones that hit you in the head like an anvil. Is that what mourning is? The hole ripped through you by something—someone you thought would be in your life forever? I don't know. There are different types of loss, I guess. And they all carry their own weight, as though the earth has a special gravity for every individual loss.

If loss has weight, then I guess joy is the ballast. The counterweight, the lightness that lifts you up. Maybe it's love. Maybe it's hope. Maybe a person needs to hold on to all those things so the grief doesn't sink you.

I wipe the tears from my face and head inside.

EPILOGUE

"Aarrrrraayyy, you're blinking too much. I can't put the khajal on straight if you're blinking so much," my mom says as she takes my chin in her hand, steadying my face as she tries to line my eyes with kohl.

Amal steps closer to me. "It's okay, I hear the raccoon look is all the rage for prom this year."

I turn to her and stick out my tongue.

"You two!" My mom jokingly shoos Amal out. We're standing in my mom's big bathroom, lights ablaze, trying to get my face ready for the dance while my body hums with nervous energy.

"That khajal is my nemesis." I scrunch my face in the mirror. My long black hair falls in loose waves down my shoulders and is extra shiny thanks to the coconut oil treatment my mom gave me last night, so at least I have that going for me.

"You look beautiful, beta," my mom says as she grabs the moment and deftly swipes khajal across both my eyelids. Then she hands me a red lipstick. "Only wear it if you want to." I apply the color and then blot on the tissue my mom holds out for me. I smile. I look good.

My mom removes the towel she'd draped around my neck and steps back to look at me. She clasps her hands in front of her heart, her eyes brimming with tears.

I look down at my clothes. Prom was a totally last-minute decision, and when I was trying to piece together my outfit, my mom walked into my bedroom with her wedding lehenga—a rose-gold silk skirt with gorgeous flowers and vines embroidered all over it in golden thread and encrusted with tiny rhinestones. At first I resisted wearing it because I didn't want to dredge up the past, but my mom was adamant that it was okay. Plus, it's absolutely gorgeous. The matching blouse was a bit too tight, so I decided to pair the skirt with my I READ BANNED BOOKS T-shirt, because why not wear your heart on your sleeve? It is prom, after all.

"Mom? Are you sure this is okay? I can wear my shalwar khameez from last Eid. I don't want my outfit to...make you think of Dad."

My mom gives me a soft smile and steps closer to me, stroking my hair. I almost flinch when she does—it still feels a little weird to share feelings with Mom. I slammed that door shut, but I'm prying it open because it feels so good to talk to her.

"These tears aren't from sadness, they're from joy, from pride at the wondrous person you've become. Does my wedding lehenga bring back memories of your father? Of course. But looking at you reminds me of the power in making new memories, of writing the story we want."

I nod. "I don't want to hurt you, though," I choke out.

My mom sighs. "Never, beta. I'm sorry it took me so long to learn this, but I can't escape memories of your dad, no matter where I go. And I no longer want to. Because some of those memories are so gorgeous they make my heart burst." She smiles, cupping my chin in her hand, gazing at me with so much fierce love in her eyes.

"I thought taking the path of least resistance, living in a kind of denial, was the best way forward, but I wasn't moving forward. That hurt me, but worse, it hurt you and your sister. I won't let that happen again."

I will myself not to tear up because I'm afraid I'll mess up my face, and I cannot sit through that whole khajal situation again. I hug my mom, letting her wrap her arms tightly around me, inhaling the smell of her jasmine attar.

Amal comes back with a shoebox. I raise a suspicious eyebrow at her, afraid of what shoes she's chosen. She shoves it into my hands. "Open it. They're shoes, not flesh-eating worms."

"Oh my God, why so grossly specific?" I open the lid expecting a pair of teetering heels that I will in no way be willing or able to wear. Instead, I find a pair of turquoise metallic All-Stars wrapped in tissue paper. "What! These are perfect," I say, and air-kiss my sister so I don't mess up my lipstick.

"What can I say? I'm the sister with style." She smirks, and I play-punch her in the arm.

We head downstairs, my mom's wedding lehenga swishing with each step. I notice my fingers trembling. Amal spies it, too, and takes my hand and gives it a little squeeze. "You okay, sis?"

"Nerves. Ridiculous, right?" I wave my clammy hands.

"Primal scream?" she asks.

I nod. I hear my mom chuckle from behind us. I turn to her and reach out my hand. She takes it and the three of us form a tight circle. I count down from three and together we scream until we're all laughing, my uneasiness melting away.

My mom clears her throat and steps back. "Let me take some pictures of you," she says. "Stand next to your sister, beta."

Amal and I squish together and goof around while my mom snaps pics with her phone. "Now a good one! Smile like regular people, not like haunted clowns," she jokes. After a few shots, she steps back, joy written all over her face. "My girls," she says. "My beautiful girls."

The doorbell rings.

"Your date is here!" Amal singsongs as she leaps to answer the door.

"It's not a date," my mom and I say at the same time, though the butterflies in my stomach disagree.

Faiz is standing in our doorway, a shy grin on his face. He's wearing a fitted dark charcoal-gray suit with a white shirt, no tie. He looks, empirically, unbelievably gorgeous. I smile and feel my cheeks flush, and once again I am thankful for the melanin that hides my blushing. He walks inside, a small plastic box in hand.

"As-salaam-alaikum, auntie," he says, ever the respectful desi boy.

My mom smiles. "Walaikum-salaam," she says, and then drapes her arm around Amal's shoulders, nudging her to respond in kind.

Faiz's eyes sweep to me as I step around my mom and sister. "You look amazing. Love how you're rocking that lehenga," he says.

"You look pretty awesome yourself."

He opens the box, and there's a wrist corsage with a spray of small pink roses set into some greens.

"It's so pretty!" I gasp as I lift it out of the box and slip it over my left wrist, those butterflies showing zero signs of calming down. I bite the inside of my lip as I look from the flowers to Faiz's beautiful brown eyes.

I hadn't planned on going to prom. Wasn't sure I wanted to celebrate being part of the Bayberry High School Class of 2023, didn't care about having a final hurrah. But last weekend, I was reorganizing the books in my fREADom Library and my mind floated back to what Andrew and I had talked about. How sometimes it's so hard to see what's in front of your face, or how easy it is to make up excuses when you're too anxious to see the truth that's *right there*. I definitely learned that with my dad. But there's a different side to it, too. Faiz was the truth I hadn't truly let myself see. It was too much weight, too many expectations, too many questions. But it was also him and his incredible kindness and how he sees me for who I am. I thought maybe I could stop catastrophizing for a minute and let myself have fun.

So almost without thinking, I drove to Faiz's house and knocked on his door, screwing up my courage to ask him to prom, hoping my nerves wouldn't make me puke all over his front porch. When he stepped outside, his smile warm and bright, the slight lingering scent of sandalwood soap on him, it felt a little bit like home.

"You good?" Faiz asks as we say goodbye to my mom and sister and step into a perfect spring night. Faiz and I stand in my driveway admiring each other for a moment, the space between us igniting with possibility. There's a gentle, warm breeze, and I breathe in the soft scent of green grass and the lilacs that line my street. I close my eyes for a moment. I don't know what happens next. Not for me or the school or this town or our state. The anti–book banning proposal in Springfield looks to have enough backing to pass, but I don't want to celebrate until the governor signs it. But I'm learning how to be cautiously hopeful. I'm learning that hope doesn't have to burn you. Things at home feel so much better, but still a little fragile, not like my family will break, but like we're carefully piecing all the broken pieces together again, hoping they'll hold. Handling each other with care.

Weird how life turns out in ways you could never imagine. How sometimes you have to let go of the things—of the people—you were holding on to so tightly. How you thought you were weak and alone but you find your strength and your people. How sometimes you find yourself at the threshold of a place you never expected. That can be so scary. But also exciting. And then the only thing left to do is to open the door, to believe in yourself as you take a leap of faith into the unknown.

I turn to look up at Faiz's smiling face, at his warm brown eyes. "Yeah," I say. "I'm good."

AUTHOR'S NOTE

Libraries are not neutral spaces. Nor should they be.

This ought to be clear to anyone paying attention to the rising tide of censorship that has been sweeping through the United States these past few years. Book bans, long a tool of oppression, serve only those who want to hide history, who want to perpetuate lies, who want to control what young people think, often under the guise of "parents' rights." But let's be clear—the drive to ban books is fueled by fear, ignorance, and hate. The majority of books that are being challenged in public libraries and public schools are written by LGBTQ+ or BIPOC authors. This is not merely a coincidence; it is a focused, insidious campaign to erase identities, to gaslight, and to press for private control of public institutions. No democracy should stand for this. The United States of America should not stand for this. We can't. We won't.

During a book event for my second novel, *Internment*, a (disgruntled?) reader asked me why I *hated* America. Apparently, because my work lays bare the faults in our nation, the reader assumed I must hate it. I don't. I love my country. But not in a nationalistic way built on ignorance or narrow-mindedness. I love America in the James Baldwin way, in the way that insists on criticizing this nation because I believe we can do better. Because I *know* we can do better. Baldwin told us to open our eyes to unearned privilege, to systemic oppression, to the truth.

The truth is that book banning is un-American. The truth is that if we want to call ourselves a free people, then we must fight for the right of all people to read freely. The truth is that fear and ignorance are the hobgoblins of small minds and weak hearts.

We cannot remain neutral in the face of oppression. We cannot remain silent. This is a lesson we have heard over and over—neutrality aids the oppressor, and book banners do not need our help. Go to your school board meetings. Vote in every election, big or small. Hold elected officials accountable. Speak truth to power. Pick up a book, open a doorway. Take the journey the story invited you on, be a part of the conversation. Reading gives you power. Don't ever forget that.

Resources

To learn more about censorship and book bans, please check out:

American Library Association: https://www.ala.org
Brooklyn Public Library's Books Unbanned initiative:
    https://www.bklynlibrary.org/books-unbanned
EveryLibrary: https://www.everylibrary.org
Freedom to Read Foundation: https://www.ftrf.org
PEN America: https://pen.org
Unite Against Book Bans: https://uniteagainstbookbans.org

Register to vote: https://vote.gov
Find your federal, state, and local elected officials:
    https://www.usa.gov/elected-officials

ACKNOWLEDGMENTS

My deepest gratitude and love to:

Joanna Volpe, rock-star agent and awesome human being, whose unwavering belief in my ability to write the story in the way it needs to be written has been a light.

The entire fabulous squad at New Leaf Literary, especially Jenniea Carter, Lindsay Howard, Jordan Hill, Kate Sullivan, Katherine Curtis, and my partner-in-pastries, Pouya Shahbazian.

Alvina Ling, publishing icon, my ever-insightful and lovely editor, whom I'm incredibly honored to work with.

The many, countless talented folks at Little, Brown Books for Young Readers who made this story I dreamed up a real book, especially Ruqayyah Daud, Crystal Castro, Lily Choi, Emilie Polster, Bill Grace, Savannah Kennelly, Andie Divelbiss, Nisha Panchal-Terhune, Allison Broeils, Jessica Mercado, Becky Munich, Victoria Stapleton, Christie Michel, Andy Ball, Jake Regier, Christine Ma, Jane Cavolina, Sarah Vostok, Patrick Hulse, Karina Granda, David Caplan, Sasha Illingworth, Patricia Alvarado, Marisa Russell, Mary McCue, and Cassie Malmo, for the enthusiasm and attention to detail that bring me so much joy.

Jackie Engel and Megan Tingley for ongoing support and for welcoming me years ago to the Little, Brown family.

My brilliant UK editor, Sarah Castleton, and the wonderful team at Hachette UK/Atom Books for giving me such a lovely home across the pond.

Jon Gray for the gorgeous cover illustration.

Kristin Dwyer for the creative zeal and shot in the arm when I needed it. And Molly Mitchell for keeping me on track.

Dear friends, cheerleaders, early readers, and truth tellers: Dhonielle Clayton, Joanna Ho, Rachel Strolle, Amy Vidlak Girmscheid, Sabaa Tahir, Aisha Saeed, Stephanie Garber, Gloria Chao, Lizzie Cooke, Anna Waggener, Sajidah Ali, Kiersten White, Katherine Locke, Adam Gidwitz, Tobin Anderson, Lamar Giles, Grace Lin, Renée Watson, and Jeanne Birdsall.

The generous authors who graciously allowed me to reference or quote from their incredible works: George M. Johnson, Brendan Kiely, Jason Reynolds, Malinda Lo, Anna-Marie McLemore, Tiffany D. Jackson, Laurie Halse Anderson, Becky Albertalli, and Mark Oshiro.

My parents, Hamid and Mazher, and my sisters, Asra and Sara. And the entire Ahmed-Razvi and Jonas clans for the stories, good humor, and support.

Lena and Noah, the brightest stars in the universe. You make the whole place shimmer.

Thomas, as ever, forever.